THE SMOLDERING VEIN

Book Three of
The Malice of Light

BRADY J. SADLER

THE SMOLDERING VEIN

Book Three of
The Malice of Light

This is a work of fiction. Names, characters, business, events and incidents are the products of the author's imagination. Any resemblance to actual persons, living or dead, or actual events is purely coincidental.

THE SMOLDERING VEIN

Copyright © 2024 by Brady J. Sadler & Twin Tale Studios LLC

www.twintalestudios.com | www.bradyjsadler.com

Cover Art by Ellie TenBrink
Maps by Mya N. Osburn
Interior Art by Ellie TenBrink & The Creation Studio
Additional Graphic Design by Chris Doughman

ISBN: 979-8-9993640-5-0 (Paperback)
ISBN: 979-8-9993640-9-8 (IngramSpark)
ISBN:979-8-9993640-6-7 (Hardcover)
ISBN: 979-8-9993640-7-4 (eBook)
ISBN: 979-8-9993640-4-3 (Deluxe Pocket Hardcover Edition)

For my buddy and first reader, Corey K.

Not sure I would have gotten this far in the series without your encouragement and enthusiasm.

VAINA

COPERA

VALE

NOVETH

EASTLUND

GUYEN

WESTERRA

KARRANE

THE
VALK SEA

LAUSTREAL

Prologue
Ithakan's Ashes

Malcolmry Sulm had rarely worn the Nazurik crown during his twenty-five-year reign as king of Copera. He didn't like how it fit his head, since it had been forged specifically for his grandfather, who—like his father—had been voluntarily bald. The golden circlet emblazoned with rubies now sat upon his thick braided hair like some foul reminder of the rebellions back home.

However, the king endured its presence while venturing beyond Copera's borders, knowing that his men would need the encouragement of riding alongside their king should that fell storm return. Even though his company feasted in the lower halls of the old tower, still he kept the crown on, so he would not forget its weight.

"Is there even much left to conquer here, Father?"

Malcolmry turned to give the princess a stern glance as she joined him at the window. Her dark eyes were fixed on the horizon where Rathen's ruins awaited their dwindling company. His royal army had been nearly a thousand strong when riding out of Nazurik on a campaign of conquest, but through rebel skirmishes, desertion, and executions, it had been reduced to just over six hundred faithful men and women.

"Walls can be rebuilt," he told her. "Towers restored. As the heir to Nazurik, you should know the true value of our quest, Kathina. The legacy of the Free Cities predates our own kingdom by nearly three generations."

She only looked at him. The way the dawn's sunlight reflected off the girl's unmarred flesh, like supple, oiled leather, reminded Malcolmry of his late wife: the true ruler of the Bronze Coasts. The memory of Queen Dreya Sulm, whose assassination triggered the rebellion against his throne, softened his mood. Instead of lecturing his heir, he just sighed and told her, "We need to claim a seat for you. Nazurik teems with lurking threats from within, and if we do not unite the other lords against some outside foe, I fear the rebels we just put down will take root once again."

"Then we'll crush them again," she replied, making a fist. Kathina had thick muscled arms; a warrior since she first bled. Malcolmry knew the girl thought only of steel and glory, as well as soft men to lay with, but he had hoped bringing her on this campaign might temper some of her more rash qualities. Thus far, it had only seemed to bolster them.

"At what cost, daughter?" He turned to face the other window looking westward. The abandoned tower they had claimed as an outpost provided a spectacular view of the western edge of Ashwood dividing Rathen and Wickham. "Putting down the Trader Rebellion undid my father's entire legacy, costing us nearly all of our Jathi alliances. Would you cut down all of Copera if it rose up against the Sulms?" Malcolmry motioned back toward Rathen. "Or would you present them a foe that makes them forget whatever grievances they have against the throne? Unite them against a foreign enemy? A true leader must consider these options before resorting to slaughter."

Kathina's gaze followed his hands, but her stubborn expression remained. "The orcs are all but broken, Father. Are they your great foreign foe? The wood elves liberated Rathen and then left its bones to rot. Are we mere crows now? Picking the choice remains from a corpse already feasted on by the victors? Is that really why we marched all this way and left the Nazurik throne open for the taking?"

By Stane, the girl is insolent, he thought. If only all of his enemies knew that it was Kathina's cruel instincts and impatient judgement that they rebelled against and not his own, perhaps they'd be dining on crabs back home—this whole campaign would not have been necessary.

But no, he wouldn't let his subjects know that Kathina Sulm had perpetrated the tragedies that had led to the near collapse of his reign. Instead, he would focus his efforts on conquest—the one thing that was proven to unite divided realms.

"My king."

Malcolmry turned from his daughter toward the voice of his key advisor.

"What is it, Chancellor Myrn?"

The elf bowed his head, first to his king, then to the princess. "Excuse my interruption, Your Grace, but Sir Einrik and his knights have captured a trader en route to Nazurik by way of the...well, the Rathaway."

Malcolmry cringed at the mention of another Shadow-taken trader, but just waved his hand dismissively. "Then string him up like the others, Myrn."

Kathina snorted in annoyance as she made her way to the wine.

"Your Grace," Myrn continued, "it's just that this particular trader is Nephillip Draunon—the king's—"

"I know who Neff is," Malcolmry snarled, not in anger, but more out of annoyance that he had almost ordered the execution of his own cousin. He had little love for the weasel, but he was technically of royal blood, which still meant something to him.

"Might as well hang him," Kathina remarked before downing a whole chalice of wine. "One less trader to join the rebellion."

"With me, Myrn," Malcolmry said, leaving his daughter to her vices. "The princess requires solitude before our march to Rathen. Let us tend to Sir Einrik and his bounty." The king led his chancellor down the winding stairs, the sounds of his company reveling lifting his spirits a bit. Once they were two floors below the topmost lord's chamber, Myrn cleared his throat.

"My king. In your wisdom you allowed me to accompany you on this quest, so I feel it is my duty to advise you against such a reckless assault against an orc-held city."

"You know as well as I the orcs are broken. They quiver in the ruined husks of the last free city in Noveth. I cannot imagine a more opportune time for recklessness."

The company's stop in Wickham had proved fruitful. Not only had the meager militia there swiftly pledged fealty to the Coperan crown after learning Malcolmry meant to purge their lands of orc and goblin raiders. But the scouts who had once apprenticed for the since-annihilated rangers' guild knew the lands of Vale much more intimately than the king's own.

His army now had more than enough strength to face a decimated city of orcs, as well as first-hand reports of the devastation that the elves from Lohkrest had left in their wake.

"I do not doubt the loyalty and aptitude of your new scouting company, Your Majesty. However, something sinister birthed that wicked storm, and I am afraid it still lurks behind those ruined walls." Myrn added in a lower voice, "I do believe the city to be cursed."

Malcolmry paused his descent to face the elf. Myrn's pale skin looked almost white with fear, and that unsettled the king more than talk of a cursed city. Myrn was not a superstitious man; he was born amongst the vampires of Caim. To see him unmanned, talking of curses, reminded Malcomry of the innkeeper back in Wickham who said the very tower they now stood in was cursed. The rangers from the town's broken guild had stayed here on their last mission before the storm came. But Malcolmry felt no malign force at work in these old stones—just the occasional draft as the high autumn winds blew from the mountains.

"We don't have the luxury to concern ourselves with curses and fell sorceries," Malcolmry explained, more calmly than his declining patience would normally allow. "Plenty of flesh and blood adversaries assail us, Myrn." He pointed toward the window that overlooked the hills leading back toward his kingdom. "My son sits on my throne so we can keep the princess from delivering any more savagery upon our own people. The admiral of Jath has been assassinated, if our spies can be believed, just as he pledged his fleet to the throne—who knows if we can expect our own navy to survive the voyage home. And now there are rumors of incarnates straight out of legends." The king's voice rose with each threat that his reign faced. "I will not quiver and fret over imagined strife when I have plenty to contend with as it is."

Myrn bowed his head in a way that almost made the king feel guilty for shouting at one of the few people in his court he could trust.

He reached out and put a hand on the elf's shoulder. "Hear me, old friend. I value your council and appreciate your concern. But when we began this campaign, we both understood that conquest was the best path toward unity. The threats within Copera continue to divide us— the traders turning against the throne, the houses turning on each other, the blasted Helm Hill dwarves starting wars just for sport!" He felt the elf cringe slightly; the king's grip had intensified as his frustration grew. Malcolmry laughed at that, patting the man kindly. "Together we will both save my reign and expand the kingdom."

With that, the king continued his descent.

"Get it big."

Tremly cringed as the orc flicked his limp manhood again. She wasn't rough like the others, but she was cruel in her own way. The other orcs called her Grush or Crush—he couldn't tell by their grunting speech—but Tremly only recognized her by the gruesome scar on the left side of her chest where she once had a breast. Her remaining one was exposed now, drawing his gaze despite his best efforts.

Maybe once upon a time, the sight of an orc breast, tipped with a big dark gray-green nipple, may have aroused a curious halfling like Tremly Boggs, but after enduring countless weeks of shameful tortures by the Aggrot orcs occupying the remains of Rathen, he knew it was no good—there was just no chance he could oblige the monster.

"I can't," he said weakly. He closed his eye, waiting for the monster to finally hit him like the others did. But instead, she just made a sound that was almost a whimper.

"No like me."

Tremly peered carefully with his one remaining eye. The room was dark, lit only by a red keyshard that glowed in the corner. The orc sat on the filthy ground. Grush or Crush looked like she might cry, which oddly made Tremly forget that he was her naked prisoner; he was repulsed by his sudden instinct to comfort her. She waited for his response, but he was afraid to open his mouth.

He refused to console his captor by saying, "No, of course I like you," or, "Oh, don't say that, my dear." Instead, he just stood there, waiting.

Finally, the orc moved to undo the filthy garment around her waist. Even though Tremly had grown accustomed to the stench of living with orcs, a fresh pungent aroma filled the small room as she spread her legs.

Tremly closed his eye again to avoid weeping like a child.

"Grush."

It was a familiar voice, one that Tremly guessed belonged to either Grush's father or brother or husband—it was almost impossible to tell relations with how the orcs treated each other. A new odor filled the room as the sound of something landing nearby in a heap caused Tremly to shrink back. He knew it was a dead body before even looking to confirm. When he finally did, he could see it was a dwarf, but it wasn't one of the Rathen slaves; he knew all of them. This dwarf had a fiery red beard to match his bushy head of hair, both caked in blood and grime.

"Cook," the male orc commanded. Tremly cautiously glanced in that direction to confirm his suspicion. Grush's father or husband or brother had a bloodied axe on his shoulder and glowered at the scene before him. "Halfling whores cook." The orc motioned to Tremly. "Fuck." Orcs only smiled in the presence of cruelty, and this one smiled at Tremly before leaving the dead dwarf to be butchered.

Grush picked up a rusty sword and swung it at a hanging breastplate like a dinner gong before grunting at Tremly. "Fuck."

Knowing his only alternative was rusted steel through his belly, Tremly crept defeatedly toward Grush's spread legs. Behind him he heard the soft patter of halfling feet, but he couldn't bear to look Suzy or Chera in the eyes with what he was about to do. Even holding his breath, the stench was physically oppressive, making him gag. But he tightened his lips, refusing to empty his stomach on her for fear that it might somehow arouse the orc even more.

"What that?"

Tremly heard the halfling women gasp in unison.

He couldn't tell which one of them answered: "W-was in his h-hand. The dwarf's…"

Tremly couldn't help his curiosity. He peered over his shoulder to see Suzy standing with her hands held out in surrender. She wore an elegant dress that didn't quite fit her, and Chera stood next to her in an equally ill-fitting gown. The orcs may have subjected many of their slaves to cruelties beyond imagination, but they at least had enough wits to treat some of their surviving cooks like people, given the monsters had no dependable way to prepare meals themselves.

Tremly saw what had drawn Grush's attention. At Suzy's bare feet was a strange rock—not a common stone, nor a keyshard exactly. Tremly felt power in the thing, even more than the glowing trinket in the corner of the room.

"Bring," Grush grunted, reaching toward Suzy with an open palm while using her other hand to guide Tremly's head down into the muck.

Closing his eye and dulling his senses as best he could, Tremly spent the next few moments trying to figure out how to please the monster with his mouth. Finally, after what felt like hours, Grush convulsed a third time and pushed Tremly dismissively away so she could drift off into a satisfied sleep.

Just as he was about to go into his corner of the room, curl up, and hope for a quiet death before waking, Tremly noticed the strange gray stone that Grush must have discarded in her passions. Suddenly entranced by the thing, he snatched it.

As he curled up in his corner, a strange warmth enveloped him, and he had the sudden urge to laugh wickedly.

"What in the Abyss is a graystone?"

Neff took another long drink of wine, motioning for his king to wait. *To wait!* Malcolmry slapped the chalice from Neff's hands. It clattered to the floor, spilling Coperan red over the tattered rug. "Tell me!"

"It's like a blackshard, Your Majesty." Neff took a deep breath, his eyes wide and wild. "You know? Those things that hold Shadowlords—or so they say. A priest told us that the graystone held a Shadowlord and...well, something else. I think it was a witch, the priests said."

"What of it?" Myrn asked from the room's door. They were in an enclosed chamber below the tower, near the dungeon where Neff had been held. "Do you have this graystone?"

"Aye," Neff said, turning back to the king. "I mean, I did. But my companion fled with it in his pack. Got picked up by the orcs that your knights scared off." Neff scowled. "He wouldn't hear anything about the stone though. Just insisted I was some sort of traitor!"

"A lot has happened since you left Nazurik in the spring," Malcolmry said. "What concern is this stone of yours anyway, cousin?"

"It should be a concern of yours!" Neff insisted. "You would not believe what that thing is capable of." He cast a nervous glance to the chancellor before leaning closer to the king. "The priest at the priory...he said it was a vessel for the Shadowlord called Ithakan."

Malcolmry was brought up in a temple devoted to Corsa; much of Copera still worshipped the Sea Maiden despite the Luminaura's growing influence over the Joined Realms, but the old wet bitch had never done much for the Sulms. In turn, Malcolmry had little concern for gods and devils, except for how their names might give him leverage over others. And the fiery name Ithakan carried more influence than other Shadowlords in the northern reaches.

"And you believe him?" The king regarded his cousin carefully.

"Aye," Neff replied without hesitation. "I could hear him when I carried the stone, his voice whispering in my head. Kolin, the dwarf I traveled with, thought I was going mad."

Malcolmry scoffed. "Maybe you are."

Neff just shook his head, his gaze going to the table between them. "I think I would prefer to go mad, cousin—I mean, Your Majesty. But when I fell asleep with it in my grasp, I could feel his power." He swallowed before adding, "And I wanted it desperately."

Tremly let himself become consumed, unable to endure the dream much longer. Even though serving the cruel orcs had hardened him, nothing could have prepared him for the visions that the stone had infected him with.

But Ithakan promised reprieve; all he had to do was submit to the Shadowlord.

After submitting to Grush time after time, Tremly found it was a small thing to promise himself to a Shadowlord.

Ithakan awoke in the halfling's body, much the same size as his previous vessel. In addition to the eons of spite he had felt for the mortals that toiled on the surface of Aetha, he also felt the misery that had been inflicted upon Tremly Boggs by the cruel creature slumbering before him.

The Shadowlord felt old powers aswirl in this new atmosphere, and he wondered how long he had been aslumber since that deceitful witch Kartha had banished him back into the stone.

Regardless of how many centuries had passed since then, he felt more power than he ever remembered, and there was almost no sense of restraint as before. It was as if he were back in the Abyss before the Netherlords had invaded, and no spells had put limitations on his devastating power.

Despite all that, as he stood up and inspected his new mortal vessel, turning over his new hands and regarding his dangling bits, he felt physically smaller than he ever had. Yet he also felt more coordinated and assured in his movements than in his previous vessel. This body was older, more learned. Less innocent and unspoiled, sadly.

The large, green-skinned creature stirred in her sleep, and Ithakan clenched those small fists, drawing on the mortal fury that his new disciple felt.

Tremly Boggs smiled as he drew ancient power that had not been felt in Aetha since the Nether War.

Wick cried in protest, but his fires came regardless.

The king's army rode hard for Rathen, driven by Malcolmry Sulm's motivating words that morning. He had lied and told his men that the scouts saw the orcs fleeing the city ruins after word reached them of the mighty Coperan force bearing down on them. The soldiers must have been still drunk from the previous night, or just eager for bloodshed, because they were quickly rallied with hardly any effort by the king.

In reality, the king didn't expect much resistance once they reached Rathen, but he wanted his men hungry for a slaughter regardless. Neff rode alongside the king and the princess at the front of the main force, with Kathina pushing her mount harder to be among the first to enter the fray. Malcolmry could hear his daughter laughing and, despite everything, that still managed to unsettle him.

When they reached the city gates, the archers sent a volley of arrows over the walls before the main contingent rode straight through the makeshift barricades. Only a few mounts were skewered on the spiked palisade, but the king saw that the riders likely survived their falls (that is, assuming they avoided being trampled, which he didn't bother waiting to confirm).

They met no opposition at the city gates, and the king wondered if his lie had had some sort of prophetic quality to it, as if saying the orcs had fled caused them to actually do so. The city felt dead, reminding Malcolmry of the one time he visited his ancestral crypt in the barrows outside Nazurik. That visit haunted his nightmares ever since, and the air hanging around Rathen's remains felt equally chilling.

They encountered the first bodies as they crossed the bridge into the city proper. Fresh orc corpses, still smoldering from whatever flames had turned their flesh black. Malcolmry saw no fires though, nor did they see smoke rising from the inner city on their approach.

Magic, the king thought, and not the kind an orc shaman wields. He reined in his horse and dismounted.

"We're too late," Kathina snarled, spitting on a headless goblin corpse before stomping on it. "The elves had all the fun. Why did they not claim the city, Father?"

"The elves were but a small company," Myrn offered, approaching the king's side opposite Neff. "They could not have done this."

"Nor did they," Neff added. "The orcs still ruled here when I was taken from the Rathaway—we could see their outriders."

The king's army continued into the city, following the trail of carnage. Finally, they came to the only sign of life within the city walls.

A peculiar one-eyed halfling stood naked in the center of what appeared to have once been a tavern. The small man's hands were aflame, but the king could see that the fire didn't burn his flesh.

"He's a warlock!" a soldier cried from within the ranks. "Archers!"

"Hold!" Malcolmry bellowed, raising a mailed fist as he stepped into the ruined building. He could hear Neff and Myrn follow him.

The halfling didn't react, his attention focused on the still-smoldering bodies at his feet. They were small, like him, only burned down to the bones.

Halfling women, Malcolmry guessed, judging from their size and the way the man looked to be mourning them.

"You stand before the King of Copera!" Myrn announced boldly. "Kneel if you be not a foe, halfling!"

The little mage raised his gaze toward them, sorrow clear from his remaining eye and trembling lip.

"Kill me," the halfling begged. "Please. Before he comes back…"

The flames enveloping the halfling's hands died then, and Neff gasped when he saw what Tremly Boggs held in one of his fists.

CHAPTER ONE

Dawn

Anika Lawson had no trouble using magic, but casting spells was something else entirely. She was learning that there were more types of magic than she ever imagined, and the practitioners of each had their own proper titles, each of which Master Audreese insisted Anika memorize. Why exactly? Anika still hadn't figured that part out, but she was determined to do everything that was asked of her while studying at the spire.

"Geomancers focus their efforts on controlling the shifting motions of the earth," the elf explained, pointing to a page in the heavy tome open in front of Anika. "The old Myrethan priests wrote the original spells that would eventually become the Geomancy Codex, which still serves as the foundation for keyshard channeling... Because?"

Anika blinked at the words on the page that had begun to blur, looking up to Master Audreese when she realized the woman had been quizzing her.

"Because they're stones?"

With a sigh, the elf pulled out the chair next to Anika, shifting her long robes to sit down. "You know, you're not an initiate, Anika. I deeply respect your desire to learn where your powers come from, but—what you are... I don't know if the Child of Light needs to begin their studies like this. You have a connection to all of this that every other beginner lacks."

Anika straightened, lowering her eyes to the book. "I need to learn as if I didn't have that—as if I were just any other initiate. Before leaving Blakehurst, I didn't even realize how much there was that I didn't know about magic. And after everything that's happened..." She swallowed, feeling a strange sense of shame having to admit weakness. "I don't want to lose control again. I have twice as much power coursing through me now, with no real fundamental knowledge of how to wield it or where it even comes from. The least I can do is understand how those who have to work doubly hard for even a fraction of that power are able to control it.

"Besides," she continued, "with the city's mayor still pressuring me to serve her as an official advisor…so many people already know I'm the Child of Light. I can't run from it anymore. Like Ransil said, word travels faster in Vale than anywhere else. We have to assume that everyone will know what I'm capable of, so I need to be prepared."

When Anika glanced up from the book, she saw Audreese was actually almost smiling.

But the elf just said, "Very well. Then let us move on from geomancy to aeromancy, since that will likely be more relevant to your current training at least."

As Audreese stood up to continue the lecture, the library door opened inward to reveal the new High Mage of Raventhal Spire, Quinn Olivick, and his faithful companion these past two weeks, the halfling Ransil Osbury. It was as if her mention of his name had summoned her old friend back to the spire.

Anika smiled at Ransil, nearly leaping out of her chair to greet him.

"When did you return?" she asked, forgoing any formalities in front of the tower's new boy-ruler.

Ransil wrapped his arms around Anika's neck when she knelt down to embrace him. "Last night. I was told dawn was your study time, and we didn't want to interrupt."

"We were just about to take a break," Audreese said, placing a reassuring hand on young Quinn's shoulder. "I trust the visit to House Grale proved fruitful?"

Ransil rested his small hands on the pommels of his daggers, nodding his head while also tilting it to either side, as if he didn't want to confirm one way or the other. "Eventually. It seems our new Lady Mayor intends to rule from her own home, sending one of her advisors on the city's council in her stead—at least for now. However, the favor Raventhal required from House Grale's ample reserves would only be rendered as payment in return for a bit of adventuring."

Anika looked from the halfling to the boy High Mage, just now noticing a few scrapes and bruises on each of their faces. "What did they make you do?"

Quinn smiled brightly, looking every bit the ten-year-old trouble seeker he was. "We had to fight gnolls!"

"Gnolls?!" Audreese and Anika exclaimed together. The savage beastfolk were known to once be a common threat in Vale before Anika's time, but they had since been driven back into Lohkrest, and then beyond to Guyen, from where they had first come. The hyena-faced mongrels were strangely devoted to fire and used it to raid and ruin wherever they went.

Ransil sighed. "It seems recent events have drawn out the more unsavory monsters from beyond our borders. Farms and hamlets along the edge of Lohkrest have been raided by gnolls, kobolds, goblins, and worse all along the Bracing River. Lady Grale promised to fund the city's rebuilding efforts if we pledged Raventhal's blue and red mages to protect the countryside." Ransil drew one of his knives and spun it, checking its edge. "But first she required a show of good faith by having us expel a small band of gnolls from a small outpost on her borders."

"Quinn," Audreese began sternly, "this sounds far too dangerous an errand. It is not becoming of you to take on such lowly quests at such risk to your own person. You are the High Mage of Raventhal Spire now. Do you think Konrath went about adventuring once he swore his oath?"

"That's what I'm for," Ransil said with a wink at the elf. "And I told him so. Many. Times. But he wouldn't have it. So I allowed him to support me, but kept him far from harm's way."

Quinn shrugged away from Audreese's hand, straightening his ill-fitting red robe. "I know how they see me—just an upstart boy, a weak replacement for someone like Konrath. But when we returned to House Grale with the gnoll leader's head, they cheered my name and called me Quinn the Courageous! They even threw us a feast!"

Ransil snorted a laugh. "That they did. And loaded up our cart with enough coin to finish the tower's repairs, along with a letter of apology to the Luminaura that the Lady Mayor will not be funding any of the cathedral." Ransil grimaced at Anika while delivering that last bit of news. "I was hoping you might be willing to take that particular report to the priest."

Anika shook her head at that. "I haven't seen Avrim of late. He oversees the cathedral night and day." She shifted her gaze toward Audreese, with whom she had already confided her concerns. "He's avoided me whenever I leave the spire. And Deina's even worse, spending most of her time in the woods outside the city."

Anika noticed Ransil avert his eyes, shifting his feet. *What are they all hiding from me?*

"Never mind," the halfling finally said, turning toward Quinn. "I'll go find him and let him know his new role as Sathford's beacon may be postponed a while."

"Let me go change first," Quinn said, moving to shrug out of his sweaty robes.

"No," Ransil said, reaching up to put a hand on the young boy's shoulder. "You're needed here. We've been gone long enough, and surely Master Groaves could use your help running this place. I'll go speak to Avrim alone."

"Are you sure you don't want me to come along?" Anika asked. Judging by how the halfling hurried out of the study, she already knew the answer; she just wanted to hear him lie again so she could be sure.

When he got to the door, Ransil looked over his shoulder and gave her a crooked grin. "You looking to get swarmed again out there, kid? You're famous now, Ani. Sit tight and keep learning those spells. I'll join you for dinner in the hall."

I can tell you what he's hiding from you, Stane whispered, his voice a slithery snake in her mind.

"No," she replied in a small breath.

"Huh?" Quinn turned toward her.

She looked at the young High Mage and then to Audreese. Something about the way they looked at her made her uneasy, so she just quickly said, "No more studies today. I need some rest."

She left the two rulers of Raventhal staring at each other in confusion as she hurried toward her quarters before Stane's laughter caused her to lash out again.

"Praise the beacon!"

Avrim Kaust shied away from the passerby, knowing that the cheer would soon be accompanied by a dozen others. It had become impossible for him to walk the streets of Sathford without being hailed as the Savior of Sathler Bridge, even when he was dressed as a commoner like now.

"Illuminate his path!" Another cry was taken up, followed by two others just like it. Avrim awkwardly raised a hand in greeting to those he passed: a gnome sellsword who asked for a blessing, two dwarf artisans who could have been twins pledging to join the builders to help raise the new cathedral, and about a dozen of the city watch who had fought by Avrim's side during the assault. They all wanted something from him that he didn't know how to give, so he settled for pleasant smiles and nods as he kept his pace.

Once, his heart may have swelled in the face of such glory thrown his way, but now Avrim felt it sink deeper into his chest with each encouraging shout. It was as if each prayer thrown his way brought back the sensation of the heavenly power flowing through him as he faced the undead hordes in that very city.

And that power was too much for any living person, no matter their station. All it did was make him feel unworthy and remind him of all the terrible things he had done to "earn" it.

To his relief, the crowd thinned as he reached the more devastated part of the city, which rested under the shadow of Raventhal. There, merchants and guards were replaced by masons and laborers who tended to the rubble, clearing the streets so trade could resume as swiftly as possible. The only one of the Five Casks in Bridge Quarter that was damaged during the assault was the Riverstone, but now that it was repaired and operating again, Avrim knew where he might find his wayward friend.

He pushed open the doors, not surprised to find the Riverstone's common room to be mostly empty this early in the day. Neither was he surprised to see Deina Brasson sitting alone in a corner, nursing a pint, while her axe, Harvester, leaned against the empty chair. The keyshard set between the weapon's blades pulsed with a slow green rhythm and, as expected, Avrim felt that same veil of power envelop him as he stepped toward the dwarf.

"Good morning, dear beacon," came a jovial voice from behind the bar. Avrim looked to see the heavy human woman whose name he couldn't recall cleaning a stein with a rag. "Can I bring you a pint?"

"No thanks," Avrim began.

"The Light would turn it to water 'soon as it passed his lips," Deina announced in a slurred voice. "Purify the corruption! No mere mortal is our blessed beacon, Sandra. No!" The rest of what she said was lost in her cup.

Avrim didn't even want to think about how many pints the dwarf had drained to get that drunk—he honestly couldn't recall ever seeing the woman get overly affected by ale.

"I thought I might find you chopping wood again," Avrim remarked, approaching her warily; he didn't want another encounter like their last one. "Our lumber stores grow meek."

Deina picked up her tankard once more and tipped back what was left into her gullet. She slammed the empty mug down and reached for her weapon. "Right away, dear beacon."

"Deina," he said, motioning for her to remain seated. "Please, a moment."

The dwarf eyed him lazily as she slouched back into her chair. A gnome girl snuck over to refill Deina's empty drink.

"I think she's had plenty," Avrim told the tiny attendant. The gnome's eyes darted between man and dwarf until Deina gave a dismissive wave to send her away.

"The Light comes to the rescue again," Deina mumbled, covering the jab with a forced belch.

Avrim allowed that, pulling out one of the free chairs to join her. "How long is this going to continue, friend?"

"Seems like it's finished now. Just letting me tummy settle before I take this 'ere mythic weapon out to fell some sacred trees for yer chapel, friend."

"You know what I mean, Deina. We all grieve with you. Melaine was a true companion, and it's important we honor her sacrifice. But this can't go on."

Deina didn't react as he expected. Even as he said the words, Avrim braced himself for the fiery retort, telling him he knew nothing of her sacrifice and how he didn't understand how much the woman meant to her. In fact, if he were being honest, he hoped she would lash out at him—anything to awaken the old fire that burned so hot in the dwarf he once knew.

But instead, Deina just stared at the table, breathing slow and steady. Harvester continued to give off that faint green glow that pulsed with the rise and fall of its bearer's chest.

"We only get one, Avrim," she said finally, still not meeting his gaze. Tears were welling in her eyes. "I ain't never truly loved someone before, and I thought them bards' songs were ripe shit for the pluckin', as they say in New Hold." She sniffed and wiped her nose on the back of her thick hand. "But all those rhymes and poems and songs those little dandies prance on about..." She began to shake so slightly that

Avrim couldn't tell if she was chuckling or sobbing. But when her voice broke, he knew which. "I get it now—why so many of them songs warn against even falling in love in the first place. Because when it's gone…"

Just as Avrim was about to reach a hand out to pat the dwarf's, Deina pushed herself to her feet and threw Harvester over her shoulder.

"Deina," he began.

The dwarf just raised a hand to quiet him as she marched toward the door. "Just let me be useful, dammit." As she pulled the door open, she glanced back at him with tear-filled eyes. "She died being useful. It's the least I can do."

Avrim hung his head, wishing he could feel better about his small victory of getting her away from the drink. But Deina's grief was only one of the thousand troubles awaiting the new beacon of Sathford.

Another of which snuck into the Riverstone moments later.

"She still grieves?"

He looked up to see Ransil Osbury approaching, looking as if he had just gotten in from the road. Avrim nodded. "Please tell me you bring good news from the Grales. I could use a bit of levity."

The look on the halfling's face was enough to confirm what he already feared.

Letting his frustrations get the best of him, Avrim slammed his fist on the table. A crash from back in the kitchen told him he had startled the little gnome barmaid; he didn't care. He wanted all the glass in the city to crash down. He wanted the whole world to crumble in that moment, but the feeling passed as quickly as it came.

"Sorry," he said to Ransil, who had jerked back.

"I wasn't eager to bring you the news. But I thought it would be best if you knew sooner rather than later." He pulled a chair out to join the priest at the low table; he still barely got his chin over the surface. "I don't know what that means for the cathedral…"

"It means," Avrim sighed, leaning back, looking to the ceiling and rubbing his forehead, "that the city and the Church are going to come to blows, and I'll be caught in the middle. You know as well as I do that the Archbeacon will take news of Gwynna withholding coin from the cathedral as an open act of defiance. Luriah has grown used to having her way, especially with the queen at her back. And after the invasion…Darrance will expect me to step in on their behalf. I'm convinced that's why he put me in this role, so he wouldn't have to deal with this very situation."

Ransil let out his own exhausted breath. "I do not envy you, Avrim. There's a reason I stayed out of these affairs… What I wouldn't give to be back in Blakehurst, where my biggest concern was having enough game for a stew or whose birthday would be needing a cake next."

Avrim actually smiled then, glad to have the small man's company again. There was something about Ransil Osbury that comforted him, and it seemed to be a quality that others saw in him as well, because he was well-liked in the city and trusted by nearly everyone. When he turned his gaze back, he saw a concerned look on the halfling's face.

"What is it?"

"Anika says you've been avoiding her."

Flashes of Renay Lawson's bloody face went through his mind at the mention of Anika's name, and he had to look away. He hadn't confided the truth of what really happened in Oakworth to anyone, and it continued to haunt him, eating at his heart. The mere mention of Anika's name took him straight back to The Harvest Breeze, when he stood over the corpse of her murdered mother.

The mother that had tasked with killing her own son.

All because of the Light.

"She's going to suspect something," Ransil continued. "I need to know you won't tell her about Gage."

"I won't," Avrim replied sharply, still averting his eyes. "As I said when I healed you, I agree that she should not know what happened. She wouldn't understand. If she found out her brother tried to kill you…well, that would make the whole prophecy much easier to fulfill."

Ransil got to his feet. "She can't know, Avrim. Whether or not we believe that insane warlock that Corvanna summoned, or that Anika somehow knows she can stop all this, we cannot set her on that path. Do we agree?"

He nodded to Ransil.

"I need you to say it," the halfling insisted.

Avrim slammed his fist down on the table again. "I said yes, dammit!"

The halfling didn't jerk away this time, his calm expression unbroken. But there was something in his eyes that Avrim didn't like.

There was a shadow that wasn't there before.

Now, Avrim thought, and he couldn't be sure if it was his own thought or the Light itself. *What are you hiding?*

Anika retreated to her chambers. The day was still young, but she felt exhausted from waking up so early. She would have preferred if her mind was a bit sharper when she met Ransil for dinner. She intended to find out what the man was keeping to himself, especially if it had anything to do with her brother. More than likely, it was something concerning Gwynna Grale or the gnoll situation that he didn't want to burden her with, but Ransil had been strangely silent in regards to her brother since the invasion.

Thinking of Gage brought a strange cramp to her stomach. She sat down on her cot and put a hand there, as if she could feel whatever afflicted her. But there was just tight muscle, a result of little appetite and maybe tightening her body too much when trying to contain the world's most ancient powers.

She lay down on her back, staring into the dusty rafters of the ceiling. She had chosen a room on the first floor with the initiates— where she felt she belonged—so it was rare that she could enjoy such a quiet moment to herself. Normally, there would be excited young mages scrambling around, practicing cantrips, and sharing gossip about their peers.

In that silence, Stane came to her again.

He promised her power, answers to her questions.

Thinking of Ransil's deceitful expression made her wonder if today might be the day she finally relented.

Unless, she wondered, thinking about the time Stane came to her in Karrane, upon the altar, *I already have…*

CHAPTER TWO

Light the Way Home

Layla Abrigale regarded the approaching cityscape with a mixture of anticipation and dread. She couldn't help but fear having to face Queen Sopheena and convince the woman that she was still her faithful Court Mage despite killing her only other Court Mage. However, the thought of finding and flaying the lecherous Desmond Everton once more kindled within her a fiery need for vengeance.

As she stood there observing Merithian's stately towers, from which sapphire banners snapped in the ocean breeze, she heard the damn whistling again.

The Lord Mayor of Waneport paced the deck of *Revery*, blowing a jaunty tune through his perfectly pursed lips as if they were out on a pleasure voyage and not plotting treason against the most powerful seat of the Joined Realms.

Just looking at Jaffron Casryk filled Layla with a heaving rage that only deep, controlled breaths could restrain. Part of her wondered if the elf was the true reason she felt the desire to peel the skin from a foe; even looking at him now, Layla had trouble not picturing Valix's head spinning from dead shoulders as it trailed an arc of blood to disappear into the watery abyss. But she reminded herself that Desmond was the one that set her on this twisting path of misery—she must focus her wrath on him.

But he killed Valix, Stane told her, his voice carried by the breeze from the Racivic Sea. *You can avenge her now, Layla. You've accepted my power before. Use it again to push this pompous high elf overboard and be rid of him once and for all.*

"Do you still want to kill me?"

Layla stiffened, wondering if Jaffron had somehow heard Stane's whispers as well.

Yes, Stane said.

"Does it matter?" Layla asked, trying to ignore the malicious presence within her. She gripped the gunwale and tried to let the sea breeze calm her. "It seems we have use of each other still, so even if I wanted you dead, it would have to wait."

Jaffron made a sound that could have been a laugh as he leaned over the railing next to Layla, resting his elbows as two of his bodyguards took position farther down from them. "I think I'd prefer my fellow conspirators wanting me dead—it makes them more dependable. It takes a certain restraint and dedication to work with someone whose throat you'd like to slit. In a way, it leads to more trusting fellowships."

That sounded absurd to Layla, but she declined to get into a debate over it.

"Do you mind if I ask you a question, Lady Abrigale?"

Why would you mind appeasing the bastard who removed your lover's head from her shoulders?

When Layla didn't answer, she could feel his gaze turn from the sea to her.

His voice changed slightly as he asked, "What do you truly know of Stane?"

The mention of that name silenced the voices in her head, as if it had some control when spoken aloud. She turned slightly to regard him, looking for any mockery on the Lord Mayor's face. There was none. It was a genuine question, one that she found she had no easy way of answering.

"I know it's a name that has been falsely used throughout the ages," she began. "His book...speaks to me, in a way. I cannot read it—not truly—but Valix..." Layla looked away, watching the shores of Noveth grow nearer. "Valix said only Kartha could read it—that no one else in the Joined Realms can make sense of its arcane contents."

"Aye," Jaffron said, following her gaze. It was eerie hearing the man speak with no mirth, and it disarmed Layla, making her eager to know why he had come above deck suddenly after having spent so much of the voyage steering clear of her. "Kartha the Cursed, Kartha the Cruel—Stane's whore is the only one who can make sense of his nonsensical scribbles. Without her, that book is about as useful to the queen as her husband's cock."

Layla snorted at that, coughing to cover it up. She didn't want Jaffron to think they were amicable now—drinking companions that could squash their grievances, make merry over a carafe of wine.

She vowed in that moment not to let that happen. It would cheapen

Valix's murder, somehow forgiving it.

Fortunately, the elf didn't seem to pay Layla any mind. His gaze was distant as he added, "I've been looking for her in these accursed visions—but I'm not my father. Nor am I my sister. Beatrim likely knew already where the old witch hid, but now it's on me to make sense of these—" He pushed himself back from the railing, grabbing his head with both his hands in sudden pain.

Layla recoiled.

"Ahhh!" Jaffron cried, clearly afflicted with something. He jerked his head toward her, glaring at Layla through the clenched slits his eyes had become. "What did you do?!"

Layla looked at the bodyguards who approached either side of the Lord Mayor, their hands on their swords.

"Nothing!" she cried.

"Back!" came a booming voice from the other side of the ship. Layla turned to see Maze emerging from below. "Get back from them," they commanded the bodyguards. "He's having a vision!" Maze was dressed in baggy sailor's clothes, and they jogged over toward the elves. "Can you hear him, Layla?"

She looked from Jaffron to Maze, not sure who they meant. Was she supposed to be hearing Stane? Or Jaffron's thoughts? Layla just shook her head, far too confused to sort through all her racing thoughts.

"It's her!" Jaffron screamed in agony. One of his bodyguards drew her sword then, stepping toward Layla. The Lord Mayor waved his arm between them. "Not her, you cunt! It's Kartha! The witch!" Jaffron fell to his knees, still clutching at his head as if he could suffocate whatever it was that was torturing him.

"It's not supposed to work like this," Maze said, turning to Layla. "Can you help him?"

"How?!" Layla wasn't a priest or healer or sage. None of the magic she mastered in the Arcania had anything to do with prophecies or visions, and after what Desmond had done to her all those years, the last thing she ever wished to do was meddle in someone else's mind. "What's happening to him?! How can I help if I don't know what—"

"Someone's trying to block him," Maze interrupted, their voice strangely calm as the Lord Mayor of Waneport doubled over in agony. "Like an Oather's armor dampens a spell—if he's trying to find Kartha, he needs to break her defenses."

Layla's mind raced, thinking back to her training in the Arcania. She focused primarily on elemental magic and spells that were either used in battle or crafting. The one time she broke an enchantment was when Fainly Lopke challenged her to disarm a ward he placed on a locked door. But she had witnessed the gnome cast the ward, making it possible to undo it.

Jaffron screamed again and fell to his side, his wonderful boots pounding a painful, erratic rhythm on the ship's deck. Sailors were gathering around to witness the torment, but no one moved to help him. It was as if none of the onlookers cared much about the sea lord's fate.

"Hurry!" Maze called, their voice finally betraying some emotion.

Layla knelt down, unsure of how to stop whatever was happening. She carefully put her hands over Jaffron's, forgetting how much she despised the man in this moment of urgency. She closed her eyes and concentrated on seeing those delicate threads of magical energy. Almost immediately, she saw it: a nearly invisible web of dark power that was completely foreign to her. The world fell away as she entered a familiar trance.

During her short time at Raventhal Spire, she had heard that all mages worked magic in their own way. Spells could be learned and rituals could be replicated, but the actual act of harnessing raw magic was a deeply personal and individual experience. Her own way of studying magic was by finding these threads—the ones that connected the unseen parts of the world—and figuring out how they linked what she wanted to happen with the actual happening.

Layla traced the dark threads, her mind weaving together a hammer to smash the clouded glass that obscured Jaffron's vision.

Pressure had been building in Layla's mind as she finished breaking the spell, and it all released so suddenly that she was thrown away from Jaffron, slamming back to reality as her body landed in a heap on the chaotic deck of *Revery*.

"South!" Jaffron shouted. Layla could hardly hear him over the thundering feet of frantic sailors and Maze's continued cries. "Turn south! To Waneport!"

"Jaffron! What'd you see?" Maze helped Layla to her feet as they shouted over their shoulder at the Lord Mayor. "What's in Waneport?!"

"The queen will have to wait," the elf replied, shoving the ship's captain toward the gathered crew. "We need to get to Stelmont before the Arcania realizes they've got Kartha and Archmage Lopke sitting in a cell under the Vestige."

Kartha thrashed awake, startling Bennik, who had just finally started to drift off to sleep. Since his recent imprisonment by the harpies, it was rare the man allowed sleep to take him while he was rotting in a cell, and he felt the sudden urge to kick the woman for ruining the promise of slumber.

"What was that?" Fainly Lopke sat up from the dirty straw pile that served as his bed. The white hair that remained around the side of his head stood on end, making him look absurd. "Ivy?"

"I've been seen," she said in a hushed voice, as if a spy lurked in the shadows of their cell.

Bennik Lawson hadn't known the woman long, but she sounded more terrified than he thought possible for someone of her...nature. What kind of nightmare could startle someone like the last daughter of Arkath?

"The High Sanctum?" Fainly asked.

Bennik pushed himself up from the ground, his legs and back aching. Looking beyond the bars, he could see that the jailor had likely gone to get drunk again. They were alone for now.

"No," Kartha replied, sitting up to rub her temples. The woman's breasts were exposed again, and Bennik averted his eyes from those strange green nipples—he swore she refused to wear proper clothing just to make her cellmates squirm uncomfortably. "It can't be..." She hung her head as Bennik tossed the gnome a threadbare blanket. Fainly draped it over Kartha's naked shoulders.

"Tell us." The Archmage's voice was strangely out of character, almost gentle.

Kartha looked up to both of them with her emerald eyes, regarding them with suspended dread. "When I last encountered Sauthorn, the man threatened to reveal what I shared with you in Arkath. He knew about Stane's time in the city, and of our relationship. It's why I had to leave Velcarthe before joining the Purveyors." Her gaze became distant. "Now that I think about it...I don't think the Unthroning would have happened if it weren't for him..."

"Who is Sauthorn?" Bennik asked, though when he said the name aloud, it felt familiar on his lips.

"The prophet," Fainly answered, his eyes still narrowed on Kartha. "He was said to be the last—the Disciples of Stane hunted the others, accusing them of stealing their lord's powers of precognition."

Now Bennik remembered. The Brightmother in Blakehurst had mentioned Sauthorn's name occasionally; given she was an elf as well, Bennik always had a strange feeling that maybe the mysterious figure was a relation.

Though he found it unlikely that this Sauthorn's relative was in his own town.

"Why would it matter if he's seen you?" Fainly asked. "You said he already knew your secrets—what is the concern now?"

"The concern," Kartha said, the fear leaving her voice, replaced by her usual condescension, "is that I purged the man's memory before fleeing Velcarthe. I couldn't let him live with such knowledge of my past—my ties to Stane. He should have no clue who I am or where I would be—he shouldn't even know my name anymore." She got up, letting the ratty blanket fall away from her pale green flesh. She held Bennik's gaze so he wouldn't look away. "Also, he's dead."

"I'm just a squire though," Jak insisted as Sir Paul Stone shoved a pot helm toward him. "I mostly just helped Dame Strallow with her armor, and...um, attended her...at night."

Paul laughed at that as he adjusted his gorget. "Oh, I bet you did. Kasia's got a way with her squires—that's certainly no secret. But that's done now. You're an honorary part of the Vestige's household guard." He jammed an armored elbow painfully into the side of Jak's chest. "Trust me, kid. There are plenty of little harlots at The West Wind that get weak in the knees for a guard of the Vestige." He swatted at Jak's codpiece, barely missing it. "They'll think your balls are little keyshards and that measly cock of yours is a magic wand." The drunk Oather laughed heartily at his own wit.

"Sir Stone!" High Mage Stacy's voice was shrill and panicked. "There's another group of them coming up the hill! There's a torchbearer and some with bows—I think they intend to smoke us out!"

There were shrieks beyond the walls, and Jak felt his heart thud against his chest. His instincts were to go check on the halfling girls, but he remembered they were back at the inn where they were likely much safer. The cultists hadn't seemed too interested in Stelmont proper, only attacking the Vestige with their beastmen.

"Stupid bastards," the Oather spat, reaching for his morningstar that he had not cleaned since yesterday. Jak could still see blood along the weapon's pitted sphere, and what looked like torn flesh hung from one of its spikes. Paul shoved a sword into Jak's hand and the boy's stomach turned. "Just stick by me, boy. We'll send the dwarves in first this time—just swing that thing at any of the Wickans that come your way."

"Wickans?" Jak had heard the term earlier that afternoon during the first assault.

"Fanatical worshippers of Wick," Stacy said impatiently. "They've been growing in number since this Combustress started flashing her bits for any desperate scoundrel who can wield a torch."

"They're looking for some fire," Paul growled, "we'll give 'em fire."

Jak's hand trembled as he followed the armored Oather out of the tower's small armory, but the sound of the dwarven boots thundering up the undercroft stairs soothed his nerves. If there was one thing he'd prefer to be between himself and an enemy host, it was a band of battle-hungry dwarves.

"Oi!" one of them cried as they emerged from the dark. It was Vlanna Hains, the axe maiden who came to the Vestige looking for a pyromancer she believed killed her brother in the mines. "Not without us!"

Sir Paul Stone motioned toward the barricaded entry just beyond High Mage Stacy Augustine. "After you, m'lady. We'll be right behind you. Just save some for the boy, yeah?" His laugh sounded more forced this time.

Vlanna slammed her heavy, double-bladed battle axe against her small round shield before calling to the five other dwarves behind her. "This tower is under Clan Hains' protection! It shall not fall to the Combustress!"

Jak noticed a subtle look shared between Paul and Stacy then, which he suspected had something to do with the two of them misleading Vlanna somehow so the New Hold dwarves would provide protection. With the Vestige cut off from Andelor, there would be no help coming from the new Archmage. And it seemed Stacy only had a paltry few untrained mages in her ranks.

The dwarves went about unbarricading the door that separated them from a glorious battle, and Jak followed Paul toward Stacy.

"You reckon it's the prisoners they want, or the keyshards they brought with 'em?"

Jak barely heard the Oather's whispered question, but he couldn't misread the High Mage's annoyed reaction.

"Does it matter, Sir Stone? They aren't getting either. These fanatics have been burning out hamlets along the Wane Coast since last year. They're just mad arsonists that need to be put down."

The Oather nodded, watching the dwarves work. "Just seems strange—those two came in all burned up, then that brawny one with the shards... Next thing we know, they're all hellbent on taking the tower."

"Take one of them alive this time," Stacy suggested, but her tone sounded sarcastic. "You can ask them all the damn questions you want."

With that, Sir Stone led Jak toward the open doors just as the dwarves hurried through on stunted legs, waving their weapons overhead as they entered the smoky haze outside.

The Combustress watched from the hill. Next to her, Dureen Cleaver snorted a laugh, pointing at the New Hold dwarves falling for their trap.

"Told ye no Hains would resist a brawl," the dwarf sneered. "But ye still haven't told me how you aim to deal with that Oather, Kindled One. He can nullify yer spells, can't he? Last time he put out all those torches without much more than a twitch of his stupid mouth."

Veronitha Blaithe lowered her hood; the setting sun painted her ruined scalp in soft glows of yellow and orange, making her copper Xe'danni skin radiate in a way that earned her namesake: *The Combustress.*

A foolish title, Veronitha knew, but it was the type of name that one would be hard-pressed to forget—the type of name that served useful when forming a cult.

"No," she said softly, inclining her head as the battle began. The first volley of flaming arrows were poorly aimed—of the dozen acolytes that had offered to sacrifice themselves to the Combustress that night, only one or two had even used a bow before. But that did not concern Veronitha, since the arrows were just for show. Her eyes were fixed on the bald human woman with the flaming fists—she suspected that would be the chosen one.

"No?" Dureen shifted on her feet, impatient as always.

"Did you think the trap was for them?"

Dureen looked up toward her fiery master, then turned back to the screams coming from the woman's followers at the base of the hill. The New Hold dwarves had only lost a single fighter to the second volley of arrows and were now engaged in fierce melee with her undisciplined cultists. The Oather and his squire approached without much urgency.

Veronitha could tell the dwarf was still struggling with the plan— which was precisely why she kept it to herself until now. Her followers were faithful and fervent, but they remained as such due to a certain degree of ignorance.

Case in point: The sacrifices below truly believed they were carrying out Wick's desire to engulf the world in flame so it may be reborn. However, their final act was merely in service to Veronitha's own burning desire for power.

"Are we not going to the tower?" Dureen sounded nervous to hear the answer.

"We are not," the Combustress said over the sound of her followers being slaughtered. The dwarves made short work of the cultists—all but the burning fist monk who had come from Guyen. Her other servants fought with swords, cudgels, and daggers (for as much good as it did them), but the woman that appeared to be her chosen one kept the attackers at bay with her bare hands.

Even if they were on fire.

The Oather finally arrived, his armor radiating the magic-absorbing aura that made Veronitha cringe even from this far away. His presence extinguished the monk's hands, and she was quickly subdued by the remaining members of the Hains Clan. The Oather shouted something that caused the dwarves to lower their weapons.

"My chosen one," Veronitha said, pulling her hood up over her burned head. "Come, Dureen. You must get back to New Hold at once."

"That's it?" Insolence crept into the woman's voice. "They're taking

Havina prisoner! I thought we needed to find keyshards!"

The Combustress smiled when she turned away, knowing those shards were now truly within her grasp.

Below deck, Layla tried not to dwell on the memory of her previous voyage with Valix. It was hard not to think of the Xe'danni woman while in surroundings that were so similar to the ones they made love in. But now that she was walking to see the woman's killer—whose life she may have just saved—Layla tried to clear it all from her mind.

Of course, it was no good. When she stepped into the captain's quarters and saw Jaffron's face, all she could think of was Valix's head tumbling into the ocean all over again.

"You have my thanks," the Lord Mayor said to her when he saw Layla appear in the open doorway. "Although, I may be cursing you soon—I have a feeling you just opened the floodgates." He was abed, laying atop the elegant covers that displayed extravagant Caimish patterns. Jaffron took a sip from a golden wine glass and then set it down on the small table near the captain's bed. "Could you see it?"

Layla shook her head, assuming "it" was a vision of the old crone they sought. She saw nothing of Jaffron's prophecies, only the effects of them—namely the Lord Mayor fumbling around the deck of the *Revery* shouting commands until Maze had the half-orc sailor Otter knock him to the ground; the elf had been abed since, demanding wine and commanding the young swab girl to constantly empty his privy.

"She's in disguise," Jaffron said, staring into his bedsheets as if he could see the witch now. "Some kind of illusion—it must be. It makes me wonder if I had seen her before, but didn't realize it because I expected a withered old cunt, not some buxom green-skinned nymph."

Layla didn't know what to make of that, so she just crossed her arms and leaned against the doorway, hoping Maze would arrive soon; she had no desire to parlay with Jaffron Casryk alone.

"I saw something else," Jaffron said, looking up to Layla. His lips didn't move, but something in his gaze felt mocking or sinister, as if he were grinning at her without moving his lips. "A bloody page..."

Layla averted her eyes, glad to hear Maze's footsteps approaching.

"I take it the wine has calmed your nerves, Lord Mayor?" Maze put a gentle hand on Layla's shoulder. "And you've thanked our Court Mage for untangling that arcane knot the witch made of your mind?"

"Don't call me that," Jaffron snapped. "We shan't play the queen's games while she's in Andelor and we're on our way back to the Wane Coast."

"Speaking of," Maze said, sliding past Layla to enter the cabin and find a seat at the small table, "where exactly in Waneport is our quarry?"

"It's not Waneport," Jaffron replied. "She's being held in the Vestige. Outside Stelmont."

"Can't say I've heard of it," Maze said, pouring themself a glass of wine.

"It's part of the Arcania," Layla offered, having visited there once when she and Desmond had to hunt troglodytes that were raiding the coast. "Stelmont is a village within the Steddlewood."

"Do we know why she's being held?"

Jaffron slid his legs over the edge of the bed, his high boots knocking against the wood floor. "She's taken some other form—I can only suppose. Given, if it was an illusion, the High Mage at the tower would likely have broken it."

"You said a green-skinned nymph?" Layla asked. "Like a Daughter of Oakus?"

Maze's eyebrows raised at that, but they continued drinking their wine as their gaze darted between Layla and Jaffron. Layla was discomforted by such a show of surprise from someone like Maze, who tended to be the one with the answers.

"Perhaps," Jaffron replied absently, pushing himself to his feet. "It would be ideal if we could get there while she was still a prisoner—would make this whole ordeal much less complicated."

"And how's that exactly?" Maze inquired, setting an empty wine glass back on the table.

"The vision," he began, making spherical motions with his hands near his head, "it's cloudy. But I could sense Kartha's concern that the Old Ways had collapsed." He looked at Layla suddenly. "And the Archmage was imprisoned with her."

Layla straightened at that, pushing herself away from the doorway. "You saw Fainly Lopke? The Archmage is held prisoner?"

Maze stood up as well. "How's that possible?"

"That's just it," Jaffron said, all the arrogance and swagger gone from him now; he was just a lost elf at sea like Layla. "He's not the Archmage anymore…"

Fainly snapped his fingers at Bennik. "Get me up!" He pointed to the high window from which screams and clashing steel came through. "Let me see!"

Bennik ignored the gnome, taking a look for himself. But Kartha knelt to lift him up, and the Archmage could see the tail end of a short-lived battle.

"It's the cult again," Bennik said. "Brought more fire this time. Are those gnolls?"

"The Combustress has been a plague on the Wane Coast since we chased the troglodytes off," Fainly offered. But his attention was on the restrained woman who seemed to have been taken prisoner—perhaps a possible new cellmate. "That one's hands aren't burned."

"A Guyenese monk," Kartha offered. "The old temples of Wick trained them how to focus their fists into flaming weapons, before those Corsan priests flushed them all out of the swamps."

Bennik turned to the gnome then. "Can't you set your hands on fire? Or summon something to break down those bars already? Or are we just to rot in here while my children face the end of the world alone?!"

Fainly sighed as he looked up at the man. "Typical soldier—thinking magic can solve all your problems. Just look out there, Lawson! We break out of this cell, then what? You and our naked friend here going to take care of all those blood-hungry dwarves or that wretched Oather? Maybe those gnolls lurking back by the trees, eh? You think your bare hands and Kartha's new tits will make potent enough weapons against all that while I'm all but expended?"

Bennik just stared back out the window, watching the surrendered monk get dragged back toward the Vestige while the dwarves tended to the fallen.

Kartha put the gnome down. "He's right, Lawson. I'd be worthless in a fight anytime soon. We would both need to use the feysleep to fully recover after the events in Arkath, and I dare not risk that while the new Archmage schemes in the Arcania."

"That Vera," Fainly growled, pacing across the cell as he pulled at his wild hair. "Should have never let that Stane-sucking heathen into the Arcania!" The only reason he had was because they had no Xe'danni at the time, and there were whispers that the Child of Shadow had risen there. The High Sanctum was convinced they needed someone with intimate knowledge of Velcarthe's underworld; Fainly had no reason to argue their case. *How foolish I was*, he thought miserably.

As if reading the gnome's mind, Bennik sulked back to his side of the cell and mumbled, "I need to get out of here and find my children."

"We will," Kartha assured him. "Because they will need us."

Fainly looked at Kartha and then to Bennik, who regarded the woman curiously.

But she just added, "All of us."

CHAPTER THREE

Beneath the Surface

Andelor was both wondrous and terrifying to Gage. While most of his time since arriving in the capital had been spent underground, the rare times he and Robin roamed the streets were enough to make him certain that he was born for city life. He felt a bitterness toward his home of Blakehurst, as if he had been hidden away from the splendors of the world.

"I feel like we could walk these streets for years and I still wouldn't see half of what this place has to offer," he told Robin.

"Well," Robin said, giving him another bite of the sausage they had purchased from a halfling vendor, "there's no reason why we shouldn't stay, is there?"

Even though the meat was juicy and delicious in Gage's mouth, the notion that they might be able to relax and enjoy the sights and sounds of Andelor reminded him that, in reality, they couldn't. The image of Ransil Osbury getting stabbed in the back still haunted him, and he knew there was no straying from the path he had already embarked on. His sister would find out eventually, then she would piece together what really happened to Elza back home.

If she hadn't already suspected him of killing their mother, it would be all but a certainty to her at that point.

Gage knew there was no going back.

"Would we join the Guild?"

Robin gave him a surprised look. "Wasn't that the plan? Escape the drudgery of small-town life? Find adventure? Take whatever we want?" He motioned toward the bustling streets of Andelor's market district. From where they sat, under the shade of a bright red awning outside an alehouse, they had a view of the four main streets that joined to create Andelor's famous market square. Huge, brightly colored wagons rolled by as more people than Gage had ever seen in his entire life shouted, haggled, and kept the economic wheels of the queendom in motion.

Gage nodded slightly in hesitant agreement, allowing himself a small smile despite the worries racing through his mind. The more of the city he experienced, the less he allowed those worries to trouble him. After his time with Desmond and everything that happened in Sathford, he felt his past in Blakehurst was someone else's life; it felt so long ago, so foreign. At that moment, he only just realized how hard it was for him to even remember his father's face.

Though he desperately wished he could forget his mother's.

As Gage thought of Renay Lawson's dead face, he diverted so far from the present that when Robin placed a hand on his shoulder, he jerked away and stood up, knocking his chair over.

Robin looked up at him, the sausage they had been sharing knocked to the cobblestone walkway in a greasy splatter. After peering over his shoulder to make sure no one was in earshot of them, Robin asked, "Was it him again?"

Gage pushed his hair out of his eyes, also looking around to ensure no one paid them any mind. The world around them was busy with its own problems and cared little for a brooding, small-town hunter and his half-elf lover.

"Who's him?" Gage asked, knowing perfectly well who Robin meant.

The half-elf stood up, drawing his gray hood up to cover his long blond hair. He surveyed the merchants and customers doing their business as he shouldered up to Gage.

"The scion," he whispered as he took Gage's hand. "You dreamed of him last night—tossing and turning. I'd be lying if I said it didn't make me a little jealous."

The mention of Desmond Evertone and the half-elf's reassuring touch awoke a flurry of emotions in Gage, and he turned to kiss Robin, long and deeply. He felt both of them stiffen as he drew their bodies together. When Gage finally broke away, he could see his own desire reflected in Robin's half-lidded eyes.

"Should I still be jealous?" he asked through smiling lips.

Gage cocked an eyebrow.

"If the mere mention of that man awakens such lust?"

They both shared a welcome laugh, turning to continue their afternoon walk, hands linked.

"It's not him," Gage finally said. "At least it wasn't just now—

fortunately I haven't been remembering my dreams of late."

"I can only assume that's for the best," Robin offered. He motioned down a side alley. "This way. We're supposed to find the next passage."

Knife had insisted that they both learn the ways back to the conclave. Her reasons were unspoken, but Gage assumed it was a common step in the Guild's recruitment process. Robin had already begun dropping random hints that they were being tested ever since they arrived from Sathford, but the topic had yet to be officially broached. Knife seemed properly distracted with court affairs ever since word arrived from the north that King Sulm of Copera had invaded Vale and taken control of Rathen.

"I was thinking of my father," Gage admitted. "All this talk of Rathen made me think of the harpies. Perhaps my father..."

Robin tightened his grip on Gage's hand. "Maybe he's dead like your mother."

Gage froze.

Pulled to a stop as well, Robin looked over at him, confused. "What'd you say?"

A black shadow melted from Robin's hairline, spilling over his face like blood. As it covered his features, his confused expression changed to wicked mockery. "I said, maybe I gutted him like I gutted your slut mother! Do you remember? When I buried a blade in her back and we watched the blood drain from her whore-flesh?"

Time froze for Gage as he stared at the ruin of Robin's face. All the animosity that he remembered feeling for Robin over the death of his mother returned. He had buried it deep since Sathford, but it burst up into his chest like a ghoul digging itself from a grave. A sudden spite awoke in him over the fact that they were now with Robin's mother in her domain—it was as if Gage had been abducted by them and forced to endure the taunts from the one person he thought could make him truly happy.

"Gage?"

Blinking, he saw Robin's face was now as it should be, if not a little disturbed.

"What did you say?"

Robin just blinked. "I said maybe we should talk to my mother. She might be able to help us find him."

Gage covered his face, trying to forget what he had just seen. He didn't want to hold onto the grief any longer. It felt like it wasn't even his to begin with. His mother had tried to kill him and Robin saved his life—it was the Shadow trying to blind him to the truth. He relaxed when he felt Robin's hand on his chest.

"Seriously, Gage," he whispered. "I'll go with you to find your family. If this is not where you want to be—"

"No," Gage said, dropping his hands and looking into Robin's eyes. "This is exactly where I want to be. With you. The Shadow isn't going to drive me away." He put his hand over his heart, covering Robin's. "It tried to before—in Sathford. But I'm not going to run from it anymore."

Robin kissed him again, more softly than before. It filled Gage with warmth, replacing the icy hatred that the Shadow tried to infect him with. Robin smiled as their lips parted. "Then let's find that passage before Knife sends a crew after us."

Even though she wore her mask, Knife felt naked at the great round table. It had seemed strange to her that Sopheena would invite her master spy to an open war council, but since she was hiding her sister's husband's bastard son in the sewers, Knife didn't feel inclined to refuse the summons.

"Shall we begin?" the king asked from across the table, still actively avoiding Knife's gaze. He knew his son was in the city, but neither had he tried to see him nor did Knife make the effort to introduce them. Robin was her own burden to bear—she felt love for the boy certainly, but she was practical enough to acknowledge him as a burden, one she intended to take responsibility for.

Luriah Vaughn made a show of yawning, delicately covering her mouth with a gloved hand. "It would seem our new Archmage follows her own agenda. However, I don't believe her absence warrants a delay in discussing such pertinent matters, Your Majesty."

"Agreed," the queen said from her seat next to the king. Wearing a shimmering purple gown that plunged low, displaying her pale chest, Queen Sopheena looked more fit for a ball than a war council. She motioned for more wine as she nodded toward Markus Durrask. "My lord husband, the king, shall relay the news we have just received."

Knife watched as her sister tipped her drink back, wondering if it was her fourth or fifth glass that morning. Sopheena did not often partake in such extravagances, further convincing Knife that she knew about the affair.

Markus rose and assumed a stately posture. "It is no secret that Copera has had eyes on Rathen ever since the orcs sacked it. However, we have received word that Malcolmry's army has brought the monsters to heel and claimed the city for his own, in Nazurik's name."

"What else would you expect from a bunch of savage sailors that worship Corsa?" Luriah's voice had an edge to it that reminded Knife of the woman's bath she had interrupted; her mask hid the smile that memory brought to her lips. "I say we rally all the warships in the Merithian ports and lay siege to Nazurik while Sulm wages war with the Bone Hill cretins."

The council chamber doors swung open then as the new Archmage glided in, carried by soft foot falls obscured by her wide red robes.

"Forgive me, my queen," Vera Mourgael announced in a tone that said she wasn't truly sorry at all. "Undoing my predecessor's enchantments has proven to be much larger of an endeavor than expected." She found a seat next to the Archbeacon as she inspected the other vacant seats. "Are the high lords not joining us?"

"Soon," Queen Sopheena replied, taking a sip of wine. "The king and I thought it prudent that we discuss plans for dealing with the rebel king before the high houses begin quibbling about who should rule over Rathen when it's wrested from Copera's traitorous grip."

"Very well," Vera said, placing her skeletal hands on the table. "Is that the matter at hand? Shall I assemble battle mages to join the throne's army?"

Eager for war, this one, Knife thought. "Diplomacy serves as a superior first volley," the Guildmaster said aloud, placing her fingerless-gloved hand on the table atop a small dagger. "That or assassination." She turned her masked face toward the king. "Depending on the crown's desires."

Markus cleared his throat. "We have sent an envoy by way of Harkand. High Lord Wexley has dispatched his eldest son, Sir Alaston, to carry the queen's demands, avoiding the Rathaway."

"I wish you would have conferred with the Church," Luriah interjected. "My paladins are well provisioned in Sathford, and the new Lady Mayor has already approved the new cathedral. Would you not agree that a company of paladins carrying the mayor of Sathford's own words would send a better message to these villains?"

"Lady Mayor?" Vera asked, looking from the Archbeacon to the royal couple. "What happened to Karlton's steward?"

Knife leaned forward, elbows on the table. "It seems whatever strange insect poisoned the Lord Mayor somehow infected each of his successors. The high houses were convened; each and every lord and lady backed Gwynna's nomination—Lord Janthy was not even a consideration. Not that he cares, I'm sure." She motioned to the chamber's high windows. "His wife's appointment gives House Grale control over the Valeway and the Bracing River."

"Yes," Sopheena added, rising to her feet. "And along with the Wane Coast and the Bracing River's mouth under the control of high elves loyal to their elven queen, it seems Vale is more united than ever."

Knife eyed her sister, wondering if this convenient regime change in Sathford had somehow been planned without her knowledge. If so, why would the queen have even sent the Guild to treat with Karlton? *Did you mean for me to fail, sweet sister?*

"Do we have a full account of what happened in Sathford?" Vera asked, her eyes fixed on Knife.

The tension that settled between the council members was palpable, but Knife let it hang there as she reclined in her chair. She hadn't shared the specifics with her sister yet, beyond cursory details about the Luminaura's defense of the city.

"I'm still waiting for one of my agents to return," she lied. Crawl was likely dead, but the woman had surprised Knife many times before with her resilience. "My own account is limited, as I had to expedite my escape before the Old Ways were closed to me." The last part was directed at the Archmage. "I would not have made it back if it wasn't for the Court Mage I encountered."

Sopheena hid her surprise well. "Which one? They were supposed to be in Jath—why were they back in Vale without reporting to the throne?"

"As to that," Knife said, offering a gesture of empty hands, "I cannot say. Desmond Everton was tight-lipped, and the invading undead shortened any report I may have wrenched from him. He did tell me the elf mage had fallen in their quest."

This time, Sopheena did not hide her reaction so well—Knife could tell the news grieved her, and not just because a fellow high elf perished.

"What quest?" Vera inquired. "Was the Arcania aware of some operation in Jath?"

"It concerned the throne," Markus replied gruffly. "Besides, this council was called to discuss the pressing matter of King Malcomry Sulm's invasion of Vale. Let us restrict our discussions to that for the time being."

"Indeed," the Archbeacon agreed. "While we await word from Lord Wexley's diplomacy efforts, I will send a dove to Sathford—our dear High Warpriest, Hope Kandelot, perished in the battle, but we have raised our brave First Paladin to the station. Sir Darrance Moore will muster the Light's army should it turn to war in old Northlund."

The crown did not object to the proposal, and Markus called the council to a close before further matters could be presented.

"Would the Guildmaster confer with me further?" Sopheena refilled her wine glass while the other council members took their leave.

When the sisters were alone, Knife removed her mask and regarded the queen. "Is Luriah Vaughn your new Master-at-Arms?"

Taking a long sip, Sopheena locked her icy gaze on her twin. When she lowered the glass, she ran her tongue slowly over her lips before speaking. "Where's the book?"

Knife kept her expression as blank as she could. "Desmond failed. I can only assume he died in the Sathford invasion—he looked grievously injured from whatever happened in Jath."

The queen regarded the closed door. "So where does that leave us, sister?"

Knife stood up. "Well, it seems we have little choice now. I'll go to Velcarthe myself—" *Where my son will be safe from you*, she thought "—much like I suggested originally, if you recall."

"The Court Mages were spies for Fainly," Sopheena snapped, finally dropping her regal facade. "It was the wiser choice—we needed you here in case any more of Aberheim's bastards tried to stake their claim."

"And now?" Knife asked.

Sopheena regarded her. "Does it have to be you?"

No, Knife thought, *but I have to get your husband's son away from you*. "If you want it done right. I know the Xe'danni underworld better than most. Even with the Old Ways compromised, there's still a gate leading to Karrane. Fainly thought it secret, but one of the gnomes in the High Sanctum was found compromised with one of my younger agents. I can sail from Pyram and be in Velcarthe before the whole Rathen situation is resolved."

"Won't you need the new Archmage's leave to travel by gate?"

Knife motioned to her sister. "A decree from the queen should suffice."

Sopheena looked into her cup, swirling whatever remained, her expression displeased. Though, if it was due to the plan or lack of wine, Knife truly couldn't say.

"We are still aligned, sister?"

Knife was taken aback by Sopheena's tone. She had felt a rift growing between them, which Knife attributed to her secret affair with Markus—one that she still truly didn't know if Sopheena knew about. However, there was a desperation in the queen's voice—something that sought reassurance.

"We both swore to free Mother," Knife said. "I will die before I see that promise unfulfilled, sister. In that, we are forever aligned. She locked herself in that place to save us from Father. We owe everything to her."

The queen nodded, allowing herself a subtle grin. "Then go, sister. Find Stane's wretched writings while I figure out how we're going to interpret them."

Knife drew her mask back up, but before she put it on, she glanced back at her sister. "Do you still intend to sacrifice him?"

"If I must," Sopheena replied without hesitation. "You know the costs as well as I do—we are not true royal blood, not in the way Markus is."

Knife opened her mouth to speak, thinking how easy it would be to tell her twin about the affair. If she were willing to let the king die, surely she could forgive the affair...

Instead, she put her mask on. "I'll prepare to depart tonight."

Queen Sopheena poured herself more wine as her sister slipped back into the shadows.

Gage liked Wisp. She reminded him of the blacksmith back in Blakehurst. Bruck wasn't as chatty though, nor did he have a habit of breaking into random songs during conversation, much like Wisp did presently. However, the dwarves both had a calming, reassuring presence that Gage needed now more than ever.

"...and if you find yourself lost," she sang, her shrill voice carrying over the laughter from the other side of the table. Robin held up his cup of bogwater, swaying back and forth to the rhythm of the dwarf's drunken tune. "Follow the shit until you get to the place where rogues can rogue!"

The gnome twins laughed at that. The woman (that Gage thought was named Flip) spilled her own drink as she tried to applaud the dwarf's performance.

The conclave echoed with their merriment and Gage found that he quite liked the sound; it quieted the voices in his head.

The Shadow's voices.

The half-orc with the smooshed nose crossed the narrow catwalk to where Gage and Robin sat with the other thieves. "Knife needs the boys."

"Bloom, come have a drink," the gnome (who must have been Flop) said. He patted one of his small hands against Gage's back. "If the boss needs these two for a job, at least send them off properly!"

"That bogwater tastes like the runoff from your sister's crotch," Bloom replied in his nasal voice.

That brought a round of laughs from the table, but when the half-orc jerked his head back toward the narrow bridge spanning over the steaming refuse (which Gage was still shocked had little more odor than a sweaty man), the merriment died a bit.

"Knife don't like waiting."

Gage followed Robin as he slipped from his seat and moved to follow the half-orc. Even though Gage didn't necessarily fear the Guildmaster, more dread filled him with each step he took across the flowing filth.

Making their way toward Knife's parlor, Gage reflected on how the conclave was not at all what he expected. For whatever reason, he imagined the thieves of Andelor scheming in grand, labyrinthine halls, decorated with all the spoils of their clandestine operations. But the underworld of Andelor was a damp, dark, and cobbled-together slum that barely seemed livable. Also, there were only a handful of agents that he knew of so far, and while Wisp and the gnome twins were pleasant enough company, Gage was disenchanted thus far by the Guild life.

Somehow, that changed when they entered the parlor. Knife sat at the head of the long council table and Gage's breath caught in his throat.

Her scarred face was bared, and she wore an expression that Gage couldn't exactly interpret. But the vulnerability he saw in her gripped him, making him eager to hear what she had to say. As he approached, he could tell she was likely once a lovely high elf, with the expected pale skin and sensual curves that artists so enjoyed replicating. But the ruin of her face had turned her into something else…something hateful.

The Shadow still whispered to Gage as he neared Knife, but he was able to ignore it in her presence somehow.

"We need to leave," she said, motioning to the chairs next to her on either side of the table.

"What do you mean?" Robin asked. He sounded unconcerned, as if Knife were just being ridiculous. "We just got here. We haven't even learned all the passages yet."

"I warned you when we left Sathford," she said, watching them take their seats. Bloom waited at the other end of the table. "It's not safe for us here—not safe for you." She looked at her son, but Gage felt like the warning was meant for him as well. He wanted to argue the point; he felt safer here amongst the thousands of people in the city than he did anywhere else. He needed the crowds, the noise. It was able to drown out the darkness inside him. They needed to stay. Otherwise, his mother's ghost would find him again.

"Where are we going?" Gage asked instead.

Knife looked at Bloom. "Prepare for a long journey; first by gate and then by ship. Myself and two agents. You will command in my stead, unless Crawl somehow returns from the dead."

Bloom just nodded and slipped into the shadowy hall beyond the parlor's door.

"We are going to Velcarthe," Knife said, turning to face Gage. While he had never seen the queen, he had seen her likeness in paintings and sculptures—the Guildmaster was like a shattered mirror reflecting Queen Sopheena's face. She wasn't as scarred as Desmond, but whatever had defiled her beauty had done so in a very specific way—as if her face was meant to be broken into three unequal sections.

"Xe'dann?!" Robin asked excitedly. He smiled at Gage, and his eagerness was infectious. It did feel like the promise of adventure, and Gage let himself become eager.

"It's a dangerous place," Knife warned, placing a hand on her mask as if she meant to put it on, but her hand just rested there.

"Then why are we going?" Gage asked, the words coming as if of their own volition. "If we're not safe here, I mean—will we be safer in a place like Velcarthe?"

"Yes," Knife replied immediately. "Because my sister is not there."

Gage was so consumed with Knife being Robin's mother that he didn't think of the wider implications of other important relations— the least of which was royalty. Robin's aunt was the ruler of Vale.

"Your sister is Queen Sopheena." It wasn't a question, although Gage wanted to hear a confirmation, as if that might make it more believable.

Knife let go of her mask, looking back at her son. "You are of noble blood. My sister and I made a promise long ago to sever our noble ties." She smiled. "Fate is wicked though, and it forced her to become queen in order to make good on our promise—we knew no other way to carry out our true ambition."

"And what is that?" Gage asked, somehow dreading the answer.

Knife stood up, putting on her mask. "To resurrect our father, Count Delucar. And in turn, the vampire lords of Caim."

CHAPTER FOUR

The Eldercrowns

Geneva felt their approach.

It was a deep unease, similar to when the Old Ways began to fall. But while that had been like some forgotten grief, this felt more thrilling—as if something that had slumbered far too long was finally waking up, eager to uncoil itself.

The trees nearby shook violently enough to shed their leaves, and Geneva knew her friend up in the branches had felt it too.

"He's back," Rhenal said before he appeared from above. His green leathers came down in a blur as he landed silently near Geneva, his emerald cloak billowing down in his wake. "And something's wrong. He's not alone."

That was obvious to Geneva; her Lexeth would not disturb the old wards unless he meant to alert the Lefayran scouts. Or he traveled with a clumsy human. Likely both, considering the prisoner from Rathen had gone missing.

"Get Shareen," Geneva said, drawing her knives. "I'll see what trouble he brings."

Fortunately, Rhenal only hesitated for a moment—likely just as eager as Geneva to see what manner of excitement could actually breach the Waywards. But she reminded him of his duty to the First Scout with a nod and he slipped into the trees to find the healer.

Geneva didn't hesitate. Lexeth had left Lefayra without warning, leaving her only a brief note demanding that she not follow him. Not only was she concerned with his wellbeing, but she looked forward to slapping his beautiful face for letting her worry so much.

She knew the Greenway well and navigated the thicket without so much as disturbing a branch. The uneasiness intensified, and soon she heard the troubled breathing and dragging feet that certainly did not belong to her wayward lover.

"...a moment," a strained voice said. "Damn you, elf, not all of us have your inexhaustible vigor! Those blasted gnolls have sapped me!"

Geneva hurried toward the sound, suddenly convinced that the grumbling human was the Eastlunder they had rescued from Rathen—the one that Lexeth had stolen away from the Eldercrowns without explanation. The thought angered her once more, unable to fathom what reason her husband had for deceiving her.

She broke through a hanging copse and came face to face with her intruders.

"Wick's burning shaft!" An old man in tattered robes fell back into Lexeth's sturdy embrace. "Why aren't you up in the trees like the others?!"

Geneva could see blood staining the old man's garments. "You're hurt." She sheathed her knives, making an effort not to look at Lexeth lest she strike him. Instead, she reached out to help his elderly human companion back to his feet.

"I'll be fine," the man said, straightening himself with some effort. "Can't say as much for my heart—I think you stopped it for a moment there."

"We were attacked at Falcon's Reach," Lexeth told her. "Reston was caught by a gnoll blade."

Now she did look at him. She had heard the name Reston Mauer, but had never associated it with such a grizzled, hunched figure. Waurane always spoke of him with such reverence that Geneva imagined him to be a hale Eastlund knight in the prime of his life. Seeing the old man's wound also reminded her of the recent gnoll sightings.

Gnolls were pushed out of Lohkrest nearly a decade ago—their likes were not seen this far west of the Eastwood. She still dreaded to find out what had drawn them back. Though Geneva supposed she shouldn't be surprised the two encountered the monsters; the Eldercrowns spoke of their increased threat at the last Covenant, ordering new wards be placed along their borders.

"I said I'll be fine," the man repeated. "I just need a damn drink—and no more sips from the stream. I require elven wine, Lexly."

"Lexeth," the elf corrected, and Geneva couldn't help but grin despite the circumstances. Certainly gnolls invading and the last surviving member of the Keyguard arriving were not pleasant omens. But her uneasiness abated, replaced by the reassuring calm that Lexeth provided in abundance.

As they set on their path toward Lefayra, Geneva finally felt composed enough to speak to her partner.

"You said nothing in your note of going after the Keyguard."

Reston harrumphed at that, but stubbornly continued leading their trek while the elves conversed.

"It wasn't entirely planned," Lexeth said. "Bennik, the man we saved from Rathen, led me to him. The Eldercrowns were right about him—he is tied to the prophecy."

"Then why did you steal him away?!" Geneva snapped, looking over her shoulder. "And where is he now?!"

"He's off undoing that damn prophecy," Reston interjected, whacking a hanging branch out of his way. "Have your elders build some damn roads already!"

Geneva looked from the old Eastlunder back to Lexeth, awaiting a more detailed explanation.

But Reston prattled on. "Besides, we don't want the Child of Light's father in your city with a betrayer lurking about."

Lexeth's sharp intake of breath caused Geneva's heart to skip a beat. Then Reston's shout of alarm did it again.

Shareena already had her deft hands on Reston to check his injuries, and Rhenal had an arrow nocked when he emerged from the thicket, scanning behind the group for any threats.

"Let's get him home," Lexeth said, casting Geneva a nervous glance. "I don't know if they're still following us."

Back in Lefayra, Geneva reported to the scout commander within the Elmery, which was the tall, fortified tree that served as the wood elves' barracks. When she was done with her update, Nyrith asked her pointed questions about Lexeth.

"Did he have keyshards?"

"Was he being evasive about where he went?"

"What did he say?"

"Did his companion look suspicious?"

Geneva answered as well as she could, but she found Nyrith's questions a bit odd—not once did she ask about Lexeth's wellbeing.

"Stay with him," Nyrith said. "I will meet with the Eldercrowns who remain in the city. Do not leave your quarters."

That was even stranger, but Geneva nodded her agreement; she was mostly just eager to return to Lexeth and find out where he needed to go without telling her. She left the Elmery and navigated the descending walkways toward the small apartment she shared with him. On the way, she encountered Rhenal.

"How's the old man?"

Rhenal nodded. "He's tough. Took a wicked slash from a gnoll blade, but Shareen is having more trouble with his attitude than the wound."

Geneva snorted at that. "Have you spoken with any other scouts?"

He stepped closer, looking over his shoulder as a blacksmith passed by them with a friendly nod. "Shara asked for you when I was leaving the apartments—she said she saw Lexeth and wondered if I knew where he went." He puffed out his cheeks and raised his eyebrows—how he normally looked when he was concerned with something.

Geneva nodded, thinking back to all of Nyrith's questions. It was as if the scouts were more concerned with Lexeth's return than they were with his absence. But Geneva just patted her friend on the armored shoulder and continued on toward her home.

She was glad to not encounter any other scouts along the way, but by the time she reached her door, all the anger from Lexeth leaving without telling her had returned.

She threw the door open, unlatching her bow and unfastening her quiver. Lexeth was mostly undressed in the apartment, wearing only his underpants as he used a basin of water on the table to clean himself. The sight of water dripping down his sculpted stomach muscles weakened her resolve.

Her physical desire to ravish the man persisted, albeit tempered by the desire for him to survive the encounter.

"I have to go check on Reston," he began. But as Geneva tossed her gear into the corner loudly and pulled at her cloak, Lexeth straightened. He opened his mouth to speak, but she rushed forward, pushing both of her gloved hands against his bare, muscled chest and driving him back into the wall.

"Let me explain," he began, but her lips were over his before he could say more. She kissed him fiercely, felt him react through the thin layers separating them. He wrapped his powerful arms around her, pulling off her intricate armor piece by piece.

There was a common belief that elven passions were more

controlled and less animalistic than other people in the Joined Realms, due to elves having longer lifespans and less urgency driving their endeavors. However, this was proved baseless in the apartment belonging to Geneva and Lexeth. The elves stripped each other bare, bent and folded each other into perplexing positions as Geneva grinded out all of her anger and frustrations on Lexeth's hard body.

There would be time enough for words later.

When that time came, Geneva arose from their floor and used her hand to cup a mouthful of water from the basin, drinking eagerly.

"You'll never do that again, Lex," she said through quivering breaths.

He gave one of his discreet laughs. "I don't know—if that's the punishment for sneaking off with another man, maybe I should do it regularly."

She spun on him, her face devoid of amusement. "After what happened to your sister—leaving alone with an outsider." She looked down when she saw how those words had stung him. "I'm sorry...but you can see why this was hard for me."

He rolled to his feet and moved toward her, smoothly and silently. He didn't reach out—not yet. "I know, and I'm sorry. Back in Rathen, when we rescued Bennik Lawson—"

"The Eastlunder?" Geneva hadn't yet learned his name.

Lexeth nodded. "Before he passed out, he looked at me in a way—I felt the connection before he even told me. He was the one Farrah mentioned—the one from Blakehurst. She had visited him before, had even taken me there when I was too young to really understand. Reston confirmed it: He is the last member of the Keyguard."

That word sent a strange chill down her spine and she oddly felt her nipples stiffen again. She crossed her arms and shifted uncomfortably. "Him? One of the Keyguard? I thought they were all old drunkards living in broken castles."

Lexeth shook his head. "I never told you—Farrah made me promise... Besides, I never really thought it would concern us here." He motioned to their elegant apartment, decorated in deep, dark wood with swirling green and silver patterns. "But our father was a member of the Keyguard, when they tried to reform."

Something about Lexeth's face changed then, as if Geneva found him less recognizable. "You never thought to tell me any of this?"

He looked at her sharply. "Of course I thought to! My sister made me swear. You know how the Eldercrowns are when it comes to keyshards. Wood elves are forbidden to meddle in such matters—what happens beyond these borders is not our concern. Could you imagine if they knew our father was secretly a member of the Keyguard? What do you think they would do with me?" He finally reached out and took her hand. "What do you think they would do to you?"

Geneva relaxed, letting her arms fall as he drew her close. She couldn't stop thinking of all the questions Nyrith had asked. Something felt wrong. Never in the past twelve years had she doubted her trust in Lexeth, but now she wondered what else he hadn't told her.

There was a knock at the door. Both elves slipped on enough clothes to be presentable, and then Geneva opened the door inward.

Nyrith stood there, fully armored. She was flanked by two members of the city guard who both had their blades drawn.

"Lexeth," Nyrith said, as if Geneva weren't even there. "You are to come with us immediately."

"Good," Lexeth said. "I must speak with the Eldercrowns at once."

"The Eldercrowns are dead," Nyrith said flatly. The guards moved forward to take Lexeth into custody. "You are to be tried for their murders."

Chapter Five

Taking Stock

Ransil Osbury felt oddly alone as he navigated the busy streets of Sathford, surrounded by activity. That morning, he had attended a meeting between the new High Mage of Raventhal Spire and the city's reformed council, which likely contributed to the loneliness he felt—there was no other place he could feel so unseen and ignored.

Since the assault, the rule of the city had fallen onto House Grale, the oldest and proudest house in the region. However, Lord Janthy Grale entrusted the city's rule to his elven wife, Gwynna, who couldn't even be bothered to attend the council in person. In her stead was one of the most beautiful elves Ransil had ever seen, Eldercrown Cethany. Why an Eldercrown would be serving as a Lady Mayor's stewardess, Ransil couldn't begin to guess, and the rest of the council didn't seem eager to ask questions with so many other pressing matters to discuss.

Throughout the meeting, Ransil felt completely out of place. But Quinn had insisted the halfling accompany him.

"You have to be there with me," the boy pleaded. "Even Konrath would bring Master Audreese with him. It's customary!"

Ransil could only object so much. While the boy was exceptionally intelligent and gifted with magic, he was still a boy who did not have a father—Ransil got the impression that Quinn saw him as a sort of surrogate now that the previous High Mage had died. As Ransil now passed by an excited human boy begging his own father for another sweet from a dwarf baker's cart, he thought of his own father back in the Acreage.

It had been years since Ransil had been back home in Bramble Nook, and the last time he left was not on the best of terms. Hule Osbury would likely toss his son out on the stoop if Ransil even set foot in The Nosy Gnome—or at least that was what he told himself whenever the notion of returning to the Acreage would come unbidden to his mind.

As Ransil turned down the hill toward the spire, thoughts of fathers and sons inevitably led him back to Bennik and his children. Recent events had reassured Ransil that he likely had never had a better friend than Bennik Lawson. While he cared for the man's children, it was the love he had for Bennik himself that made it impossible for Ransil to allow Gage and Anika to leave Blakehurst without him. And now that Bennik may be dead—a hard truth that Ransil had yet to truly accept—it was as if he were the children's sole guardian.

It made the knife Gage buried in Ransil's back that much more painful.

"Halfling."

Even though he had already seen another dozen halflings scurrying about the streets of Sathford, he still stopped and turned out of habit.

"You're alive," Ransil said with intentional detachment.

Kasia Strallow took a long pull from the wineskin before nodding. "Disappointing, I know. It seems you have the boy's ear." She looked strange without her armor, almost like a beggar, which emboldened Ransil's response.

"That I do, and I told him to reject your offer without consideration."

Kasia looked out over the Bracing River, nodding as if she had both expected and deserved that. "I didn't kill them, you know." She glanced back at him. Even though she looked drunk, she did not slur her words. "Your nieces. I told Jak to take them to Andelor—to the Arcania for safekeeping."

"They were safe with my cousin," Ransil replied through clenched teeth. "Their mother."

"Are you quite sure about that?" Kasia stood up, towering over the halfling. "Do you know half of what your motherly cousin has done in service to the Guild?"

"Can't imagine it's much worse than what you've done in service to the Arcania."

Kasia pursed her lips as she glared down at him. "I'm no mother. That life forever eludes me. After I had to watch a warlock turn my own mother into a whore to service his entire coven, I swore I'd never bring someone into this world that could be so ruined because of me. I made that same bastard hollow out my womb before I bled him dry."

Ransil felt his expression relax at that unexpected admission, but he refused to yield. "Whatever Dolly did before having those girls doesn't matter. They changed her—I spent my entire life getting her out of trouble, but once she settled down in Oakworth..." He trailed off, not even sure why he was trying to explain this to the Oather. Kasia Strallow wasn't someone he needed to appease; she was the one asking him for a favor, not the other way around. But when he looked back up to her, he noticed her expression had softened as well.

He no longer saw the Lady Commander of the Oathers. He saw a drunk woman telling an old halfling cook that she was barren. Ransil couldn't help but feel sad for her.

"I shouldn't have done it." Her voice was almost a whisper and her gaze was distant. "I failed in Rathen and I didn't want to fail again. I knew Scratch—I knew Dolly had the stone; it wasn't the first time she interfered with my affairs."

"That justified kidnapping her children?"

That earned a fiery look from Kasia, but it quickly passed and she maintained her calm presence. "I got Jak's brother killed in Rathen and I acted rashly—I told him to keep the girls safe, and I trust that he has done so..." She looked toward the river. "Wherever he is."

"And what exactly do you require of the High Mage?" He looked out across the river in a show of detatchment. "Should I tell him to accept the audience you've requested?"

She looked back at Ransil, hopeful. "Raventhal hasn't had an Oather in over nine years, not since the last one betrayed the Oath of Sorcery."

Ransil was taken aback by that. "You want to pledge yourself to Raventhal Spire?"

She tossed aside her wineskin, straightening. "I mean to find Jak and the girls. And with the new Archmage cutting off the towers, I don't suppose he made it back to the Arcania." She gave the halfling a look he couldn't quite discern. "Besides," she added, "I'm sure you don't believe the incarnate alone was the cause of what happened here. That assault and the Lord Mayor's assassination... There is witchcraft here that needs rooted out." She crossed her arms. "What better place is there for someone like me?"

Ransil considered that a moment, knowing that he'd much rather have Kasia Strallow as an ally than a foe. But that wasn't his decision. "I'll talk to the boy," he finally said.

Kasia's face twitched as she tried to hide her surprise. "Thank you, Ruse—I mean, Lord Osbury."

"Ransil," he said, raising a finger. "But I'll make sure your first task will be finding my nieces, so don't get all excited about hunting witches should Raventhal have you."

"Understood," she said, shaking out her hands as if she had just exorcised a demon from her body. "Now, unless you have the time and inclination to attend to me in such a capacity, perhaps you might direct me toward the best place to find a pillow boy in this city…"

Ransil left without a word.

Anika tried to wake herself several times, but she couldn't escape Drastil Manor. Each room was a different agony, and the one she traversed now was a rancid scene of primal lust. The atmosphere was like that of a slaughterhouse, with death lingering in the air. Yet the sounds of carnal pleasures echoed loudly.

Her memories of Lekan Nafir were poison, still awakening in her that thick desire that had released her from grief in Pyram. That very same desire now repulsed her after learning what kind of man the majest truly was.

She walked as a stranger through the halls, seeing herself—Anika Lawson or Anika Voth, whoever she truly was—acting out the memories, fantasies, and horrors that lurked in the slumbering recesses of her mind. The Child of Light presently wrapped her naked legs around Lekan's waist as the majest thrust himself in and out of her, groaning like the living corpses that had invaded Sathford from below. The smell was overwhelming as Anika watched her dream-self roll her eyes back in her head, overcome with passion; overcome with dread.

Wake up, Anika begged, not sure who she was speaking to: the version of herself on her back, or the one that had fallen asleep in the Raventhal library. *Please wake up.*

The pungent smells might have once been intoxicating to a seventeen-year-old in the throes of lust, but to Anika now they were the smells of rot and sickness. Her stomach heaved and she felt like retching.

"Kalany," Lekan said between grunts. But it was Stane's voice.

Anika could never forget the voice of Stane.

"It's Anika," she said angrily, stepping over the naked figures as they neared a climax. "Anika!"

Beneath Lekan's convulsing body, the dream-Anika righted her eyes so they looked directly into her own. That face changed into Stane's. He smiled wickedly at her as he thrust her writhing hips toward Lekan. The majest shrieked in sudden agony, pulling himself away from his lover. As he arose, Anika saw that his manhood was gone; in its place was a terrible bloody ruin, a waterfall of gore splashing down his perfect thighs.

Anika, Stane said, his quiet voice almost deafening over Lekan's pathetic wails. Anika couldn't pull her eyes away from the majest as he doubled over, a pool of blood spreading from his wound, staining the lush purple rugs below.

"Anika."

Wake up, she begged again. *Just wake up!*

Anika, a voice said in her head now: Stane, penetrating her thoughts like he had on the altar in Pyram. *I can free you from this, from these men like Lekan who want only to use you.*

"Anika," some distant voice said.

Just follow me, Stane said in her mind again, the naked form of herself with his face now changing into Stane's body completely. *We are joined,* he continued. *Me, you, and your sweet brother, Gage.* His manhood arose, betraying his eagerness for her to submit.

"No," she said, pulling back from his hand as he held it out to her. "Wake up!"

"Anika?"

"Please!"

"Anika!"

Small, familiar hands pulled her out of Stane's reach.

"Are you all right?"

Anika felt the soreness in her limbs as she turned in the chair to see Ransil Osbury looking up at her. The halfling's big eyes were full of concern and his beard looked thicker, with more gray hair than she remembered.

She looked around to see that she was indeed still in the library, but her friend's appearance and the tightness in her limbs made her worry she had slept longer than was natural.

"Is it time for the council?"

Ransil's face broke into a smile then. "That was this morning, Ani."

He looked at the pile of books on the table—arcane tomes and translated spellbooks. "Did you spend all night in here?"

She yawned and twisted to stretch her back. "At least one. I'm sorry I missed the council—why didn't you send for me?"

Ransil motioned to the table. "I felt like you've had plenty to worry about lately. Besides, I'm not in a hurry to put you in front of our new Lady Mayor's stewardess just yet." He crossed his arms. "Eldercrown or not, I don't know her well and trust her even less than that."

Anika smiled at that, comforted in the fact that she had such a loyal friend looking out for her. However, the halfling responded with a frown.

"We need to talk about Gage."

Anika's heart sank. She looked at her studies spread across the table, knowing that her brother was truly the reason for her desperate need to harness her powers. "I know we do..."

Silence fell between them, with the only sound coming from the ravens that nested outside the library's open windows.

Finally, Ransil moved to scratch the back of his neck and motioned toward the open sky with his other hand. "After everything that happened in Oakworth... Your brother may be dangerous, Ani."

"It's not him," she said, more angrily than intended. Frustrated, she pushed herself away from the table so she could stretch her legs—suddenly she felt so confined; the blue skies outside were calling desperately to her, each day louder than the last. "I need to save him—"

"What if he doesn't want to be saved?" the halfling interjected. "I'm not saying to give up on him, but at what point is he truly lost? He abandoned us during the invasion. If it wasn't for the Shadow-taken Guildmaster, I'd be rotting in the undercroft with..." He trailed off, looking up to Anika. "I'm sorry, I didn't mean— Quinn and I nearly died getting here after Grip robbed and abandoned me..."

Emotion overcame Anika as she heard Ransil's voice break. The old halfling was a rock throughout her life, and he always seemed unbreakable to her. But Gage's betrayal had brought the halfling lower than she truly understood until now.

She went to him, kneeling down to hug him. "I'm so sorry that happened, Ransil. But we have to remind ourselves it's the Shadow— Gage is my brother. He might be the only family I have left. We have to believe that he's still the same menace that used to steal a slice from the pies cooling on your window."

"But what if he truly is the Shadow?"

She pulled away to look him in the eyes, her hands still on his portly waist.

"I just mean... You believe now," he said, cautiously, "you are the Child of Light."

She let her hands fall from him. "I know I am, Ransil. And if Gage is the Child of Shadow, the world expects me to kill him and repeat this cruel cycle. You don't have to remind me."

Ransil scratched his head. "I'm no expert in these matters, Ani. As far as I'm concerned, you're the one to advise any of us on matters of Light and Shadow, and I'll follow you wherever you need me." He reached a small hand up to place on her cheek. "But I saw his eyes down there... He was already taken, Ani. And I don't know how we get him back."

She sat down, crossing her legs. "When I was in Karrane, down in the Fathoms...there was an altar."

Ransil sat down next to her when he heard the word. "Altar?"

Anika concentrated on the decorative rug's pattern below them, trying to remember how the huge rock had looked—so much of the events had blurred. "That's what they called it—this massive keyshard jutting up from the earth."

Ransil waited for her to continue.

"I think—I believe my being in Karrane somehow summoned it...or awakened it. I was having these dreams, and then when I got near it..." She looked up and saw the confused expression on Ransil's face. She shook her head, defeated. "I don't know how to explain it, Ransil." She motioned to the table above them. "That's why I asked Master Groaves to train me. I keep thinking, if I'm the Child of Light, shouldn't I learn what all of this comes from? I mean, what if the Child of Light before me just accepted this power and let it guide their path wherever it wanted, like—" She dropped her hands in her lap. "Like maybe Gage did with the Shadow."

Ransil opened his mouth to speak, but the huge library door groaned open behind him. Audreese and Quinn entered, both of them giving Anika and Ransil curious glances.

"Are the tables not adequate?" Audreese asked.

"Ransil!" Quinn said excitedly, hurrying over to him. "Do you feel like hunting some monsters again?"

"What now?" Ransil asked, bouncing up to his feet in a way that made Anika wonder if the halfling had somehow procured an elixir of youth from the spire's vaults.

Master Audreese stepped forward, tucking her pale hands behind her black robes. "One of our Accepted was serving in New Hold, a dwarf named Grianna—quite an accomplished geomancer. She was helping excavate one of the new mines when her team struck a deposit of keyshards."

"In a mine?" Ransil asked. "Are keyshards commonly mined? Aside from blackshards on Suthek, that is."

"It's not unheard of in the mountains," Quinn replied. "Caves collapse on old monster lairs or spellthief hideouts. But what Grianna found was something different...almost like a natural deposit." He pointed to Ransil. "Like Suthek—which is not so common in the dwarf lands."

During all of this discussion, Anika was picturing the altar of Eyen below Pyram. She imagined another storm brewing in the south, similar to the one Corvanna birthed. Her heart began hammering in her chest.

"Has something happened to New Hold?" she asked.

"To that, I cannot say," Audreese replied. "Grianna just returned from her trek up the Valeway, but the keyshards meant for our vaults were taken from her. She barely escaped with her life."

"Don't tell me," Ransil said, an edge to his voice. "Gnolls?"

"Sounds like it," Quinn answered, a bit too gleefully for Anika's tastes. "Grianna was traveling with a merchant caravan that broke off for Oakworth. She continued on foot, but had to make camp just south of the river. That was where she was ambushed."

"She's all right?" Anika asked Audreese.

The elf nodded. "Fortunately, she went against her nature and fled, just arriving at Sathford this morning. Which means the gnolls couldn't have gotten far—perhaps they even have a lair along the southern banks of the Bracing River. We've heard reports of creatures lurking about with the increased trade barges taking stock back to Andelor and Merithian."

"So we should get moving," Quinn said, motioning for Ransil to join him.

"Wait, Quinn," the halfling began, but Audreese finished for him. "It's not befitting for the High Mage to risk his life on such things;

we have several qualified Accepted here that can accompany Ransil, should he even accept this task."

"Are you telling me Konrath wouldn't have handled something like this himself?!" Quinn burst out. "How can I be High Mage if I don't prove myself out there where it counts?"

"I'll go with them," Anika said, getting to her feet.

"Ani," Ransil began again.

"You'll need me," she insisted. "And I'm sure Master Groaves would agree with me—I need to start practicing what I'm learning here."

"I do agree with that assessment, my lady," the elf replied.

"It's just Anika. I'm not royalty—I'm your student."

Audreese actually almost smiled at that.

"I'm going too," Quinn said stubbornly. "I've been a student here longer than her, and now I'm the High Mage, so I make the rules. Right?" The boy looked defiantly at the elf.

"You can come," Ransil agreed. "Just so long as you understand that out there, I make the rules."

The ravens outside the library window cawed in agreement.

CHAPTER SIX

Aimless & Adrift

Desmond watched as the old halfling performed her prayers. He pondered why someone like her might still pray to Oakus—a god that she had helped dethrone and encapsulate—but he kept the inquiries to himself. Her presence alone was a constant reminder of Fallon Shaw, and that grief was enough to quell any snide japes he might otherwise make toward the first Scion of Stane.

A breeze filtered in through the damp leaves, shaking loose morning dew, and Desmond raised one of his scarred hands to catch a drop. The pure water dried up between his ruined fingertips, and something about that sight became too much for him to bear. He arose.

"Are we done here?"

Ruke turned to face him, the halfling's strange eye twitching. Something about her gaze stripped him bare and he shifted uncomfortably. She made a motion with her hands—a circle from her forehead to each of her breasts, and then her mouth—before standing. She fixed her tattered brown robes as she made her way toward him.

"Now you're eager?" She grabbed her staff that leaned against a tree. "Ever since Sathford I've felt like I've had to drag you along, but now I'm the one holding you up, eh?" She stalked past him without waiting for an answer.

Desmond followed her out of the glade, trying to quell the immense rage he felt for this diminutive woman. In his mind, she was still the one that drove him to murder, making him believe he was carrying out some divine will by trying to goad Anika into killing him.

"There's a chance we can still reach New Hold," Ruke said, waddling in that way of hers down the hill away from the trees. Hollowood was a cursed place that Desmond would not miss, but something about traveling along the open Valeway was even more unsettling for him. "That is," she called over her shoulder, "if those legs of yours still work."

He narrowed his eyes on her, feeling suddenly tired of her peculiar attitude that drifted between ambivalence and mockery. "How about you just go to New Hold without me?"

The halfling stopped and tilted her head to the side like a parent who knew they had to explain something tedious to their child. For some reason, the thought of aggravating her in that way pleased Desmond; the woman had barely told him anything since Sathford, only that it was imperative they find the other scions. It made him want to upset her, however petty a desire that might be.

She turned around slowly, walking halfway back up the hill. "We don't have to enjoy each other's company, Desmond. I chose you to be a scion because I could sense not only your power, but your rebellious nature." She smiled as she motioned up to his place on the hilltop. "It is that very nature that's causing you to mistrust me. But we are the Scions of Stane now, whether we like it or not. And together, we can usher Stane back to our world." Her eyelid twitched as she held out her small arms in a shrug. "Divided, we shall be responsible for the continuing cycle of wars, tragedies, and devastations tied to the malice of Light."

Something about that phrase physically struck Desmond, as if he had just been hit by a lightning bolt from the sky. "What is the malice of Light?"

She eyed him curiously, as if she had expected the question while still finding it peculiar. "The Light is the most destructive force in the world," Ruke said. "In all worlds. It burns all who oppose it, but it craves opposition; elsewise it may die out, burning alone with nothing to worship it."

Desmond felt like he was at a sermon back at the Chapel of Morning in Verenshire, but Ruke's words actually *felt* more captivating to him; even though he didn't really understand her meaning, he could sense the truth and importance of them.

"The malice of Light," Ruke continued, "is the end of the world that myself and the other Purveyors set in motion. When we attempted to give Light to the world, we didn't understand the trap Stane had planted for us."

"What trap?"

Ruke shook her head; even though she smiled, he could tell she was afraid. "I don't know. Stane is a trickster, a master of deception. Look what he had you do in Oakworth. The only way we can figure out how to stop the malice of Light is by working together. And whether Stane is friend or foe, we need him, because only he knows the truth."

"But what is the malice of Light?!" Desmond's patience had run out. This woman spoke in riddles and cryptic phrases. "Is it a weapon? A person? A spell?!" He was waving his arms around exaggeratedly.

Ruke's smile faded when she said, "Yes, it's all of those things."

Desmond could only stare at her, his mouth working but no words coming. After looking toward the southern horizon where New Hold awaited them, he finally managed to ask, "What does that even mean, Ruke?"

She turned to continue their trek. "It means that Anika Lawson will destroy the world unless we can stop her."

They arrived at New Hold late in the afternoon and Desmond was quite impressed with the settlement. He had never been this far south, and the stories he had heard of the dwarven city—if it could even be called a city—always conjured images in his mind of a small mining town formed out of cobbled together shacks surrounding crude holes dug into the ground.

Instead, they were greeted by tall stone walls that encircled gabled roofs and fortified turrets. Red and gold banners flapped in the breeze, proudly displaying the crossed pickaxes that were the arms of the United Clans of New Hold.

Seeing those arms made Desmond wonder, and after a league of not speaking with her, he asked Ruke, "Who rules here?"

The halfling glanced up from the Valeway's packed dirt to regard the city gates. "Your guess is as good as mine these days. But I suspect either Clan Cleaver or Clan Brasson, though the Brassons had plenty of rivals. I'd wager some queens on the Cleavers."

Desmond wanted to ask her how she knew any of this considering it must have been over three hundred years since she walked the Joined Realms. But instead, he asked, "Will we be welcome? The Scions of Stane come to break bread with the noble dwarf clans that were displaced by Myretha's wrath?"

Ruke chuckled at that. "Perhaps you better draw your hood and we play the part of a traveling leper and his healer—that way none will peer too closely at those nasty scars of yours."

He obeyed, pulling the tattered hood over his frail white hair. "You've still yet to tell me why we're here."

Ruke looked over her shoulder at him, eye twitching as usual. "Looking for the next scion, who hopefully isn't as dead as you were."

"Halt!" a thunderous voice bellowed from the gates. A short, armored figure approached. Desmond had thought the dwarf was a statue flanking the gates with how still they had been, but now it closed the distance at a brisk walk.

"Good afternoon," Ruke called in a jovial voice. "My name is Helga the healer, down from the Shatterwood, my good dwarf. My companion is unwell—he's not catching, mind you—and we had hoped to take shelter in your city. We have queens."

"Do we?" Desmond hissed under his breath.

Ruke gave a stiff shake of her head as she awaited a response from the guard.

"Aye, shelter we have." The guard stopped their approach, raising the visor on their helm to reveal a bearded dwarf that eyed them from afar. "Are ye cultists? We'll find out—may as well just tell me now and save us all the trouble."

This time, Ruke turned to Desmond, giving him a look of confusion. "Don't recall joining no cult," the halfling replied loudly; Desmond noticed she began adopting some of the dwarf's accent. "Not unless you count the Luminaura—may the Light bless you regardless."

The guard harumphed at that. "I don't mind the Light none, just wary of the Wickan heathens in these parts—those following the Combustress. Figured you seen their handiwork along the road—been burnin' every house and hovel they come across. All in the name of that Combustress bitch."

Something about that name caused Ruke to take notice; Desmond saw just a slight jerk of her head and rise of her shoulders. Instinctively, his hand went to his breast, reaching for the small notebook he used to carry so he could make a quiet note of the name. It was no longer there, reminding him he was someone else now. He would just have to remember to press Ruke later.

She knew whatever this Combustress was. Desmond could only assume it was either another scion or an incarnate—neither prospect appealed to him, but he remained silent as instructed.

"I can assure you we follow no Combustress, my lord," Ruke replied. "Not unless such a person has a cool pint of ale and some toasted bread to buy me affections first. That goes doubly for you, my lord."

The guard laughed jovially this time. "I ain't no lord, healer—just a lowly watchman. But you'll find what you need at The Red Anvil near the market." He turned over his shoulder. "Open the gates!"

The huge wooden doors creaked open at that, revealing a much more elegant town than Desmond was expecting—dare he actually call it a city. The main thoroughfare was paved with smooth stones leading down a wide avenue of shops and homes. He could see the market down the winding road, bustling with dozens of dwarves and some other folk.

"If your companion coughs or spews, we may require he stay outside the walls," the guard said, turning back toward the gates. "But he'll be well cared for regardless."

Ruke motioned for Desmond to follow. "He's on the mend, with a special tonic of my own creation. But he knows how to keep his toils to himself."

The long walk into town gave Desmond time to admire just how impressive dwarf craftsmanship was. He had traveled from Eastlund to Jath, and all the way north to Farhelm Mountains, but he had never seen such an organized and structured settlement as New Hold. The roads were paved with purpose, as if every part of the place was meticulously planned. How many cities in the world could claim that? Century after century, war after war, all the grand settlements had been ruined and rebuilt, stacking new atop old.

This place, he thought, was one-of-a-kind.

When they passed through the gates, Desmond had to adjust his hood so it wouldn't fall back and reveal his face. He couldn't help but stare up at the immaculately smooth stone walls and the pristine hanging banners. He felt like a giant as they navigated the thoroughfare, which was bustling with dwarves and halflings (or gnomes—he could never tell them apart), with only a smattering of taller folk.

He hunched as he followed Ruke, feeling as if he should avoid drawing attention to himself. But the busy dwarves didn't seem to care about him; they were focused on their various tasks. Desmond walked as if in a trance; the disciplined nature in which the dwarves went about their day was almost hypnotic, and as he followed Ruke, his mind wandered to Fallon, of all people.

The druid was possibly one of the only people he could consider a friend. Yet he had repaid the girl's kindness with apathy during their time at Raventhal, and then betrayal in the Old Ways, when he had tried to guide the Child of Shadow as Ruke guided him now. Thinking back, he could hardly even remember what he hoped to achieve with Gage, or by killing Anika's lover. It was as if all those memories belonged to someone else—someone vile.

Desmond's mind was a murky pool that he did not want to fall into, so he shook his head and focused once more on their current path.

"There it is," Ruke said, pointing to a large hanging sign shaped like an anvil. "I remember this place." Her voice was quieter, distant. Desmond stooped even more so he could properly hear. "The name didn't sound familiar, but that sign… I remember it."

"Are they magically repressed?"

Ruke raised an eyebrow when she looked up at him.

"Your memories," Desmond continued. "Maybe I know a spell—"

"Ain't like that," Ruke said, still keeping her feigned dwarven accent. "You ever wake up in a strange place and forgotten how you got there? But then after a few glances around it all comes back?" She motioned dismissively with a hand. "Well, it's like that, only I been asleep for a few centuries, so it's just going to take me a little bit longer to figure out where the blazes I am."

Desmond wasn't convinced that couldn't be remedied with magic, but he was honestly slightly relieved to not have to find out. After dying in Jath, he had been afraid of working any serious magic. There was trauma there that he wasn't anxious to face anytime soon. Silently, he followed the halfling into The Red Anvil.

The doors opened to the pleasant sound of two singers performing a jaunty ballad that Desmond knew; it was a popular one at the Riverstone in Sathford, but he never recalled its name. The singers looked like dwarf siblings: a yellow-bearded man and his golden-haired sister. The inn itself was bustling, full of mostly dwarves but also a good number of smaller folk and about a dozen humans. Desmond noticed a striking wood elf in green leathers eye them momentarily before returning to her conversation with a portly human woman.

"Act naturally," Ruke said to him, her low voice barely audible over the Anvil's merriment.

Desmond wanted to laugh at that. His natural inclination would be to turn around and retreat into the nearest library—if dwarves even cared for books. But he followed the halfling up to the bar regardless.

"Afternoon! Uh—yer friend unwell?"

Desmond didn't meet the short bartender's gaze, but Ruke answered with a dismissive affirmation.

"On the mend, he is. Came down from Hambury where an apothecary mixed up a remedy. Me own healing is more limited to wounds and injuries, not illness such as this."

Desmond glared at her from beneath his hood. *Already getting your lies mixed up,* he thought. *It was Shatterwood, not Hambury! Maybe she's lost more of her mind than she realizes...*

The dwarf man behind the bar nodded, satisfied, but Desmond could feel the man's eyes still on him. "Well, glad to hear the worst is over, aye? Are ye heading back home to the Acreage then?"

"That is the plan," Ruke replied. "We thought about finding work here while my friend, Denny, finishes recovering, but it sounds like things 'round here are a bit tense at the moment, what with the cult and all."

"Aye," the bartender replied. "Ye could say that. Between Dureen going off to hunt the Combustress and the collapsing mines, things ain't been exactly calm. But that also means there's plenty work if you do stick 'round."

"We heard about all them problems," Ruke replied. "But what about these mines? Still open?"

The barkeep explained that several mines in the surrounding hills had fallen in on themselves, burying several teams of miners—he offered an ale to them both in honor of the fallen.

"Since then," he added, "Clan Bronkite had taken charge in Dureen Cleaver's absence, opening up three additional mines in the Rethil Hills—which is where you could find work, I'm sure." He eyed Desmond doubtfully. "Perhaps chronicling if ya'll be studied folk, or healing any miners that forget to duck under a shallow pass."

"That's good to know, friend," Ruke replied.

"Call me Hank," the dwarf said. "Can I tell me daughter to prepare a room for ye? Two rooms, mayhaps? Most of these fine folk are locals, so we've got plenty of space."

Desmond certainly didn't have any queens on him, and he suspected that Ruke—who had just emerged from some other celestial realm—likely didn't either.

Ruke gave Desmond a quick glance before leaning closer to Hank. "Unfortunately, we were accosted on the road…"

"Oh no," Hank replied with genuine concern. "It's that damn Combustress, I tell you. Her followers have burned their ritual fires in so many nearby lairs, they've smoked all the vermin and thieves out to raid us hardworking folk."

"Ah!" Ruke reacted dramatically, selling it well. "I say… 'tis a shame! Not even us meek and ailed folk are safe!"

Desmond thought the woman could find good work in an acting troupe; she seemed to have quite the knack for it.

A boisterous dwarf woman knocked on the counter for Hank to give her two more pints for some other guests. "Come now, Pa! Thirsty patrons here!" She gave Desmond a wary eye before smiling at Ruke. "Don't go gettin' me old man started on yackin' or he won't stop!" She gave Ruke a wink and a smile while Hank thumped two full tankards on the bar.

"I tell you what," Hank said, wiping his hands dry on a towel. "If ye be staying to look for work, I can rent yer room on the promise that you'll be settling up once ye make yerself whole here in New Hold. We value the will to work more than coin itself, and I ain't gon' let your recovering companion curl up in some stable when we still have spare beds."

"That's mighty kind of ye," Ruke said jovially. "I believe we'll take ye up on that offer, Hank." The halfling pointed up to a painting that hung behind the bar. "Forgive me prying, but who are those women there holding up that red keyshard?"

Hank didn't even turn to look at the painting, he just crossed his arms and leaned away from Ruke in sudden surprise. "Now, how can you come from the Acreage and not know Lena Osbury?" He laughed heartily. "I reckoned ya'll had statues of the woman down there in Bramble Nook! Ain't she a proper legend down there as well?"

"Oh, certainly," Ruke said with a laugh of her own. This time, Desmond could hear the dishonesty in her voice, but if Hank did as well, the laughing dwarf gave no indication. "Lena is indeed quite the local legend. I was referring to the other; the Xe'danni human with her."

"Korinthy?"

Hank's query summoned a cheer from nearly the whole common room. "Korinthy Blaithe! All hail the Seeker of Fire!"

The chant was followed by the clapping of hands and the clanking of tankards. Desmond got the impression that the practice was fairly commonplace here. Hank pounded on the bartop with his massive hand, laughing as he explained, "Korinthy Blaithe and her valiant halfling warrior helped defend New Hold from a mad wizard who tried several times to burn the city down. He wielded a great keyshard that could summon towering flames—it was Korinthy and Lena that defeated him and saved the city, using the madman's own stone, no less!"

In the recesses of Desmond's fractured mind, he recalled such a story. It must have been at least twenty years ago when Larasyn Melth betrayed the Arcania and became the Red Renegade. However, he had never heard the details of Larasyn's defeat.

Hank offered them both another pint on the house as a peace offering for his having to return to tending the bar. Ruke and Desmond found an empty table in a shadowed corner.

"That's our next scion," Ruke said quietly into her cup.

Desmond's eyes darted to the painting again, seeing the rendition of the human archer and her armored halfling companion, both of their arms held up to bear the weight of the floating oversized keyshard above their heads.

"Which one?" Desmond asked. "Korinthy or Lena?"

"Neither," Ruke said, her eye twitching rapidly as she regarded the painting. "It's her child we need to find."

CHAPTER SEVEN

Losing Grip

The dark elf lounged below deck, keeping to herself. She had been asleep when *Revery* diverted its course back toward Waneport, but she was not surprised to hear that fate decided to lead her back toward Ransil yet again.

Secretly, she was thrilled with the prospect of seeing him once more, even if it would be for the last time. But she also knew that he would likely try to kill her once he laid eyes on her.

Like that would be so bad, she thought, interlacing her fingers behind her head as she leaned back farther. Thinking of everything that had transpired since she left Andelor, she was starting to wonder if she'd just rather have the love of her life put her out of her misery than have to sort this fucking mess out. She had already lived much longer than she felt should be allowed, given what happened to her bloodline. And the closer she got to reclaiming her birthright, the more she dreaded actually going through with it.

Maybe that was why she crossed Ransil so often, as if she were just begging for him to kill her outright. The notion brought a morbid smile to her lips.

There was a soft rap at her door. "Grip?"

The voice sounded unfamiliar, so she drew one of her many knives as she melted from the makeshift hammock into the shadows of the cargo hold.

"Are you there?"

She could tell now it was the elf witch, but she had no idea what that one would want with her, especially given the nature of their meeting. Her curious mind got the best of her, and she reached for the door's latch. Layla recoiled slightly when the door opened. She had one hand on the Arcanian mark hanging from her necklace while the other one held the *Book of Stane* tucked under her arm.

"Sorry if I woke you," the elf said. Her tone implied she actually meant it, which Grip found odd. Something had weakened the girl.

She sheathed her knife and crossed her arms. "I think I've gotten enough beauty sleep on this little voyage. What would a Court Mage need with a Guild agent in the middle of the sea?"

"We're not really in the middle," Layla began. "I could see Waneport before coming down here. We should be ashore by nightfall." She glanced down at the book, shifting her feet slightly like a boy at his first brothel. "That's actually why I'm here..."

Grip leaned back against the support that jutted up from the middle of the hold. "If you're hoping for a tour of the city, ask the Lord Mayor. I don't plan on sticking around once we reach the coast."

That drew Layla's gaze. "What do you mean? You're leaving?"

Grip snorted lightly. "I know you'll miss me, but do think fondly of our time together in my absence...especially that time we spent down here when you were my prisoner."

Layla didn't laugh at that, which made Grip feel cruel—well, *more* cruel than she usually felt. *The girl had just watched her lover get beheaded*, she reminded herself; regardless if the bitch deserved to lose her head, Layla most likely didn't deserve to be mocked after having witnessed it.

"Where will you go?" she asked.

Grip considered lying to her, but she wasn't feeling particularly clever at the moment. "I'm going on to Andelor as planned, even if I have to ride there. I don't feel like stepping through another gate anytime soon with what's happened to the Old Ways."

"Will Maze let you go?" Layla released the Arcanian mark and hugged the book to her chest. "I mean, back in Jath—weren't you both conspiring against the queen? And now, what? You'll just go back to serving her sister?"

Grip chuckled at that. "Serve? You think I serve Nipheena? Tell me, do you even know how those twins managed to thwart their own father's conquests?" When Layla didn't answer, Grip pushed herself away from the pillar and motioned behind her toward Caim. "The Xoation army was fractured—half sworn to the princess and half to the vampires. Count Delucar had all of Caim on a silver platter, and all that stood in his way was a host of dark elves led by an exceptionally lovely heir to the throne."

Layla's eyes grew wide.

"I don't serve either of the twins," Grip snarled, not hiding her annoyance at such a suggestion. "But that doesn't mean I want their father returning, so I will stay as close to them as possible to prevent that from happening." Her thoughts went back to Ransil and, with sadness washing over her, she added, "Whatever the cost."

Layla stared at the floor as she considered that. When she looked up, she said, "I've read plenty about the vampires—the devastations on Caim. I can understand not wanting to revisit that, but with Xoatia fallen and all of the Racivic Sea dividing the Joined Realms from its ruins..." She shook her head in confusion. "Why would it matter if he returned now? What is left on Caim for them to conquer?"

Grip knew the elf was thinking about her former partner—the one she flayed on Jath. However, she was unsure what that had to do with Count Delucar or Grip's ambitions. All she could think to say was, "I haven't given up on Xoatia. And when I return, it will not be the kingdom of blood that Count Delucar hoped to raise."

Silence fell between them, and for several breaths they just swayed together as the ship rocked its way toward safe harbor.

"Can I come with you?" Layla finally asked.

Grip was taken aback, not really sure how to process the request. Not waiting for her, Layla stepped into the cargo hold.

"I pledged myself to Stane on Jath," she admitted with glistening eyes. "Valix saved my life, and I think part of me attributed that to Stane—she gave me an escape, you know? And on the voyage back—before... I heard him. He's been speaking to me ever since." She looked down at the book again. "And I'm afraid if Maze finds Kartha... If these writings are translated..."

Grip considered that for a long moment as the bells on deck rang out to signal their approach. She looked up into Layla's eyes before asking, "What is it you're afraid of?"

The elf's expression shifted toward confusion. "I'm afraid of being used again."

Grip laughed low and wickedly. "We're all being used, Layla. Whether Stane's using you to fight dragons, or the queen's using you to recover old books, or Knife's using me to threaten barons... If we're not useful, what are we?"

The other elf's brows furrowed. "There has to be more to life than that. Don't tell me you're running off just to be used by someone else—to do someone else's bidding."

Grip thought of Ransil then, even though the halfling had never used her (unless she asked him to, that is). She didn't want to tell this woman that it was Valix's execution that had made Grip realize she needed to go find Ransil—everything else could wait. And he would likely be going to Andelor.

The bells continued ringing above and Grip nodded in that direction. "We should be in Waneport soon. Then Maze and Jaffron will expect you to bring the book to Kartha—do you feel no obligation to see your part through?"

"Don't you?"

She scowled at Layla. "Before all of this, I was on my way to inform Jaffron and the queen that the Shrouded were in play at Oakworth. I've already played my part. Casryk has the proof."

"What about Delucar?" Layla sounded desperate, as if she needed Grip to give her a reason to stay her course. "You're Xoatian. Do you want the vampire lords to return?"

Grip struggled to keep her face expressionless. In truth, she did want that, so she could kill the bastard herself, instead of just sealing him away like his daughters did. But she knew she'd be back in Caim before there was any chance of that happening.

She just needed to find Ransil and give the man a proper goodbye. He deserved that much.

"You need to see this through, Layla. I know what it is you fear; I can see it in your eyes. You just realized you came to face Desmond again, but now that you're this close, you would rather run than stand before him."

The elf's eyes blazed then and she stepped forward. "How would you know?! Has the Shadow clawed its way into your mind? Turning you into some pleasure slave to serve the whims of a cowardly man?!"

Grip tried to disguise her sympathy, knowing what the woman dealt with but also knowing she had a certain reputation to maintain. "Not exactly."

Layla exhaled, her breath ragged. "I don't know what I'll do when I see him," she said softly. "I just know this book is going to lead me to him. If he's actually alive after what I did to him…" Her eyes glistened with tears. "I don't know what I'm afraid of, but I do know that I'm just tired of being controlled." She looked directly into Grip's one good eye, pleading. "Can you understand that?"

The sporadic bells up on deck became a constant clamor, signaling the ship was dropping anchor in the Waneport harbor.

"Let's go," Grip said, motioning toward the stairs behind Layla. "We both have places to be."

Grip found Price lurking in Wharfside again at dusk. This time, it was her that caught him unawares.

"Any news from below?"

Price started, glaring at her down the length of his bird's beak nose. "I would ask you." His eyes darted toward the opening of the alley. Grip had caught him counting queens in his gloved palm—just as she suspected, the Guild ruled the dark recesses of Waneport and Price had grown accustomed to feeling safe and secure in their confines. "You were the one bound for Andelor last we met. I take it you returned with the Lord Mayor?"

"Just tell me what you've heard." Grip crossed her arms. "I've been stuck on a ship from here to Caraby and back. What have I missed?"

Price pocketed his coins and rose from his seat on a battered barrel. "Another incarnate, they say. Struck Sathford. If the whispers can be believed, your little Ruse finally ran out of luck." He clicked his tongue as if describing someone falling and scraping their knee. "Those halflings seem to have more lives than cats though, so who knows?"

Grip lost all sense of time and place as those words slowly registered. She imagined Ransil lying dead on some grimy bridge in Sathford, or floating face-down in the Bracing River.

In a flash, she grabbed the man by the cloak and slammed him up against the building. Someone gasped out on the street, but Grip paid it no mind—she just glared at the man who claimed Ransil Osbury was dead.

She felt the steel of his knife against her bare belly, exposed by her vest riding up. But again, she cared about nothing aside from the truth.

"Easy," Price said, smiling cruelly. "I didn't kill the prick."

"What happened?"

"I wasn't there. I'm just telling you what I heard. And unless you want me to see if your guts are as Shadow-stained as your flesh, ease up, elf."

Grip didn't ease up; she couldn't. "Just tell me."

"I heard Knife has some new recruit. You know how these things go. If she offered someone Ruse's old position, there's an open bounty.

Must have been pure chaos in Sathford—would have been nothing for someone to put a blade in a washed-up halfling thief."

Grip's hand moved like a striking cobra, snatching Price's blade from his hand and burying it in the wall behind him, pinning him with his cloak.

"Hey!"

Moving just as fast, she pulled her satchel from beneath her own cloak and slammed it into Price's chest. "Give that to her. It's everything she needs on the Shrouded—all the high houses that conspire with the Shadow."

She reached into her pocket and produced her Guildmark—the ring that Ransil gave her back in Caim when he asked her to marry him...the one she could never bring herself to wear. Each agent had to sacrifice their greatest treasure to be their Guildmark, giving it over to the conclave's enchantments.

But now Grip truly gave it away, flipping it toward Price as she released him. He caught it deftly, as if to prove he wasn't so easily bested in agility.

"You know she won't let you quit," Price said, almost more in fear than with any sense of authority. "She needs you."

Grip turned to walk away. "Well, I don't need her. Not anymore."

Layla stared at the book, wondering if she should just leave it with Maze and wander off to explore the world on her own. She truly wanted to accompany Grip wherever the dark elf intended to go, but she could make do on her own. After a few weeks of rest, she might be able to comfortably work magic again, possibly finding new employment with a high house.

As she silently wondered what kept her in that seat in that dimly lit tavern, something about the book made her feel desperate to know what secrets its pages held.

And that's how Maze found her an hour later.

"Get some food, Layla."

Blinking away from the tome, she regarded Maze, opening her mouth to say that she would be leaving in the morning. But the words didn't come. Instead, she just shook her head.

"You've been at sea far too long, girl," Maze insisted, setting a bowl of various cheeses and dried meats on the table between the two. "We'll leave at nightfall and make camp on the way to Stelmont."

Layla surveyed the common room while Maze explained the plan. Each of the weary sailors, eager merchants, and hopeful adventurers that ate and drank around her began to look like Desmond Everton— a roomful of pale sorcerers with ash smeared around their eyes, all staring at Layla accusingly. Maze's touch startled her, causing her to almost jerk out of her seat. Layla met their eyes before closing her own tightly.

"He's everywhere," she said, pushing her fingers into her eyes and shuddering. Layla heard Maze scoot their chair around the table, felt a gentle hand on her shoulder.

"That's Stane trying to deceive you, child."

Maze's voice was soft and soothing, though somehow Layla heard it perfectly over the din of the common room.

"He wants you to stray from the path, which means you are the right one."

Layla opened her eyes to ask, "How do you know?"

"Because otherwise he would wait and watch—he only interferes when—"

"No," Layla interrupted loudly. "I mean how do you know anything about Stane?" She laid a palm on the book. "Have you read this book? Have you heard his voice? It seems like no one has ever encountered Stane or read his writing, but so many claim to know so much about him."

Maze regarded her while listening, calmly nodding along. "You're not the only one that hears the voice of Stane, Layla. Though he hasn't spoken to me since I renounced the Disciples, there was a time when he tried to keep me from my purposes."

"You were a Disciple?"

Maze nodded, their gaze shifting to something distant and unseen in the tavern's shadows. "In another life. I was Maythan Krusayne— and you wonder why I changed my name, eh? I served as an archer in the Vaustren army before I deserted and joined up with the Disciples of Stane in Velcarthe."

Layla was stunned. She always assumed Maze would likely have an interesting past, but she wouldn't have pinned them as a Disciple.

"He spoke to you?"

Maze nodded. "Often. I was a *he* then, but he insisted on referring to me as *she* and *her*, as if it held some sort of power over me. After abandoning those terms, I began to see through his lies and eventually found myself free of Gravern's grip."

Layla looked at the *Book of Stane*, wondering what Maze might say if she told them just to take it from her so she could wander down the Wane Coast and be free of all this. But that strange yearning to know what those pages said remained—she couldn't take her hand from it. "Grip is leaving."

"I expected as much," Maze replied. "She's done her part and she has other obligations in Andelor. I also expected you might want to return with her."

Layla turned toward Maze, feeling like she had just gotten scolded by one of her Raventhal professors. But Maze just gave her a knowing smile.

"I'm relieved to see that book has its hooks in you," they said.

"Why?"

Maze laughed. "Because I'm going to need your help. This Kartha we seek is, well… She's a cranky old bitch."

Layla couldn't help but laugh. The levity allowed her stomach a chance to grumble, and she took a bite of cheese from the bowl as the conversations around them continued on.

"What's so funny?"

Layla turned to see Grip—*Has she been crying?* she wondered. The dark elf had a pack slung over her shoulder.

"Heading back to the Guild?" Maze asked.

"No," Grip said, casting Layla a curious glance. "I just quit. I'm going to Sathford."

Maze gave Layla a smirk. "Seems we'll be sharing the road then, at least to Stelmont."

"Seems that way," Grip said, turning to leave. "If Jaffron's coming, he's not sleeping within arms' reach of me."

Layla looked around, smiling. Desmond was nowhere to be seen.

Chapter Eight

Morning Light

Brace dreamed of fire.

Despite the icy cold in the cell that night, he managed to sweat through the sparse rags covering his burned body. It was a nauseating sensation, so he clung to sleep as long as he could, despite the nightmares.

His cellmate's voice pulled him from the freezing fire of his nightmares.

"Will you not speak?"

"Ugh," Brace managed, his mouth feeling parched and raw. He rolled over weakly, the bruises from the Oather's questioning sessions aching with every shift of his muscles. "Melaine?"

His sight adjusted to the faint moonlight filtering into their cell. It was then he realized the half-orc was not speaking to him.

"You look unwell," Melaine continued. "Did the Oather question you as well?"

Brace pushed himself up, still struggling with the tightness in his flesh. The High Mage's healing kept him alive for the Oather's interrogations, but it did little to relieve the pain from the fires that had scarred him in Oakhold.

Melaine's glinting eyes turned to Brace as he eased himself into a sitting position. She nodded toward the shadowed form seated against the opposite wall. "She must have been one of the attackers. With the gnolls."

Brace regarded the shape. "Aye. Sure caused a lot of racket—much good it did. Are you human? Elf?"

No response. The only movement came from her steady breathing.

"Them robes," Brace said, more to Melaine than the stranger. "She's either a witch or a Shrouded, I say. I don't like neither prospect. And if she's a mage openly attacking one of the Arcania's towers, then she must be one of them followers of the Combustress."

"Don't even say that name," Melaine whispered. She got to her feet, the black irons on her wrists and ankles clattering loudly in their meager confines. "The Oather will most likely take it as some sort of admission."

"That one doesn't need an admission," Brace replied, turning to regard the cell door that Melaine peered through. The jailor was likely off whoring again; they were as alone as they could hope to be. "He's convinced we're one of them."

"One of who?"

The woman's voice was meeker than Brace had expected, like the question of a child. He ran a hand over his scarred scalp—which only retained half of his hair on the right side—wondering if this mysterious woman was afraid.

"The cultists," he replied. "You follow this Combustress, right? The one that's burning up the countryside and sowing distrust along the Wane Coast."

"The one who sent me to free you."

Brace heard Melaine's irons clatter as the half-orc stepped into the moonlight. His unexpected companion cut a mighty figure. Even in their prison rags, she stood like a proud warrior who wouldn't hesitate to carry a fool like him through consuming fire. In that moment, he was reminded how much he owed her, and the sudden thought of this new prisoner either harming or threatening Melaine caused Brace to get to his feet. Since he was just a man, he wasn't shackled with the black irons like Melaine, who the Oather suspected was some kind of orc shaman.

"What do you mean?" Melaine asked.

The woman began to rise from her darkened corner, the moonlight revealing a human that Brace assumed looked much like himself: burned-away hair and angry, wrinkled flesh where fire had melted it like wax. The hair around her brow was gone, and what remained on the back of her head was ratty and unwashed. She wore ashed robes that the Oather had talked about when questioning Brace, asking where he had hid his before invading the Vestige.

"She will free all of us," the woman said, stepping the rest of the way into the moon's light. Brace could see tears in her eyes. Her face twisted in agony as if moving pained her as much as it had pained him.

"Something's not right," Melaine said.

Brace turned toward her to see the half-orc holding up her wrists, staring at the crude black cuffs that were clamped around them. She looked up at him, fear in her wide eyes.

"She's doing something…"

The prisoner made a strange groaning sound that drew Brace's attention back to her. What he saw made him cringe away toward the wall. The woman's face contorted as she hunched over, holding her stomach with both hands.

"She can burn it all away," she groaned, letting out a jagged, pained breath before continuing. "The Combustress is the only one who has survived Wick's flames… The only one who can summon the cleansing fires to rid the world of corruption."

During this soliloquy, Brace watched the stranger with a mix of sorrow and fear. It seemed like this woman was dying before his eyes, and he didn't know if he could—or should—help her. He was a vacant shell, just there to witness whatever madness was about to play out.

Melaine let out a sharp gasp, pulling Brace's gaze away from the other woman. The half-orc clenched her fists, drawing her lips back in a snarl as if the irons were burning her.

"What is it?" Brace moved toward her, but Melaine drew back.

"Don't," she warned. "The enchantments on these… They dampen magic. But whatever is happening…" Her eyes went back to the woman who was now doubled over in pain, groaning. "This is power beyond their control."

A ripping sound caused the woman to straighten suddenly. She screamed in agony as flames burst from her torso, spraying fiery blood at Brace and Melaine.

"Light's mercy!" Brace shielded his face from the warm droplets of the woman's innards. More hideous sounds made him squint his eyes tight against whatever horrors happened across the cell. The sounds were enough for him to nearly empty his stomach.

"Gods!" Melaine cursed.

Brace didn't want to look, but he knew he had to. Those sounds were sickening, and when he saw their source, he screamed like a terrified little boy.

The fire reduced him to a helpless child—frozen in fear as he watched the concentrated inferno consume the woman. Once he looked, he couldn't turn away. The scene was a mesmerizing nightmare.

Voices shouted a warning from somewhere outside the cell. "Attack! To arms! The cultists have returned!"

Brace barely comprehended those cries. His world was limited to the burning woman before him. Melaine moved toward her, but the flames licked out as if wanting to keep her at bay. Brace remained motionless, smelling burning flesh, taking him right back to the encounter with the incarnate in Oakhold—when it was his time to burn.

Somehow the woman kept her balance as she stiffened and convulsed in turn while the fire engulfed her limbs. The sickening ripping sound grew louder, and from within the flames, Brace saw...something.

It was like curtains parting to reveal oblivion within the unnatural fire. That blackness grew wider, like a woman giving birth, and eventually revealed a glimmering red eye.

My keyshard, Brace thought immediately, but remembered that his stone was locked away somewhere up in the tower, not kept in the guts of a Wickan cultist. Despite the realization, he still watched that keyshard that looked so much like the one his father had bequeathed to him as it tore the woman's body open, spraying blood and fire across the cell.

"What in the Abyss?!" Melaine cursed. Swords clashed outside, signaling the start of a battle. "It's a gateway..."

Brace saw it too. The keyshard released a small gust of fiery wind that pushed him back against the wall. When he returned his gaze to the new prisoner's body, he was shocked to see she was still standing. Even though her body was torn in two by the magic she had smuggled within her, she kept her balance. He had just enough time to wonder if the woman had swallowed a keyshard in order to carry out her bizarre ploy before the gateway began to reveal a strange scene—what appeared to be a cave.

What if she didn't want to smuggle a keyshard in here? Brace thought, seeing a tall figure in that cave's flickering torchlight lower their hood. *What if she wanted to smuggle someone in?*

"Wait," Ransil instructed, motioning for Anika to stay with the boy. She had her knife out and he saw the subtle glimmer of magic swirling around the enchanted blade. He spun his own knife so its blade was downward, making it much easier to bury it in a gnoll's back if needed.

That is, the halfling thought, *if these two oafs could step quieter.*

Ransil followed the sounds that had originally drawn them from their camp in the middle of the night. They had ridden nearly a full day from Sathford, east along the Bracing River, following the trail left by the gnolls.

As Ransil slid down a shallow incline on his backside, he heard the unmistakable sound of a skirmish. The grunting, snorting sounds of his prey turned into panicked squeals.

A familiar voice barked threats between heavy blows. "Burn my lumber, will ye?! Slobberin' wretches!" There was a choked whinny that followed, like someone had kicked a dog.

Ransil bounded to his feet when he got to the bottom of the hill, slipping through the tall weeds to see Deina pulling her axe free from a monster's shoulder. Her foot was on the thing's chest as she tore her enchanted weapon from the corpse. Five gnolls lay dead at the dwarf's feet. She regarded Ransil calmly, as if she had been waiting for him to arrive.

"I thought you'd still be in Sathford," Ransil said, sheathing his knife. He motioned to the gnolls. "Did you find any keyshards on them? We've had a robbery."

"Deina?!" Anika's voice sounded close enough to startle Ransil; she had followed him toward the ridge, not keeping Quinn far enough away from danger. "Is that you?"

"Keep your voice down," Ransil hissed over his shoulder, feeling as if he were a wet nurse wrangling children. He moved toward the gnolls as Deina kicked the one at her feet over, nudging the purse that hung over its shoulder.

"Feels empty," the dwarf said, motioning to the others with Harvester; the axe glowed with a faint green aura as the keyshard affixed between its double blades pulsed. "These others didn't even carry weapons."

"I was hoping to follow them to their lair," Ransil replied. "What brought you so far from the city, Deina?"

"Oh, apologies, Lord Osbury," Deina mocked. "I forgot to ask for your leave. I saw these furry bastards setting fire to me stock of timber near the bridge—for no other reason probably than to watch it burn!"

Ransil nodded. "So you chased them all the way out here? Normally I'd thank you, but I needed to find out where they were going."

Anika gasped behind them as the dwarf inspected a gash on her arm. "Are you all right, Deina?"

The dwarf looked up from the wound and smiled. "Just fine, Lady Lawson. Sorry if I startled ye. Someone's gotta keep these filthy vermin in line."

Anika gave a light chuckle as she descended the hill, holding Quinn's hand (much to the boy's chagrin). "It's good to see you. How is Harvester? Any more strange visions? Here, let me heal your arm."

Ransil shot her a look before turning back to Deina, curious what visions the dwarf had been having in regards to the axe. From his understanding, the weapon was forged similarly to Anika's knife—affixed with a greater keyshard in the presence of an incarnate—but beyond that, he wasn't aware of any visions tied to the thing.

"All's well," Deina said dismissively, letting the Child of Light mend her. "It functions as well as I need it to." She motioned to the dead gnolls, the keyshard in Harvester leaving an emerald trail in its wake. "I don't need Oakus to cut down the likes of them."

Anika placed her hand over the bloody gash on Deina's muscled arm and soft blue light enveloped both. Ransil turned away, still not able to come to grips with the girl's power.

"Do they have the keyshards?" Quinn asked, untangling himself from Anika's grip. He stepped up next to Ransil to observe the slain monsters. "Or any other loot?"

"We're not out to loot monsters," Ransil snapped, feeling even more like a nursemaid with all this chattering so near danger. "There's a keyshard hoard nearby and we need to find it."

"Are you going to help us?" Anika asked Deina, inspecting the ugly red scar that replaced the bleeding wound on the dwarf's arm. "Our company could use a bodyguard."

Secretly, Ransil hoped the dour woman would refuse and take herself back to Sathford. Ever since Melaine was killed in Oakworth, Deina had become either drunk or unpredictable (usually both). She spent most of her time either chopping wood for the new cathedral or drinking herself into a stupor at one of the Five Casks.

"May as well," Deina said, hefting Harvester over her armored shoulder. She didn't sound enthusiastic about the idea, and Ransil had a strange feeling that she only agreed to it because she could sense the halfling's unease.

"Should we have a name?" Quinn asked. Ransil saw that he was being genuine, and he felt slightly guilty for cringing over the absurdness of the suggestion. "You know, like the Keyguard or something."

"Why not?" Ransil mumbled to himself, his eyes darting between Harvester and Stormender. "Someone's gotta guard these things."

The Combustress strode out from her follower's ruined carcass, which was still held suspended in the air—whether it was burnt to such a crisp that it had become rigid, or the spell worked on the keyshard simply defied gravity, Brace couldn't begin to guess.

He was too busy watching in shocked awe as the cult leader strode through the wreath of licking flames. He was still paralyzed by what he witnessed, but he was aware enough to realize that Melaine must have been stunned as well, since neither of them moved.

While he couldn't speak for the half-orc, Brace knew what kept him too horrified to move, and it wasn't the bald and bloodied Xe'danni that now stepped into full view. The lashing flames were what kept him against the cell's wall. He hadn't seen fire since it tried to consume him in Oakhold, not even the flame of a candle. Just looking at the unnatural fire produced by the hollowed-out corpse, he could feel the icy pain of the inferno that had nearly ended his life, and his body reacted by locking up completely.

"You've touched fire."

Brace jerked his eyes toward the Combustress. Even with the burns marring her face, she was still beautiful, and he had enough sense to feel foolish and embarrassed as he cowered from the heat. The woman's gaze found his, and the fire shrunk back when their eyes met.

"And yet you fear the flames?"

Melaine's irons clanked in response to the woman's voice. "Neither of us are accustomed to them bursting out of a person."

The Combustress turned her gaze to the half-orc as the smoldering remains of the cultist finally crumbled to ash behind her; however, that fiery portal remained suspended behind the newcomer.

"You've both been burned. You have endured Wick's blessings, haven't you?"

"You call this a blessing?" Brace asked, his voice not as confident as he had hoped. He held a shaking hand up to his ruined face. "Do I look blessed?"

The Combustress smiled at him; it wasn't a mocking or condescending smile. It seemed genuine, despite the circumstances. She stepped toward him and raised a flawless hand up to his cheek, touching it gently.

Brace nearly melted again.

Outside, the sounds of battle continued to rage. But the Combustress only had eyes for the burned chaplain.

"Are you here to offer us to the flames?" Melaine took a step forward, clearly not as terrified of the fire as Brace was. "Like your follower there?"

She turned from Brace to regard the pile of smoking ash, her tattered red robes swirling through the fire without catching—Brace could tell they were enchanted, but how they retained their powers in the presence of the magic-dampening irons around Melaine's wrists (and probably the bars of the cell door), he couldn't begin to guess.

"Iris played her part well," the Combustress said. As if the words were an incantation, the keyshard that was suspended in the air clattered quietly to the ground as the portal caved in on itself. The encircling flames shrank away as the woman bent to retrieve the stone. "It is no easy task to swallow a shard of this size."

When she held it up, the sense of familiarity Brace felt allowed him to finally peel himself from the wall. The fires had died away, so he felt safe enough to approach her.

"So is this where you kill us?"

She turned to him, a surprised look on her face. "Kill you? I was hoping you might join me so I could get you out of here."

"Are you saying you came here to rescue us?" Melaine asked. "Find that hard to believe."

The Combustress held Brace's gaze, unsettling him. "I came here to release the Vestige's grip on what doesn't belong to it." She turned to Melaine then. "Do you belong here? If you do, feel free to remain in this cell."

She flourished her arms then, throwing them wildly toward the black bars of the cell's doors. An explosive burst shot from her outstretched hands with a force that knocked Brace and Melaine back against the opposite wall. The sounds of battle were muffled by the screech of metal and the tumbling of stones, and Brace once again felt like he was in Oakhold as it collapsed. He struggled to breathe through the lingering smoke and the clouds of dirt that filled the confined space.

But when he felt the gentle hand on his shoulder—with powerful fingers that helped him to his feet—Brace was able to take a deep, reassuring breath. He straightened to look into his savior's eyes, knowing somehow that the Combustress was someone that he could easily devote himself to.

This time, Ransil allowed his companions to follow him toward the mouth of the cave. Anika crept along on his right side while Deina followed closely behind Quinn, who Ransil insisted at least remain behind them.

"The tracks didn't lead in there," Anika whispered. "Do gnolls typically hide out in caves?"

Ransil considered that. He was no expert on gnoll habits, having only had to deal with them in southern Westerra, near the Karranese wastes. He had also forgotten that Anika was an experienced tracker, having gone hunting with her father since she was a little tot. "It may be worth checking regardless," he told her. "Even if the thieves aren't inside right now, there may be some signs of their passage."

He took Anika's silence as agreement and pressed forward into the awaiting dark.

"Do you want to try what Master Audreese taught you?" Quinn whispered as they entered the cave. Despite the early daylight outside, it was dark enough underground to possibly make navigation tricky.

Anika sheathed Stormender and knelt down. "Don't blame me if I singe anyone's hair again," she replied. Ransil watched as she contorted her hands, mumbling something to herself. He could feel that same rising energy emanating from the girl—the energy that reminded him how far they had come from Blakehurst—and he couldn't help but feel impressed and maybe slightly scared that the young tanner was now in training to be a mage.

Light bloomed in Anika's palm, similar to how the priest Avrim would summon divine power. However, Ransil had never seen such controlled illumination. The bright white sphere that she conjured was not like the blinding sun that the Luminaura were known to wield; this was something much less raw, more practiced.

Ransil heard Quinn gasp and Deina mumble something under her breath.

"Have you done that before?" Ransil asked.

"In a way." Anika got back to her feet and gave the halfling a sidelong look. "But only with Audreese helping me."

"Well, take care, Ani," he warned, inwardly cringing at how parental he sounded. "I don't believe most first-year mages at the spire are able to wield that kind of power."

"Most first-year mages aren't the Child of Light," Quinn added, sounding much older than his nine or ten years.

They continued into the cave, Anika's light keeping the shadows at bay. The passage twisted inward, leading them farther underground. Bones lined the walls; mostly old animals, but Ransil noticed some halfling or gnome skulls that made the hairs on his arm stand on end. He chose not to make his companions aware of those grisly remains, allowing them to keep their steady pace into the depths.

"Are those ashes?"

Ransil looked in the direction Anika pointed, her glowing hand directing him toward a trail of blackness wrapping around the next bend.

"Aye," the halfling replied. "Seems like the kind of thing you'd find leading to a stash of red keyshards."

"I'm not sensing any," Quinn said in a strained voice.

Ransil looked back at the boy to see his face contorted. He had drawn out one of his own stones—an amber keyshard of Syrina, gripped in his small fist. It was said that all keyshards were linked in a way, and they could sense each other if the wielder knew how to listen; but only extremely advanced mages could tap into those hidden leylines.

Quinn Olivick may have just been the most advanced mage in the world, for all Ransil knew; the boy was a wonder.

Anika led them farther toward the blackened trail, but Deina pushed herself forward before they reached the bend in the passage.

"Lady Lawson, let me." The dwarf held Harvester in both hands, the axe giving off its own strong green glow. "I feel the roots of this place, and something doesn't feel right."

No one argued, and Deina led them into the horror that awaited them in the cave's lowest chamber.

As the battle continued to rage outside the tower, Brace and Melaine followed the Combustress up the stairs. The woman hadn't said much after freeing them from their cell, but she kept a slow pace as if to give the prisoners plenty of time to consider following her.

Brace and Melaine had exchanged unsure looks before making their way through the blackened rubble that was their prison door. Now they walked in silence, though Brace felt their shared uncertainty. Neither of them had any love for the Vestige, after the tower's Oather had begun torturing them for information on the very woman now rescuing them. But were they really following a cult leader? To what end?

"Are we free to go?" Melaine asked, causing the Combustress to pause at the top of the stairs. When the woman turned toward them, Brace could feel unmistakable power; it was no wonder she led a cult of fanatically devoted pyromancers.

"You don't look free," she said, sounding more sad than Brace had expected. Her gaze went from the half-orc's black manacles to her eyes. "Where do you hail from, half-blood?"

"Wickham," Melaine replied without pause.

She smiled at that. "There are some in this world that would question fate. But how could it be anything but preordained that you are this far from your homeland, which just so happens to be Wick's homeland, only to be rescued by his messiah?"

"Is that what you call yourself?" Brace asked. He did not seek to provoke her, but since he joined the Luminaura he had endured his fill of self-proclaimed messiahs.

"It's what I am," she replied, unbothered by his rebuke. "Just as you are a slave to the Light, guilted into doing whatever it is the Archbeacon proclaims your purpose to be."

"So you would have us follow your proclamations then?" Melaine shot back.

"I have no proclamations, half-blood. Wick has touched us both— us three," she corrected, giving Brace a cold look. "I offer salvation in his name, but I do not require you to take it. He requires me to burn this tower down after claiming Kindler's shards that he has laid in my path." She turned away from them to continue her climb.

Melaine started but froze when the Combustress raised a hand aswirl with dancing red threads of magic. A loud clank drew both the prisoners' attention to the anti-magic chains that now fell from Melaine's limbs. They shared a shocked look before gazing back toward the cult leader.

Brace could hear footsteps pounding above: sounds of a retreat.

"If I were either of you, I would choose a side quickly," the Combustress called behind her, "as there are only two in the battle ahead: those who rise from the flames and those that smolder to ash."

Brace looked back to Melaine, but the half-orc was already following the cultist.

The vast chamber smelled sweetly of cooked meat, but when Ransil's vision adjusted to the unnatural light from Anika's hand and Deina's axe, he felt his stomach turn.

"Myretha's mercy," Deina whispered, the words echoing in the darkness above the site of slaughter. Dead gnolls were strewn across the ashen floor, arranged in a concentric pattern around a charred box in the center of the chamber. The blackened skeletal remains of what Ransil could only assume were once people were positioned haphazardly at four specific points surrounding the gnolls.

"This was a ritual," Quinn said, his voice strained but certain. "The gnolls must have brought the keyshards here to fuel...whatever this was."

"I know what this was," Ransil said, stepping carefully toward the box. The gruesome scene threatened to spill his stomach into the ashes, but he bit back the bile and squatted over the black container.

"Careful, Ransil," Anika warned from nearby.

"Stay back," he countered, looking at a trail of ash that spiraled away from the box. "I've seen this before." *I just can't believe she's still alive*, he thought to himself. With one digit exposed from his fingerless gloves, Ransil broke the trail of ashes leading from each cardinal direction; he knew the arcane trap would trigger if he opened the box without breaking the pattern.

"You know what you're doing there, halfling?" Deina's voice sounded distant, as if she were backing away from a potential explosion.

"In theory," he replied, tracing his ash-covered finger over the blackened exterior of the box. It was the same one he found in Caim, he was sure of it. "But just in case," he warned, looking over his shoulder at Anika and Quinn, "stay behind Deina."

They did.

Ransil opened the box slowly to reveal a familiar, exquisite red Caimish dagger: a confirmation of who had certainly orchestrated such a gruesome spectacle.

"What is it?" Quinn asked.

Ransil drew out Emberance, the familiar blade gleaming under the light of the other two Keys of Transience in the room. It was a broad knife in the hands of a halfling, but Veronitha Blaithe might have treated it as a pocketknife when she placed it in this box.

But if she had done that, she had done it as the Combustress, and not the sweet young girl he had known all those years ago in the Acreage.

"Is that…" Anika's question was lost as Ransil turned to face his companions, holding the enchanted knife between them.

"It's not what we came for," he said. "But it confirms my fear about who's behind this…massacre."

"Who?" Anika asked.

The Combustress led them to the High Mage's quarters. Stacy Augustine was watching out the high window, shouting commands to the defenders of the Vestige.

"Get back out there, cowards! They're just a bunch of fanatics!"

Brace felt like he should say something to the woman, to alert her to their presence. Despite being a scout, he was not generally in favor of cowardly ambushes. But he just watched and waited for the Combustress's command.

"Where are the keyshards, High Mage?"

Stacy spun around to face the Combustress. She eyed Brace and Melaine in turn until her smoldering gaze settled on the cultist.

"How did you get in here?"

The Combustress reached her arms forward, jerking her hands in awkward motions as flames burst from her palms. The High Mage cried out, shielding her face from the assailing inferno.

Brace wanted to scold the cultist, tell her to spare the woman. But he couldn't shake the image of High Mage Augustine watching approvingly as her Oather tortured him. So he gave her the same treatment as the summoned fire encircled the High Mage.

"Please!" the woman screamed, backing up to the window. She flailed her arms, likely trying to cast a counterspell, but it was no use; the Combustress was too powerful. All Stacy Augustine could do was back away until she was forcing herself through the window just to escape the arcane fire.

"Enough!" Melaine shouted, but it did not stop the Combustress. From the edges of his vision, Brace could see the half-orc move to stop the duel, but fire bloomed and knocked her away.

Brace could only watch as the High Mage threw herself from the tower's window to escape a more tortuous fate. Her descending screams unmanned him, and it was all he could do to keep his footing and not drop to his knees in sorrow.

"That was unnecessary!" Melaine strode toward the Combustress, but when the cultist turned to regard her, the half-orc shied away from that awful gaze. The pair could only watch as the Combustress strode across the scorched quarters to retrieve a leather satchel from the High Mage's desk.

"The final shards of Kindler," the cultist said, turning toward Brace and Melaine. She held the sack up for them to see, as if it explained everything. "I was called to deliver your salvation by these. Now I can finish the ritual."

"What ritual?" Brace asked, convinced that he didn't really want an answer.

The Combustress just smiled, pocketing the shards and leaving the High Mage's quarters to burn from within.

CHAPTER NINE

A Call to Duty

Bennik saw the battle was lost. The cultists had somehow allied themselves with gnolls, which made absolutely no sense to him. He had fought plenty of gnolls during the war in Westerra, when the beasts invaded the border towns, and he had plenty of first-hand knowledge of how stupid and cruel the monsters were. They weren't creatures that responded to bribes or threats, concerned only with their primal fascination with fire. He had even seen a pack of gnolls throw themselves into a burning building in the throes of battle.

Gnolls had no allegiances, not even to the other members of their pack.

How a group of fanatical Wickans managed to join them to their cause, Bennik couldn't begin to guess. *A shared love of fire?* he wondered, refusing to believe it could be that simple.

"This may be our chance," Kartha said from the other side of their cell. "That was the Oather screaming out there. You hear it? And those other sounds— I know what choking on your own blood sounds like. This tower is lost. We must make our escape while we still can."

"And how do you suppose we do that?" Fainly asked, motioning for Bennik to give him a boost up to the window so he could see Sir Stone's miserable death for himself. "Unless those beasts rip out these Sutheki bars, I'm still not going to risk any magic in these confines."

"These things can't nullify the old magicks," Kartha snapped back. "You know that."

Bennik picked up the Archmage, struggling to keep the gnome balanced as the little man peered over his shoulder at her. "Be my guest then, witch!"

"Oh, to the Abyss with you, wretched man!" Kartha shook the iron bars of their cell. "You know what will happen if I try! Do you want every Disciple of Stane or Shrouded assassin knowing just where to find us?!"

"Precisely," Fainly replied, with palpable pleasure in his voice—Bennik could tell this was a man who lived to win arguments. "What we do now is wait while these morons slaughter each other. Gnolls are simple creatures—they'll take whatever shiny red rocks the tower has and disappear back into the woods." He squirmed out of Bennik's hold and added, "Then, we can make our escape in peace and quiet."

"No!" Bennik snapped, thinking of Reston's keyshards—the pieces of Kindler. He wouldn't let them fall into the hands of gnolls or zealots, not when he was just entrusted with them.

A scent caught Bennik's nostrils then, and he turned to look at Kartha, who had smelled it as well.

"And what if the tower is burning?" she asked. "Perhaps then we might hasten our flight?"

Jak scrambled back into the village proper. He heard the flaming arrows hiss by, only a hair from the side of his face—he could feel their heat as they passed. The grunts and howls from the gnolls had fallen far enough away that he no longer feared them—but he still feared the Wickan archers who somehow had control over the monsters.

Monsters were one thing; he had defended Blakehurst from the occasional goblin ever since he could hold a sword. But the prospect of such weaponized monsters unsettled him greatly.

After seeing Sir Stone fall to the gnoll chieftain's axe, Jak and the dwarves from Freehold fell back toward the Vestige. But then the High Mage fell from the tower, landing in a gruesome heap atop an unfortunate dwarven crossbowman.

That was when the full retreat was sounded. He hadn't even spared a glance back toward the tower to see if High Mage Augustine and her surviving mages followed. All he could do was follow the dwarves as they cleaved through the fastest of the gnoll pursuers.

"Whoa there!"

Jak slowed to an awkward stop as he reached Stelmont's gates. Two watchmen held polearms to block the New Hold dwarves from entering the village.

"Let us in," one of the warriors snarled. She was holding her arm, hunched over in obvious pain. "Bastards burned me and me husband!"

"Well, don't be bringing your wizard troubles to our door," the watchman spat back. He pointed toward the hill where the Vestige loomed, black smoke billowing from its high windows. "Seems your tower is burning as well! Go tend to that and keep your quarrels where they belong—which is far from our gates!"

"I need to get inside!" Jak had to shout over the angry response from the dwarves who had just risked their lives defending the nearby academy. "The halflings! I'm responsible for those kids!"

"Aye," the other guard replied, a broad-faced woman with a huge mole under her nose. "The brats are fine—but you bring your trouble in here and that could be a whole different story!"

"Look!" One of the dwarves was pointing back at the Vestige. Jak risked a quick glance over his shoulder and immediately noticed what the man saw. "The gnolls are fleeing! The battle is done, you dicks. Let us in and tend to our wounded! We nearly died protecting your tower!"

"Ain't our tower," the woman said, easing her posture as the other guard stepped aside to open the gates. "That place ain't been nothing but trouble for us since the reeve let the Arcania recommission it. If you ask me, I preferred it when bandits used to squat in it—give me flesh-and-blood criminals over these witches any day."

None of the dwarves had anything to say to that, eager as they were to get behind the village walls before the guards changed their minds. Jak was the last one through the gates, which were slammed shut behind them.

While the fighters from New Hold made their way toward the Everbright Church that overlooked town square, Jak sheathed his shortsword and hurried toward The Thistle & Bough. Even in his haste, he noted how strange it was that the village appeared entirely unaffected by the fighting that happened just a stone's throw away from their walls. He wondered if this had become such a common occurrence with the cult that the villagers felt completely content just going about their daily routines while the High Mage and the Oather did battle with the Wickans.

The lanterns glowing in the inn's windows obscured Jak's view into the place, but he could hear the halflings laughing inside. Opening the door, he found them in the common room sharing a small loaf of cinnamon bread, giggling as they poked it with a couple dull, buttered knives. They both looked up from their silly game of slapping each other's knives away—two innocent, identical faces, reflecting every ounce of guilt Jak felt since leading them into Oakhold on Dame Strallow's orders.

"Hi, Jaky!" they both said in unison. The sweetness of their voices made him feel even worse, if that were at all possible.

"Hey there."

Jak turned to see Shelly, the human woman that ran The Thistle & Bough's kitchen. She was a thick-limbed matronly figure that Jak quite liked. However, now she looked at him as if he were a vagabond.

"You're not bringing trouble here, are ya?" She pointed to the open door. "I heard some commotion outside the gates this morning."

Jak shut the door, stepping toward her. "The tower's been attacked four times since yesterday. Why are the guards not helping with the defense?"

Shelly strode past him to peer through the windows. "We don't get drawn into the Arcania's conflicts. It's a rule. The reeve told the High Mage himself—if those wizards want to study their spells out there on the hill, they can do so under their own protection. Not since the second Aberheim have we had to tolerate the whims of a wizard in our town."

Jak wasn't sure what to make of all that, but he looked back at the halfling girls knowing that he could no longer keep them here. He also wasn't sure he wanted to take them to the Arcania any longer, with this new Archmage cutting the towers off.

"I need to take them back to their mother."

"Mommy!" both girls exclaimed, scooting off the bench to run toward Jak. The one he thought was Sadie grabbed the hem of his tunic, jerking it excitedly as if he were hiding Dolly Osbury up his sleeve.

"I wanna see Mommy, Jak! Please!" She had the beginnings of tears in her eyes.

Yet Jak couldn't help but smile and pat the small girl's head. They were such brave little girls, only truly crying a handful of times since he kidnapped them. It took everything within him to push down the vileness he felt toward his actions back in Oakworth. But what choice did he have? He was squire to the Lady Commander of the Oathers. The High Sanctum would have him executed as a traitor if he did not follow Dame Strallow's command.

"You can't go now," Shelly said, motioning to the village walls outside. "It's too dangerous out there."

Jak didn't want to tell her that it was likely more dangerous *in*

Stelmont with the tower fallen. He doubted the gnolls would content themselves with just burning the empty Vestige.

As if his thoughts were an incantation, a horn blew outside, long and shrill.

"Oh no," Shelly gasped, moving toward the other window to get a better look at the town's main gate.

"What's that?" Jak asked, dreading the answer. He felt the halfling girls desperately hugging his legs, each of them whimpering.

"It's the alarm!" She glared back at him. "You led them here."

Fainly screamed, falling back onto his makeshift bed as he grasped his temples. The door to their cell clanged loudly against the opposite wall as stonework from the broken frame fell in chunks.

Bennik—who had been shielding his eyes against the arcane blast—waved the cloud of dust from his face, staring in utter amazement at the hole the gnome had created for them. Never before had he been present for such a display of arcane destruction. While he had assumed someone who had risen to Archmage of the Arcania must be a powerful mage indeed, witnessing such awesome magical prowess in person was enough to take his breath away.

"Impressive," Kartha said, kneeling to help the gnome up. But Fainly smacked her hands away, grabbing the sides of his head again and rolling away. She stood up again to survey their escape route. "Honestly, I'm surprised you're still alive, Fainly. This shouldn't have been possible…"

Fainly just kept cursing and groaning in response.

"I'll get him," Bennik told her under his breath, motioning toward the stairs. "We need to find those keyshards before we leave. Reston entrusted them to me. Scout up the stairs to make sure no one is coming to check on the racket we just made."

"We?!" Fainly growled before sucking in a painful breath. "*We* didn't just cause any racket, Lawson! I single-handedly defied the very laws of magic just now—I've never heard of anyone pushing through Sutheki iron like that!"

Kartha was already mostly up the stairs as she called back, "Unless you want that to be your last great feat, get off your wrinkled ass and let's get out of here."

Fainly allowed Bennik to help him up, and they followed the green-skinned witch up to the main floor. As Bennik had predicted, the place looked abandoned. There were signs of a hasty defense, with tables knocked over to block doorways and rolled-up rugs tucked under closed doors. But the main doors were thrown open to reveal the site of a battle on the hill. Small fires burned where the cult's fiery arrows struck the tower's dilapidated gates.

Bennik's heart sank as he saw several young mages in lifeless heaps, some of their robes still on fire. One of them had wild, bushy hair like Gage, and he had to turn away to avoid breaking down and stalling their escape.

"Well," Fainly said, "if they weren't already convinced we were aligned with this Combustress, I think this will put the final nail in that coffin."

"Speaking of," Kartha said, motioning to a heap on the ground. Bennik approached the smoldering remains to see the unmistakable red robes that denoted Stacy Augustine as the High Mage of the Vestige. Her skin was blackened to a crisp, but something about the shape of her face reminded him of the looks she had given him during those torturous interrogations. He didn't feel the same sorrow for the woman as he did for her students.

Bennik looked up to see flames licking out of the window that Stacy had likely fallen from. It was clear to him that the tower was breached, and whoever had done so was also the one who assassinated the High Mage. Something told him this wasn't just some random cult attack—this felt tied to their own presence here.

"It looks like we're free to go find that scion now," Fainly said, making to descend the hill.

"The keyshards," Bennik said, turning to go back into the tower. But Kartha grabbed his shoulder with a powerful hand.

"Don't go back in there, Bennik. You're no good to your children if you're buried under this tower—that fire is going to burn everything down to the stone walls."

He forcefully shrugged out of her grip. "Can't either of you do something?! Summon some rain! Call in a gust of wind to blow out that fire up there."

"Have I not performed enough tricks for you already?!" Fainly spat, glaring at him with watery eyes. "Besides, you know as well as I do that whoever lit this bitch on fire and shoved her on top of that poor dwarf there already stole your damn shards. There won't be anything but cinders up there now!"

Bennik wanted to argue, but he knew the man was likely right. He certainly couldn't *feel* the keyshards any longer.

There was a crash inside the tower as one of the floors caved in, as if to emphasize Kartha's warnings.

The three of them shied away from the entrance as a spray of cinders and dust were thrown through the open doors.

Before Bennik could properly mourn the loss of the keyshards Reston had entrusted to him, there was a shrill horn blast from Stelmont. The three of them ran to the crest of the hill to see a shadowed group of assailants charging toward the gates.

"Are those the gnolls?" Kartha asked.

Bennik knew the answer, but he was already rushing toward the town's defense and couldn't spare the breath to answer her. He heard the gnome shout after him.

"What are you doing?! Now's our chance to sneak away and find the scion!"

Bennik called over his shoulder, "The scion will follow Wick's incarnate. Where better to find them than in the fire?"

Jak joined the defense of Stelmont, holding the line with the same guards that had so recently tried to keep him out of the village. The gnolls came in a ragged band, no organization and no leadership. There were archers posted along catwalks behind the village's low walls, thinning out the besieging monsters by nearly a third before the true fighting even began.

Unlike the battle outside the Vestige, Jak pushed to the front and spilled blood this time, putting down two snarling gnolls. His sword cut into their coarse brown fur, their bestial faces twisting in agony as they fell to the humans and dwarves that defended Stelmont. It was his first true battle, and he welcomed the fearlessness that accompanied the chaos.

Blood pumped in Jak's ears, making him deaf to any sense of cowardice that might have caused him to stall or misstep during combat. Something had overtaken him in the midst of the battle, making him feel like a true soldier—a proper knight. Whether it was seeing the defenseless looks Sadie and Kadie gave him before he left the inn or a feeling of vengeance over the deaths at the Vestige, he couldn't quite say; but he found bravery in ample supply.

It wasn't until the tail end of the fighting that Jak saw the prisoners from the tower join the skirmish: the gnome wizard, his green-skinned apprentice, and…

"Bennik?!" Jak shouted much louder than he intended, but the fighting was coming to a close and his blood had risen to a fever pitch. Anika and Gage Lawson's father slashed a small knife across the throat of a flailing gnoll, sending a spray of blood across the damp grass.

Seeing the man brought back a sudden, hazy memory in Jak's mind. It felt like a dream, but he had never suddenly remembered a dream like this—vivid and unbidden. Something about it felt like magic…

———◇———

"Now listen," Sir Paul Stone said, lowering the drink from Jak's lips. "I need you to focus on this part carefully, son."

Jak's stomach spasmed from restrained laughter, but he followed the Oather's orders, setting his drink down.

They were in the Vestige's dining hall, alone except for a mage in a hooded green robe. It was the night before the attacks.

"You listening, boy?"

"I hear ya, sir," Jak said drunkenly, his vision blurring. "Does the High Mage have any more of this stuff?"

Paul laughed, carefully lowering the cup back to the table as he leaned closer to Jak. His breath was heavy with garlic and some herbs that Jak couldn't quite place. "We'll get you plenty, kid. I just need to make sure we understand each other. The man you said you knew—what was his name again?"

"Lawson," Jak said, hiccuping. "Bennik Lawson. A tanner from my hometown."

"Right," Paul said, leaning closer, his voice becoming a whisper. "That actually wasn't Bennik Lawson. You actually have no idea who that was. He's likely one of those cultists, which is why we need to lock him up." He leaned even closer. "You hear me, son? You. Do. Not. Know. Him."

Jak hiccuped again, his vision blurring more. "I know. I told you, sir. I don't know who that was." He hiccuped as he held up his drained cup again. "Can I get some more?"

Paul patted him on the shoulder. "Usually takes another cup or two, but sure, let me see what I can scrounge up for you, kid."

"Jak?!" Bennik Lawson threw his knife into the neck of the last gnoll, the monster spasming as it fell to the ground, dropping its crude blade. "Is that you?!"

Sheathing his sword, Jak approached the man in disbelief. Was this the cultist that Sir Stone had warned him about? The one that had delivered keyshards of Wick to the Vestige just as the Combustress had begun her assault on the tower?

The questions he asked himself triggered a memory—or was it the echo of a dream? Had he known Bennik was one of the prisoners? *No,* he thought, watching Bennik step toward him with wide eyes, mouth agape. *I would have known...I would have stopped them from hurting him.*

"Quiet, boy," High Mage Stacy Augustine said in that dream-like reflection. "You don't know any of them. Just watch these lights, see them spin?"

"You and your mind games," Sir Stone scoffed, dragging the bodies out of her study. "Just leave the boy some of his wits, I could use a squire."

The memory faded, leaving only emptiness and grief.

As dozens of questions raced through Jak's mind, the very real memory of Anika's father bringing a stack of furs to the Warner manor during the coldest winter of their lifetime reduced him to tears. He moved toward the approaching man that had been imprisoned and tortured in the same place he had defended, and by the time Jak reached Bennik's arms, he was a sobbing ruin.

Some time later, the defenders of Stelmont were in The Thistle & Bough celebrating the victory over the gnolls. Bennik and Jak sat in a corner to discuss the strange events that had led them here.

"I'm truly sorry for your brother," Bennik said, reaching out a hand to pat the boy's wrist. "You both were such dutiful sons—you should get back to Blakehurst and be with your father. His grief will consume him. He needs to know you are safe."

Fainly set a mug of ale on the table, startling Bennik, who hadn't seen the gnome approach the high table. Jak regarded him nervously as well, but Fainly just climbed the stool and said, "At least there's some perks being this close to New Hold. Best ale I've ever tasted."

"I can't leave," Jak said to Bennik, drawing his hand away from the man's touch. "There's something I swore to do, and I can't break my oath."

Fainly scoffed at that. "Aren't you one of Strallow's boys? I know what kind of oath the Lady Commander would have you swear, and you'd best break it as swiftly as possible."

Jak held Bennik's gaze, ignoring the Archmage's mocking words. "My brother died serving the Arcania. I won't soil his sacrifice by failing my charge."

Bennik didn't have a good response to that, knowing how important oaths were to Oathers. He had been a soldier himself, sworn to the King of Eastlund before Menevere became infested with rival claimants to the throne, so he knew exactly how stubborn an oathkeeper could be.

"You do know who I am, don't you?"

Jak looked at Fainly now, as if just noticing him for the first time. Bennik recalled Jak Warner being a slightly slow boy, and it seemed his wits were still a bit lacking. After a slight delay, the boy's eyes widened and he stood up, bowing his head. He looked up at Bennik, also reacting as if seeing him for the first time.

"Apologies, Archmage," he stammered, looking back to Fainly. "I did not recognize you. I swear! I don't see many gnomes... I mean, not that— I just..."

"Sit down," Fainly said, looking around at the attention Jak was drawing from the other revelers. The surviving dwarves certainly didn't notice, however, caught up in challenging each other to who could better honor their fallen through drink. "Besides, I'm not the Archmage anymore, as I'm sure you've heard." He took a drink of his ale, wiping his chin with his sleeve before adding, "So now you need to figure out: are you serving the true Archmage, or the upstart who the queen put in my place?"

Bennik watched Jak's face twist at that, and he realized the subtle trap that Fainly had just laid.

"He's right," Bennik added. "There's never been a different Archmage since the Arcania's founding, and since Fainly was never officially removed by the High Sanctum, he still commands the Oathers."

Fainly just kept drinking while Jak's gaze shifted between Bennik and the Archmage.

Ivy joined them across from Fainly, setting two mugs of ale on the table as she looked at each of them in turn. Jak leaned slightly away from the strange woman as if he expected her to curse him.

"So," Fainly continued, slamming his empty mug onto the table. "What'd Kasia make you swear to do? Aside from warming her bed?"

Kartha coughed into her ale, choking. She glanced at Fainly and then at Bennik. "What'd I miss?"

Before Jak could answer, two tiny girls rushed the table, saying, "Jaky Jaky Jaky!" They grabbed his leg under the table, and in response his head snapped warily toward Bennik.

"Are those...?" Bennik slowly stood, waiting for the boy to confirm what he already knew.

"Their mom was stealing keyshards for the Guild," Jak whispered, his eyes darting between each of them as he reached down to corral the halfling girls.

"Then they should be with their uncle," Bennik began angrily. He was moving around the table toward Jak, fury in his eyes. "Are you holding them hostage for Strallow? Is that your oath that you cannot break, Jak?!"

"No!" Jak began, but caught himself before having an outburst. He was trying to get up from his seat, disentangling himself from the halflings. "I mean, I didn't want to!"

"This is madness," Fainly commented, remaining in his seat. His voice was loud enough to quiet many nearby conversations. "She had no authority to apprehend children, not even when the Oath of Sorcery has been broken. Where is their mother?"

Bennik stopped behind Kartha, waiting for Jak's reply. The two halfling girls were hugging either of the boy's legs protectively, fear in their eyes as they regarded the furious man towering over them.

"In Oakworth," Jak admitted. "I was taking the girls to Andelor, but that was before the attacks."

"Of course!" Fainly exclaimed. "Oakworth!"

Bennik looked at him, still seething. "What about it?!"

The gnome's eyes held a hint of childlike wonder, as if he had just glimpsed a secret his parents had hidden from him. "That's where we'll find the next scion!"

CHAPTER TEN

Legacy of Fire

Tremly Boggs awoke in the woods with only hazy memories of elves, blood, and maniacal laughter lingering in his confused thoughts. He lifted his head from the comfortable grass to see black leathers covering him from neck to toe, curved blades strapped to either hip.

There was a distinct feeling of lost time, as if his body had left him behind and his mind was just catching up. Everything was as hazy as a dream, yet he felt neither rested nor weary. He knew he hadn't been slumbering; his limbs felt more limber than he could even recall. Sitting up, he suddenly felt the odd sensation that he somehow changed bodies with someone—as if some witch cursed him. Instinctively, his hands explored his person to ensure that wasn't the case.

His eyepatch was enough to convince him he was still Tremly Boggs, but something gleaming on his chest drew his remaining eye's gaze.

A small medallion hung from his neck; a device with two crossed halberds wreathed in heather. The arms of Nazurik.

The black leathers. The knives.

He was dressed like a rogue, which brought back a memory that felt like his own, but with his fragmented mind, he couldn't be too sure.

◆

"The elves have been here," Malcomry Sulm's daughter explained, motioning to the various arrows scattered across the courtyard. Coperan knights strode in the opposite direction on either side of them, inclining their heads to the princess and giving Tremly wary looks while they tended to the wreckage. There were still plenty of burned orc bodies yet to be cleared away, and many of those corpses had arrows jutting from their heads and necks—arrows that were mostly unharmed by the flames.

Tremly knew enough about the Lohkrest elves to know that their arrows were masterfully crafted (and most likely enchanted); it would take more than fire to destroy them—even if that fire came from a Shadowlord. He wasn't sure if he found that knowledge troublesome or reassuring. He had no reason to fear the wood elves, but if any of them remained in or around Rathen, it would likely mean further conflict with the new rulers.

Ithakan laughed in his mind, but Tremly closed his eyes and forced the terrible presence down. The initial orc massacre had seemed to satiate the demon's thirst for devastation, but in the days that followed, Tremly had trouble controlling the urges. He was being pushed toward violence, which was an altogether unnatural inclination for someone like him. Especially when the only real nearby target for such violence was Kathina Sulm, who never let him out of her sight.

"Is there a problem, halfling?"

Tremly looked up at the dark-skinned warrior, the crossed golden halberds on the breastplate of her crimson armor gleaming in the morning sunlight. She was hard and ugly, but had a presence that made him want to fall to his knees and beg for her mercy. The only thing that allowed him to retain his composure was the Shadowlord's suffocating ego, refusing to yield to the princess regardless of how badly Tremly wanted to give in.

He managed a curt nod, still feeling ridiculous in the noble attire the Coperans dressed him in. "There's nothing wrong, Princess Kathina. You're right, it had to have been the elves."

The woman snorted. "Don't call me that."

Tremly worked his mouth, struggling for a response, but she talked right over him.

"A princess sounds like some little useless damsel sitting around waiting for her cockless prince wonder to rescue her from dull, pampered drudgery." She sneered at him. "Do you take me for some useless damsel, runt? Some little wet harlot who needs your rescuing? Who will fawn over your tiny pecker?"

Tremly kept his eyes downcast, cringing in preparation for a devastating blow to his head.

But it never came.

Instead, Kathina snorted a laugh as she turned to continue their walk through the ruined streets of Rathen. Coperan craftsmen sorted through the wreckage on either side of their passage. Tremly kept his head lowered and followed, feeling abashed despite the infernal grumbling in his mind—Ithakan could not abide this submissive role Tremly had struggled to maintain since his initial meeting of Malcomry Sulm's royal company.

"You're a halfling," Kathina announced, as if she had just noticed. "Which *means you can cook, yes?"*

"I can," Tremly said honestly. *He was far from a good cook, when ranked amongst even the worst artisans of the Acreage, but he certainly knew his way around a kitchen. However, Ithakan's seething disdain refused to let him admit his shortcomings to Kathina.*

"Then you will be my personal cook," she said, looking over her shoulder. *"In Copera, secrets are kept well between rulers and their cooks."* She motioned toward the broken battlements of Rathen. *"And now that this is a Coperan city, certain traditions should be maintained, yes?"*

Tremly nodded, keeping his eyes downcast. Ithakan raged at the halfling's meekness, but the demonic presence failed to take control of the body, still weakened from the exertion of massacring the orcs.

And Suzy. Sweet Chera.

He could still hear the women screaming for him to save them while the infernal menace within Tremly merely howled with fiery glee. He closed his eyes as Kathina turned from him, the sunlight glinting off her armor reminding him too much of the inferno that consumed his friends.

They continued their walk through Rathen as the king's men shook the ashes off the last free city of Vale.

———◇———

As he struggled to his feet presently, Tremly surveyed the surrounding trees. Something about the clearing gave him the sense that he was supposed to be here—as if the terrain itself had purpose, and it was chosen specifically for a pressing task.

He just couldn't remember what it was.

Ithakan spoke to him in fiery curses, but his mind was a fuzzy cacophony, allowing him to tune the Shadowlord out. While the last handful of days felt lost to him, he still remembered the day he killed his tormenter Grush or Crush—the orc woman who tried to make him some sort of love slave. He almost felt bad for burning her alive—it was as if she didn't know better, like she had been just a child that didn't know it was cruel to mutilate a bug.

Tremly had heard orcs despised other peoples, which meant the prospect of coupling with a halfling should have been repulsive. But Grush (or Crush) had seemed genuinely infatuated with Tremly, in her own sick way. Thinking of it in that way turned his stomach, and he almost retched.

"She raped you," Ithakan said wickedly, this time his voice crystal clear in Tremly's head. "And I made her pay! So give yourself to me in restitution, mortal! Make me whole and submit!"

Tremly grabbed his temples until the horrid voice quieted. When it did, he looked around again with his one good eye. Wherever he was, it felt like he had—at one point—intended to be here. He couldn't say why he felt that way, but some deep-seated instinct told him he had found his path.

Leaves rustled behind him, and he instinctually drew his knives, spinning to prepare for an attack. After a long breath, and when it was clear that no danger would reveal itself, he hazarded a glance at his blades for the first time.

They were coated in fresh blood.

Naya had taken to wandering through Lohkrest Woods while the druids went about their schemes in Gwynna's manor. Even though she felt disconnected from the Shrouded during her prolonged stay in House Grale's lands, she could not deny the security Lord Janthy's domain offered. The presence of the Order of Oakus gave her a voluminous shadow to hide within. Still, she required the solitude that these excursions provided her, otherwise the druids and their incessant bickering would drive her to violence.

That would not do; she needed allies more than ever, now that her precious Mawsurath had fallen.

The memory of her child's demise reminded Naya of the Shadow's ultimate betrayal. She had truly thought she had found allies in Desmond and Gage: the Scion of Stane and the Child of Shadow. The loss of Mawsurath ached all the more with the knowledge that Naya had foolishly allowed herself to trust again.

But none of that mattered now.

She needed to find the next incarnate if she hoped to finally sway the Child of Shadow to the Shrouded's cause. Without him, that little Karranese bitch would bring them all to ruin.

Those thoughts drove her onward as she pressed deeper into the forest, farther than she had ever dared to go before. Only last week she had ventured into a misty glade, drawn to the heavy magic she felt lingering on the air. The wood elves were known to leave enchantments on their boundaries, and Naya was eager to feel their innate power—perhaps she could draw from it.

Ever since falling into the Nethering, she hadn't fully recovered. It was as if the Shadow was reluctant to open itself to her after she had failed it so badly.

However, that enticing glade became a deathtrap as enormous spiders descended on her from the thick leaves above. She had fumbled for the magic knife Renda gifted her, dropping it in her haste—she still wasn't used to only having one hand. And then her flight was thwarted by the webs that hid in the dark crevices. Naya would have died in that sticky prison if it hadn't been for the serendipitous arrival of the gnolls.

Bless those stupid, aimless mongrels! she thought, remembering how grateful she had been.

Rumors of fires raging along the borders of the forest had proven well founded, and Naya did her best to keep still as the horde of gnolls tore into the two giant spiders; it was as if those overgrown hyenas were in a rabid frenzy, using their crude clubs and stone axes to smash the great arachnids into heaps of steamy, sickening goop.

As quickly as the gnolls had come, they tore back into the woods in a flurry of braying snarls, ignoring the spiders' black-robed dinner that still played dead in the webbing.

The memory of that encounter almost made Naya turn back around to the druids' hideout, but something still drove her onward. It was as if her desire for a change in the monotony of the past few days was manifesting itself into the form of something that lay just beyond the next row of trees.

Or the next row. Or the one after that. When nothing materialized after the next break in the trees, Naya finally decided she had better turn back before the sun fell any farther.

And that was when she heard the noise.

It began as a gasp, followed by frantic, troubled breathing. Then she heard whispered voices, like two people arguing while trying not to be heard. Despite those efforts, she did hear them, if only barely.

As she followed in the direction of those sounds, Naya came to a trail of small footprints, like a human child or gnome had run through the soft earth near the path.

"What did I do?" the voice asked, jolting Naya. It sounded as if it had come from just over her shoulder. But she crouched and looked in every direction, not seeing anyone with her.

The whispering continued ahead, so she slowly crept toward a gap in the copse. Pushing aside the vegetation revealed a bizarre sight.

A halfling rogue sat in a small clearing. He was a portly, older man, looking awkward in the black leathers that a Guild agent might wear. He had an eyepatch and a ratty beard, with his long hair tucked back into a knot. It looked as if he were in a daze, unsure where he was.

Naya held her breath as she watched him, feeling far too close for the man to not have heard her approach. Though he did look awfully distracted. He sat motionless, only his head tilting to either side as if considering a very difficult decision or trying to remember something.

"I couldn't have killed them all," the man whispered. "The Eldercrowns…"

"You didn't," another voice said, much deeper and more sinister than the halfling's—yet it seemed to come from the same source. "I did. It's me Kathina wants, not you. What could a fat little runt like you do without my help? Just submit and be done with it, coward."

Naya nearly collapsed, catching herself on a nearby branch. She sucked in her breath and became still again, hoping the halfling hadn't heard her.

But he had—he was up on his feet, knives drawn and looking for a foe. She silently called upon the Shadow to conceal her, much like the Lawson boy had back in the baron's keep. While she had always been able to conjure a void to remain unseen, just being in Gage's presence had given her even more mastery in the art of concealment.

The one-eyed halfling looked straight in her direction, but the darkness enveloping Naya wouldn't allow him to spot anything other than the surrounding trees. She watched as his gaze went back and forth, finally settling on his outreached blade. Whatever he saw there must have chilled him to the bone…

"It can't be," Tremly said again. As if speaking those doubts aloud was an affront to his possessor, Ithakan reached out to take control of his mind once more. Tremly tried to resist again, but it was no use, the Shadowlord grew more powerful the longer he stayed dormant.

The repressed memory of assassinating the Eldercrowns came back to him all at once, and Tremly dropped the murder weapons so he could claw at his brow, hoping to somehow stop the massacre from replaying in his mind. He tried to scream, but he couldn't hear anything over the pounding of blood and the laughter of Ithakan. With his eye closed, the tranquil surroundings fell away to the oppressive shadows of his recent past. In that darkness, he thrust his blades down, again and again, into the flesh of unsuspecting elves.

The rulers of Lefayra.

How he had come to be among them, he had not the slightest clue. But he killed them all indiscriminately from the silent shadows, driven by a power he didn't understand.

The scene played through his mind as forcefully as a sharpened blade through the gut, and it didn't seem to matter how much he tore at his hair or his ears or his beard, he couldn't free himself from its grasp. He was forced to watch the executions over and over as he fell onto his back, kicking his legs wildly to no longer hear the dying sounds of the Eldercrowns.

Eventually, his efforts to stop the maddening guilt paid off, as silence returned to the glade—enough for him to hear the approach.

Rolling for his blades, Tremly's unnatural reflexes allowed him to prepare for an attack. But as his vision cleared, he saw a one-handed priestess standing before him in a position of surrender. She spoke so quietly that he shouldn't have been able to hear her, but he did—as if she were whispering in his ear.

"You're Shadow-taken, aren't you?"

The woman's accent was unfamiliar to Tremly, but her voice was kind, soothing. It banished the terrible memories of Lefayra. "I don't know what that means," he replied, "but if you're here to rob me, I have nothing but these knives—which I'm afraid you cannot have. They belong to the new rulers of Rathen." Tremly didn't know where the words came from; it was as if he was just reciting them by instruction.

The woman smiled, as if he was joking. "I need nothing from you, halfling. And certainly nothing from Rathen. But perhaps I can give you something?"

He raised an eyebrow, still expecting an attack. "And what's that?"

"Parity," she whispered.

The word didn't mean anything to him, but it somehow further calmed the raging torrent inside him. Ithakan responded to her voice, as if she spoke a secret language that only he understood. For some reason that angered Tremly, but he allowed himself to relax, lowering the knives. "What does that mean? Parity?"

She lowered her arms as well, cradling her stump of a wrist. "It means I can sense the Shadow has chosen you—it has drawn me here, so that I might guide you on your new path."

Tremly tasted something acrid in his mouth, so he spit it out before asking, "Guide me? What new path?" The woman's face changed into that of an Eldercrown—a beautiful elven woman who looked up at him with terrified, innocent eyes just before they were splashed with blood. He turned away from her.

The woman took a step toward him. "Is there someplace you seek?"

He laughed at that, a weak airy chuckle. "The past, perhaps. Before the siege. Anywhere but back to Rathen, I suppose."

"What's in Rathen?" She took another step and he did nothing to stop her. "Something waiting for you?"

Tremly shook his head. "Nothing for me. The Coperans have taken what remains, and that wicked princess somehow— I think she made me kill the Eldercrowns." Part of him couldn't believe he freely admitted that to this stranger, but deep down he hoped confiding in someone—anyone—would free him of the ghosts. Even now they screamed in agony as he killed them over and over and over in his mind.

The robed woman didn't respond immediately. She just watched Tremly with those strangely caring eyes that somehow also regarded him with sinister intent. Or maybe that was just Ithakan trying to deceive him? Regardless, he felt compelled to explain further.

"I don't remember what happened—how I got here. I only have broken memories of elves, blood, and..."

"Gnolls?"

The word flooded Tremly's nostrils with the smells of burning fur, smoldering flesh. He hadn't remembered encountering any gnolls, but ever since he was a boy he always pictured them as walking dog-people—wicked, hunched creatures that knew how to make fire and bring misery to the civilized world. And hearing the word spoken aloud cast the creatures into his terrible visions. Whether she put them there or simply revealed their hidden presence, Tremly couldn't say. But there certainly was much more to this woman than met his eye.

"Were you there?" he asked. This time, he took a step toward her.

She shook her head slowly, keeping eye contact with him. "I've seen gnolls in these woods—it was a curious thing, as I understand they typically keep to the woods and swamps in Guyen. There have been recent reports of them moving east, and I suspect…" She took yet another step toward Tremly; he only slightly recoiled this time, taken aback by her intensifying gaze. "I believe you drew them here."

He kept his eye narrowed on her. "How? What am I to them?"

There was reverence in her eyes when she said, "Because I believe you are Wick's incarnate."

Those words shattered Tremly's internal defenses, and Ithakan once more infected his mind with another repressed memory…

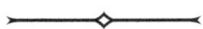

"I've been here before," Ithakan assured him. Tremly wasn't comforted though, and remained hidden behind the statue as an elven sentry passed by. The demon's thoughts were relentless and foreign, but sometimes sentences became clear to Tremly, and something about the atmosphere in Lefayra allowed the halfling to better understand the demonic presence inside him.

"Go now," the Shadowlord instructed once the guard was out of sight.

Tremly felt powerless to resist the command and slipped around the corner to let his silent feet carry him down the hall. There was almost no conscious thought to his movements; he was pulled toward Ithakan's desires like some sort of gleeman's puppet on invisible strings. Tremly just wished he could remember what his new master's desires were, beyond this mental anguish.

As he slipped into more shadows to sate Ithakan's thirst for blood, he fell into a dream within a dream, another memory…

His last conscious thoughts before Lefayra were of Rathen, serving as Kathina's cook for about a month before she began testing him.

"I can sense something in you," she had told him one evening, after he brought her a heavy tray of roasted lamb and onions braised in dark Coperan wine. Tremly was surprised to discover that he wasn't as bad a cook as he remembered; the Acreage would have been proud—of the cooking, that is, not the demonic possession. "The Shadow speaks to me."

Ithakan chuckled in Tremly's mind, but back then he hadn't been sure if those noises weren't just him going crazy—what else could they have been? He just stared at the princess as she tore into her dinner, keeping her cold eyes on Tremly as she spoke with mouthfuls of food. Like most nights, she forced him to watch her eat so she could lecture him more about things he did not fully understand.

"Back in Nazurik, the Shrouded hold sway." She leaned forward, eyes peering

toward the dark ends of the empty dining hall before falling back on Tremly. She lowered her voice as she added, "My fool of a father never treated with them, which is why those fucking rebels took root in the city. He could never understand the usefulness of fear." She smacked her fat lips as she sucked juices off her sausage-like fingers. "The Shadow priests taught me how to listen to the dark—to hear the whispers of the Shadowlords and sometimes even the Dark One himself. Only those without fear can understand their words—truly appreciate their power."

Tremly only vaguely knew about the Shrouded or the Shadowlords, never having been one to go out of his way to worship either of the great powers. However, he could feel the reverence in the woman's words, and it unsettled him even more than the burning laughter in his mind.

"We shall test you," Kathina added, tearing herself more meat from the shank on her tray. "If the Shadow has chosen you, perhaps we can strike the elves down before they grow bold enough to try and take this city from us."

"They didn't try to take the city," Tremly replied. The withering look he got from Kathina made him regret opening his mouth, but he felt compelled to tell her: "The elves tried to rescue us—they only attacked because of the incarnate."

"Incarnate?"

For a moment, Tremly thought the princess was mocking him, but the woman's face wore a look of genuine curiosity.

He swallowed before asking, "Have you not heard of the incarnates?"

Kathina laughed, reclining in her great chair as she took a drink of ale—it sloshed over the rim and spilled down her pudgy cheeks. "When would I have heard of such things? While I fought against the rebels in Nazurik? Or as I marched down the High Road to liberate these worthless ruins?"

She slammed her drink down and added, "All I know about incarnates is that the Light priests talk about them as if they're more feared than Shadowlords." A wicked smile pushed her pockmarked cheeks aside, revealing crooked teeth riddled with food. "That is the fear I was talking about—fear we can use."

"How did she test you?" Naya asked, her good hand working a small mortar and pestle in her lap. The halfling sat close enough to watch her prepare the potion, but just out of her reach; he also still kept his blades bared. Naya knew they would be useless in a fight, even against a one-handed priestess, but if it made the man feel less pathetic to have a sharp weapon between them, so be it.

"I don't remember exactly," he replied. He kept his eyes fixed on the mortar as it crushed the herbs, grains, and animal semen that would clear his mind (as long as he allowed the concoction to take effect before retching it up). "I only remember pieces...almost like fragments of a forgotten dream from childhood. And even those pieces are hazy."

"This should help," Naya said, sniffing harshly to loosen up enough phlegm. She spat it into the mortar, hoping it would join the dried mixture enough—she had no desire to extract fresh ingredients out here with only one hand. She may be desperate, but there were limits to what she would do—even in pursuit of another incarnate...

"Why are you helping me?"

Naya tried not to smile, but it was just too much effort. She could not hide her excitement, and she saw no reason to lie to the man more than she already had—that approach failed miserably with Fallon Shaw. She needed to earn this man's trust before the druids got to him first. While Renda would certainly ally with the Shrouded to take down the Luminaura, Naya did not feel compelled to remain a pawn in that game—she served the Dark One and would continue furthering the Shrouded's cause, even if she had to trick the druids into it.

But she couldn't risk deceiving the incarnate, so she opted for the truth this time.

"I believe I was meant to help you, Tremly Boggs."

The halfling jerked his head up at that, tightening the grip on his knife. "Did I tell you my name?"

Her smile softened. "Yes, you did. And you were set on my path just as I was set on yours. It seems your captivity with the orcs continued with the Coperans, and this Kathina Sulm—she is not known to me, but if she is truly a Shrouded, perhaps it was her that led me to you." She stopped working the mixture and set it aside. "She may not know it yet, but Princess Kathina has saved your life, Tremly Boggs."

He clenched his eyes at that, as if hearing the princess's name was enough to pain him. Naya could only assume the "testing" was some repressed trauma, which would not be surprising. When it came to the Shadow, power was drawn from pain, either physical or emotional. She would have to choose her words more carefully to earn the man's loyalty.

"I'll need to start a fire to finish this elixir," she said, motioning toward the surrounding trees. "Would you mind gathering some wood? We'll need to make camp anyway, with the sun going down as it is."

With only a slight hesitation, Tremly got up and sheathed his knives, adjusting the belt over his round belly. As Naya watched him disappear into the woods, she grinned much more wickedly. The power that hung around the halfling remained in his wake, and she was able to easily conjure a second hand of solidified fire.

Her eyes grew wide as she watched her new blackened fingers flex, coils of orange and yellow flames licking from the smoking joints at each knuckle. The only way she would be able to work such pyromancy was if Wick's incarnate had come forth.

And that infernal being whistled a jaunty tune as he dutifully gathered firewood for her.

CHAPTER ELEVEN

The Brightening

The Brightway Cathedral's bells rang out for the first time in Sathford that morning. Loud clangs, echoing across the noisy streets, announcing a new dawn.

For better or worse.

The cathedral blocked out the rising sun even though the building wasn't close to finished. The outer structure had been reinforced with thick oaken pillars where two great bells had been raised. Those bronze monstrosities now chimed loudly as Avrim wiped sweat from his brow.

"Your friend stopped bringing in lumber," the gnome foreman beside him remarked, pulling his little gloves off. "I've never known a dwarf to shirk their duties... That is, unless there's fightin' need doing."

Avrim looked down at the man, raising a skeptical eyebrow. "Deina is grieving the loss of her partner, Lyle. She is allowed the occasional recess. Besides, she's largely responsible for those tree trunks holding the walls up. Perhaps a few of the Tolle Collectors' convicts would be able to pick up the slack?"

Lyle rubbed his sparse scalp, nodding. "Certainly, Beacon. I meant nothing by it. Just hoping she is well is all. We don't see her in the Riverstone much anymore."

Heavy breathing drew Avrim's attention away from the foreman as their only remaining mage limped up the stairs. Harmony was a tall, wiry elf whose limbs always looked to Avrim like they might snap in half. Now, she leaned heavily on the makeshift railing that ran along either side of the stairs, clearly exhausted.

Avrim and Lyle both moved to help her. Together, they led the girl up to the landing that overlooked their side of the cathedral.

"What are you still doing here, Harmony?" Lyle sounded more annoyed than concerned. "I promised that young spire-master of yours that none of his wizards would be harmed on my watch. You were supposed to be resting!"

"I'm not harmed," the elf replied, easing herself down on the top stair as she pushed her long auburn hair back from her sweaty brow. Even in distress she managed to speak like some mythical princess. "I'm just a bit worn out is all."

"This is more than worn out," Avrim said, putting a hand to her damp brow. The Light allowed him to feel the ailments of others, and he could quickly tell it was more than just weariness afflicting her.

He turned to look back toward the construction for any sign of trouble, but all he saw was workers going about their tasks: dwarf masons carrying heavy stones from their carts, various sizes of convicts working in their shackles, and a few elven artisans overseeing the finer details of the cathedral's outer architecture. "What were you doing?" Avrim wondered aloud.

"The same as usual," Harmony replied, sucking in a pained breath while taking a skin of water from Lyle. "Simply moving a pallet of bricks up to Grevan—felt my shard weakening, so I took a break from aeromancy." She produced a dull red keyshard of Wick from her robes, showing it to Lyle and Avrim. "Figured I'd help with the forges instead... Pyromancy's always been a little easier for me." She closed her thin fingers around the stone and returned it to her pocket.

Lyle held out two upraised palms in expectation of further explanation. "And?"

But Harmony was looking up at Avrim, fear in her eyes. "I felt something trying to claw into my mind—some kind of power I'd never felt before. I've heard some mages experience...intrusions, like sudden surges in power that shouldn't be there. I should have let go...not tried to push it..."

Something cold filled Avrim's lungs. Whatever she was describing reminded him of how he had felt in Oakworth, with the baron's daughter, and then in Blakehurst, when he was apprehended by the Oather in the reeve's manor.

Had Harmony felt the Light's wrath like he had? Had it chosen her as well?

An unexpected anger rose within him, as if she had intruded on a private affair—one she had no business being a part of. Something deep down made him clench his fists, hoping that whatever unsettled her wasn't the same thing he had experienced. That communion was his, and his alone.

It felt almost like...jealousy.

"What was it?" Lyle asked.

Avrim jerked his head toward the gnome, afraid the man had seen through him. But the foreman was more concerned with the mage.

Before Harmony could respond, they heard the sound of hooves pounding across the bridge. Avrim moved toward the top of the stairs so he could see—it was Sir Darrance Moore, the new High Warpriest of the Luminaura. As curious as he was about Harmony's experience, he could sense the urgency that drove Darrance, and he quickly descended the stairs to meet the man near the cathedral's gates.

Crossing the courtyard, Avrim felt dread increasing with every step, already mourning the loss of a simple morning of work.

"We have a problem," Darrance said as he dismounted. He was fully armored, except for his helmet; his blond hair was sweaty and matted, as if he had been sparring in the yard again. It seemed all he did these past weeks was either train the Luminaura's new recruits or bicker with the Lady Mayor's elven stewardess, Cethany. If someone hadn't known any better, they might assume that the High Warpriest was avoiding his new duties…

"What is it today?" Avrim couldn't help but feel spiteful of the Church's constant problems, cropping up like relentless weeds since his appointment. It all further disillusioned him in regards to his new post as beacon, but he tried not to dwell on that now.

"A dove arrived," Darrance said, pushing his hair from his forehead as he approached. He climbed the steps and joined Avrim on the small catwalk to share the rest privately. "The Archbeacon has ordered the reclamation of Rathen. Immediately."

Even just the name of the city still managed to send a chill through Avrim. His time in the duke's manor continued to give him nightmares, and the recent accusations from the Oather in Blakehurst had torn those wounds back open. "I thought we were focused on retaking the priory first? What does the Church want with a ruined city?"

Darrance narrowed his eyes. "A beacon of the Luminaura should know: it's not for us to question the Archbeacon's decree. The incarnate has defied the Light by openly attacking one of its sanctuaries—we cannot let it rot under the reign of orcs and harpies. We have been given our orders, Father Kaust."

Avrim bit back his response. He doubted anyone in Andelor truly cared who ruled over the remains of a city that didn't even belong to the queendom of Vale, but he knew the pride that was associated with the Luminaura losing one of its original seats of power. Luriah Vaughn would not let that insult go unpunished.

Many of the free cities that originally broke away from Eastlund kept faith with the old gods, using their temples to Wick, Oakus, and Corsa as symbols of their traditions. Rathen was the first to embrace the Light, and the Luminary said it was that decision alone that protected the city, leading it to become the most prosperous and only Northlund settlement to survive the Nether War.

Regardless of what he thought, Avrim knew Darrance was right; it would do no good to question the will of the Church, especially now that it had gained such footing in Sathford. He felt trapped enough in the city, but under Darrance's gaze, he felt judged and sentenced—forced to keep his wavering faith in line despite the compounding misgivings.

"We're to lead the paladins north on the morrow," Darrance said, sensing Avrim's wandering thoughts. "I trust you're recovered from the invasion?"

Avrim wasn't certain he had done anything of the sort, at least not mentally. He still dreamed of the Arkathian hordes bursting up from the city streets, devouring citizens before turning to ash under his divine wrath. Those dreams were almost worse than his nightmares of Rathen, because he awoke from them with lust rather than fear.

He turned away from the High Warpriest to regard the cathedral again. "We're both to lead the campaign?"

Darrance clicked his tongue, clearly expecting the question. "I trust you want to be on the front lines, after how you handled the incarnate of Oakus here."

Avrim resented the notion that he somehow enjoyed being used as an instrument of the Light's fury—*The malice of Light needs a Shadow to banish, else it will only burn itself*, a voice from his dream echoed in his mind, summoned by Darrance's assumption. Instead of taking the bait, Avrim turned away again to observe Harmony, who still hung her head in her hands while Lyle offered her another drink of water. He leaned over the catwalk's railing, watching a dwarf mason chipping away at a chunk of marble.

"Something's happened to one of our mages—I thought maybe we should report it to the spire."

Darrance spat over the railing. "I can't imagine it is more pressing than an entire city of monsters growing their strength for a possible attack."

Now it's an attack? Avrim thought, wondering what the true purpose of this whole reclamation was—but he knew it was a useless endeavor to inquire. Even if Darrance knew the Archbeacon's schemes, he doubted the man would confide in his pawn.

Before Avrim could press the matter, he noticed he had lost the High Warpriest's attention; the man was peering over Avrim's shoulder at something happening on the Sathler Bridge beyond the construction yard.

A crowd had gathered, offering half-hearted cheers and words of encouragement to a group of figures Avrim certainly recognized.

"There she is!" a dwarf shouted from the cathedral's grounds. "Where's our lumber now, Deina?!"

"Waiting on yer damn cart out there, Clint," Deina hollered back. She held Harvester up with one hand, motioning toward the trees outside the city walls. She earned several hoots from supporters who clearly recognized the enchanted weapon; it had earned as much reputation in town as Anika's Stormender. Besides the annoyance he felt over Deina publicly waving around a Key of Transience, Avrim couldn't help but smile seeing his friend in a better mood. He wanted nothing more than to join them.

Darrance said something as Avrim moved to greet his friends, but the beacon couldn't hear the High Warpriest's words over the growing clamor. He hadn't seen Anika in almost a week, and she looked like she had been on some sort of important errand with Ransil and the High Mage of Raventhal himself.

Avrim stopped mid-step toward the group.

The same chill he felt with Harmony returned. He peered over his shoulder toward the elf. She clearly felt it too, looking from him toward the gathering on the bridge. Whatever had bothered her—whatever caused the unease that also infected Avrim—had been brought into Sathford by his companions. Whether knowingly or unknowingly, they carried doom with them.

"Something wrong?"

Realizing he was drifting, Avrim blinked and saw Deina staring up at him. But his attention was immediately diverted to the source of his concern.

Ransil Osbury.

"Father Kaust," Anika said. "I can call you that now, right? Instead of Brother?"

Having trouble pulling his gaze from the halfling, Avrim nodded absently before finally turning toward the Child of Light. "Officially, yes. But in your company, I still prefer Avrim."

Anika smiled at that, but the happy expression quickly faded as their eyes met. *She knows I feel it,* he thought. *She's the Child of Light; she can feel the taint as well.*

The halfling's voice cut through his panicked thoughts. "If you'll excuse us, we need to get to the spire," Ransil said, casting Avrim a worrying gaze as he attempted to pass. But Darrance blocked him, motioning toward the crowd.

"What's the meaning of this, halfling? I won't have you riling the citizenry up while the Lady Mayor's stewardess has entrusted the city's peace to the Luminaura."

Avrim wanted to round on the man—not just to correct the way he spoke to a hero of the city, but also because he wanted the chance to speak to Ransil alone regarding whatever it was he had brought into Sathford. Being this close to the halfling, Avrim was more than certain the little man carried the object that had so affected Harmony.

Ransil mumbled something in response, but it was overpowered by the blast of horns coming from the city's main thoroughfare. The chatter died down, and all attention turned to a rider accompanied by two messengers with brass warhorns.

"High Warpriest Moore and High Mage Olivick," the messenger announced, "you've been called to an urgent council with the Lady Mayor!"

Audreese Groaves sat uncomfortably in the presence of Raventhal's newest Oather, who stood like a sentry near the council table. Her armor had been returned to her, and Audreese found that she cared little for being in its presence. While her Arcanian Mark would keep her safe from its wards, there was nothing about Sutheki blackiron she found comforting.

The same could be said for the woman wearing the antimagic armor.

Dame Kasia Strallow was a rigid woman, which was likely how some would have described Audreese herself. However, the Oather carried an air of wickedness about her that went beyond mere standoffishness. Her face may have been lovely, but the vacant expression it wore made it discomforting.

Neither of them spoke in the empty council chamber as they waited for the arrival of the returning Lady Mayor. Gwynna Grale had been mostly absent since her appointment following Karlton Tolle's death. The lack of an heir made the succession troublesome, but due to the chaos following the attack on Raventhal Spire, Janthy Grale was able to rally enough support from the high houses and, with a written decree from King Markus Durrask himself, Gwynna was installed before the smoke had settled over the aftermath.

"May I ask you something?"

Dame Strallow's voice startled Audreese; not only from its suddenness, but more due to its unexpected softness.

Turning in her seat to face the Oather, Audreese nodded.

"Are you able to truly devote yourself to someone who you have never met or who was not appropriately installed?"

A difficult question, considering Audreese couldn't tell if she was speaking about the Lady Mayor, her stewardess, the new High Mage, or the elusive Archmage that had recently closed the Old Ways.

After considering for a moment, Audreese said, "I suppose I find the prospect of devoting myself to any one person in that regard problematic." She couldn't help thinking of Konrath as she added, "I devoted myself to the spire rather than the Archmage himself, who sat in Andelor and rarely thought about Raventhal outside of his annual tour of the academies. I suppose you could say I devoted myself to the High Mage, but he earned that devotion—it wasn't just expected of me given my position."

The Oather listened intently, nodding along as if all these concepts were completely new to her. Audreese found it oddly endearing and, for the first time since she had known the woman, she didn't feel animosity toward her. Or her wretched armor.

The brief silence that followed was interrupted by echoing voices just barely muffled by the closed doors. Audreese couldn't put a face to either of the shouts, but she could only guess it was the stewardess, Cethany, and some other retainer. However, she was shocked when the doors were thrown open to reveal Gwynna Grale, red-faced and furious.

"Who gave you leave to lurk in here?!"

Shocked, Audreese turned to Kasia, who looked just as taken aback by the outburst. She stiffened her posture, if that were even possible.

"We were summoned," Audreese explained as calmly as she could.

"I didn't ask for a fucking Oather!" Gwynna turned to face the elegant elf that followed her into the chamber. While Gwynna was disheveled and exhausted, Cethany, the exiled Eldercrown, was a picture of grace. She still wore the headdress that marked her as one of the rulers of Lefayra, but her gown was more in the stylings of Vale, as opposed to the wood elf fashion. She flowed into the council chamber as distinct counterpoint to Gwynna's jerky presence.

"Dame Strallow serves Raventhal now," Cethany informed the Lady Mayor calmly. "With the new Archmage's appointment, I thought it would be time to reassess how the Oathers are assigned between the academies." The two elves shared a strange look that Audreese took note of, wondering if the two also shared a concern over Archmage Vera's recent installment.

Gwynna glared back at Kasia, but said no more on the matter. She strode toward her seat at the head of the table. "Where are the others?"

Others? Audreese wondered. But she didn't have to wonder long, as more footsteps echoed down the hall.

"That must be them," Cethany said, once again seeming much too calm in comparison to the Lady Mayor. "Please have a seat, Dame Strallow. You have a seat on this council, but not as its guard." Several figures were led into the chamber as Kasia took a seat across from Audreese.

Sir Darrance Moore carried his helmet under his arm, still looking sullen ever since his constant companion, Brace (who Audreese had quite a fondness for), had tragically fallen in the battle of Oakhold. Sathford's newest beacon entered, walking shoulder-to-shoulder with the High Warpriest. Behind the pair were the three familiar but unexpected faces of Ransil, Quinn, and Anika, with the dwarf Deina following behind.

"Is that everyone?" Gwynna snapped, waving a hand for the guards to close the doors. "Perhaps we can begin now."

The High Mage took Konrath's old seat, displaying a level of confidence Audreese had not yet seen in the boy. It made her wonder what had happened outside the city. She looked at Anika, who gave her a curt nod as she took a seat on Audreese's other side. The halfling stood against the wall with his arms crossed, a bundle of rolled leather tucked neatly under his arm, out of sight.

What have you found? Audreese wondered as she tasted the subtle sourness of magic in the air. There was a hint of ash, making her hopeful they had found the stolen keyshards.

"My lady," Darrance began, setting his helmet on the table. "Welcome back. I trust your journey was pleasant. However, I'm afraid we must part again. The beacon and I are to prepare the Light's forces to march north. Rathen has waited long enough, and the Archbeacon has decreed it must be retaken immediately."

"The Archbeacon can take Rathen herself," Gwynna remarked dismissively, her fervor leveling out now that she was seated in the mayor's chair. "You will march by my leave and my leave only, not Andelor's."

Those words landed on the High Warpriest exactly as Audreese imagined they would. The following silence was brief and uncomfortable.

"You dare—" Sir Moore began, but Father Kaust raised a hand to stay him.

"The Luminaura answers only to the Archbeacon, Lady Grale. Save the queen herself, none can defy her orders. Nor does the mayor of Sathford outrank the High Warpriest on matters of holy conquest."

Audreese watched the Lady Mayor's reaction to that lecture carefully. The woman seemed to have expected such a retort, and her elven eyes narrowed on Father Kaust as another discomforting silence followed his words. Finally, Cethany cleared her throat.

"I'm sure the Archbeacon can appreciate our current circumstances. The city of Sathford was in the Church's debt after the invasions of both incarnates."

"Exactly," Darrance interjected angrily, but before he could utter another word, the Eldercrown continued calmly as if he hadn't spoken at all.

"But given the cathedral that our esteemed new mayor has invested in the Luminaura, as both a token of gratitude and continued mutual interests—not to mention the supplement of Sathford militia that helped your paladins repel the invaders—it seems prudent for her Luminescence to fully garrison this new fortress of the Light until such time as its construction is complete."

Each member of the council (aside from Cethany herself and Gwynna) looked from one perplexed face to the next. It seemed none of them could believe what they were hearing. The new rulers of Sathford were using the very gift they had presented to the Church as a trap to defy the Archbeacon's decree.

Audreese couldn't hold her tongue any longer. She laid her own hand on the table to draw Gwynna's attention. "Wasn't it just last month that you used this council to request troops to your holdings? And now you want to keep them here behind the city walls while Copera is threatening Vale's borders and the Eldercrowns continue to ignore our summons?"

"The Eldercrowns are dead," Cethany said flatly, as if delivering news of a tomato cart losing its wheel.

Those words filled the chamber with gasps and murmurs. Audreese felt her chest caving in, her mind scrambling to grasp any memories of the wood elf rulers that she hadn't seen since she was a child—she couldn't even picture what the city of Lefayra had looked like anymore, nor could she recall the faces of her siblings.

Lexeth, she thought, wondering if the city had fallen and she had lost another of her kin.

"How's that possible?" a voice from behind her asked.

Ransil Osbury approached the council table, placing his bundle atop it. He glared at Cethany as if she were the one that had murdered them.

"Aren't you an Eldercrown?" Darrance added.

"It seems there's another incarnate," the Lady Mayor said to Ransil before turning to Darrance to add, "And she was an Eldercrown before she was exiled for defying their foolishness."

Something felt wrong to Audreese, beyond just the shock of hearing of the wood elf rulers all dying together. There was an eerie calmness to Gwynna now, when just moments ago she had been riled up and eager for an argument. And Cethany, being an exiled Eldercrown, delivering the news of her order's sudden demise...

"An incarnate?" a whispered voice asked, just loud enough to be heard over the other members of the council.

Audreese turned to Anika Lawson, the Child of Light. Her most important pupil was still in her seat, but her hands gripped the armrests as if to restrain herself from flying straight for the wood elf domain.

Gwynna turned to her, leaning forward with her elbows on the table. "It's said a great fire was started from within their chamber. No wards were triggered, as if the Shadow itself gave the assassin passage, along with the invading gnolls." She moved her gaze to each of the other council members in turn. "And with those savage beasts burning up the countryside, it seems most likely that our incarnate of Wick has already been chosen and decided to remove Lefayra from the ranks of its opposition."

"That's not possible," Anika said. All eyes turned to her.

"Why's that?" Cethany asked, the hint of emotion finding its way into her voice finally.

Anika suddenly looked unsure, turning to Ransil and then Deina before answering. "I don't know exactly, but…" Her eyes strayed toward Ransil's bundle, and Audreese got the sense that whatever it contained held the reason for Anika's doubt. "I felt something with the other incarnates. It was as if I knew when they came to their power." Her words sounded hollow, as if she were just trying to fill the silence.

"What is that?" a new voice asked.

Everyone looked at Kasia Strallow, whose eyes bore into Ransil's wrapped bundle on the table.

"A delivery for the spire," the High Mage replied, sounding nearly a decade older than he actually was. "It does not concern the council at this time—not until it is properly examined."

"We'll be the judge of that," the Lady Mayor decreed. "Let us see, halfling."

Ransil Osbury looked from the mayor to Anika. As gruff and competent as he normally appeared to Audreese, the small man now had the look of a rabbit cornered by foxes.

"This is hardly relevant," Quinn continued.

"If those are keyshards," Kasia interrupted, pushing herself away from the table to stand, "your Oather should be informed of them immediately, should she not?"

Ransil said something under his breath as the council members began talking all at once.

"Enough!" Gwynna shouted, slamming a fist down on the table, silencing them all. Despite the woman's diminutive size, Audreese observed, she certainly carried authority well. "Show us the damn thing already, or I'll have my guards lock you up with the rapists!"

Somber anticipation fell over the gathered as the defeated halfling reached over to uncover the leather-wrapped parcel.

Bright red fire was revealed.

Ransil's memory flickered at that moment. Like a spark between flint and steel igniting a campfire, the fateful night returned to him from nearly fifteen years ago—when he and Grip set Veronitha Blaithe on the path that would eventually consume her.

Since their first meeting in the Acreage, Grip had been a curse on Ransil Osbury, one that would doom a vengeful daughter to a life driven only by fire and misguided hatred.

But even as the memories flashed through Ransil's mind while he stared into the red gem fixed just below the dagger's blade, he couldn't regret his fateful encounter with Griphelia Shu'wath. If she hadn't hired him to steal his mother's keyshard from that Gustopher Hawn fool, he might never have learned the truth about his mother.

Without her manipulations, he never would have found Lena Osbury's hidden messages to her son, sent from beyond the grave. He never would have discovered the bravery that lurked beneath the restlessness and resentfulness he felt toward his father—so content was Hule Osbury to remain in the boring, safe, quiet, perfect haven of the Acreage, that old fool! Maybe he never would have spent all those years in the Guild, preparing him to protect the Child of Light when she needed him the most.

In a way, he owed Grip everything.

Despite her taking everything from him.

Yet even if young Ransil Osbury had been given the knowledge of Grip's rampant cruelty fifteen years ago, it would not have prevented him from following his heart when it came to her.

Which is why he failed his mother when it mattered most.

He failed to keep Veronitha from the truth that Korinthy Blaithe had died trying to bury.

He failed to keep Veronitha from becoming the Combustress.

The memories faded like smoke as Ransil's mind returned to the present, wrestling for reasons why he brought such a cursed relic into a vulnerable city.

"How could you bring that here?!"

Avrim Kaust was on his feet, glaring down at Ransil with an

accusatory arm pointed toward the revealed blade. The moments that followed the mayor's command to show the item to the council were loud, angry, and confusing. However, Audreese observed the object with calm fascination. She had expected a handful of chipped keyshards coming from New Hold, not an enchanted Wickan dagger.

"Avrim, listen," Anika began, but the priest turned toward the Oather instead.

"Can you ward this thing, Strallow? One of our mages at the cathedral felt the Shadow at play, and now I know why! We cannot let this go unmarked."

"Hang on! Wait!" Quinn's boyish cry cut through the madness. "Let him explain first!"

"What's there to explain?" Cethany asked in a soft voice, just above a whisper. "Unmarked enchantments can't be privately kept, as you certainly well know. It's the Oather's duty to confiscate it until it can be properly affixed. What else is there to say?"

"This is a Key of Transience."

They all turned toward Ransil Osbury, who wore a look of weary defeat. He stared at the dagger as if it were about to levitate in the air, spin around, and then bury itself into his heart.

"It's true," Anika said, getting to her feet. "We found it in a cave near the river, where we tracked the gnolls. It looked like a ritual site— a circle of flame around this knife in a sealed box."

"They were trying to break it," Audreese said, drawing all their eyes. But her own sight was locked on the weapon. It was a bright red dagger with a yellow-gold edge to its blade. A shimmering, polished ruby was set where the blade met the decorative crossguard. In many ways, it reminded Audreese of Anika's own Stormender, the Key that was forged from Eyen's blessed Skythe. But this new one, while appearing more elegant, felt much less powerful than Anika's.

"They did break it," Anika added, as if sensing Audreese's evaluation. "But it shouldn't have been made in the first place—it shouldn't have been possible." She drew Stormender from the sheath at her hip, holding it out for the council to see. "As I'm sure you've all heard, I forged this before using it to slay Eyen's incarnate. At the time I didn't fully realize what I had done, but after researching with Master Groaves at the spire, we determined that I was only able to forge the Key because the incarnate had absorbed the rest of the pieces of Skythe." She spun the knife and held it up to show the sapphire embedded in the blade. "This was the last shard, and only one of the Children could have used it to forge a Key."

"So that can't be a Key of Transience?" Darrance asked, pointing to the knife Ransil had tried to hide from them. "At least, not like yours?"

Anika gave Audreese a quick glance before turning back to Ransil for further explanation. The halfling hung his head for a moment before looking up to the Oather.

"Strallow. You knew me as Ruse—a dead man who once foolishly served the Guild. I'm just Ransil Osbury now, and I have no reason to lie about Knife's affairs."

The council members shared looks amongst themselves, not fully comprehending the point. But Ransil continued, staring at the weapon on the table.

"I originally came to Andelor in search of a dark elf, one who tricked me into stealing the keyshard that enchanted this weapon. That was the only reason I joined the Guild, and it would later be the reason that I left. I come from a line of Wickan priests on my mother's side, and the piece of Kindler you see here seemed destined for me…though *cursed* seems a better term."

"Are you saying you've had this since you left the Acreage?" Kasia's voice sounded strange to Audreese. Not having known the woman as anything other than an acquaintance, she couldn't be certain, but it almost sounded like the Oather was hurt by the discovery.

"I didn't have it," Ransil replied. "The Combustress did. Because I stole it for her."

CHAPTER TWELVE

Three Farewells

Gage crept through the Shadow.

The darkness was an oppressive comfort, like a heavy blanket in the dead of winter. Yet it didn't keep the dread at bay, which hounded him with every silent step he took toward his blond-haired prey.

Anticipation.

He felt the eagerness for the kill, twisting his insides, making him erect. It was exciting and revolting all at once, but he pressed on through the nightmare, determined to have his vengeance.

"Why?" Robin asked, his voice a disembodied plea from the darkness. His meek voice made it all the more exciting.

"Because you killed my mother," Gage said with a sneer, loosening and then tightening the grip on the same dagger he had used to kill Ransil Osbury. "If I don't close this circle, it'll consume us all."

The mists up ahead of them took on the shape of his target: Robin's mother, the Guildmaster. Knife's hips swayed seductively as she walked away from them, her face forward so Gage couldn't see the mask.

"It's better this way," he thought aloud, his voice a snake's hiss. "This is how we'll be free."

"No," Robin whined, sounding like the boys they had both been back in Blakehurst—scared and eager, wanting to show the world how much they mattered while not wanting to face the reality of how little anyone else would care whether they lived or died.

Knife's back was within reach now, bared pale skin yearning for ruin. All he had to do was bury the blade. Gage could feel how bad the steel in his grip wanted to pierce the woman's skin; it ached to be inside of her.

To be inside of him.

Gage turned the blade downward, raising it in a way that could set himself and Robin free. But before he could summon the courage, he felt gentle fingers wrap slowly around his wrist.

No, not his wrist.

He awoke with a gasp, feeling Robin's hand beneath the sheets, stroking what his wandering fingers found.

"Sorry," he whispered thickly. "It looked like you could use some help there…"

Gage lay back, exhaling slowly. The tension from the dream felt different now—felt welcome. He put his arm around Robin as they pulled their bare bodies closer against the chill beneath the city.

Together they eased the hard emotions that had built up within Gage, letting him slowly forget the terrible things he desired to do to Robin's mother. When they were finished, they both rolled out of bed to prepare for the day's journey.

"Are you nervous?" Gage asked as he watched Robin arrange several knives on the bandolier his mother had given him. "About going to Xe'dann?"

He raised an eyebrow in response. "What's there to be nervous about? The ocean?"

Gage shrugged. "I've never been outside of Vale. Hardly been out of Blakehurst. Not really sure what to expect."

Robin scoffed. "That's the whole point, right?"

Gage smiled. They had always talked about leaving the monotony of Blakehurst, but that was before everything had gotten so confusing—before he had murdered Elza, the innocent gnome merchant; before Robin had murdered his mother.

He felt his fingers clench into a fist, rejecting the visions from his dream from returning.

As if reading Gage's mind, Robin motioned toward the door to their chamber. "Mother said she would be back before noon, so we should be sure we're ready."

"Where'd she go?"

Robin waved a dismissive hand. "Said she had to say goodbye to a few people."

Gage looked up into the shadows above, feeling as if he had become lost before they even had the chance to leave.

Knife slowly lowered herself by rope into Luriah Vaughn's chambers, using the bustling of the servants to easily cover any sound she might have made (though she made none). Normally, she wouldn't have infiltrated the Lighthold in the middle of the morning, but time was of the essence.

"Don't drag the Archbeacon's sheets!" one of the maids shouted, causing a young halfling to scramble to pick up the bedding from touching the carpeted ground. "Light, defend!" the surly maid continued. "You've been doing this too long to make such a mess of it, Yelna!"

Knife waited until they were clear of the chambers before she took a seat in the darkened corner, where she would wait until the Archbeacon returned from her breakfast.

She used the time to consider what she would say to the woman; they were past the idle threats and subtle warnings that Knife usually relied on. The time had come for more direct methods.

When the Archbeacon arrived, Knife made her presence known immediately—she stood up and said, "I'm leaving for Xe'dann immediately and I need you to do something for me."

Luriah Vaughn barely reacted, closing the double doors to her chambers and slowly making her way to the table where her wine waited for her.

"Are we friends now, Guildmaster?"

Knife sighed. "We both know who the new Archmage is, and who she serves. And we both know the queen doesn't care." When Luriah looked over her shoulder at her, Knife added, "If you want me to handle the Dark One so they don't interfere with your own plans, then you'll need to take care of a matter here in my stead."

Luriah kept her eyes on Knife as she poured herself some wine. She raised her eyebrow and nodded toward an empty cup, offering the Guildmaster a drink. Knife gave a curt nod of her own, pushing her mask up so she could partake.

"If you want me to act as Guildmaster while you're gone," Luriah began, holding out the offering of Caimish dark red, "I'm afraid I must protest. Regardless of how much our interests align, there are certain tasks that are just not befitting of my station."

Knife allowed herself a slight chuckle as she took the drink; there was a certain degree of ridiculousness to all of this. Until recently, it would have seemed preposterous to her that she would be asking a favor of the Archbeacon of the Luminaura, let alone even sharing a drink with the woman.

But the world continued to become a ridiculous place, and there was no time to stop and consider it all. Instead, Knife tipped the cup back and let the dark liquid do its work. It reminded her of home, back when she and Sopheena would sneak into their family wine cellar to partake of the Xoatian vintages. Simpler times that made her feel both wistful and angry at the same time.

"I take it things in Sathford took a turn," Luriah began, refilling Knife's drained cup.

"I should ask you. Seems your forces are busy constructing your next foothold there. Meanwhile, my sister's puppet has been assassinated and Grale's whore of an elf-wife has taken the mayorship for herself—knowing perfectly well my sister cannot oppose the station without causing chaos amongst the high houses." She tossed back her next cup, already feeling her head swim. "I still have suspicions that she is in league with the druids, though for what reason I couldn't begin to guess."

"And the Child of Shadow?"

Knife casually set the cup down, lowering her mask back in place so the Archbeacon would hopefully not catch her hesitation. "That's why I'm going to Xe'dann. The Child of Light was in Sathford during the siege, as I'm sure your doves informed you. We overheard the girl claim that she planned to train in the spire until she was ready to hunt the Child of Shadow in Velcarthe."

The lie was based on enough truth that Knife was able to tell it more casually than expected, even though she had never found deceit to be all that difficult for her. Perhaps it was because she knew what her son's lover was truly capable of—that's what made this gambit feel so perilous. But mostly, she suspected, it was just the mere presence of her son in the city that was truly throwing her off her game.

Luriah finished her own drink, setting the cup down as she crossed her arms under her breasts and leaned against the table behind her. "You truly mean to bring the Child to me?"

Knife let out a small laugh. "Don't presume too much, Archbeacon. The queen has need of the Child of Shadow as well. What kind of sister would I be if I delivered such a high ransom to the Church instead of the throne?"

Luriah's eyes narrowed.

Knife savored that look for a moment before adding, "Though, coincidentally, our father's remains reside in the same depths as

Charlton Vaughn's, so it seems we'll just need to make sure we are all in the right place at the right time."

That part was at least true, which anchored the many deceptions Knife would have to weave throughout Andelor before departing that afternoon.

"What is it you need from me then?"

"You're to request an audience with the queen in three days, telling her you know about the bastard her sister conceived with the king."

Luriah straightened at that, but Knife continued as if what she spoke wasn't treasonous betrayal.

"You can name whatever sources you want, but what matters is that you tell her your High Warpriest—the one who died in Sathford—killed the boy before she met her end." Again, there was enough truth to the tale that it would more than serve her current needs. "You will tell the queen that the king's infidelity is an affront to the Church and demand that Markus Durrask be dethroned and exiled from Noveth immediately."

The Archbeacon just stared at her with a face that was nearly devoid of emotion. "Why?"

"Because it's the truth," Knife replied, producing a rolled parchment from her vest affixed with a simple wax seal. "You can give her this if she asks for some proof. It should be convincing enough."

Luriah carefully took the scroll as if it contained poison. "Is it true?"

Knife felt the sting of a tear in her eye as she turned away. "Does it matter?"

The Archbeacon didn't reply as Knife retreated back to the shadows.

Gage heard the voice again. He watched Robin for any indication that he had heard it too. But the half-elf's attention was focused on something at the end of the alley.

You used to be so alike, it said in the same threatening tone it used in Gage's dreams of matricide. *No mother, only each other.*

Someone shouted out on the street, drawing a wave of distant laughter. Robin turned to him and said something, but Gage only heard his own wicked thoughts.

You'll lose him just like you lost your family, it warned. *He's here for his mother, not for you. He killed your mother, isn't it only fair you kill his? Then you will only have each other again. It would be just like before: simple.*

Gage pushed his hair back, leaning his head against the damp stone wall. It took everything he had not to slam his head back into the hard stone. He knew these were not his thoughts, but the more they came to him, the more sense they seemed to make.

It's the Shadow, Gage thought, remembering the dark presence that crept into his mind back in Sathford and Oakworth. He knew it was trying to twist his mind.

No it's not, the voice mocked. *The Shadow doesn't speak reason, and you know I do. Your sister knew it as well, when I told her she had to come back to Sathford to kill you.*

Gage jerked to his feet.

"What is it?" Robin turned to him, setting his pack down. "Did you see her?"

"No!" Gage recoiled, not meaning to shout. For a moment he wasn't sure if Robin was talking about Anika or Knife, but either way, Gage didn't want to think about seeing either of them. Some presence in his mind wanted him to kill them both, and he was suddenly flooded with relief when he felt the reassuring weight of the bag over his shoulder.

It meant escape.

"We should leave."

The words were out of his mouth before he realized, but hearing them was a revelation. *Yes,* he thought. *If we leave now, alone, I won't have to kill anyone. We can just disappear. The Shadow—or whatever is poisoning my mind—can't use me for whatever it means to do.*

Robin smiled crookedly. "We are leaving." He put a hand on Gage's shoulder, leaning close. "She said to meet her here and we'd go straight to the gate."

Gage put his hand over Robin's, squeezing it desperately. "Why don't we just go alone? We don't need her. We can just take a ship to Jath, find work in Caraby. Away from all this." He motioned to the city beyond, but really he just hoped he could escape his own thoughts—they seemed to have gotten worse in Andelor.

Robin's smile took on a nervous quality as he waited for Gage to better explain why they would run from the Guild's leader who had saved him from the High Warpriest of the Luminaura. When none came, Robin wet his lips and glanced over his shoulder to make sure nobody had heard Gage's suggestion.

"What are you talking about? Why would we leave without her? She's the one that suggested we go to Xe'dann—she's the one with the connections there."

Gage felt Robin's hand start to pull away, so he gripped it tighter. "But we don't have to even go there. We can go wherever we want, Robin. We can start our own life, away from—"

Robin yanked his hand back suddenly, his expression hardening. "Away from what, Gage? Aren't we already away from everything? Your parents are dead, your sister likely wants you dead, and we can't go back to Blakehurst after what happened with that gnome."

"Elza," Gage said softly, staring into the Shadow that gathered behind Robin.

"What?"

"Her name was Elza."

There was a crash near the mouth of the alley, but neither of them paid it any mind.

"What is this, Gage? Is this about your mother?"

"My mother you killed?"

For a moment, Gage wasn't sure if he said that aloud or if he had just heard it in his head again. But when he looked up and saw Robin waiting for a response, he knew the answer.

"I know why you did it, Robin. This isn't about that…at least I don't think…"

"Tell me then. What are we running from, Gage? Because I thought we both wanted the same thing, but now it sounds like maybe this is only what I wanted."

"I dreamed I wanted to kill your mother."

The words came out before Gage could decide if he wanted to tell him, as if his heart decided the matter before his mind.

After a moment of silence, Robin asked, "Do you?"

Gage didn't answer; he just stared at the grimy stonework that ran down the length of the alley.

"Because I killed your mother?"

"The Light killed my mother," Gage said, the words once again coming from a hidden source of truth within him which he couldn't seem to access until now. Hearing himself say it had a soothing effect, quieting the malicious taunts in his mind. He finally looked up into

Robin's eyes. "It wasn't you that poisoned her, Robin." Anika's face flashed in his mind before he added, "It was the Light."

Knife didn't bother sneaking into the Arcania. While she would bet her blackshard against any of the Lightwards the Luminaura employed to protect against intruders, the most prestigious institute for magic in the entire world was not a place she was in the mood to infiltrate.

Besides, it was past time she presented herself to this new Archmage properly.

"Did you have an appointment?" the young guard asked. She was an elf too, wearing the four colors of the Arcania draped over her armor. Knife could see her eyes watching her nervously from behind the helm's visor.

"As I'm sure you're aware, I have a standing appointment. Tell Archmage Vera that the Guildmaster wishes to speak with her."

The title caused the guard to blink, but she didn't otherwise give any indication that she heard this masked woman admit to being the head of the biggest criminal organization in Vale.

"Wait here."

Knife didn't have to wait long. Just moments after turning and walking through the shimmering veil of magic, the guard stepped back through and motioned for Knife to enter.

This was the part Knife dreaded. The last time she had used a magical portal—aside from a gateway—was just moments before her death. But she knew this would be her only way to leave Andelor on her own terms, so she swallowed and stepped through. The icy sensation only lasted half a breath, and when Knife opened her eyes again, the deep violet, shimmering surface had dissolved and she was in the Archmage's chamber.

Vera Mourgael stood over a large desk covered in books, her back to the Guildmaster, as if to prove how little she feared the woman.

"To what do I owe this... Oh, what would you call it? Shakedown?" The dark-haired woman peered over her mantled shoulder, those almond Xe'danni eyes stripping Knife bare with just a glance. "I don't suspect you're here for enrollment."

"I need to use one of the old gates to get to Karrane," Knife said, pacing around the table to see if she could make sense of any of the books Vera seemed so interested in. But it was no use; Knife had little patience for magic, especially books about magic.

"The gates have been dismantled, as I'm sure you've heard. The Old Ways posed too much of a threat with my predecessor—"

"I know what you've told the queen," Knife interrupted. "She doesn't need to know about this trip, as I won't be returning. I just need to know you'll let me and my two companions reach Pyram without intervening."

Vera looked up from her studies, the hint of a smile on her dark lips. "Just what happened in Sathford?" She held Knife's silent gaze for a moment before closing the book she had been reading. "No, I don't suppose you would tell me. But you have my word. I have no use for you, nor do I have any use for the remaining secrets you seem to know of in Andelor. So, go down to the lower sanctum and take the fourth door on the left, the one with the bowl of sand marking it." She snorted a laugh. "Fainly Lopke was not the most cunning gnome."

"I have a favor to ask as well."

Now Vera laughed. "So this *is* a shakedown?"

Knife ignored that, eager to be done with this exchange. "Being rid of me will serve your cause well, Vera. The Shrouded would have assassins here on the morrow if they knew the Disciples of Stane had control of the Arcania."

The mirth died on Vera's face, but she held Knife's gaze defiantly.

"I have no cause to draw them here, mind you, but the queen sent her mages to recover his fucking book. It's only a matter of time until they are drawn here, whenever the mages give away their mission. That is…unless I can get to Xe'dann and kill their master."

This time, Vera's eyes widened in disbelief. "And that's what you intend to do? Assassinate the Dark One?"

In a single flawless motion, Knife produced a dagger from her vest and flung it down into the table. Vera reacted almost as quickly, drawing her hands into a protective spell that shimmered with faint purple energy between the women.

"If you agree to help me, Gravern's greatest adversary—aside from Stane himself—will be dead before the next dove returns from Andelor." Knife spun another blade through her fingers as Vera let her shield fade away.

"What do you need?"

Knife told her, and in response, Vera laughed again. But there was little humor in it.

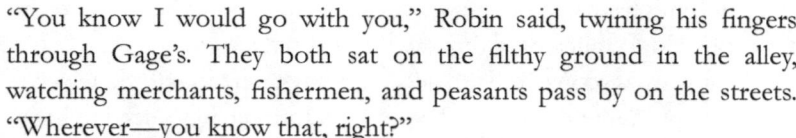

"You know I would go with you," Robin said, twining his fingers through Gage's. They both sat on the filthy ground in the alley, watching merchants, fishermen, and peasants pass by on the streets. "Wherever—you know that, right?"

Gage nodded. "You're right though. I don't have anywhere to go, especially not with you." He laid his head on Robin's shoulder, enjoying the silence that had settled in his mind after opening up to him. "I already ran—after everything that happened in Oakworth— and look what happened."

"None of that was your fault, Gage."

Wasn't it? he thought to himself. He was the one that stole the keyshard from Elza and put them all on this path. *Was the Shadow working through me then?* Or was it working through Robin, who had encouraged his thieving habits? *Stop!* he told himself, hoping to quell the voices from returning again.

Robin shifted forward so he could look at Gage, as if sensing his thoughts. "Neither of us decided on being here—none of it was planned. You didn't ask to be the Child of Shadow, just like you didn't ask for your father to bring Anika back from wherever he found her."

Something inside Gage reacted to that. Was it relief? A confirmation of his deep-seated, shameful belief that his sister brought misery upon his family? If she hadn't come to Blakehurst, would their mother have become so consumed with divine wrath? Would the Shadow have ever sought him out to make him its servant?

Gage felt weightless all of a sudden. His fingers swelled, and he was overcome with a distinct sense of disembodiment. It was as if Robin had given voice to a dark truth that he had buried for so long that its release was almost too relieving for Gage to bear.

"Gage?"

He blinked, seeing Robin as if for the first time. The boy he had fallen in love with was now a grown man. His blond hair was tied loosely back with a purple band, revealing his half-elven ears. There was the hint of facial hair above his upper lip and along the edge of his chin, and his eyes were enough to stall Gage's heart.

He reached up to touch his cheek, pulling his lips to his own. Gage was reminded of their first kiss, when they were cleaning Ransil's kitchen with only the faint light of a single candle to guide them. Back then, he had been shaking, nervous that he wouldn't be able to perform such a simple act properly.

Gage wasn't shaking now, but it felt just as new and exciting, making his body eager for Robin's touch again. But before they got carried away, Gage broke from Robin's lips so he could look him in the eyes to say, "I love you."

When the half-elf smiled at him, Gage saw Robin's face turn into his sister's. "I love you too, Gage. And nothing's going to come between us anymore."

Valiant Keep was louder than usual as Knife made her way up the hidden staircase. But she supposed that wasn't too strange, considering everything that happened in Sathford. And if the rumors of King Sulm taking over Rathen were true, there would likely be plenty of activity preparing for possible war.

Despite the circumstances, she was relieved to finally be getting away from the myriad of problems that afflicted her sister's reign. Only a tinge of guilt kept her from fully embracing that relief, but her sister would probably not lose sleep worrying about Knife's wellbeing, so she tried to remind herself that Delucar's daughters were no longer bound to each other.

Nypheena was free.

She smiled as she ascended the last flight of stairs and pushed the section of wall that would give her access to the queen's chambers.

That smile faded when she saw the king.

"What are you doing here?"

Knife looked around, seeing no one else in the brightly lit chamber. "I'd ask you the same thing. My sister is usually alone at this hour."

Markus moved swiftly toward her, grabbing her shoulder and pushing her back to the wall. "Haven't you heard? Rathen has fallen. Again. The high lords are calling for war and Sopheena is likely to give it to them."

Knife didn't resist; just held the king's gaze. "And you think this is my doing somehow? We both know the Church was behind Rathen—all of this is due to the Archbeacon's grasp for power."

Markus' grip softened slightly, but he didn't yield completely. "I'm not blaming you, Nypheena. But now is not the time for these games. You shouldn't be here—"

"Which is why I'm leaving," she finished for him. "I just came to tell the queen that Bloom will be serving as Guildmaster in my stead—unless Crawl survived the battle at Sathford, in which case she is to take command upon her return."

"For how long?"

Knife reached up and removed her mask. "Indefinitely."

Markus let go of her, his hard expression melting into shocked sadness.

"You know I can't keep him here," she whispered; but she didn't say, *But I can't live without you, which is why I set your exile in motion.* She reached up to lay her gloved hand on his bearded cheek, feeling every sleepless night of the past fifteen years all at once. "And I can't stand to see you anymore now that I have him back in my life. So I'm taking him to Velcarthe."

"Xe'dann?! Why?! You can take him to Merithian, where I can visit."

Knife felt the first tear as she shook her head. She knew that even if Markus sought them out after his exile, he likely could never love her unless a literal ocean separated them from Sopheena—it was a childish, foolish gamble, but the only gambit Knife had left. Somehow, deep down, she believed they could have a life together with their son.

"There are things I must do. Should Sopheena eventually recover *The Book of Stane*, we still have to find Ruke, and there's only one other being that I know of who can find her."

Markus blinked his own tears away. "I know you need to free your mother... I know what it means for you and Sopheena. But can't it wait? Can't you give us more time?" He reached for her hand, but Knife drew it away.

Part of her wanted to tell him that things had escalated well beyond just Allista's rescue or Count Delucar's vampirism—their son was in love with the Child of Shadow. But the King of Vale did not need to know any of those things. At least not yet. She would save those truths for Markus Durrask the Exile, should they ever meet.

"Tell Sopheena that I'll send word once I discover what's become of Ruke." She put her mask back on before Markus could see the rest of her tears. "And tell her that no matter what," she looked into his eyes one last time, "I'll finish what we started."

CHAPTER THIRTEEN

Digging Into the Past

The rooster's crow made Desmond jerk awake.

He sucked in a painful gasp when his lower back flared up, yet he smiled. Having never endured manual labor, the unfamiliar ache in his muscles was both new and surprisingly pleasant. After only a few days in the mines, he had a new appreciation for the dwarven diggers that swung heavy pickaxes all day, inexhaustible in a way that Desmond found inspiring.

Given everything he had been through—allowing the Shadow to work its way through him so he could turn Layla into a carnal zombie, then getting flayed only to be resurrected by the omniscient devil known as Stane—Desmond thought he had lost the ability to be inspired. Mere existence had felt like a burden to him.

And yet, as he swung his legs free of his comfortable sheets, enduring the sweet agony coursing up his thighs, he had never felt so alive. He couldn't help but wonder if this was why his brothers detested him so much for not joining them in the sparring yard or taking more of an interest in hiking through the woods with them.

There was a soft tap at his door.

Desmond pulled on the short pants that Hank had loaned him to replace his tattered robes and went to open the door.

"Gods," Ruke said, recoiling from the sight of his bare torso. "You certainly were torn completely apart, weren't you?"

Desmond didn't bother looking down to the cacophony of scars crisscrossing his body in patterns he had almost memorized by now. "I'll be down shortly."

Ruke pushed her way into his room before he could shut the door. "The mines are closed today. Besides, we have other matters to tend to."

"Closed?!" Desmond was surprised by how much that devastated him. He was actually looking forward to breaking stones with Vraston and the crew. "Why?"

"Clanmother's decree," Ruke said, closing the window and covering it with the curtains. "She returned late yesterday, and there are rumors she was near the Wane Coast where all those fires are breaking out—I'm convinced she's a cultist."

"The Combustress?"

Ruke nodded. "What do you know of her?"

"Mostly what you've told me: some disciple of Wick who has taken her love of fire to new levels of mania."

The halfling's gaze became distant, staring past Desmond's legs. "I'd hoped it wasn't her, but the more I've learned while you toiled in those dwarf holes, the more I'm convinced it is."

"What are you talking about?"

"The scion," Ruke said, still focused on something that wasn't in the room with them.

"The Combustress?" Desmond was surprised. He had assumed she would be Wick's incarnate. If someone was that obsessed with the god of fire, it seemed likely they would be the one that gathered enough of his keyshards.

Ruke finally looked up into his eyes, and Desmond saw something there that unsettled him: She looked afraid. "I believe her name is Veronitha Blaithe."

That name sounded familiar to Desmond, but he couldn't quite pin down where he had heard it. Before he could inquire further, there was a commotion from downstairs.

"What's the meaning of this?!"

It was Hank, the proprietor. Desmond and Ruke exchanged looks before moving toward the door. Desmond grabbed his tunic as his companion slipped through the door and down the hall.

By the time they reached the stairs, the clear sounds of conflict arose from down the stairs: shouts, shattering dishes, and the wet thuds of fists on flesh.

"You can't do this!"

Desmond descended the stairs just behind Ruke, but they both stopped when they could see the cause of the ruckus. Several similarly armored dwarves were accosting a struggling patron—one of the dwarven miners that Desmond had worked beside.

"You were told to stay out of the Cleavers' mines," one of the armored dwarves said before smacking the restrained miner again with a heavy open hand, drawing blood from the man's mouth. "Dureen has made herself perfectly clear!"

"I'll not have this violence in my establishment," Hank commanded from behind his bar, flanked by armed Cleaver soldiers. "If Dureen wishes to charge Stanson here formally, I'm sure he'll gladly face the Masonry's judgement. But I won't abide by this abuse under my roof!"

The armored dwarf that struck the miner raised a stubby finger toward the innkeeper. "You shut your ugly trap, Fowler scum. Your clan dried up—you have no grounds to speak demands to a Cleaver that way."

Hank moved around the bar, puffing out his chest defiantly. The air tightened around Desmond, and he felt his own lungs seize up. It wasn't like the comforting ache that affected his limbs—this was raw adrenaline, reminding him of the few battles he had fought by Layla's side in service to the queen.

He clenched his fist and began descending the steps, but Ruke grabbed one of his wrists.

"Wait," she whispered.

But then everything went wrong.

Before Ruke even had the single word out of her mouth, Hank confronted the Cleaver soldiers only to catch the butt end of an axe in his face. Blood sprayed upward in a cruel arc, and Desmond tore his arm free from Ruke in a sudden rage. He leaped the rest of the way down the steps, landing awkwardly on his stiff legs but refusing to let that slow him down. He was already moving his claw-fingered hands in the tensed way that allowed him to focus on the darkest spells that Fainly Lopke had cursed him with.

Desmond dug deep within himself—beneath the layers of arcane knowledge that High Mage Konrath had taught him, and even deeper than the mastery he had gained in the Arcania under the Archmage's tutelage. He reached into the Shadow that had turned him first into a monster and now into an instrument of Stane.

The dark energies from the Abyss responded eagerly and, as Desmond stepped toward the scuffle, he unleashed the thorny black whips that wrapped around the necks of all five of Clan Cleaver's finest.

Almost in unison, the dwarven guards dropped their axes, shields, and bloodied prisoner so they could try to tear the strangling apparitions from their windpipes.

Ruke screamed something behind him, but Desmond ignored her, choosing instead to revel in the horrifically pleasant sounds of his new adversaries choking on their own blood.

It didn't take long for the Shadow to dig its familiar claws into Desmond. Despite the discomfort that came from trying to harness such chaotic energies, there was also the intoxication that he knew all too well. Like a confusing book that a reader would grow more fond of the more they came to understand it, Desmond didn't want to let go of the fell powers that ravaged his mind.

"Desmond!" Ruke's voice managed to finally penetrate the consuming vortex of emotions that fueled his sorcery, causing him to break his concentration. He turned to face the halfling, feeling a different type of uneasiness. When he saw her, he realized how she had broken through.

A green aura surrounded her as she rotated her hands around an invisible sphere—a prayer to Oakus. The sound of cracking branches overpowered that of the choking dwarves, and Desmond felt the drunkenness fading away. Whatever the halfling was doing, it was countering the spell he had woven.

"Kill 'em!" one of the dwarves commanded between gasping breaths. "Kill the little witch and her Shadow priest!"

Desmond turned back to face them but swayed on his feet. Not only had the impulsive spell taxed his mind, it also seemed to have sapped his strength; he could barely stand, let alone fight half a dozen dwarves.

As if sensing Desmond's dread, Hank shoved one of his tables in front of the guards as he got back up to his feet. "I said not in my establishment!"

Two other patrons who had been watching the spectacle joined Hank to stand against the Cleavers, each of them spitting their own threats until the common room was a din of guttural curses.

The Cleavers recovered from the Shadow vines slowly, watching Desmond warily while they rubbed their necks; none of them seemed eager to meet the challengers.

"Come on," one of the Cleavers coughed. "Report this to the Clanmother—let her arrange their executions. No mercy for the Fowlers!"

Their leader snarled at Desmond as he backed out, spitting blood at the feet of the defiant dwarves helping the injured miner to his feet.

"What have you done?" Ruke asked quietly from behind him. "This place was already a tinderbox…"

Desmond turned to ask what she meant, but the miner who had been charged with trespassing began riling up the other dwarves once the Cleavers were gone.

"This can't go on any longer, fellas. I know Zakrin and his crew were murdered down there, and I were just lookin' fer evidence. I dunno how they figured I were down there, but—"

The dwarves began shouting over each other, each one's voice stoking the fires that Desmond could now see had just been waiting to ignite.

"We have to go," Ruke whispered, tugging on Desmond's sleeve. "I know an uprising when I see one. And with the Cleavers in control of the town guard, this whole place is about to become a giant prison until the miners can be contained."

Desmond allowed himself to be dragged from the common room; Hank and his patrons were too busy planning their revolt. It wasn't until just that moment that all the signs of these troubles were revealed in Desmond's memory.

Each day, as he worked in the mines, Desmond would hear grumblings about Clan Cleaver and how they had gone against tradition by claiming ownership over previously neutral sites. And the name Zakrin had come up before, spoken with the reverence of a martyr. Having been so focused on the unfamiliar rush he got from the arduous work, Desmond failed to inquire further about the strange events that befell Zakrin and his crew.

It was too late now.

Desmond followed Ruke out of the inn and into the bustling streets of New Hold. The Cleavers had left chaos in their wake, with several carts overturned and about a dozen more dwarves cursing as they gathered their spilled tools, soiled produce, and other goods that fell victim to Dureen's angry soldiers.

Ruke pulled his sleeve. "We need to get to the mine before the Cleavers reinforce it."

"Why?" But when Desmond turned toward her, he saw the halfling already hurrying toward the city gates. He had no better idea than to follow her.

A lone guard stood sentry outside the mine, just over the Renthil Hills to the east of New Hold. Desmond knelt down beside Ruke; from their position behind a copse, he could see the dwarf who blocked their way to the mine posed almost no threat.

"I don't suppose you have any qualms about harming total strangers?"

Something in the halfling's tone felt mocking, so Desmond didn't reply. Though, he had already lost his taste for violence after what had happened at Hank's. He looked up into the morning sun, finding it oppressive.

"Why don't you tell me why we need to get in there?"

Ruke sighed, turning to face him as she stepped behind the bushes, ensuring she was screened from the lazy dwarf standing guard. "I realize we haven't discussed the nature of the scions—what we actually are, and why Stane needs us." She pointed to her chest with two fingers. "But I know you feel it here, just like I do. I know he whispers to you, just on the edge of hearing. And you don't know what he's saying exactly yet, because if you did, you wouldn't be asking me why we're here."

Desmond stared blankly at her, waiting for the point.

"The truth is, Desmond, I also don't know why we're here. I just know we're supposed to be. I'm the first Scion of Stane, and I have no memory of what our purpose is. I chose you as the sixth scion, but I can't recall why. I banished myself in that stone, knowing that I was important enough to survive the centuries and unite the scions."

"If you don't know what we are, then why should we want to unite us?" He tore his shirt open. "I'm a monster, Ruke. The woman I tormented and violated killed me in the most horrific way I could imagine, and it wasn't even half of what I deserved! Then I came back and—" His emotions finally caught up with him as he thought of Anika and her friend Matty. "I killed him!" He covered his mouth, glancing through the bushes to make sure the guard hadn't heard the outburst; they were still beyond his notice.

"You!" he said, rounding back on her with a lowered voice. "You made me believe that Anika had to kill me so I could be free from this. You made me that monster!"

The look Ruke gave him was calmer than he'd expected; it implied that she had known the outburst would come.

"Like I said before, Desmond. That was Stane. He is clearly manipulating us, which is why we're here. I need to remember why I chose the scions before Anika or her brother are able to set them on the same path we're now on."

Desmond shook his head in disbelief. "How can you not remember something like this? You clearly remember who you are and that you had something to do with Stane and his scions, but you truly know nothing beyond that?!"

"What do you remember about your life, Desmond?"

He scoffed, but then when he opened his mouth, prepared to regale her with the saga of his life, he realized there were only faint patches in his memory. Like a threadbare blanket, he could tell pieces of his life were there in his recollection, but not enough to warm him against the existential dread building up inside him.

"Now imagine that handful of hours you lost," Ruke continued, "compounded into days, years, decades… How much do you think you could hold onto once the Nethering swallowed you up?"

Desmond had no response to that, but he could only imagine with how fractured his own mind was, Ruke's must be infinitely worse.

She sensed his sadness and rested a small hand on his exposed chest. "I can't take away your wounds, Desmond. But I can acknowledge them and share in your grief—I have wounds of my own, even if you can't see them. And now is the time that we can try to set things right—both of us. Because we are in this together."

The camaraderie Desmond felt with Ruke then made him blush and look away. It had been longer than he could even remember since someone had actually been kind to him. Perhaps because he was never kind to anyone else, but he didn't dwell on that thought. Instead, he appreciated Ruke's words and nodded. "So what do we do?"

Ruke moved her hand and turned toward the mine. "We need to get past that guard—whether we kill him or capture him, we can't have him running off to Dureen. She'll already be looking for us, but we need some time alone in there."

"Why?"

She looked at him. "I'm starting to remember. It's why I came to you this morning. While you were digging with the crew, I was studying the New Hold chronicles for mention of Korinthy Blaithe and Lena

Osbury, because Hank's mention of them was what first triggered these flashes in my mind; they could be memories, but I can't be sure, as there's no way I would personally have interacted with either woman."

Desmond remembered the day they had first arrived in New Hold, when Ruke had been so bothered by the mention of Korinthy Blaithe.

"You said it was her daughter," Desmond said, eyes distant, focused on the past. "Do you mean Korinthy's daughter or Lena's?"

"Korinthy's. Lena had no daughters, just a son…at least, I think—though I don't rightly know how I know that."

Desmond didn't press the matter. "Do you want me to incapacitate the guard?"

She gave him a shrewd look. "Are you able to? After what I witnessed back at the inn…"

Desmond waved that away. "Not the Shadow. There are other spells. Wait here."

As Desmond crept around the bushes, he was relieved to see that the guard had become even more detached from the present circumstances; he had taken a seat on the ground, leaning against the hard earth of the mine's hill. As he approached, Desmond reached into the depths of his memories of Raventhal Spire to ensure that he remembered the spells taught to him by High Mage Konrath and Master Audreese. He managed to grasp some level of familiarity, even though he couldn't remember the specifics of learning magic at the spire.

A particular lesson came to him, when Master Audreese had been instructing him in the undercroft, during one of their evening sessions that shaped the way Desmond approached spellcraft.

"Each spell is a promise to yourself," the elf had told Desmond. "Magic takes a piece of you, so anytime you beseech its power, you are surrendering yourself to the unknown essences of the world, hoping to get something in return—even though it's you who must take the power."

He wasn't sure why that particular moment survived the ravaging of his memories, but it must have been significant, even if he couldn't fully appreciate it at the moment.

As they neared the mine's entrance, he could clearly see the guard had dozed off, and Ruke motioned for Desmond to act.

The Shadow was still present in him, and it urged him to put the lazy fool down, but the memory of Audreese's face allowed him to resist. He whispered a name that he couldn't remember ever speaking aloud: Lathanna. It was a word of power, conjuring mists that swirled from his hands. Like a dozen insects leaving an interwoven trail of vapors, the spell sought out its target, swirling around the slumbering dwarf's face. The misty streams found their way into his nostrils, disappearing like snakes returning to ground.

Ruke stopped, looking back at Desmond. "Lathanna...the druid?"

"I had a friend at Raventhal." He didn't say Fallon's name, afraid it might conjure more emotions than he'd care to deal with—the grief over strangling Anika's lover was still fairly raw. "She had a strong connection to Oakus."

Ruke smiled. "I wonder if I ever heard her prayers." She looked back at the slumbering dwarf guard, now slumping fully to the ground. "You're full of surprises, Desmond."

He followed her into the mines just as the horns of New Hold began to blare out.

Ruke felt the altar's presence, even though she didn't know what it was. *Maybe I once did,* she thought, navigating the tight passage with the faint green glow of her spell. She heard Desmond curse behind her as he likely hit his head on an overhang again, but she was too focused on the altar that awaited behind the cave-in.

"Here's where they were digging." Ruke motioned to discarded tools and a pair of hand axes. "The Cleavers took them unawares and likely questioned them to give up that poor chap at Hank's."

"I take it you know what's beyond there?"

Instead of responding, she just stepped toward the blocking rubble and placed her small hand on it; the heat almost made her pull back, but she kept it in place, as if hoping her memories could be burned back into her.

Even if her flesh melted, Ruke couldn't turn away from what called to her.

Desmond said something, but his voice was so far away—a faint echo against the raging fires in her mind. She had never been drawn to Wick, but now it was as if the old god had burned every trace of Oakus from her heart, and she only felt fire where she had once felt...

What had Oakus even felt like? she wondered, having no actual memory of it.

"We can't trust you, Stane—not after what you did to Corsa."

Ruke spun around. "What?"

Desmond recoiled. "I asked what you were doing. Isn't that stone hot? I can feel it from here... It's like a furnace."

Looking at her hand, Ruke saw red and angry flesh. The stone had certainly burned her, but she hadn't felt it in the slightest. Even now, as she flexed her fingers, the pain just wasn't there.

"We have to get through," she said, still staring at her charred palm.

"Believe me, Wick, it was for the best. She was going to betray us. If I hadn't sealed her away, you'd be the one trapped in an altar."

Ruke looked up to her companion, not seeing his lips moving, as someone else spoke the words in her mind. It was almost like a memory, but much louder.

"I can try something," Desmond mumbled, raising his hands but not touching the stones as Ruke had. "Stay back."

"They're not altars, they're prisons! That's why you had us make them, isn't it? It was your plan all along. Admit it, Stane."

"Calm down, Wick." That voice was eerily calm, as if whatever the argument was about was just a huge joke. "I told you before, if you want to become a god, you need to have an altar—each of you. You think Oakus is *trapped* in the jungle? No, he's worshipped there! Just like Corsa, though now she can't interfere with our plans."

"They're not our plans, Stane! They're yours! You used us, just like Myretha warned us!"

"Ruke? You may want to back up."

"Ruke," Stane said, his voice a lower whisper now. "These aren't your memories—leave them be."

"What are you talking about?!" Wick's words seared into her mind, and Ruke grabbed her temples, doubling over in pain. "Who's Ruke?!"

Desmond's voice pierced through. "Ruke?"

"Quiet!"

As requested, Ruke was granted a reprieve from the assaulting voices; but it did not slow her racing heart. She looked up to see Desmond staring down at her, frowning in confusion.

"Sorry," Ruke said, getting back up to her feet. "Go ahead."

Desmond's gaze only lingered on her for a moment before he returned his attention to the blocking cave-in. He wove a spell with intricate hand movements, commanding the rocks to give them passage, which they eventually did. Ruke watched in wonder, still surprised by the young man's power. She had seen plenty of wizards in her time, but—unless the holes in her memory had removed such individuals—she had never seen one with such natural command over magic.

Except maybe Fainly Lopke, but she couldn't remember entirely who that was.

As the rocks moved away, the sight beyond took Ruke's breath away.

"What is that?" Desmond stepped into the pulsating crimson aura surrounding the massive red keyshard.

"It's an altar," Ruke said in a voice that wasn't her own. That voice knew exactly what she saw, despite her own eyes not truly recognizing what it was. "The true source of the old gods' power."

Desmond turned to face her with an expression of doubt. Ruke could read the questions racing through his mind, but she had no answers for any of them; he must have known as much, because he didn't give voice to any of them.

Instead, the two Scions of Stane stepped deeper into the chamber, enveloped by Wick's devouring rage.

Dureen Cleaver strode quickly through the gates of New Hold, her soldiers close behind, axes drawn. The city erupted into chaos behind them.

"Who's guarding the mine?!" she shouted, breaking away from the main road, heading toward the hills.

"Ulrik," one of them replied between heavy breaths. "The rest of us had to apprehend the trespassers."

Dureen glared over her shoulder. "It took all eleven of you to handle a few fat miners?"

The guard who spoke had no response to that.

They found Ulrik sprawled outside the entrance to the altar's hiding place—the one the Combustress had entrusted Dureen to protect against discovery. Dureen stepped over the slumbering guard, dragging her heavy boot clumsily against his face; it did not wake him.

The tunnel was brightly lit, sending a stinging pain through Dureen's large stomach. Whoever had infiltrated the mine had found a way to break through her clan's barricade—the Combustress would not take kindly to the news of someone finding the keyshard vein.

"Spread out," Dureen commanded, pointing to either side of the altar. The guards kept their distance from its smoldering aura, searching the tight chamber for any sign of the intruder.

"No one's here," one of the soldiers reported.

Dureen felt something that could have been relief, but it wasn't enough to chase the scowl from her face. "Seal it off then. This time, bring the whole tunnel down." She grabbed one of the guards nearest her, snarling into her face. "And no one hears about this. Kill the miners."

Dureen turned from the altar just as the image of two figures faded into its smoldering depths—a gaunt man in robes and a diminutive woman, searching their fiery surroundings for some sign of where they had been swept away to.

CHAPTER FOURTEEN

Kindler's Hearth

Melaine grew concerned with Brace.

Since escaping the Vestige, there had been multiple opportunities to break away from the cult leader, but her companion found an excuse to stay with their rescuer each time.

"We should at least see where her followers meet," Brace had said the first time, when the Combustress had gone to pray during their first night at camp. "Don't you think that would be useful to know? Especially if this has anything to do with what happened in Oakworth."

There had been logic there, Melaine could admit that, but she still felt like the man wasn't being entirely forthcoming with her when it came to the mysterious Xe'danni woman who insisted she would see them unharmed to her sanctuary.

"Besides," Brace had said the next night, "I don't mean to let her keep my father's keyshard. She may think it belongs to her now, but I mean to have it back before we part."

They all felt like hollow excuses to Melaine, who wanted nothing more than to be on her way back to Deina Brasson; that was assuming she had survived the encounter with the incarnate, but Melaine had to believe she did—it was all she had to hold onto.

Just thinking of the dwarf made her even more anxious as they emerged from the Steddlewood during a late afternoon. The Wane Coast stretched before them just below the cliffs, and the western horizon was all ocean. It was the first sight that truly made Melaine realize how far they had traveled from Oakworth.

"This is too far west," she said, having grown tired of keeping silent on account of Brace Cobbit; while they had shared a cell, she wasn't prepared to fully abandon Deina on his account. She turned her gaze toward the Combustress, who slowly lowered her tattered hood and regarded the horizon that lay ahead.

Something about the way the sunlight reflected off the woman's skin unsettled Melaine. Aside from the gruesome burn scars that covered her bald head, discoloring her Xe'danni flesh from a light ochre to a muddied brown, there was an aura around the woman that seemed to sap Melaine's desire to confront her.

It wasn't cowardice, she realized with sinking horror—it felt like reverence.

"How much farther?" Brace asked, his voice meek and burdened with shame. "To your sanctuary?"

Without turning her gaze, the Combustress raised a scarred hand to the cliffs. "There's a path down the ridge. We can be there before nightfall." Finally, she turned toward the half-orc. "Though you will have trouble reaching safety if you turn back now. Not even my gnolls are allowed to traverse the Steddlewood at night. The great spiders from Hollowood are known to venture out this way when darkness falls."

"I'll be fine," Melaine said, instinctively reaching for her bow that wasn't secured across her chest as it had been before getting captured. She doubted her own words when she remembered they were unarmed. She and Brace both had daggers that they recovered from the battle, but she wasn't necessarily excited to test her abilities with such a short blade against who knows how many bandits or monsters lurking in the forest.

"Very well," the Combustress said, moving toward the cliff. "But do be gone before sundown, as my people are under orders to eliminate any trespassers. You may be mistaken for one if you're not with me."

"Trespassers?" Melaine looked at Brace, searching for support. "Do you own this land? Are your people authorized by Waneport to execute innocent travelers?"

The Combustress turned to face them, her singed robe flapping open in the breeze to reveal her only partially clothed body, which was also burned, head to toe. "This land belongs to Wick—his authority is all that matters now. He entrusts us to carry out his will, which you will see should you accompany us to Kindler's Hearth."

"Comb— I mean," Brace stammered as he stepped forward.

"Call me Veronitha," she said; Melaine thought she saw the hint of a smile on the woman's lips as she glanced at the burned chaplain. "Veronitha Blaithe."

Growing up in Wickham, the name Blaithe was spoken of almost as often as the old god himself. Korinthy Blaithe was a hero who fought to recover Wickan keyshards from those that would abuse the fire god's power. Melaine could see from Brace's reaction that maybe those legends were just as popular this far south—the man seemed to be utterly enchanted by this woman who claimed to be a heroine's descendant.

"Blaithe?" Melaine asked, her hand still clutching the phantom bow that was not strapped to her chest. "As in Korinthy Blaithe?"

The Combustress turned her unnaturally gold eyes on the half-orc. *Had they always looked like that?* Melaine wondered to herself, realizing she had been avoiding the woman's gaze since her first appearance from her follower's bowels. Somehow she had been convinced the woman's eyes were as red as her robes might have once been.

"My mother," Veronitha said in a voice that would brook no argument on the matter. "The Seeker of the Burning Altar."

Melaine knew the ballad well. And while she supposed this woman could very much have some relation to a Xe'danni hero that she had never met, the odds felt too unlikely for her to just believe the stranger. However, she was in no position to really question the claim. Having seen what the Combustress could do from the confines of a blackiron cell, she had no desire to witness her capabilities with over a dozen Wickan keyshards she had taken from the tower she burned.

"You won't be harmed on the way to Kindler's Hearth if you come with me," she informed them, turning back toward the cliff. "However, I cannot guarantee your safety if you travel onward alone or venture back through the Steddlewood." She knelt down near the cliff before adding, "You have some time to decide. I must perform a ritual to alert my people that we're coming, else they will release my pets."

Your gnolls, Melaine thought. She did not wish to trust a person who would call such savage creatures pets. Even though gnolls were not as common in the north as in Guyen, Melaine was no stranger to the atrocities the monsters were capable of; she could think of no other force that could tame or control a gnoll than the burning powers that Veronitha wielded—only control over a blazing inferno could earn the loyalty of such savages.

"You should come," Brace whispered, stepping toward Melaine with his back to the Combustress. "She didn't have to let us out of that cell; why do you think she is inviting us to her sanctuary if she meant us harm?"

"I'm not worried about her harming us," Melaine replied, less silently. "I'm worried she will try to deceive us into joining her order. This is a cult of fanatics that have been burning down farmsteads and villages all throughout Vale. You heard them talk about it at the Vestige."

Brace glanced over his shoulder at the woman who bowed her bald head in prayer, overlooking the calm Racivic Sea. "What if it's all just rumors? Shouldn't we find out for ourselves?"

Melaine realized that Brace made a very valid point (even if he wasn't thinking entirely with his proper head). She knew that Deina was the main reason she wanted to turn around, but just thinking about the stubborn dwarf reminded Melaine who the woman she had fallen in love with truly was.

Deina traveled with a priest who she was sworn to protect. Melaine looked at Brace's ruined face; the flesh that had melted in cruel streaks reminded her that he had tried to protect her from the flames in Oakhold. She may have died without him having taken the worst of the inferno. Didn't she owe him just like Deina owed Avrim for saving her life?

She looked toward the Combustress and motioned to the strange supplication the woman was performing as she said, "Don't expect me to do any of that. But you're right: we should see for ourselves just what this cult is about."

Kindler's Hearth was a precarious chapel built upon an outcropping that was far too high from the beach below for Melaine's taste, while also too low from the cliffs they descended—the perfect place for a secret cult to convene.

Eventually, the three of them reached the end of a steep incline that gave way to the plateau upon which the chapel stood in ruins.

"Seen better days," Melaine remarked.

"The Kindler built this place with his bare hands," Veronitha said with reverence. "He loved a Corsan priestess and faced his temple to Wick toward his Lady Bane—the only one who could quench his flames."

"Romantic," Melaine remarked, wondering where the entrance to the place was—the building was more a pile of bricks than anything else. "Did his Lady Bane also knock down his house?"

Brace exhaled sharply to try to reign in Melaine's attitude, but the half-orc ignored him; she was already doing enough to earn the man's respect, she wouldn't humble herself toward the leader of a cult as well.

"What do you know of the Kindler?"

Something in the way she asked that made Melaine stop mid-step. There wasn't challenge in Veronitha's tone, it was more like genuine curiosity—as if she truly wondered how much Melaine knew about the most legendary Wickan priest that ever lived.

"I'm from Wickham, where the Kindler was born. The company of rangers I served operated out of the Kindler's first chapel in Ashwood. There is likely little I don't know about Rowen Klein."

Veronitha smiled at that as if impressed. "If you know his true name, then I suppose you know enough. However, did you know he was the head of a secret order that opposed the Keyguard?"

Melaine looked toward Brace, wondering if she heard the woman right. "Opposed? Rowen was a member of the Keyguard—he was the one that helped them recover the shards of the sword he took his name after."

Veronitha let out a gentle laugh, one that seemed to say, *Oh, dear sweet child, how little you know.* Instead, she just looked back at the crumbling chapel and said, "He didn't just take the sword's name. He became the sword, in every aspect. He became a Key of Transience, through the joined belief of his followers—they lent their faith to him, and with it he forged himself into a celestial embodiment of existence itself."

The wonder in Veronitha's voice oddly made Melaine want to guffaw wildly—it just seemed so comical, especially when talking about turning a person into a Key of Transience. *This woman is mad,* she thought. *How did I let Brace talk me into following her down here?*

But when she saw Brace's reaction, all humor left Melaine. She could tell that the man was falling under this woman's spell. Whether it was his own fascination with Wick through his father's keyshard (that she had stolen), the fact that they both wore scars of their union with the fire god upon their faces, or just simple carnal lust.

Almost in spite of the scars, Veronitha Blaithe was certainly beautiful; Melaine could not argue that. But if Brace was leading them into a cult so he could potentially lay with its leader, Melaine would have to take the man's balls since he couldn't be trusted with them.

"You doubt me?"

Melaine realized she had been wearing her misgivings on her face, and she looked away from the woman, trying to bite back everything she wanted to say; but it was too difficult.

"I do," she replied. "I think Rowen truly believed he became a god's relic, because priests tend to hold a high opinion of themselves. But yes, I do doubt that he truly became a Key of Transience."

"Why?"

Melaine was losing her patience with the conversation and chose not to hide it as she rounded on Veronitha with outstretched arms. "Where do I start? If he could become a Key of Transience, how come no one else has since then? Why was he the first? How would you even know, given he died, what? Four hundred years ago now?"

"Melaine…" Brace began.

She turned to him, letting her arms fall back to her sides in defeat. "You're a man of the Light, Brace. Don't tell me you believe this woman's tales. Doesn't it contradict your entire belief that the old gods gave way to the Light by giving pieces of themselves to the world? What value would the Keys have if some mortal man could turn himself into one?"

Both Brace and Veronitha stared at her, making Melaine feel like some sort of priestess herself, giving a sermon. She sighed, not even sure why she let herself get pulled into this discussion—let the crazy woman believe whatever she wants; what was it to her?

"You have a void, don't you?"

Melaine narrowed her eyes on the Combustress, daring her to make this personal.

"There's a fire in us all," she continued, her mocking expression changing into something that may have been compassion. "I can feel yours is burning hotter now—you feel it too. But it's not rage you feel toward me or your companion, is it?" She stepped toward Melaine, and the half-orc could feel the heat that surrounded her. It was oddly comforting, calming. The anger she felt just a moment ago melted away like wax from a candle's flame.

"You feel loss," Veronitha added.

Deina's face swam in Melaine's thoughts—she could almost feel the dwarf's powerful body yield under her own timid touch. She shifted uncomfortably under Veronitha's gaze. "How would you know what I feel?"

"Because I felt like you when I first came here—when I first learned of the Pyric Path."

"The Pyric Path?" Brace's voice held a childlike wonder, which would have worried Melaine if she hadn't been so distracted by Veronitha's cryptic words.

"Wick deals in truth," the Combustress replied, turning back toward the ruined chapel. "His most devout disciples are given the Sight if they survive the Pyric Path. My people train for it below, hoping to risk their lives in pursuit of it, but only a few will ever truly find it." She looked over her shoulder at Melaine. "I knew when I saw you both in that cell, you were destined for the Path, should you wish to embrace it for the sake of your loved ones."

"Our loved ones?" Brace asked. "What if we ain't got loved ones?"

The Combustress smiled at Melaine. "She does. And she'd do anything for her."

The woman earned her namesake by waking a fire within Melaine, and when Veronitha Blaithe turned to lead them toward the Path, the half-orc moved to follow.

Kindler's Hearth was as much a ruin within as it was without, and the trio had to navigate a tight passage that was lit only by a small flame burning in Veronitha's open palm.

"I had assumed the Combustress might have a brighter presence," Melaine remarked quietly to Brace, but the man just grunted in reply. She kept her mouth shut the rest of the trek down the cramped staircase.

Soon they heard the low growls of beasts, which Melaine could only guess were the gnolls that Veronitha had called her pets. She instinctively gripped her knife as they reached the bottom of the stairs.

"Keep quiet," the Combustress whispered. "They won't harm me, but I have lost a few followers who crossed this threshold unwarily."

Melaine once again felt ashamed to be following a person who would so callously lead her own people into danger. But she obeyed, following Brace and Veronitha through a dark archway into a dimly lit vestibule.

The growls intensified as she saw several shapes melt from the shadows, taking the form of hairy humanoids with long, muscular arms and arched backs. They paced in the dark, waiting hungrily for a misstep.

Without warning, the Combustress snapped her fingers and sparked a flame out of thin air. The gnolls snarled in response, shrinking from the light, circling the trio as they crossed the monsters' domain. Melaine saw bones and half-chewed limbs with rotting flesh scattered across the messy stone floor. She wondered how many of Veronitha's followers these savages had fed on.

"This is the only language they understand," she whispered to Melaine, then turned to Brace. "They worship the flame almost more than you worship the Light."

He said nothing to that, but Melaine felt something in that tense silence—and it wasn't just the gnolls' hungry growls.

They reached the other side of the chamber after what felt like far too long of a time to have traveled such a short distance, and Veronitha closed a heavy door behind them, letting the conjured flame go out.

They no longer needed it.

"Light above," Brace said in soft amazement.

The heat caused Melaine to squint more than the light; it felt like they had stepped in front of a furnace. Kindler's Hearth was nearly volcanic.

"Below," Veronitha corrected. "Wick's illumination is all you'll find down here." There was a loud metallic click as she secured the door behind them. While Brace admired the stone walls of the hallway before them, his eyes following the intricate veins of liquid fire that flowed through the place, Melaine turned back toward the Combustress to see the woman removing a black key from a lock.

"And that illumination will give you the truth you seek." She turned around and gave Melaine that cruel smile. "Well, one of you at least."

The sounds of movement from the other end of the hall drew Melaine's attention from Veronitha, her hand instinctively going for her dagger again. But a different hand that was too hot to be human grabbed her wrist.

"You'll want to save your strength," she said with amusement while Melaine watched several robed figures stride toward them, blocking any passage.

"What is this?" Brace asked, his voice finally finding the command that Melaine remembered from Oakhold. "You said you wouldn't harm us!"

Calmly, as if speaking to a child, Veronitha reminded him, "I said you wouldn't be harmed on the way here."

"You piece of shit!" Melaine struggled against the hot hands, but there were too many restraining her.

"This is Wick's first test," the Combustress said, still unbothered by their struggle. "Neither of you come to us as a true Wickan. And just as he had to cast his own true love into the flames, you must prove your faith by giving the other to the Path below."

Melaine managed to free her arm and draw her knife, but as she brought it down on Veronitha, the Combustress's arm moved like a snake and caught it. She tried to yank her arm free from the cult leader's grasp, but the woman's hold was unnatural and unyielding. Her skin was hotter than any of the other cultists'; solid fire.

"She means for us to kill each other," Melaine snapped at Brace, wanting the man to feel every ounce of his own foolishness for leading them into this trap. *But who is the bigger fool?* she wondered, forgetting how she even let herself follow them. That only fanned the flames of hatred she felt for her cellmate.

"Nonsense," Veronitha laughed. "I only need one of you to kill the other—how else will I know if you're worthy to join our cause?"

Melaine glared at Brace; in that moment, she resented just how badly she wanted to play this bitch's game.

CHAPTER FIFTEEN

Trials

Geneva found Reston Mauer sipping a cup of tea on the terrace. He was not what she had imagined, having only heard of him through Lexeth's stories. But she knew humans aged much quicker than elves once they lived past forty or fifty years old.

"How is he?" Reston asked, not taking his weary eyes away from the lush greens of the Deloreth Valley. Geneva could hardly blame him; she had been raised in Lefayra, and even she had trouble pulling herself from such a marvelous view.

"Funny," she replied, "he asked how you were."

Reston snorted before taking another sip. Despite his haggard appearance, he had a strong posture, refusing to lean on the elegant railing as he observed the wood elves' realm. "He always asked me to come visit him here. I suppose I should have, long ago. Before all this mess." He finally turned toward her, looking every bit his age under the light of the setting sun. There was a sadness to him that made Geneva want to weep—she had always been too emotional, even for a wood elf. "When is his trial to begin?"

"That's why I've come," she replied. She hesitated, reaching a hand out for the banister that Reston refused to touch. The polished wood held many memories for Geneva, but she imagined it was more like the iron of a jail cell to Reston, who was held against his will by the Eldercrown Guard. "You've been summoned to testify before the assembly."

He gave her a sneer. "Testify on whose behalf?"

She expected his skepticism. With how secretive Reston Mauer was in regards to his relation to the Eldercrowns (both individually and as a group), it was no surprise that he would not be anxious to speak before a sage, especially in regards to such an affront to Lefayra.

"My husband's, of course." She nodded toward the valley below. "Waurane does not want to hold a wood elf accountable for such an atrocity, Reston. She won't be looking to incriminate him; she just wants to know the truth." She glanced at him over her shoulder. "Do you truly think I'd have offered to escort you if I felt she intended to accuse Lexeth of both treason and murder?"

"Hasn't he already been accused?"

Geneva shook her head. "You know how impulsive Kreith is; he took it upon himself to arrest Lexeth so there would be no chaos. As much as I hate to say it, Lexeth made the most sense—not that I condone them tossing him in a cell, obviously. But you must admit, the timing of all this felt circumspect."

Reston nodded slowly. "Almost as if it had been made to appear so..."

She considered that as well. But why someone would want to elaborately frame an old Eastlunder and a Lefayran scout, she couldn't begin to guess. Just as she couldn't begin to speculate who (or what) slipped into Lefayra and slaughtered all of the Eldercrowns, only to escape back out again without being noticed.

As if reading her mind, Reston stepped forward with his hands behind his back and asked, "What about the eighth?"

"You know she's left." Geneva certainly hadn't forgotten about her cousin Cethany, who had abandoned her post with the Crowns when they discovered her ties with the exiled druids. "I refuse to believe this was her."

"Someone is trying to sow chaos though," Reston continued. "Do you not think the Order of Oakus would benefit from the Eldercrowns no longer standing in their way?"

"In their way of what?"

"War."

Footsteps echoed from the chamber behind them, and Geneva turned to see a row of four Eldercrown Guards stepping out onto the balcony.

"I said I would bring him."

None of the guards spoke in reply, but one of them—a young woman who Geneva had remembered shouting at the day Lexeth was taken away—gave her a poisonous smile.

"It's always war," Reston said sadly as he turned away from the peaceful valley. "Let us go get this over with, shall we?"

The assembly met in the wide circular chamber outside the Elmery. Reston and Geneva were escorted through the hushed crowd that had gathered around the sage.

Waurane Thirrow was a wood elf who had seen more winters than Reston, but she looked almost as young as Geneva. She had pale skin that was clothed in loose lavender silks cinched by silver bands, and her hair hung in tight silver curls. Regarding the old man with kind emerald eyes, the sage betrayed the hint of a smile that told Reston she remembered the last time they had shared a room well enough.

"Thank you for joining us, Lord Mauer." Her voice held much more age than her flesh suggested.

"Everyone here knows I'm no lord," Reston said, regarding the elven faces that were already judging him from every angle. "Lords are not held captive."

"In times of war they can be," she replied, not unkindly. "Do you not see the massacre of our highest council as an act of war?"

"Where's Lexeth?" Geneva interrupted, stepping up to the table that was now flanked by three Eldercrown Guards on either end. "Shouldn't he be here if this testimony is truly on his behalf?"

"I'm here."

Lexeth stepped from behind two guards. He wore the elegant device that bound his wrists—the wood elves' version of manacles that Reston somehow found more cruel than iron chains. The scout didn't look mistreated, which wasn't too surprising since he was mostly being held captive as a farce. Either way, Reston did not like seeing his friend this way.

"Let us begin," Waurane said from her seat at the table. "If the assembly would remain silent during Lo— Reston Mauer's testimony, our chroniclers will add today's hearing to our collection of evidence, and we will be one step closer to finding justice for our slain kin."

The silent chamber remained silent, reminding Reston how unnaturally civilized wood elves were—if they were in Menevere, riots would have already been in full swing.

"Perhaps you can begin by explaining what brings you to Lefayra."

Reston glanced at Lexeth before taking a deep breath to begin his tale. "I came here to meet with the Eldercrowns to discuss Lexeth

Groaves' admittance into the Keyguard." Someone in the assembly gasped, but a stern look from Waurane prevented anyone else from making a sound. Reston could feel the young scout's eyes on his back, but he paid the prisoner no mind as he continued. "The time has come that we must restore the order to its proper place, and I know of no other wood elf more deserving of a place in its ranks."

The sage cast a brief glance at Lexeth before returning her gaze to Reston. "Had you discussed this topic with any of the Eldercrowns before coming to such a decision? I would have trouble believing that either Ulrith or Vanna would concede to such a thing, given their own history with the Keyguard."

Reston nodded wearily. "I didn't say I expected to be granted my request, only that it was my purpose in coming here."

"And should your request have been denied?"

"Would I have killed your leaders? No. I have few enough allies left in the world as it is, their collective deaths are a grievous wound to the Joined Realms." He placed a wrinkled but sturdy hand on his breast. "I pledge everything I have to helping you bring their deaths to justice."

Waurane inclined her head slightly as if considering the truth of his words, but Reston knew the woman believed him. This whole testimony was as much of a farce as Lexeth's arrest, but Reston had no immediate course of action now that the Crowns were dead; so, he played along.

"We have heard from the accused," Waurane finally said, motioning to Lexeth. "Now we would like to hear from you: Why was the refugee from Rathen absconded from his quarters?"

Reston resisted the urge to turn toward the shackled elf as he answered, afraid he might bend the truth slightly if reading the man's face wrong—he intended to keep his testimony as honest as possible.

"I suppose he wouldn't have been able to find me without Bennik Lawson—or wouldn't have known to look for me at all. Up until now, the Keyguard remained a secretive order. But with the incarnates rising and the Scions of Stane emerging, that time has passed."

This time, more than one gasp escaped the assembly, and the sage did nothing to quell it—she was too focused on Reston at the moment, boring into him with disbelieving eyes. For some bizarre reason, Reston savored the discomfort his words brought; it reminded him that the Keyguard had not been so forgotten that their return wouldn't go unnoticed.

That is, if he could truly bring the order back from the decades of dormancy.

"What do you know about the Scions of Stane?"

Reston narrowed his eyes, wondering why the woman had focused on that one piece—he thought this would have to do with the Keyguard and the murder of the Eldercrowns, not old prophecies. But it occurred to him that he had no recollection of ever discussing the topic with Waurane during any of their meetings—though, to be fair, they had done little in the way of talking back in his more virile days.

"I know there are two by now, with four more to reveal themselves." He motioned at nothing behind him. "Assuming the incarnates are dealt with accordingly."

"I mean the nature of them," Waurane pressed, her calm gaze steady and unyielding. "The Keyguard was torn apart from within due to the conflicting views on Stane—whether he was the self-proclaimed Illuminator or the deceiver that used the Purveyors of Light to carry about his great betrayal of the old gods."

Reston chuckled. "Oh, he can call himself the Illuminator all he wants. You know as well as I, the Light isn't inherently the truth—it can be used to reveal lies just as easily as fact. Stane is and always has been a snake—his nature is confusion and chaos."

Reston turned to the assembly to make sure all the seated elves in the chamber could hear him well enough. "When that bastard split himself into six parts, hoping to break free from the Abyss where he belongs, he charged the only surviving Purveyor with choosing his scions. These are the individuals that truly hold the power of his return, and I came here to beseech the Eldercrowns to allow me to train Lexeth Groaves to join the Keyguard." He looked back at Waurane, whose gaze still hadn't changed. "Because we are the one truly united force that can meet the threat of Stane."

"Are you saying Stane is responsible for the incarnate that destroyed Rathen? Or the one that corrupted the druid in Sathford?" Waurane's face finally shifted slightly, as if she truly didn't know the answer to that.

"The malice of Light," Reston said, quoting the Luminaura, "has always been the greatest threat to the Joined Realms. The Shadow is wicked, but it lacks the antagonism that drives the forces of Light into conflict, eager to burn away any encroaching darkness." He held up his crooked forefinger. "There is no one force responsible for these incarnates; they are a gathering, a tide that was directed toward our mortal shores. And I believe it was indeed Stane who manipulated followers of the Light to carry out his deceit."

"You mean the Purveyors?" Waurane arched an eyebrow, challenging him to go down that path with her again.

"They're dead and gone, as I'll soon be. No, I don't speak of the Purveyors—they were only the first to be duped, certainly not the last. I speak of Luriah Vaughn, the Archbeacon of the Luminaura." The assembly did not hold back their collective gasps this time. "She is the one that instigated the keyshard smuggling out of Copera, causing the riots in Nazurik—you think Malcolmry Sulm would have let even a single keyshard out of his kingdom?" Reston shook his head for show. "There's not a single wizard in the Joined Realms who hasn't lusted after the famous Sulm vaults, but not once in the past two generations has a single keyshard been found, bought, or stolen in the north without a Sulm taking claim of it."

Waurane rose out of her chair, quieting the murmurs that were rising behind Reston with a sweep of her gaze. She settled it back on the old man. "Just what are you accusing the Archbeacon of?"

"I'd say treason if I didn't believe the throne might have something to do with it," Reston countered, drawing more shocked whispers from the assembly. "But I charge her with drawing out these incarnates—if not directly, then through pure foolishness that would have shamed old Charlton Vaughn." He laughed. "Now that man would have at least had the decency to face an incarnate he was responsible for himself."

"Enough!" Waurane declared. Whether she snapped at Reston or the now unruly assembly, it wasn't clear, but silence fell regardless. "We've strayed too far from the crime at hand, Lord Mauer."

"Reston."

"You're a lord if I say so, old man," she snapped.

Reston pinched his lips to hide his smile the best he could—he hadn't realized he still had the ability to wrinkle the woman's smallclothes like that.

"You vouch for Lexeth Groaves' innocence?"

"I do," he said without hesitation. "He was with me in Eastlund, at my tower. Besides him being unable to physically slay the Eldercrowns, I know his character well, just as most of you must. His sister died serving the Crowns, and he would never soil her legacy by doing anything to harm Lefayra."

He turned to face Lexeth—the man looked on the verge of tears, which may have inspired the vow Reston decided to take on.

"If the assembly wants justice for the murder of the Eldercrowns, I shall personally deliver it." He turned back toward the sage and added, "I'll just need one thing from the assembly…"

CHAPTER SIXTEEN

Coming Together

Grip felt an uneasiness as they approached the unremarkable boundary of Stelmont. Serving as a halfway point between Andelor and Waneport, many might assume the place would be quite prosperous, but with so much trouble from Hollowood spilling into the Steddlewood, most travelers preferred the safety of the Valeway over the more efficient path through the backwaters of Vale, leaving Stelmont to fester like the remains of the tower they now approached.

"Well, that's certainly seen better days," Maze remarked. "Though I had heard its High Mage was a particular thorn in your old master's side." They cast Layla an expectant glance, who was scowling in confusion.

"I came here last year," she said, looking around as if someone could explain the state of the place. "It hadn't looked— Something happened here."

"I'd say so," Jaffron remarked, sounding not the least bit interested. "Unless it was the work of the witch, I say we continue on to town."

"What would a thousand-year-old witch want in a squalid village?" Grip asked, annoyed. "What we're looking for is in that scorched tower, I'm sure of it."

As if in response to that declaration, hooves thumped from up ahead, drawing Jaffron, Maze, Layla, and Grip together: four strange companions ready to meet whatever trouble rode toward them.

That trouble was none other than a familiar face that Grip was simultaneously shocked, annoyed, and relieved to see. His eyes met hers almost instantly.

"If you're here on Guild business," Bennik Lawson said as he reined in his horse, "I suggest you head back the way you came. The reeve has put me in charge of keeping the peace since the raids."

Layla stepped forward, clearly still bothered by the state of the Vestige. "What raids? Shard thieves?"

Bennik gave her a cursory glance before returning his watchful eyes to the dark elf, daring her to make a move; Grip could see the man's hand hovering over the hilt of a broad knife at his belt. "Of a sort," he replied. "There's a cult causing trouble along the coast. The Combustress. She's in league with gnolls from Guyen. They attacked the tower two nights ago. Reeve Jansen is looking to pay coin for laborers if you're looking for honest work. Otherwise, I recommend you find elsewhere to bring your trouble."

"We bring no trouble," Maze said, a strange humor in their voice. Grip noticed the Jathi accent nearly disappear as Maze added, "We were just hoping to maybe spend the night before trying to make it to the Valeway."

Bennik looked at each of them in turn, lingering on both Grip and Jaffron longer than the others. "Those are fine mounts and you look well-provisioned. Why would you be looking to linger in a backwater village that just got attacked?"

"Enough!" Jaffron declared, urging his chestnut mare forward. "I'm the Lord Mayor of Waneport, appointed by the queen herself. Stand aside."

"I know who you are," Bennik said calmly, motioning toward the hill to their side. "As does he."

Grip followed Bennik's hand toward a small, familiar figure that looked down on them from the hill. It was the Archmage of the Arcania, with swirling bands of violet energy orbiting his small hands. Identical bands of magic appeared around Jaffron and his elegant horse, as if eager to squeeze the life out of both of them.

"Wait!"

Layla Abrigale strode forward, *The Book of Stane* held out toward the gnome. "The queen sent me to find this, Master Lopke."

"And I sent her to find it for me," a voice announced from behind them.

Grip spun around, instinctively drawing a hidden blade. But she froze when she saw a Daughter of Oakus looking down at her from another hill.

Jak gave Kadie the rest of his cinnamon bun as the girl wiped her tears away. Her own snack had fallen to the floor and was quickly snatched up by Brandeline. The dog was still licking his lips and looking up at the halfling girls for more as Kadie took a bite and said, "Fank you, Jaky."

Jak smiled, once again fighting back tears for what he had put the girls through on account of a false sense of duty. Even after he had risked their lives and dragged them away from their mother, they both treated him as if he were their big brother.

It was all made worse by the fact that they were still stuck here when he should be well on his way taking the girls back to their mother in Oakworth. He wasn't even allowed to send a messenger to assure Dolly that her kids were cared for.

As if reading his mind, Sadie set her empty plate down and licked a tiny finger before asking, "When are we going home, Jaky?"

"Soon," Jak replied, looking out the common room's window to see if Bennik had returned from his patrol. They hadn't seen a gnoll since yesterday, which meant there was a very good chance that they could be on the road that afternoon if Reeve Jansen agreed to give them the mounts he promised.

"How soon?" Kadie asked with a mouthful. She reached her tiny hand out to pet Brandeline on the head; the dog gently nibbled on the halfling's fingers, licking eagerly at the honey that coated them. Kadie giggled.

Before Jak could respond, the common room door was thrown open, startling him, the girls, and the dog. One of the town guards—a girl younger than Jak by at least a few years—turned to him, gasping for breath.

"Lord Lawson has requested you at the Vestige."

The Vestige? Jak wondered, looking at the girls as if they somehow knew why he'd be called back to the burned tower. Regardless, he got to his feet and told the girls to remain at the inn until he returned.

The young guard followed him, making Jak feel uncomfortable, as if he were a prisoner being escorted. Stelmont's main thoroughfare— if the narrow dirt road even deserved the name—was deserted. The townsfolk were likely still concerned that the attacks were not over.

"Do you know what this is about?"

Jak turned to the guard, his hand resting on the small dagger at his waist, which was the only weapon the reeve had granted him. Under the late morning sun, he realized how pretty the girl was, which oddly reminded him of Dame Strallow, making him even more uneasy.

"Sorry, I may have forgotten your name…"

The girl gave a small smirk, her own hand on the hilt of her sword to keep it from smacking against her leg as she took long strides to keep up with his pace. "Claudia Jansen. I'm the reeve's niece." She motioned back to the inn behind them. "I don't blame you for not remembering me; the last time we met, you were protecting those darling girls in there—it was very brave of you."

Jak tried to smile at her, but given his discomfort, he couldn't be sure his face obeyed. They continued through the vacant town, and when they reached the two craftsmen fixing the gates—a curiously thin dwarf named Alric and a gnome with bronze spectacles named Randle—Claudia began slowing. Jak turned to her, wondering if she saw trouble. But mostly she just looked distracted, staring at the tower on the horizon.

"There was a dark elf with them," she said when she saw Jak's eyes on her. Meeting his gaze, she added, "You know? From Caim."

Jak slowed his pace as well until they both stopped there in the middle of the deserted road. He waited for her to explain. Dark elves, he had heard, were not altogether common in Vale, but he didn't understand why that seemed to bother Claudia so much.

"You ever seen one?"

He shook his head.

Looking back toward the Vestige, she rubbed the back of her neck as if something had been crawling up into her braided hair. "I hadn't either until Lord Lawson called for me to summon you." She stepped closer to Jak and lowered her voice. "Do you suppose it's true? That they're Shadowfiends?"

Jak was far from an authority on such things, but he couldn't help shaking his head. Maybe his recent experiences with those who were supposed to be "good" made him doubtful that all the dark elves in the world were wicked on account of how they were born.

"I can't imagine that's true," he managed to say. "Bennik Lawson certainly wouldn't treat with anyone tainted by the Shadow." Even as the words left his mouth, Jak felt an odd sense of shame, as if he had suddenly spoken out of turn. Regardless, Claudia just nodded.

"I suppose you might be right. Lord Lawson seems a good man; if you trust him, I have no reason not to myself."

They continued on toward the Vestige in silence, but during their trek, Jak couldn't help but ponder what Bennik was doing meeting with a dark elf—also, why he needed Jak to be present for it.

The bodies had been cleaned from the tower's hill, and even the Vestige itself looked only as ruined as it had before the attack; Jak could hardly tell there had been an assault, aside from the blackened scorch marks along the tower's windows and doors. When he saw two dwarves from New Hold carry out charred lumber, he remembered that they had already been hard at work on the repairs.

From inside, they could hear raised voices as they approached, and Jak recognized Bennik's, but he had never heard the man sound so angry. It did little to ease the discomfort that gripped him as he crossed the threshold back into that dreadful place.

"I'll wait here," Claudia said, giving him a look that he couldn't quite interpret. Regardless, it gave him the small amount of courage he needed not to flee from the stairs that led up to the High Mage's study.

"We cannot wait that long!" a woman shouted.

"I'm not asking you to wait," a voice responded, but Jak couldn't decide if it was a man or woman. Maybe it was the dark elf. He had never heard one speak; maybe they had less definition between the sexes.

Each step up the stairs was indecisive: he wanted to hurry so he wouldn't miss what was being so fervently discussed while also wanting to take his time so he could overhear as much as possible before revealing himself.

The mysterious voice continued. "I'm just saying it would be best if we allowed Kartha to regain her understanding of the text before we make any further plans."

"That's easy for you to say," the angry woman replied; her voice broke slightly, giving Jak the impression that she was young and scared. "You're not the one with his voice in your head!"

"I believe I can help with that," a small voice interjected as Jak reached the top of the first flight of stairs. He knew it was the Archmage. "I could at least dull it some. If it comes from the Abyss, where he's said to be trapped, it's a form of Shadow magic, to which I know some counterspells."

The gnome's stern words, spoken with his usual litheness, gave Jak pause.

From his position at the top of the stairs, he could see into the High Mage's study. Two figures moved about, one of which was clearly the broad form of Bennik Lawson. Jak could tell from the man's movements that he was eager to be done with whatever this council was discussing. After the man passed from view, Jak could see the former Archmage himself, standing atop a chair so he could reach his little hands up to hover over a pretty elf's head. The other pacing figure—a high elf dressed in aquamarine finery—slammed his hands down on the scorched table.

"No!"

A shocked stillness fell over the study, as well as the outer hall where Jak spied from. All eyes were on the handsome elf, but that man's eyes were fixed on something that Jak couldn't see.

"Not here," he finally said, keeping his eyes locked in place. "Let's escort the book and Kartha—or whoever you are now—back to Waneport. I don't trust this place."

"I helped build this place, son," Fainly snapped. "There's probably no place safer than the Arcania itself for Shadow magic to be controlled." Jak could just see one of the gnome's eyes from his position, but it narrowed on the elf. "Unless you have something to hide, Lord Mayor?"

"Enough of this," a new voice said. "Bennik, get your boy outside and bring him in. If he's meant to help you return the girls, he shouldn't be in the dark about all this."

It took Jak far too long to realize the woman was talking about him. Realization hit him at the same time as all the eyes he had been watching through the study doors had turned toward him. Then Bennik appeared in the threshold and pushed the burned door farther open, motioning for Jak to join them.

"This is the one I mentioned," Bennik said. "He and his late brother were squires to the Lady Commander of the Oathers." As Jak crept into the room, he could finally see all the curious members of the council. Returning to the head of the burned table with his arms crossed over his green tunic was Bennik, glaring down at Jak as if he had already done something wrong. "He will be accompanying me to Oakworth to return Ransil's nieces and investigate the scion that Fainly insists can be found there."

"I'm going too," a figure said from the one shadowed corner of the study. Jak nearly gasped when the dark elf revealed herself. Claudia's words echoed in his mind, and he wondered if this woman's presence was why the other elf had objected to Shadow magic being cast. "I owe a debt to their mother," the woman continued, her strange, mismatched eyes challenging Bennik to object. But the man just nodded.

"And I will escort the green lady back to Waneport with the book," the high elf said. "Layla can come if she wants, but maybe a little distance from the thing might cure those whispers in your mind."

"I'm not going anywhere," the strange woman's voice said. Jak turned to see the green woman in question—the one that had been imprisoned with Fainly and Bennik. Not quite a dryad and certainly not human, Jak had no clue what kind of creature she was; all he knew was that she was probably the most beautiful woman he had ever and probably would ever see—as well as the most terrifying.

She sat at the end of the table opposite Bennik, where she wielded an undeniably commanding presence over the chamber.

"As I mentioned," she continued, regarding the impatient high elf, "Kartha is well and truly dead—her body is dust. Whatever part of me is still here is fractured, and I'm still trying to piece it together. I'll need Fainly's help, but we'll both need time to recover after...well..." She motioned to their burned surroundings. "A lot has happened."

Fainly shifted in his seat. "And we can't go back to the Arcania while that usurping bitch sits in my seat and undoes centuries of meticulous work." He slammed his two small fists onto the table. "Closing the Old Ways?! Madness! What?! Are we supposed to traipse across the realm like beggars when we need to be in six places at once?!"

"This place will serve," Kartha continued. "I'll speak to the reeve and ensure he knows that we've taken command of the tower. He doesn't need to know whether or not the new Archmage is aware of or approves of our residency."

"Damn right, he doesn't," Fainly sneered, still clearly angry thinking about the woman who had stolen his post. "His town would be a pile of cinders if it weren't for us!"

"The book stays here as well," the young elf interjected, pulling a black leatherbound tome across the table toward her. She gave Jak a nervous glance as if he had come to take it away. Just as the Lord Mayor of Waneport moved to object, the younger elf turned her eyes to him and added, "Too many people have died since I found this, and I will not let it out of my sight until we know its contents."

"You will come to regret those words," Kartha said, getting out of her seat. "I may not remember exactly what those pages said, but if the dread I feel just looking at the thing is any indication, no good will come from reading it."

"We don't have any other choice," the ambiguous voice said. Jak turned and saw it belonged to an equally mysterious figure. Whether man or woman—*Or both?* he wondered—they were captivating in a way he wasn't used to. He watched as they got out of their seat, their eyes fixed on the black book that the elf mage now clutched with both hands. "Unless anyone here has any answers for what is happening with the incarnates, that dragon, Stane's Scions, and now gnolls raiding openly in Vale, I say we see what answers that book may be hiding."

No one had an argument for that, but the mayor of Waneport made a loud snort so they all knew how much effort he was putting into not arguing the matter.

"Then it's settled," Bennik said, moving around the table toward Jak. "Go see that the girls are ready to travel. And tell the reeve we'll need at least one extra sword to ride with us to Oakworth." He looked over his shoulder at the dark elf. "I won't risk Ransil's kin with all these gnolls prowling about."

"Nothing will harm them," the dark elf said, her jovial face shifting into something much more dangerous. Jak saw the glimmer of steel spin through her fingers as she made her way past them toward the stairs.

Bennik turned from her back to Jak. "Still, find another, someone we can trust." He lowered his voice and nodded toward the dark elf descending the stairs. "Ransil shared a bed with that one but still doesn't trust her."

"I heard that," she called back.

He patted Jak's shoulder as he took his leave.

Jak waited for the rest of the council to depart before he made his own way down the stairs, dodging the busy dwarves as they removed burnt wood and replaced it with freshly sanded lumber.

As Jak stepped out into the open air, the early autumn wind seemed to carry away the dread that had lingered around him while in the burned husk of the Vestige.

He heard Claudia approaching before he saw her, but when he gazed up into her curious face, he smiled boldly now and asked, "Have you ever been to Oakworth?"

Chapter Seventeen

A Road to War

Anika had found a strange sense of routine since returning to Raventhal. Aside from the looming threat presented by King Sulm's claiming of Rathen and the disturbing details she had learned about the Combustress from Ransil, there was a comforting rhythm of waking up, tending to her studies, and then meeting with the council in the evenings.

Despite the grim circumstances plaguing each aspect of her life, the steadiness of it all made it bearable.

But all that ended when the High Warpriest announced that they would be marching on Rathen.

"The Archbeacon will wait no longer," Darrance announced, trying to contain his pleasure. Anika could certainly tell that the man was eager to start a conflict with Copera, even before they fully understood what the Sulms were trying to achieve in Rathen. "It is time for action. We are to ride at dawn."

Anika looked toward Avrim, but the priest hung his head as if he were ashamed to be part of the whole charade.

"Who is *we?*" Ransil asked pointedly. "It was my understanding that the Luminaura was sent to protect Sathford."

"That we did," Darrance replied in a sharp tone. "If it weren't for my paladins, the city would be in ruins now and my chaplains wouldn't be helping build a new cathedral to replace the one the enemy had corrupted from within."

Anika noticed the High Mage inhale sharply at that, but the boy just waited for the paladin to finish.

"But to answer your question," Darrance continued, standing up to motion toward Avrim at the other end of the council table, "the new beacon and I will lead the majority of the Luminaura's strength— along with a portion of the city watch that we have helped re-garrison—north by way of the Rathaway."

All eyes fell on Avrim. Anika could tell the priest was just learning about this now.

The new mayor was the first to speak. "So it seems you called this council to officially request my leave to take my city's military on the Church's campaign." Gwynna drummed her fingers on the table, her cold eyes fixed on the paladin.

Anika could actually feel the tension in the room; it was oppressive in an embarrassing way, making her almost wish whatever incarnate had killed the Eldercrowns would burst through the doors so she wouldn't have to sit through one more of these blasted councils.

"My apologies," Darrance began, not even trying to hide the mockery in his tone. "I'm so unaccustomed to having to ask permission to carry out the Light's will that I must have forgotten to beg for your leave, Lady Mayor."

Gwynna chortled at that, but Anika could still sense the tension rising.

"What was the word from Harkan?" Ransil asked. "The reports from Wickam claim that the Coperans passed peacefully through the town on their way to fight the orcs."

"Are you suggesting that Malcolmry Sulm does not have designs for Vale?" Gwynna asked the halfling sharply. "Do you reckon he marched into the queendom on a campaign of charity? Saving our free cities so he could relinquish them back to the realm when the dust settles?"

Once more, Anika opened her mouth to reply, but Ransil was quicker.

"Of course not. We all know the Sulms are desperate—their dynasty lies bleeding, and they likely saw the perfect time to unify their splintered people by making a show of Rathen." He turned his gaze on Darrance. "Which is not wise. And despite what the Archbeacon may suggest, I would advise the High Warpriest to reconsider following the wayward king's poor example."

"Are you suggesting that the Luminaura is divided?" Darrance asked, tenor rising.

Anika could take it no longer. She stood up and asked, "Why don't I go?"

The council all turned to her, but it was Ransil's eyes she felt the most. He had talked to her before the council, asking her to remain silent as much as she could. They didn't need to stir up trouble with Lady Mayor Grale, not while the woman was so determined to keep the conflict with the Luminaura at the forefront of her new reign.

"Are you volunteering to accompany the paladins as Sathford's envoy?" Gwynna sounded intrigued, but her eyes were still warily watching Darrance.

"Why not?" Anika asked. "I'm the Child of Light. After what happened in both Oakworth and Karrane, doubtless the Coperans are aware of me and Gage… What if that's why they're here?"

It wasn't the first time Anika had considered that, but she hadn't spoken it aloud until now. And from the looks around the table, it seemed she had touched upon what many of them had already been thinking. Ransil, in particular, looked as if he had been exposed.

"We can only speculate," the mayor said, her face no longer pinched in an angry expression. "Sulm has long been rumored to be eyeing Rathen. His grandfather had a lot to do with the city's independence, so there's a history between the Sulms and the late Duke Ambrose."

"But the timing of the invasion is circumspect," Ransil added, giving Anika a sharp look. "Back in Blakehurst, Neff let slip about the rebellions in Nazurik a few times. It seems to me that something beyond an old grudge or just simple conquest has brought Malcolmry here—I wouldn't want to deliver that something to his doorstep."

"So you'd rather he march farther into Vale to find it?" Anika snapped, suddenly feeling her annoyance with Ransil grow—*As if he were your father*, Stane remarked in her mind, fueling her own disdain.

Ransil gave her a hurt look, but quickly turned back toward Gwynna. "If she accompanies the Luminaura, I go as well, along with Embrace."

Anika wanted to challenge him on both counts, but before she could, Avrim got to his feet. "We all go, Deina as well. Keep your watch, Lady Mayor."

He turned and left the council chamber before anyone could argue.

Gwynna returned to her chambers to find Renda laying on the floor in front of her hearth, a cozy fire lighting the room that once belonged to Karl Tolle.

The gnome didn't look up as the Lady Mayor entered, she just continued writing hurriedly on a scroll that was already filled with her sloppy scrawl.

"Where is Cethany?" Gwynna asked, loosening the clasp that held the emerald cloak over her shoulders. She shrugged out of the thing, revealing the flawless skin beneath. The way her flesh looked under the soft firelight somehow made her even more resentful of having to be in Sathford again. But with both Avrim and Darrance now leaving the city, she was grateful to have returned when she had.

"Praying," Renda replied, not looking up from her work. "She said something about the Eldercrowns still speaking to her through Oakus, but I think she still grieves." The gnome waved a hand as if the idea were incredulous to her. "I suppose she still blames herself for this whole ordeal."

Gwynna stiffened at that, tossing her cloak on the nearby bench. "Ordeal? You call the slaughter of the entire wood elf council an ordeal? Travesty, I say."

Renda kept scribbling. "You're entitled to do so. Their removal likely aids our cause, so I won't be so quick to call it such."

Closing her eyes against her growing frustration, Gwynna just said, "You're such a little cunt, Renda."

"As you say," the gnome retorted, dabbing her quill into an inkpot. "The last of the Eldercrowns returns."

It was then that Gwynna heard the footsteps outside, delicate slippers making their way up the spiraling staircase. Renda's uncanny senses always unsettled her. She slid over toward her desk, stepping over the gnome's sprawled body before they were joined by the last surviving Eldercrown.

"She claims she has found it!" Cethany's cry was a hoarse whisper against the sound of the door closing.

"Found what?" Renda asked, still not looking up from her work.

Gwynna poured herself a glass of Coperan red, trying to restrain her own excitement—it wasn't every day that she would be able to tell her sisters in Oakus that she had just orchestrated the perfect way to put their order in control of an entire city.

"The incarnate!"

Sudden adrenaline caused the mayor to jerk her hand, nearly spilling the glass of wine, red as blood. She set it down with the pitcher and moved toward the others. Renda scrambled to her feet like a child on Winter's Eve.

"Who?" the gnome asked in her own whisper.

"The priestess! Who do you think?!" Cethany sounded more

delighted than annoyed; the excitement was certainly contagious. "Naya. The Shrouded. She kept her word and—"

"No!" Renda interrupted, smacking the Eldercrown's hand as the woman gestured toward the door. "The incarnate! Who?! What is it?! Myrethan? Wickan?! Tell me it's Corsan…"

Cethany shook her head and looked toward Gwynna. "It's a Shadowlord, she claims."

Both women gasped and looked at each other, as if the other had an answer.

"What does that mean?" Renda asked. "An incarnate not tied to an old god?"

"Stane," Gwynna said. Just hearing the name in her own whispered voice gave the mayor a strange sense of weightlessness—as if she had suddenly begun to float off the ground, her limbs swelling with dread.

Gwynna locked eyes with Cethany. The Eldercrown wet her lips and asked, "You felt him too?"

"Felt him?!" Renda exclaimed, her voice no longer a whisper. "What have I missed? When has either of you felt Stane, and how could he possibly have an incarnate?"

"I don't know," they both answered in unison.

"But," Gwynna continued, holding Cethany's gaze, "we'll be able to prepare for him from our seat here." She moved toward the window and threw back the curtains to reveal a perfect view of the unfinished cathedral. "The city is ours. And once the paladins march on Rathen, we can call the dryads in to deal with any uncooperative Luminaurians…"

"Naya?"

The halfling's voice pulled her back to the present and she gasped, feeling a radiating pain course through the front of her skull down the length of her spine. Communing through the Old Ways was becoming more and more costly for her, but she felt assured that the message from Cethany had been worth it.

"Are you all right?"

The man's voice was abhorrent to her—it had the quality of spoiled milk the way it interfered with her concentration. But she needed Tremly, so she bit back whatever acid she would have otherwise spat in his direction and forced a smile.

"I'm fine," she managed, easing herself up off her knees. The ground was still damp from the morning dew, which had soaked through her robes. But again, she was beyond caring.

The Dark One would not be able to deny her any longer, not after she delivered both the Disciples of Stane and the Luminaura to the Shrouded.

She turned to regard the short, ugly, one-eyed man that emerged from the trees where they had camped. He was Naya Lahmoud's providence—her pathway to ruling over the Joined Realms with the Dark One.

"What do you know of Stane?" she asked him, brushing the grass off her robes with her only hand. Her eyes watched him warily for any sign of deception—if Stane truly had a foothold in this tiny vessel, he would not want her to know about it.

But she would know—she was already mostly convinced.

Tremly just shrugged, sucking on his lower lip. "Same as most, I s'pose. First Man, they say. Fooled the Ghultans out of their dead worshipping. Wrote a book that nobody can properly read; if it even exists at all, that is." He was rattling off the facts on his tiny fingers, stopping to look back up to Naya to see if he had satisfied her query.

"Do you know how he relates to the Shadowlords?"

Tremly's eye twitched slightly, as if a part of him did in fact know. But he just shrugged and said, "Can't say that I do. Aside from the fact that Gravern banished him to the Abyss—again, if you believe the legends."

Naya cringed inwardly at that, resisting the urge to lecture the little man about the very presence that lurked inside him. Instead, she stepped forward and used her sweetest, most consoling tone to say, "Believe the legends, Tremly—legends exist for a reason. Whether or not they have been exaggerated, there is truth if you dig deep enough beneath the surface."

He nodded, looking genuinely interested. Whether or not it was Ithakan's ego that desperately wanted her to continue inflating his influence over Stane, or just a general curiosity that halflings seemed to possess, Tremly held her gaze with patient anticipation.

"Stane was indeed the First Man, but he was a flawed one to say the least. He brought magic to Aetha, stolen from the old gods. For eons without count he roamed the mortal world, raising and felling civilizations that have since been lost to history. He earned the praise of countless priests and the ire of even more. It wasn't long until the rise of ancient Ghulta drew such a figure to its underground empire, which is what put him in conflict with Gravern."

Naya watched Tremly carefully as she said the name again, but the halfling still just stared, entranced with her tale.

"No one really knows what exactly pitted the two against each other," she continued, "since so many legends exist, and more often than not, one contradicts two others. But there has been a Dark One since the fall of Ghulta, and the Shrouded have been the keepers of Gravern's greatest secret—it is why the Disciples seek to destroy us."

Tremly swallowed. "What secret?"

It was a difficult thing for Naya not to smile, but she knew that she had him now.

Ithakan.

Stane.

The incarnate.

She had them all.

CHAPTER EIGHTEEN

The Altar of Eyen

After traveling through the Old Ways and feeling the Shadow itself course through his body, Gage felt prepared for his journey to Karrane. In his mind, it wouldn't be so different from the gate they had taken below Raventhal that had whisked them all the way to Andelor.

What he hadn't anticipated was that there were many different types of gates; some were more unstable than others. And the only remaining gate to Karrane was made by an unhinged gnome wizard in the bowels of the Arcania.

"We'll need to stay close," Knife had instructed as they made their way down a perilous winding staircase. A floating violet light was their only guide into the blackness below. "Fainly had several gates hidden down here, thinking himself clever by making the realm believe he was capable of teleporting himself wherever he wanted."

Knife motioned for Robin and Gage to stop. She pulled a small orb from her vest and tossed it to the ground, where it smashed and released a strange hissing sound. Smoke plumed from below and revealed several floating strings of blue magic just above the next few stairs.

"Whoa," Robin breathed, grabbing Gage's hand.

Knife stepped carefully between two of the threads. "Goes without saying: Don't trip these."

Robin and Gage followed carefully as the smoke began to dissipate.

"Most of his magic was based in illusion," Knife whispered when they cleared the traps. "However, the little bastard knew how to hide his wards, I'll give him that."

"Who?" Gage asked, feeling as if he had heard the name Fainly before, but he couldn't say for sure.

"The Archmage," Robin answered. "Well, former. Right, Mother?"

Knife turned her masked face toward them. Gage couldn't read her expression from just seeing her eyes, but he had the sense she was smiling. That somehow unsettled him.

"He was the first and only Archmage," she explained, motioning toward the end of the stairs. "I believe he originally came to Andelor from these depths, all the way from his home in the Shatterwood."

"The Shatterwood?!" Robin's excited voice echoed into the blackness above them. He lowered it to add, "How old is he? I thought Glearia was destroyed like a thousand years ago. Gnomes don't still live up there, do they?"

"To his age," Knife replied, directing them toward a faint yellow glow that broke the haze just ahead, "it depends on which stories you believe. But with the fey sleep, he could be as old as anyone walking the Joined Realms. As for Glearia, it was never destroyed, just hidden."

Gage felt lost, both in the strange darkness below the city and with the conversation mother and son were having about distant places he had never heard of. His own thoughts were on his sister now, as if the act of distancing himself even more from her was somehow awakening a longing to see her again—to maybe explain why he had left.

Why you killed the halfling, Stane added. Gage pretended he hadn't heard the voice.

As the gate came into view, he pushed both Anika and Stane out of his mind, letting the arcane passage represent his new path in life—one that would take him far from the Shadow.

Knife insisted that Robin pass through first, followed by Gage. "I know how to keep this open if one of the wards trips. Just stay low and keep moving forward, even if it feels like there's something in your way. If you stall, the passage will consume you."

Those words echoed in Gage's mind during the long stretch of time they spent in that passage. Nothing could have prepared him for that sensation.

While the Old Ways had an oppressiveness to it, everything about the surroundings down there had still felt real to him. But this small, cramped passageway forced him to hunch over, making him feel both confined and disembodied. It was more than uncomfortable. He had no words for the sensation, nor could he even keep his thoughts straight during that bizarre trek beyond the known world.

But through it all, he could feel Robin's hand in his, keeping him anchored and moving forward.

Gage couldn't say how long they were actually in the passage, nor could he even say what his surroundings looked like—it was like a miasma of active magic circling him in conflicting directions, how he imagined being caught in a whirlpool might look.

Finally, the assault of blinding lights gave way to soft, flickering candles. But before his vision focused entirely, there was a deafening crash.

A much-too-calm voice said, "Well, who's that now?"

Gage peered around Robin's shoulder to see a human man seated behind a table. His skin was dark like Anika's, but his hair was much coarser, sprouting from his head in short tangles. There were rows of cards on the table, and the man had several more in his hands, fanned out as if he were playing a game against an opponent; but no one else was in the small room. There was just the man, the table, and shattered glass across the floor.

"Is this the academy?" Robin asked. Gage could see his hand slowly reaching for the dagger that he kept sheathed at his back.

The man returned his lazy gaze to his hand of cards, as if bored of the intrusion already. "I think it was—back when I was a kid. When people could find honest work." He picked up a dirty mug and took a small sip of its contents; he made a face like he didn't care for the taste.

Gage heard Knife step out of the gate behind them; the unmistakable sound of two blades being drawn quickly followed.

"Who do you serve?" Her voice was odd, like she had adopted an accent, but Gage couldn't place it. He reckoned that was a normal tactic to hide her identity.

"Whoever pays," the man said, playing one of his cards onto one of the rows. "Which is nobody these days. You hiring?"

"Don't play there," Knife said. "You're going to drain your hand before you can close that row. Take it back and draw two instead."

He looked up at her, the candlelight flickering in his big dark eyes. Gage thought the man was strikingly handsome, but perhaps it was just his calm presence that he found so appealing. The man's big lips parted in a smile, revealing dazzlingly white teeth.

"I didn't realize the Guild still operated here."

Knife stepped around her two companions and approached the table, sheathing her blades. "We don't. At least, not normally. I need passage to Xe'dann immediately."

"That seems unlikely with the war going on," he replied, slowly drawing two new cards from the stack near his drink.

"War?"

He nodded, choosing one of his cards to play on a different row. "Most of the fighting is kept to the desert, but the ports are locked down. Which is probably a good thing with all those pirates from Velcarthe swooping in to raid any distracted war galleys."

As usual, Gage felt completely lost with all this. There was talk about war up north, near Rathen, but they had heard nothing about a war in Karrane. Who would they be fighting? Westerra? He pictured a bunch of halfling farmers waving rakes against a swarm of Karranese soldiers.

Maybe there was some evil wizard raising an army of mummies. Gage remembered some story Matty Cullen had told him, back when he used to tease Anika about her mysterious heritage. He said majests would wrap up their dead family members in white shrouds and hire Shadow sorcerers to raise them as undead servants.

Knife seemed to be wondering the same thing. "Who is Pyram fighting?"

He played another card. "Their own. The three cities have finally finished their ancestors' work. The Trivestiture is complete."

Knife glanced over her shoulder at Gage and Robin—as if they had some sort of explanation—before returning her gaze to the stranger. "There's a civil war then? And you haven't taken a side?" She made a sound that could have been a laugh or just a discreet cough. "Let me guess: You're a fugitive, right? Hiding out in a decommissioned Arcania tower to get out of fighting."

"And you're an ugly bitch in a mask," the man said flatly, still focused on his game. "But you and your boys are free to join me if you like. Plenty of wine in the casks out there."

"If only. We need passage swiftly," Knife insisted. "I'm assuming the boy isn't out leading his armies on the field? Can I find the majest up in the city?"

"If you do, I reckon you'd pocket quite the bounty." He played another card before adding, "Nafir got himself usurped—some business with a gray priest and that creepy alchemist on his council. There was a wedding between him and some young lass that fancied herself the Child of Light, but seems like it didn't go well—not for the boy, that is."

"Anika?!" Gage stepped forward, heedless of Robin's hand tightening around his. He loosened his fingers and approached the table. "Was it Anika Lawson?"

He regarded Gage calmly, playing another card without looking at its destination. "I heard Voth, or something about her being a Drastil, but aye, Anika she was called—won't be forgetting that name."

"You saw her?" Visions of his sister flooded his mind now, breaking the dam he had been struggling to build. He was farther from her than he had ever been, but suddenly he felt like she was just within reach.

The card player nodded, finally pausing his game to regard the three of them properly. "Down in the Fathoms, that's where they had the wedding. Most of the nobles were down there. I only happened to be with the city watch at the time while my contact here arranged a job that would take us to Jath." His gaze shifted to Knife. "He said we'd be looking for some book for the Guild."

Gage looked at the Guildmaster, but the woman had no response to that.

"What happened to her?" Gage asked, turning back toward the man. "Did she marry him?"

He took a deep breath and a long drink before he spun the tale of Lekan Nafir's unforgettable wedding.

Jamira looked over the map of Karrane with the same exhausted disdain that she once regarded Anika Lawson with, back when the Child of Light was a prisoner of the previous majest.

An army of red-tipped pins marked the sites of battles, their numbers growing by the day, slowly making their way to her city. Much like every other day since the wedding, Jamira wondered just how she had gone from respected nomarch to wartime majest of Pyram, overseeing the largest civil war that the Joined Realms had likely ever seen.

Deep thunder rolled outside, building into a chest-rattling roar. With it came a gust of wind that threatened to pull the map from the heavy ornaments that pinned it by the corners on the table.

"Dear!" Stevra cried, rushing toward the open balcony doors. "The storm is waking again!" The halfling latched the two glass panes just as bright blue lightning split the unnaturally dark sky.

"It's the altar," Taliah said, for the nine-hundredth time. "It needs to be studied before what happened to Rathen happens here. And we can't study it unless we return to the Fathoms."

"You know we can't," Jamira said, pinching the bridge of her nose to keep the headache at bay. "Stevra. Wine, please. The Guyenese stuff."

"I will send for it," the halfling replied, hustling from the council chamber before Jamira's patience withered completely.

"This storm is not breaking," Taliah insisted. "We both heard what happened up north, with the storm and that business with the incarnates." She pushed herself away from the table and got to her feet, still moving awkwardly from her injuries. "Apologies, Majest, but the blasted Child of Light was to be married down there! We must see what it is!"

Jamira kept her eyes closed as she calmly instructed, "Do not call me that."

Taliah sighed. "Move past it, Kraiev. You were elected by all the survivors—accept it. You're the only one fit to lead Pyram through this."

"Through what?!" Jamira exploded, arms wide in aggressive anticipation. Lightning crashed outside again, as if responding to her rage. "What is it I'm leading us through? Nearly all of the city's fighting bodies are out in the desert answering for Lekan's failed gambit. Triune and Ithyra have likely fallen to the Shadow already—what else could explain their armies marching with basilisk, mummies, and gnolls?! And I can't even join the fighting because I'm expected to rule a city caught in a supernatural storm that seems to have no end!"

Taliah hung her head, having no answer to any of it. Thunder rolled again outside the exquisite glass that separated them from Eyen's fury.

"Maybe we can call her back?"

Jamira took a breath before asking, "Who?"

"The Child," Taliah replied, gazing up hesitantly. "We could send back that raven from Sathford. I told my chaplain to keep it in the rookery. We could ask her to come back and fix this."

"What do you suppose she could do?" Jamira asked, genuinely curious. The girl had fled the city by way of self-levitation after nearly dying upon that altar—what could possibly bring her back? "Her letter said she was studying at the spire, hoping to find answers to what that thing is. Don't you think if she had found something, she would have let us know immediately?"

"Look outside, Majest. See how dire things have gotten? Who

knows what those monsters are doing down there since we locked the Fathoms. What if they're the ones that summoned this storm and Anika could stop them? Maybe it's up to us to find something—but we won't be able to if we don't make the effort."

Jamira considered that for a long moment, wishing Stevra would hurry with the wine. She knew Taliah meant well, and there was plenty of wisdom in her suggestion. But Jamira was a soldier, a strategist. She thought about considerable losses, where strength would be needed versus a subtle approach (which she rarely believed in). The decision of whether they should open up the barricade between the city and the monsters that now prowled in the Fathoms—in the middle of a civil war, no less—seemed to be an easy one to Jamira the very first time Taliah had broached it.

Yet, here they were again, debating it yet again.

"I'm sorry, Taliah," she finally said. "We just can't risk doing that. One wrong move and the whole city could fall—if not to the creatures gathering around that stone down there, then perhaps by the riots that such a move could certainly cause. You see how divided the people are—surely you've noticed at worship! Last time I was at the chapel, Lekan's loyalists wouldn't even sit on the same side of the aisle as the Chambersworn." Jamira motioned to the harsh winds outside. "All we can do right now is weather the storm, at least until we secure the outer nomes."

The fire went out of Taliah then as another crash of lightning punctuated Jamira's argument. "I pray you're right, Majest. Because I don't know what else I or any of us can do now."

"You can let us down there."

Both women spun around toward the voice, but that corner of the chamber only held shadows. Jamira lunged toward the chair that held her sword, drawing it deftly and putting herself between the unseen threat and Pyram's only Lightmother. "Go, Taliah! Guards!"

The door to the chambers swung closed then, as if a gust of wind had blown through the closed windows.

"They won't hear you," the voice said again, coming from behind Jamira.

"It's the Shadow," Taliah breathed before the majest could respond.

A shape appeared then: a pale man in billowing black shrouds of smoke. His eyes were white slits and he wore a smug smile on his ghostly face.

"It's the answer to those prayers," the voice said again, but the man's lips didn't move. It was a woman, whispering from yet another direction of the chamber.

The Shadow spoke for him.

When the pale man's lips finally parted, he said, "My sister has sent me to free the city. Show me where the altar is."

CHAPTER NINETEEN

The Pyric Path

Melaine watched as the woman removed her rags. Despite the dire situation, there was a tenderness to the cultist's touch that reminded her of Deina. She turned away to watch the flickering light on the dirty wall, not wanting to soil her memories of the dwarf by allowing herself to take any hint of pleasure in this madness.

"Do you feel shame?"

She turned to the Combustress, who stood at the entrance to the small chamber.

"That the world can see your burns?" There was no mockery in the woman's voice, only curiosity.

"You think I care what the world sees?" Melaine looked down as the cultist gently pulled the last of the garments away, revealing the half-orc's muscled naked body. Her pale green flesh looked more human than orc in the flickering light, which somehow angered Melaine even more. It made her feel weak. "I have nothing to hide. I don't cower in crypts and abduct people for my own sick pleasures."

The young cultist who had removed Melaine's clothes got to her feet. The rags from the Vestige were folded neatly and carried in both hands like ceremonial offerings.

"You think this is for my pleasure?" The Combustress stepped forward. There was the slightest hint of anger in her voice now, but she kept her face as unreadable as ever. "Do you suppose any of this is by my design?"

Melaine held up her wrists, bound in oil-soaked rope. "Oh, I forgot. It was Wick that tied me up and forced me to kill my friend."

"No one is forcing you to do anything," she replied calmly. "Would you not have died without my help? None of this was by my own design. You and I are at the mercy of powers beyond our comprehension. All we can do is read the signs and follow the path, which is what we are allowing you to do here."

"You're insane," was all she could reply with. "Worse than any drunken doomsayer begging for a queen outside an alehouse, insisting you have all the answers." She tried to get up, but the ropes around her midsection kept her in the blackened chair. "Why don't you step on this Pyric Path with me, you bald, withered cunt-witch! I'll show you just how worthy I am!"

The Combustress didn't react; if anything, Melaine's outburst calmed her. She stared down at the half-orc, her eyes not avoiding any part of Melaine's exposed body. "I know you're worthy. Otherwise, you wouldn't be down here. As with Brace." She bowed slightly so that their eyes were level. "What I need to know is, which one of you is more worthy?"

Gnashing her teeth, Melaine tried to cool her rage, knowing it wouldn't sway this mad woman. "If you mean which of us is worthy of your indoctrination, neither of us. We won't join your cause, whatever it is."

"You know what it is."

Melaine flinched when she saw something flicker in the woman's golden eyes. As if she had peered into the cultist's maddened thoughts, a series of visions assaulted her.

The world burned in brilliant shades of ruby and gold. It was as if autumn itself had turned into a consuming entity, devouring all of existence.

Melaine didn't see it with her own eyes, but the absolute despair the vision brought was entirely hers to keep. Yet, it wasn't only dread she felt as she watched Stelmont, the Vestige, Sathford, Oakworth, Rathen, and Wickham all go up in flames; she also felt the undeniable truth that what she saw was real. The faith those fires seared into her heart was more real than anything else she had ever felt.

But she didn't actually *feel* it, not really. As she stared into those golden eyes that smoldered with a calm, calculated, patient hatred, Melaine knew she was somehow feeling the devotion Veronitha Blaithe felt for her cause.

"Now you know my name," the woman said, still unblinking. Her voice allowed Melaine to return to her own senses, not knowing if she had actually spoken the name aloud.

But did that matter? It seemed this woman had the power to meld minds, share thoughts, and inflict faith.

"It means nothing to me," Melaine told her. It was true, but she doubted that fact would survive long. Something told her that the name would somehow be one of their undoings.

"What do any of them mean?" She straightened as two hooded figures entered the chamber, their singed robes sweeping small arcs into the sooty stone floor. "None of our names will survive Wick's rebirth. Like a phoenix, he will rise from the ashes to reduce the world to cinders." She motioned toward Melaine with a slight jerk of her head; the cultists moved to untie the naked half-orc. "And only his burned children will remain to inherit his new kingdom."

Melaine watched in shocked silence as the cultists began to unbind her from the rickety chair. They left the oiled ropes joining her wrists, but she was allowed to stand.

The Combustress smiled again—a sour, crooked grin that reflected the absolute loathing that Melaine felt for her. "The Pyric Path awaits."

"The what?!"

Brace covered his manhood the best that he could. It wasn't modesty so much as ingrained propriety that compelled him—the cultist escorting him was a gnome, and her eyesight was fixed at an unfortunate height.

"The Pyric Path," she repeated. Her face was shrouded under the hood, so he couldn't really tell where she was looking, but he kept himself covered regardless—even though she had already seen all of him during the cleansing.

"Is that where you expect me to kill the half-orc?"

"You could let her kill you if you think she would serve Wick better." She made the suggestion almost boringly, talking of life and death as if they were meal options. "My husband let me kill him when we walked the Path, because he knew his own faith was fragile." She pulled up one of her tattered sleeves to reveal burns from her wrist up to her shoulder. "He couldn't even pass the first test, which both of you have already done."

"How so?" He knew the answer before he finished the question, but he hoped to stall this woman as long as possible. *Maybe I can distract her until the others come back*, he thought to himself. *None of them look like fighters. Though, if they're Wickan priests, they could likely summon fire.*

Looking down to his ruined body, he lost any desire to fight his way out of the place. But he also refused to even consider killing Melaine.

"Your burns," the gnome said, reaching a small hand out to feel the angry, knotted flesh around his waist. Her touch was delicate, tender, and it caused him to jerk away lest he become aroused. A woman hadn't touched him properly since last year in Merithian, and she had charged him handsomely for the comfort.

"You are already worthy to tread the Path," she continued, unbothered by him stepping away. Pulling her hands together, she turned back toward the open doorway where candlelight flickered down the hall. "Most prospects must endure Wick's trial before they step foot on the Path. It is a great honor to walk the Kindler's Hall on your first visit."

"Visit?" Brace scoffed, allowing himself an absurd chuckle. "Is that what this is? A visit?"

She didn't answer, only left the chamber on silent feet. Looking around the empty room, Brace saw nothing he could fashion into a weapon—certainly not with his wrists bound by oil-soaked rope.

He followed his gracious host to the Pyric Path.

Ransil stared into the blade, remembering the first time he had held it. He had less hair on his cheeks back then (and maybe less stomach hanging over his belt), but he had already become a broken, tired old man in a young halfling's body, thanks to the betrayal tied to Embrance.

Veronitha had tried to hide the dagger from him when Ransil tracked her down in Caim; she had used her mother's tragedy as some kind of shield against Ransil's anger.

But he had earned that anger. No amount of grief or sadness gave a person the right to turn someone into a monster. And that was what Veronitha Blaithe had done to Ransil.

"Is that what you've been hiding?"

Ransil concealed his surprise as best he could, annoyed that Anika had once again snuck up on him. *Surely it's magic*, he thought, but kept the suspicion to himself.

"I didn't realize I was hiding anything" he said, not turning from the object. "We found it together, Ani. Remember?"

"You know what I mean," she said, sounding every bit a sulky teenager. She walked toward the table in the middle of the High

Mage's study where Embrance rested atop an open tome. "You clearly knew a piece of Kindler had been used to forge a new weapon. Were you not drawn to it?"

That notion hadn't occurred to him. "Maybe I was," he replied honestly, unsure. "But I haven't seen this thing in over fifteen years—hadn't even thought of it since settling down in Blakehurst." He took a deep breath. "It's a part of my life that I've tried to forget."

Anika knelt down before the short table so she was of a height with Ransil. "When I was a prisoner in Pryam, they took Stormender from me. But I could always feel it—like it was calling to me. If it had been in a cave in some other realm, I know I would have found it eventually." Her voice softened slightly. "Do you not think it was the same for you?"

"I didn't come by this thing the same way you came by Stormender, Ani. Back in Oakworth, when you... This isn't the same thing. This dagger isn't rightly mine—I didn't make it."

"Well, then who did?"

Ransil turned from her, not wanting to revisit his buried past right now. "Shouldn't we be preparing for Rathen?"

"We leave in the morning, Ransil. Stop this."

He turned to her, confused. "Stop what?"

"This!" She rose suddenly, motioning to the dagger. "You've been hiding something since I woke up. You don't think I can tell?! For someone who used to be called Ruse, you're not much of a swindler. And I *know* you're not a liar." She smiled slightly. "At least not with me."

Ransil realized then that she did know about his deceit. Only, she was wrong about what he was hiding from her. Now he was faced with a dilemma: lie to her and let her believe that this whole time he had been trying to hide the existence of this blasphemous blade tied to his past, or be honest with her and reveal that her brother had likely been lost to the Shadow.

Or just continue his pathetic charade.

As if reading his mind, Anika added, "Haven't we always been honest with each other?"

Ransil looked over at Embrance, wondering if maybe the truth about the blade might distract Anika from his other secret at least.

"It was forged by Veronitha Blaithe, using a keyshard that I stole for her back in the Acreage."

"Why'd you steal it for her? Was she your friend?"

Ransil chuckled. "No, I hardly knew her. It was Grip that actually tricked me into stealing it, but then I duped her and gave it to Veronitha."

"Why?"

"Because," Ransil whispered, his mind fading to the past. "I thought it's what my mother would have wanted."

"My mother always said I was destined to burn bright," the disembodied voice said as Melaine walked naked toward the torch. "She said I would guide those who didn't know the way."

The chanting on either side of Melaine made her unsure if the shadows hid rows of cultists instead of just old stone walls, but she did not stray from the path to find out. Something told her that leaving the narrow strip of light would be worse than facing whatever waited for her at the end of the path. But maybe that was because she was still humoring herself that her and Brace could escape this place alive, together.

"I can show you the way," the Combustress continued, her voice now just above a whisper in Melaine's mind. "Just as my mother showed me the way and Wick's false prophet showed her. I will lead you toward your chance to prove your conviction—"

"What conviction?!" Melaine shouted, sick of this game. "I'm no zealot! I renounce Wick! Show yourself, coward, and I'll spill plenty of blood, if that's what you seek!"

"You know I don't."

Melaine kept walking toward the light, despite not wanting to give this madwoman what she desired. Her skin was riddled with goosebumps from the chill in the hall, her nipples tight, painful rocks. She walked toward the simple promise of warmth.

Perhaps that's all it is, Melaine thought, wanting to laugh. Maybe the Combustress had legions of devoted followers who only wanted a moment's reprieve from the crypt chill running through this cursed hall.

Regardless, she closed the distance between herself and that fucking torch, imagining that Deina would be waiting beyond it with her thick, powerful arms wide open.

"She was a warrior," Ransil said, eyes fixed on something far beyond the enchanted dagger. Anika had never heard his voice sound so...meek. "She defeated the Red Renegade before I was born." He looked up at her. "Did you ever hear about him? Larasyn Melth?"

Anika shook her head.

He returned his gaze to the dagger. "He stole that keyshard from the Arcania—claimed it was his family's heirloom, way back before the Keyguard was broken."

"My father said the Keyguard never actually disbanded," Anika replied, unsure if it was at all relevant.

Ransil just nodded. "It's up for debate, I suppose. Anyway, Larasyn was a lunatic—wanted to burn the world down so it could be rebuilt. There were two villages south of Hambury that he turned to ruin back then—never rebuilt, just ashen fields where nothing grows anymore."

Anika felt a strange heat rise within her, as if she were drawing Wick's power from the blade. It took her a moment to realize that it was just her own anger. *Curious*, she thought, narrowing her eyes on Ransil's cursed weapon.

"The first Aberheim was a staunch supporter of the Arcania," Ransil said, "and the idea of a rogue wizard breaking the Oath of Sorcery infuriated him. So he put a bounty on the Red Renegade. He would have likely sent his own armies after him, but there was trouble along the Wane Coast back when Velcarthe had designs on Vale, so it was up to the mercenaries to deal with Melth."

"Your mother was a mercenary?" That was a strange notion to Anika.

But Ransil shook his head. "She was a paladin. An old one," he added, waving his hand in the general direction of the new cathedral being raised. "Not one of the Luminaura. She was devoted to Wick, even when it wasn't in fashion."

"Wasn't that forbidden?"

He shook his head again. "Not in Westerra. The old temples stood alongside the Luminaura's new churches for a time. I was raised to light the five candles before bed, at least that's what my father tells me. I was too young to remember much about my mother before this fucking stone got her killed."

As Brace neared the torch, it took everything within him to resist reaching out for it to pull the flickering light toward him. He felt his balls desperately seeking the warmth of his bowels as the eerie chill became freezing pinpricks across his bare flesh.

This cold is unnatural, he thought. A foolish notion, he realized, considering how unnatural all of this seemed. The shadows on either side of the path undulated and reached for him, driving him to panic. But his soldier's discipline kept him from blindly fumbling for the fire.

His faith was never strong to begin with, but Brace couldn't even remotely feel the Light in this place. He felt more alone than he ever had, despite the creepy whispers that would not relent.

Finally, he reached for the torch, unable to take any more. But he stopped when he saw...

Even in the thick darkness, he could still see the oil-soaked rope wrapped around his wrists. If he got that near the flames, his arms would go up in a blaze. He moved his arms into the faint light from the fire; it traced the crooked grooves of the burns that already covered his muscled arms. He'd likely lose all his flesh if he let even a tiny spark near all that oil.

"Be not afraid," the Combustress said, her voice nearly driving Brace to his knees. It sounded as if she were leaning over his shoulder, shouting in a clawing whisper. "The fire is your salvation, just as it was mine."

He heard a roar behind him. Turning, he saw something melt from the shadows: a gaping maw with narrow lantern eyes searing into him.

"The darkness consumes," she continued, her voice a mocking, threatening, diseased worm boring into Brace's mind. "It is doubt that binds your wrists, feeding you to the Shadow."

Brace turned away from the monstrosity taking shape behind him, focusing on the torch that was now within his grasp.

"The oil is life for us all, Brace."

He took another step forward, entering the circle of light around the torch to see two levers on either side of a door. Just by looking at them, he knew that they would open the only way out of the dark hallway.

The dark-borne monster let out a guttural roar—it was within pouncing distance now, Brace could tell.

He looked down at the ruined flesh on his arms, glistening with sacred oil. The only way he would be able to open the door would be to plunge his wrists into the fire once again. If the rope was burning, he could maybe free his hands and open the door to escape the monster in time to put his burning arms out.

"Fire can't burn alone."

Brace closed his eyes and saw the memory of his father pressing the red keyshard into his unburned palm. Something like conviction was born from that image—not like the duty he felt toward the Light when he swore himself to the Luminaura. This was more primal, intimate.

This was life and death.

When the monster roared again, Brace screamed just as loud. Tears blurred his vision as he thrust both fists into the fire, feeling its icy fingers unfurl across his oiled flesh.

Howling in agony, he pulled his arms apart with every fiber of his strength. The ropes gave way and Brace grabbed either lever with his fiery fists, thrusting downward.

The door opened to reveal—

"I don't know if I'll ever learn the truth of what happened, Ani." Ransil picked up Embrance with both hands. "But I know that my mother died for this damn thing, and we cannot let Veronitha have it—for whatever she wants to use it for."

"But she left it in a cave…" Anika struggled to understand how the thing could be so important if the Combustress would have left it behind. "Would she really leave a weapon behind if she intended to use it?"

Ransil looked at her coldly. "It's not the weapon she wants." He nodded toward her own knife sheathed at her hip. "If someone wanted that piece of Skythe you used to make Stormender, imagine the ritual that would be required to unmake the thing."

She wants the shard, Anika thought, realizing that Ransil Osbury already knew who the next incarnate would be the whole time.

She clenched her fists as she regarded the little man, feeling waves of raw fury flowing into her from the dagger. It took everything she had not to scream at him, but that feeling quickly passed when she saw the tear stream down the halfling's cheek.

Instead of strangling the man, she knelt down and embraced him. The simmering rage melted into a warm comfort.

—the Shadow.

Melaine recoiled, waving her arms frantically as if she could somehow shed the flames. Despite the agony, she had enough sense to dodge the black mists that took the form of a giant maw, snapping at her with insubstantial teeth.

Turning, she saw an identical giant mouth yawning toward her, looking to swallow its burning meal whole. Melaine screamed and shouldered past the thing into the awaiting chamber. The fire enveloping her arms, clawing its way up to her shoulders, made her heedless of any other death that lay in wait. She only wanted to be free of the burning.

"Only blood can sate them," a calm whisper in her mind instructed. As if the words guided her vision, Melaine turned to see a gleaming curved knife resting atop an altar in the center of the small chamber. Several candles gave just enough light to keep the hungry shadows at bay. Feeling her skin crackle and smolder, Melaine sprinted toward the weapon, her bare feet slapping frantically on the cold stone floor.

Just as she was about to reach the knife, with no idea whose blood she could even draw with the thing, another form burst from the cloud of darkness in front of her. It was as if there was a curtain of shadow just beyond the altar, and Brace Cobbit burst through it with both his burning arms reaching desperately for the knife.

"No!" Melaine screamed, certain in that moment that Brace had already been forcefully indoctrinated by the woman that had so enraptured him since the Vestige. Memories of Deina flashed through Melaine's mind as she watched Brace's flaming, blackened fist grab the knife. She could almost taste the dwarf's firm, luscious lips as the flames now consuming her shoulder lashed at her own mouth.

In that final moment, as Brace knocked the altar over and raised the knife up to kill her, Melaine managed to smile.

At least she would die without giving in to this mad woman—she would not play her sick, twisted game.

That thought died, though, when Brace stopped suddenly in front of her, frozen by some horrid realization.

The sound of cooking flesh, snapping shadows, and whispering cultists fell silent then. And Melaine could only stare into Brace's wild eyes as he said, "Don't let her have my father's shard."

In a flash, he raised the knife upward at an angle. Brace's aim was perfect: he buried the blade into his neck so the fountain of blood sprayed over Melaine in a healing mist.

She tried to scream—not in pain, but in absolute horror. Brace's naked body swayed grotesquely as he tried to keep his head upright, aiming his body's lifeblood toward his companion. But the strength left him before Melaine could reach him with her sizzling hands.

While her arms were blackened with cracked flesh, they were free from any sort of pain as she held Brace's dying form in her lap. His blood soothed her limbs as much as it agonized her spirit.

Dozens of pairs of hands came to soothe her anguish, and she had no energy to strike them away.

Besides, with each cultist that touched her, a small patch of her seared flesh fell away to reveal a fresh layer of pale green skin, as if she were being reborn.

A new faith invaded her mind then.

And her will to fight was gone.

CHAPTER TWENTY

Changing of the Guard

Waurane upheld her end of the deal, which assured Reston once more that the wood elves were not above the primal desire for revenge—it could only be the desire for vengeance that Waurane would give up her boat and let them raid the hidden depths of the Elmery. He smiled proudly as he paced down the length of the table, which contained every piece of Lefayra's mythical treasury that he had personally helped accumulate during his younger years.

"How have all these been here?" Geneva asked in a whisper. The three of them were alone now, and Reston could tell that the two elves felt like children abandoned in a sweetshop.

"The Eldercrowns refused to fully acknowledge the Keyguard," Reston explained, his eyes moving from one enchanted artifact to the next. "But that did not mean they were not trusted allies. And while many of my fellow Guards had offered to store our findings in Menevere, Andelor, Nazurik, or any of the free cities, none of those places were as safe as here." He peered over his shoulder at Lexeth and Geneva, both of whom looked unable to take their eyes from the displayed treasures. "Do you really think all those Waywards were placed in Lohkrest just to protect your elven kin? You all have bows for that, eh?"

Neither of them chuckled with Reston.

"So, what are the terms?" Lexeth finally looked away from an ivory longbow affixed with two small amber keyshards, setting his gaze on Reston. "Waurane did not explain the specifics around my release. Are we to find proof of who killed the Eldercrowns?"

Instead of answering, Reston nodded back toward the bow. "Does that one call out to you, Lex?"

The elf returned his gaze to the weapon before asking, "What do you mean?"

"Reston," Geneva interrupted. "What is this? Can you skip through any of your riddles and get to why we're down here? Why were the Eldercrowns hiding this vault from all of us?"

"That one is called Heathener," Reston said, ignoring the question. "I never quite understood why, but it's blessed by Syrina." He laughed again. "Or cursed, I supposed."

"Reston," Geneva began again, her tone losing its patience.

"You both are to escort me to the Green Lake," he finally explained. "Waurane has given me leave to borrow her boat so that I can go to Guyen by river. It is a journey I don't mean to return from, given these old bones, but it is one that I must take if the Keyguard is to save this world from itself."

Lexeth and Geneva shared a look before turning their doubtful gazes back to Reston. He continued before they could question him further.

"Then, you both are to track those gnolls to the west on behalf of the Keyguard. Those dogs would not have been able to infiltrate Lefayra and slaughter the Eldercrowns without the help of some other force. It is up to you to find out who or what that force was."

"Are you not the last of the Keyguard?" Lexeth asked, stepping toward Reston. "Why would this task not fall to you? Come with us."

"I cannot," Reston said. "I am too old to be an active member of the Keyguard anymore. That rests with you two—which is why Waurane has given me leave to equip you both with proper instruments." He motioned to the satin-covered table covered with enchanted knives, swords, bows, axes, daggers, rings, staves, and various other armaments.

"Are you saying we're both members of the Keyguard?" Geneva asked, her eyes fixed on a pair of Myrethan hatchets.

"Don't sound so excited," Reston teased, "I'm still the senior member, and I can be quite intolerable to work for." He grabbed a long staff tipped with a sizable ruby, which trailed a fiery aura as he straightened it and tapped the floor with the other end of it. "And once I'm dead, you'll have to answer to that fucking grouch, Bennik Lawson."

The journey south to the Green Lake was a familiar trek for Geneva. However, the winding paths of Lohkrest felt completely different with her new weapons. She carried the twin daughters of Myretha in either hand—Brecka and Mara. The keyshards embedded in the weapons were identical: ashen-brown, veined with streaks of dusty gold. Unlike the gleaming keyshards tied to the other old gods, the essence of the stone goddess was bound in jagged chips of living earth.

Geneva liked the ruggedness of them. And though she had lived her life so closely tied to Oakus—like so many of the wood elves—the stories of Myretha, who carried an eternal growing child in her belly, always resonated with her. Perhaps it was because of her own inability to have children.

Her eyes wandered to Lexeth, who gently guided Reston by the elbow through the thicket, the old man grumbling as he always did. The sight made Geneva both sad and content. Her partner was such a gentle, loving spirit who would have made the ideal father to any number of children they might have had together.

But after the accident, she would never be able to become pregnant—her belly would never swell with life as Myretha's did in so many depictions of the old goddess. And Lexeth refused to sire kin with anyone else, despite Geneva's flexibility on that matter.

Was that why Reston had secretly chosen the two of them—from all the other qualified wood elves in Lefayra—to join his order? Two young warriors with no offspring to tie them down? She continued pondering such questions until they reached the final Wayward that marked the end of their safe passage.

"Stay alert," Lexeth whispered over his shoulder, nodding toward a break in the copse ahead. Geneva saw scorched brambles and large pawprints.

Gnolls.

In almost immediate response, a low growl came before rustling on either side of them.

The creatures were waiting for them.

"Do we go back?" Geneva whispered. She spun Brecka and Mara, preparing for an ambush.

"Fuck that," Reston growled, using his fiery staff to haul himself out of Lexeth's grasp. "Those wards are falling, I know you can feel it as much as I can. These bastards are here for those keyshards you carry—mine too. Let's give 'em what they came for."

Lexeth nocked an arrow and drew his new bow, the orange cat-eyes piercing through the misty haze of the woods, hungry for prey. Nearly a dozen sets of other eyes—bestial, filled with infernal hatred—appeared in response, as if Heathener had revealed them, awakened them like candles in the dark. Several of the monsters howled, striking up a chain of similar cries that encircled the border of the Waywards.

"We hold them here," Reston commanded. "Consider this your initiation. Allow not one of these wretches to breach your borders again."

Lexeth took that as an invitation to begin the skirmish, unleashing a missile that left an orange streak in its wake as it disappeared into the trees. A pitiful yelp told Geneva it had found its mark.

Chaos erupted.

The trees spewed out waves of ravenous gnolls, many of which carried clubs that burst into flame once their wielder appeared from the leaves. Geneva slipped around a great oak tree, planting her foot on its trunk on the opposite side so she could launch herself into the fray. She heard at least three more arrows from Lexeth's bow meet their marks one after the other, and Reston's maniacal laughter told her the old man was holding his own with that staff of his. She focused on her own fight, which pitted her against four savage beasts that came at her in a mass of furry appendages wielding crude torches which left streaming cinders in their wake.

Geneva easily dodged their attacks, bringing her hatchets down into two different skulls, one after the other. A brief moment of panic came over her when she realized Brecka wouldn't come free of the skull it had split, the gnoll's body nearly wrenching the weapon from her grip when it crumpled to the forest floor. But one of the gnolls that came to avenge its companion flew backward with a Syrinic arrow jammed into its throat, and the other one lost its head when Mara came up in a wide, outward arc.

The battle only lasted a few more breaths, with Lexeth's rapid shots making short work of the more cowardly gnolls that hung back in the trees to fling burning brands at the three travelers. Geneva caught sight of Reston holding his staff at his side with both hands, unleashing a torrent of fire into a trio of gnolls that almost looked excited to let the flames envelop them.

However, the sound of their dying was more than unpleasant.

They're possessed, she thought, feeling almost no remorse as she swung both of her hatchets in a downward strike to sever both arms of her last attacker—the horrid thing continued to try to attack with his snapping maw before she brought her leg around in a devastating kick that forced the gnoll to the ground so she could end it properly.

"These things travel in packs," Reston said between heaving breaths. "We should keep moving—don't want to draw the next lot to the same site. Waurane says the west Waywards are already compromised from the buggers slashing and burning trees in their wake. Best thing we can do is lead them toward the lake and let Lunath's archers help keep them at bay."

Lexeth nodded to Geneva before slinging his bow back over his shoulder and helping Reston move through the thicket.

Geneva spared one last look at the dead bodies, her thoughts wandering back to the ruins of Rathen. She would die before she let that happen to Lefayra. But how could she stop it if she were being pulled away from the only home she had ever known?

Lexeth scouted ahead during the last stretch of their journey. Night wasn't far, but there was plenty of light from the moonwell trees, whose leaves bloomed in late summer and shone brightly until winter with all the moonlight they had trapped throughout the warmer months. The short structures of Lunath were in sight.

Turning back toward his companions, he could see Geneva's eyes through the faint light of the trees. He gave her the scout signs that would tell her the passage was clear and he was pressing forward. She nodded as she guided the old man to follow.

The banks of the Green Lake were teeming with wildlife: deer that showed no fear of their elven kin, rabbits that perked their ears up at Lexeth's passage without scampering away, and other carefree critters. It seemed the invaders hadn't poisoned this place yet. That gave Lexeth a small sense of relief, but until Reston Mauer was safely aboard Waurane's craft, well on his way to Guyen or wherever in the Joined Realms he needed to be, Lexeth would not let himself become too comfortable.

Lunath was a small settlement that used to be the site of the first wood elf city—what would eventually become Lefayra before the first Eldercrowns ordered their seats be moved farther north, where they said the heart of the forest resided.

Despite the settlement's unremarkable architecture compared to his home, Lexeth always had a fondness for Lunath. Maybe it was because he was named after Lunath's husband, the first Eldercrown of Lohkrest. Whatever it was, he couldn't help but smile as he neared the gates.

"You're lucky my sister didn't put an arrow in your eye."

Lexeth smiled wider as he turned to face his old friend, who silently slipped to the forest floor from the trees above. "With her aim? There are more pressing fears in these woods lately."

"You can say that," Kurn replied, the swirling tattoos on his bald head reflecting the moonpetals. "Hope you put any fires out on your way down—these fucking gnolls…"

"Lexeth?!"

Kurn's sister, Treesa, was next to leap down from the thicket above. Proving her brother a liar yet again, she carried no bow, just her favored knives at her hips. She moved swiftly to embrace him with a painful hug.

"What's it been, a year?" She pushed him away suddenly, gripping his shoulders to regard him with a serious expression. "We were so sorry to hear about your sister…"

He nodded sadly, peering over his shoulder to see how close Reston and Geneva were. "Yes, she will be deeply missed. But that's sort of why we're here…"

"We?" Kurn spun around to see Lexeth's companions. "Belated honeymoon, Genny?"

Once the elves got him settled on the boat, Reston allowed himself a moment of much-needed contemplation. He watched the still waters of the Green Lake, trying not to listen to the low voices of Lexeth, Geneva, and their sibling friends. The shipwright didn't bother Reston, she just focused on preparing the vessel for its long journey.

Longer than they realize, Reston thought, more sadly than he had expected. This trip was certainly a long time coming, but could anything truly prepare a man for his last journey?

He rested the staff across his weary lap. The scorched length of wood that had been his dear friend's seemed the proper companion for the voyage. The Red Renegade may have been dead, but Reston could still feel Larasyn's spirit imbued in the weapon. He ran his gnarled fingers down its length, remembering all the times he had tried to convince his colleague that he had looked too deep into the fire.

You were never good at listening, Melth, Reston whispered morosely. He didn't wipe away the tear that followed the groove of wrinkles around his eye.

"Pardon?" The shipwright stopped her work, looking up at him with a half-coiled rope in her hands.

"I trust Waurane's instructions are clear?" He kept his eyes on the staff, remembering Larasyn Melth for the man he had been, not the twisted monster his faith in Wick had driven him to be. "This craft shall not be returning."

"Yes," the woman said stiffly, returning to her work. He could tell she did not approve of the instructions, and he felt a certain amount of guilt at the thought of depriving her of such a remarkable vessel. But some things had to be done properly. "You do know how to guide this through the rapids? The waters can get a bit rough on the way out of the woods, just before it splits at Hammerdale Falls."

I'll be long past caring at that point, he thought with a smirk. But he just said, "Aye, lass. I'm looking forward to a little excitement."

She snorted a laugh as she finished her work.

"You sure you don't want us to come along?"

Reston turned to see Lexeth standing at the shoreline with his lovely wife.

I choose them well, he thought, admiring how the young elves looked with their sharded weapons. He gripped his own in a futile effort to pull his own youth back from the clutches of uselessness. But it was only a passing notion—he had accepted this fate a long time ago.

And there was a certain comfort to it now—now that his work was mostly done.

"You have a quest before you both that is far more important than watching me heave your fine elven cuisine over the edge of this little boat." He motioned back toward Lunath. "You're to track those bastards westward, looking for their master. Look for any Wickan priests or shardthieves that favor a bit of fire." He raised a finger. "But most importantly, find Bennik Lawson. He's in charge now. I'm too old for all of this, and whether he admits to it or not, he knows the way things should go. He is the Keeper now."

The two elves shared a look as the shipwright finished her work and took her leave.

"Go on now," Reston said, getting to his feet so he could shove off before changing his mind on any of this. "We all have places to be."

"Until we meet again, Reston Mauer," Lexeth said in that proper way that wood elves spoke when any type of ceremony could be carried out. "May the moon guide you back to us."

"Thank you for bringing him back to me," Geneva added, giving the old man a smile that could warm his grave until bones were all that remained of him.

He nodded, turning before they could see his tears. "Go on now. We're all that's left of the Keyguard, and the world needs us."

He used Melth's staff that was once known throughout Vale as Ruiner to push the small boat away from the elegant dock. He didn't look back at the elves, keeping his nearly blind eyes focused on the glowing haze ahead.

There were sounds from Lunath behind him, calls from Lexeth and Geneva, and the strumming of several harpists that made his departure melancholic and proper.

He waited until he was consumed by the mist of the Green Lake before he lay down one final time. As he ignited Ruiner and used his feet to kick the bundle of straw out of his pack, he spoke the words that he had practiced since long before he knew what they actually meant.

"In darkness we die to give others the light. In Wick I confer, by his flame I will rest. Let my ashes be the path so those who follow are not lost. Your flames are not mine to keep, only to carry until it consumes me..."

He exhaled the fire from Ruiner, wondering if Melth could have done the same in the end, or if the coward made someone else do it.

Reston reminded himself that the Keyguard could only exist if he weren't around to fuck it up again. That thought was the only thing that allowed him to keep his legs still as the excruciating fire took hold.

He knew this was the only way he could truly show Bennik the truth about the Light.

He only hoped the bastard would listen to the flames when the time came.

For the sake of his Children.

For the sake of the world.

Reston Mauer lay still as Wick devoured him, finding peace in the fact that he wouldn't have to see Guyen again.

He hated the swamps, ever since that one mosquito feasted on his balls.

The last thing he heard was his own laughter, wry and deeply satisfied.

CHAPTER TWENTY-ONE

Growing Desperate

Bennik awoke with a start, pushing himself desperately away from the campfire. Fainly peered over at him with a raised eyebrow, his wild white hair sticking out in all directions around the sides of his head. Darkness surrounded them.

"Did the warmth disturb your slumber, Lawson?"

Bennik rubbed his eyes, realizing it had all been a dream—the boat, the fire, the sensation of watching his own flesh crackle and split like roasted mutton. It had likely just been his mind running wild with the idea that gnolls now roamed throughout Vale, openly burning whatever they pleased. And here they were, sleeping out in the open.

Already his company had encountered two separate bands of the monsters, each group setting fire to a different homestead. Grip had sighted them both while scouting, so they were able to make quick work of them. Bennik regretted not taking up either offer from the farmers they rescued; he knew they needed to make haste, but sleeping in a barn suddenly felt like a welcome alternative to their current camp.

"Guess I'm developing an aversion to the heat," he replied, giving the gnome a weak smile. "The hearth had burned down before I knocked off." He looked over to see Jak and Claudia still on their watch, walking the perimeter of their little camp, tucked inside the edge of the Steddlewood's tree line. There was no sign of Grip.

"Yeah, well, I can still spark a fire," Fainly said, warming his hands. "Despite this lingering ache in my noggin from breaking you out of that cell, it seems I still have some use."

Bennik sat up, knowing it would be useless to try to get back to sleep—that dream had been more than disturbing, and he'd rather deal with a groggy day than revisit the sensation of being burned alive. "How long do you think it will be until you're back to how you were?"

Fainly closed his eyes in obvious annoyance, making Bennik regret the question. However, the gnome spoke calmly. "I need the feysleep.

I don't know if I'll be able to properly get over this...whatever this is. It's all new to me. Perhaps it's tied to the Old Ways, or maybe these incarnates are infecting the very threads of magic itself. Whatever it is, I have more limits than I'm used to, and it's not the best time for that sort of obstacle."

"You could say that again," Bennik replied, absently watching Jak and Claudia laugh about something in the distance. The two halfling girls were snoring peacefully beside him, oblivious to the entire world carrying on around them, with all of its compounding problems. Bennik couldn't help but think of his own children, out there wrapped up in the cruel prophecy that had separated them, pitting them against one another.

"Tell me about Oakworth," he said, hoping to divert his mind from despair. "You said we'd find the scions there."

"I said that's where we'd find the scions," Fainly corrected. "Whether or not any of them are physically there remains to be seen. But Ruke found her stone in the depths beneath that town and— though I haven't seen it myself—I suspect the altar is there."

"An altar?"

Fainly turned toward him with a raised eyebrow. "*The* altar. The source of Oakus' power."

Bennik just stared at the gnome, waiting for more—he could tell there was plenty the little man wanted to say on the matter.

"Where do you think the keyshards came from, Lawson?"

Knowing full well this was some kind of trap, Bennik played along. "The Purveyors. When they brought the old gods low, they shattered the Keys of Transience, along with any relics or altars associated with the gods."

Fainly scoffed, turning back toward the fire. Bennik saw shapes in those flames, faces from his past, but he didn't disclose that to the Archmage. "That's what the stories want you to believe," Fainly explained. "But the truth is, those Keys of Transience were just pieces of a greater whole. The essences of the old gods once had a physical presence in this world in the form of huge stones." He glanced back at Bennik with a sly grin. "Imagine giant keyshards, if you will. Massive precious stones that the original keyshards were chipped from. Back then, many quested for a piece of these altars. It was said only the most worthy could chip a piece of an altar away to create a keyshard, and that single piece contained a miniscule fragment of the associated old god's powers."

Bennik wondered why he had never heard this tale. Naturally, he was skeptical of Fainly Lopke, as it seemed very in character for the man to create some elaborate lie just to make a fool of someone who wasn't as studied as him. Regardless, Bennik was intrigued and listened intently in case it pertained to his children.

"I suppose it was believable enough," the gnome offered with a dismissive wave of his hand. "As far as explanations go. People seek reasons, so if something is even remotely believable, we are eager to accept it, right? Well, every object tied to an old god suddenly exploding during the Unthroning makes for a much more exciting tale. In truth, the keyshards were always just that—shards from the altars."

Bennik felt a weightlessness in his chest, a sensation that could only be attributed to the feeling of loss—the loss of what he once understood to be fact.

Fainly seemed to sense the man's discomfort, smiling wickedly by the light of the campfire. "You're asking yourself if I'm serious, aren't you?"

"I've never heard anything about such altars," Bennik said flatly. "Altars are things that people make to worship the gods, not the other way around. If what you say is true, I'd ask why you didn't think to mention this sooner. Or why people weren't still questing for such altars."

Fainly shrugged. "It's a fair question, and one that I would expect from one of Reston Mauer's pupils. However, not even Reston knew about the altars. There aren't many that do. Because the altars have been nothing more than colorful hunks of rock since the Unthroning. All of their power had been given back to the world thanks to the Purveyors of Light, siphoning the gods out of their cradles on behalf of some madman's prophecies."

"Stane."

Bennik hardly ever spoke the name aloud. Even now, secluded in the woods with a bright fire and reliable companions, the name filled him with an indefinable dread. He was hardly a man of faith, but had he believed in the power of salvation through a divine being, he was certain that Stane would somehow stand in clear opposition to that; more so than the Shadowlords themselves. After what he had heard from Kartha—and seen with his own eyes in the ruins of Arkath—Bennik was even more certain that Stane represented true evil in the world.

As if reading his mind, Fainly turned away from the fire as he explained, "I've been thinking of our time in Arkath—what Kartha divulged to us. We glimpsed behind a curtain that so many scholars have dedicated their lives to simply proving the existence of. There are hundreds—maybe thousands—of books written about Stane, but never has it been posited that he sought to father a messiah. I mean, I had my own suspicions, of course, but that realization made me wonder…"

The gnome had begun pacing in front of the fire, but now stopped to stare at Bennik. "What if it wasn't Stane who orchestrated the Unthroning? What if it was Kartha?"

As shocking of a suggestion as it seemed, Bennik couldn't sort that one out. It was surprising that the notion wasn't presented before, considering Kartha was the only one who could read the text. "Why would she want to help Stane?" Bennik asked. "She knew he cursed her daughter, ruined her home."

"Precisely," Fainly replied, holding a stubby finger up. "It would seem a scorned woman might go to great lengths for revenge. What if the Unthroning was a blow against Stane, disguised as his will? It's said he was banished to the Abyss, and something had to be in place to keep him there. That's how it works, right?" He pointed his finger back into the Steddlewood. "Those numbskulls at the Vestige locked us up and those damn blackiron bars kept us banished. It seems to me, most likely the altars are what once kept Stane banished—if we assume the old gods were truly channeled during the banishment."

"So what would drawing their power into lesser stones do?" Bennik asked, not sure he even remotely followed the gnome's epiphany. "Would draining the altars of their power make it easier or harder for Stane to escape the Abyss?"

Fainly made an annoyed face and waved the question away. "I don't even think that's what all of this is about. Whether Stane's trapped in the Abyss, walking the world, or back where he belongs in the Nethering, his will can still be worked—he is inevitable in that way. He's always been a part of Aetha in one form or another. But what is telling is how the old gods have responded to all of this. With their powers all spread throughout the world in the form of the keyshards, they'd likely want that power back—back in their altars."

It wasn't lost on Bennik that they were on their way toward one of these altars, drawn there as if by some strange twist of fate. "So you're saying we're carrying out the will of Oakus by convening at his altar? Or would it be Stane's will?"

Fainly's eyes were distant, twinkling in the firelight. "That's the thing, isn't it, Bennik?" His eyes focused on him, the corners of his mouth pulling away in a wry grin. "What if they're one and the same?"

The Fathoms echoed with the sounds of war. It wasn't the large-scale military campaign being carried out on the desert sands of Karrane above ground; this was an underworld slaughter.

Gage slipped from shadowy alcoves to darkened recesses, slitting the throats of monsters and cloaked people alike. Knife said they were grayfolk, devoted to some cruel man known as the gray priest. So he tried not to hesitate when it came to ending their lives with a slash of his dagger. Each killing strengthened his conviction that he was ridding the world of evil.

Not even considering that he might be the evil one.

The darkness helped cloud him from that truth.

It was easier than he expected to detach himself from his feelings—the emotions that normally burdened him when he could be seen by others. There was a freeing sense of exhilaration that filled the void of conscious thought, and it swelled to bursting the longer he remained in the Shadow.

However, Robin's voice would occasionally recall the ignored pain of each killing, filling Gage with guilt once more.

"He's over here, Mother!" the half-elf's voice echoed down a wide passage, followed by the wrenching caw of what had to have been another gargoyle dying. "Look out! Basilisk!"

Gage spun around in the cloud of Shadow that clung to him. His black eyes could see clearly through the inky void, and he knew he wouldn't have to worry about his companions as he saw the majest leap forward in her gleaming crimson armor. Jamira Kraiev slashed down with both sabers and dark blood sprayed across the sand-blasted stones of the passageway. Ahead of her, Robin and Knife sprinted toward Gage, Jamira's soldiers following in a tight formation, keeping any surviving monsters at bay.

Gage let the Shadow fall away as Knife slowed to a stop before him; he could see her wide eyes regarding the carnage laying at the Child of

Shadow's feet. The Guildmaster didn't say anything, but Gage could see the reverence in her eyes. It may have been fear, but whatever it was, it gave him a sense of pride, which overpowered the remorse that he did not want to feel. Part of him wanted to question if it was the Shadow again that didn't want him to feel, but Robin's hand on his shoulder drove the thoughts away.

"Are you all right?" His eyes were fixed on Gage's, not the butchery below. Gage wiped the blood from his face and smiled.

"I can feel it, just over that bridge."

"The altar?"

"We need to go back!" Jamira called from the front of the line blocking the passage. "There are more coming! We need to resupply!"

Gage ignored the majest, turning toward the blue glow of the altar. He knew he was walking in Anika's footsteps, and something about that angered him, spurring him onward. It was as if she had beat him to his rightful spot, reminding him of that one time she tried to cut in line at Elza's wagon of sweets. But she wasn't here now and he was, and that was enough to drive him toward the power that awaited him.

The rest of the sounds in the Fathoms fell away as Gage quickened his pace through the twisting passages, more narrow and less finished. It was like a network of mines, with several new branching paths each time he turned a corner. But whenever the tunnel split, he knew exactly which direction to go. Before long, he was standing before the altar of Eyen, which was guarded by nearly a dozen harpies.

One of the feathered, feminine monsters raised its wings in a warning, clearly trying to scare the invader away. Almost without hesitation, Gage reached out for the Shadow that trailed behind him, but before he could use it against his foes, one of the other harpies took to the air with a screech.

Lightning struck the altar from the darkness above, rejecting the gathering Shadow with a smoking hiss. Gage was thrown backward by the force, dropping his bloodied dagger. His vision blurred from the impact as his body struck the chamber's wall.

"Gage!" Robin's voice was almost as shrill as the harpy's. As Gage's vision cleared slightly, he saw Robin diving on top of a flailing harpy, the half-elf slamming his dagger into the monster's chest as it clawed at him to be free. Behind that struggle, three other harpies were struck out of the sky by the spinning, glinting discs that could only have been the Guildmaster's throwing knives.

Gage managed to get back to his feet, once more drawing the Shadow from farther down the hall; he gathered it in his two clenched fists, staring defiantly into the depths of the huge sapphire stone jutting up from the broken ground. So much power filled him that it lifted him off the ground. Black tendrils like crooked webbing latched him to the chamber walls, lifting him higher and higher, filling him with more power than he thought possible.

When Gage heard Robin scream in pain, he unleashed everything. The sound of a thousand thunderbolts ripped away the vast darkness above, pulling down an avalanche of sand and bricks and light. The world above was falling down on them, burying the harpies in blinding, heavenly brilliance.

Turning from the sudden illumination, Gage had only a moment to glance back at the altar, witnessing the moments of his sister's wedding played out in a separate window of time. When Stormender was jammed into Eyen's crystallized form, Gage's body was launched skyward through the opening he had just created with the Shadow.

Robin's desperate cries were lost on him as the deafening sounds of the open sky took him back to the sister that he now knew he needed to kill.

Grip nearly stumbled, feeling a sudden wave of dizziness. She steadied herself on a nearby tree, looking around to see if something had been following her through the woods.

She saw only darkness and heard only crickets. There wasn't some sorcerer behind her casting a spell; she hadn't tripped some hidden arcane trap designed to inflict her mind with visions.

No, she hadn't been that fortunate.

Her heart skipped a beat, but then began to thunder.

"Shit."

She spun on her heels to run back toward camp, knowing that the blood of Luishen running through her veins was one of the few things she could truly trust.

That and Ransil Osbury.

The trees whipped by her as she picked up her pace, feeling the Shadow's presence like an arrow flying overhead, racing toward a target that only she could protect. The light from the campfire came into

238 ~ BRADY J. SADLER

view, and she slowed her pace so she could catch her breath.

Fainly and Bennik were sitting by the fire with their backs to her; both of them turned when she approached.

"We need to go now," she said.

Bennik got to his feet. "Gnolls?"

She shook her head. *How can I explain this?*

"It's the altar, isn't it?"

Grip felt her eyes widen as she looked at the Archmage. She knew she shouldn't be shocked that the little man would have known about the altars, but it didn't change the fact that he had hid the knowledge well, from her and the Guild at least.

"You felt it?"

Fainly scrunched up his face, clearly not sure. "I felt something. Ever since coming through that gate from Arkath, I've felt this...presence in my mind. And when I remembered that the altar of Oakus was so nearby, I could only assume that was it."

Then you didn't feel the Shadow claim Eyen's altar, she thought, not sure if she wanted to divulge it yet. She looked at Bennik, knowing his kin would be in the dark without Griphelia Shu'wath.

But they didn't have much time.

"Listen," Grip said softly, noticing the halfling girls stirring under their heavy blanket. The two young guards were coming back from their patrol, and she didn't want them to overhear. "We can discuss this later, but just know that the altars sway one way or the other—Light or Shadow. Whichever side claims it, the old gods' powers respond accordingly." She nodded toward Bennik. "Your daughter must have found Eyen's altar first to awaken it, but now it seems your son has turned it to the Shadow."

"What does that mean?" he asked, stepping toward her with panic in his eyes.

But the young guards had joined them, their eyes eager for news.

"I'll show you," Grip told him, nodding toward Fainly. "Let's get to the next altar before he does."

Thankfully, the Archmage understood, grabbing Bennik's wrist to urge the man to wake the halflings. Grip felt more naked than she ever had, but the quicker she got Ransil's nieces to safety, the quicker she could go to be with him.

She couldn't think of anyone else she'd want to be with when the world ended.

CHAPTER TWENTY-TWO

Echoes of Eyen

Anika jerked her eyes to the sky, away from the marching paladins whose rows stretched across the entirety of the Rathaway. The vision felt too real, like a memory, long-forgotten, suddenly rushing back. Once again, she was flying from the Fathoms from beneath Karrane, the wind whipping through her hair, sorrows left behind for the world below to deal with.

She felt the same exhilaration that had brought her from one tragedy to her next. But as she searched the sky, she didn't see some distant version of herself hurling through the infinite blue. All she saw was the gray autumn clouds settling over the city of Sathford behind them.

"Somethin' wrong?"

Anika jerked her head back toward Deina, the dwarf casting her a curious glance from the back of her donkey. Smiling, she just shook her head. "Thought I heard something."

Deina held her gaze for a moment, skeptical. But then Ransil rode up between them on his own mule. "Last chance, Ani. You sure about this?"

Anika thought of the reserved looks the halfling had been giving her over the course of the last few weeks, the clear indication that he was hiding something from her. "I don't know, Ransil. Is there something I should know?"

He feigned a look of surprise. "What do you mean?"

"I mean, is there something you haven't told me? Why I shouldn't want to help Sathford prevent a war?"

The halfling made a show of turning in his saddle to look at Deina, as if he had no clue what Anika was talking about—she knew it was all an act. He knew. *Oh, he knows*, Stane repeated. *He knows, but he won't tell you.*

"You've been actin' quite odd, kid," Deina said bluntly, earning a glare from Ransil, but that didn't bother her. "I know things haven't been easy, but you need to keep your head on straight."

Anika was aghast. "*My* head? Deina, we've barely even seen you since the assault! You've been either taking out your anger on any tree you can find or drowning yourself in ale."

Deina's face darkened, but she didn't deny the charges.

"We don't have to do this now, Ani."

She turned her fury on Ransil. "Of course we don't! Let's just keep it all bottled up, Ransil! We don't need to tell each other anything—like whether or not we know about magic knives, or Guild plots, or anything else that could get our friends killed!"

Stane's cruel laughter echoed in her mind as she glared at her two friends, appalled by how she was talking to them. But she couldn't find it in herself to apologize, not with how much she was supposed to be taking on while also dealing with dangerous secrets being kept from her.

"Come on," Anika spat, jerking her reins to urge her mount away from the two. "We have a long ride to Rathen."

"There are riders up ahead," Tremly said. He descended the hill in a way that made Naya wonder if Ithakan had fully claimed the man. His limbs had a frail quality even though his steps were sure, as if he were buckling under the weight of sinister forces. It was unsettling to watch as he jerked his body toward the priestess.

"We can wait for them to pass before continuing on to Rathen," he said.

"We're not going to Rathen." Naya stepped past him to make her way up the hill to see for herself, even though she knew what came.

"But you said we needed to return the graystone." He followed her back up the hill. "It came from Rathen."

"No, it didn't," she said, not eager to explain everything Ithakan told her last night while Tremly slept. The halfling was snoring when she had prepared the ritual, but by the time it was complete, the Shadowlord was laughing maniacally through the halfling after explaining to Naya how she could usher him into the mortal world. In the morning, Tremly awoke without any knowledge of the discussion.

Now she settled for just telling him the basics. "It came from the priory, which is where Kathina is going."

"Kathina?! The princess?!"

She heard Tremly stumble behind her, surprised by the revelation, mumbling his panicked concerns. The oddness of it all wasn't lost on her, considering the news had come from the man's own toothless mouth. But demonic possession was a peculiar thing, so she did not dwell on the oddities.

"Hush now, Tremly. Stay low and let me do the talking."

Exhilaration filled Naya as she crested the hill, feeling like she was literally climbing out of her recent failures—everything seemed to finally be falling into place.

"Priestess!"

Despite knowing it would come, the voice rattled Naya's chest, nearly causing her to stumble. Tremly's small hands kept her stable and, for a passing moment, Naya nearly felt guilty for what she had to do. But the heir to Nazurik's bellowing call strengthened her resolve, so she untangled herself from the doomed halfling and returned to her ascent.

"By the Shadow, show yourself! I've come as you've bid. And if it turns out you were truly just a drunken nightmare, I may just be forced to slaughter my company in your name."

There was a raucous guffaw at that. "We didn't make you drink, Princess."

"Don't call me that!"

"Why are you expecting Kathina?" Tremly whispered behind Naya. "Why has she come this far south from Rathen?" She missed a step and fell back into his supportive hands again.

"Because I summoned her," Naya said, pushing herself away from the halfling, partly out of urgency to greet her newest ally and partly just to be done feeling the remorse that Tremly's touch gave her.

Naya reached the top of the hill as one of the other members of Kathina Sulm's company made some other snarky jest about the woman's drinking.

There were just under a dozen soldiers on the Rathaway, each on horseback with crimson armor over their brown skin. The princess of Nazurik was easy to spot, since her helmet was just a flared faceplate that left her long braided hair hanging over her ornamented shoulders.

"You must be the woman of my dreams," Kathina Sulm announced as soon as she saw Naya. "I expected you to be a bit taller, but I guess…" she began as her gaze shifted away from Naya. "Well, if it isn't my little scullion. When you didn't return from that little errand I sent you on, I suspected that my faith may have been misplaced."

The chatter amongst the princess's men died down then, as all attention turned to the top of the hill.

"Your faith," Naya called down to the fighting force that she would need to bend to the Shroud's will, "is perfectly placed, Kathina Sulm. Allow me to show you how I can deliver to you all of Copera."

After a long stretch of uncomfortable silence, Anika could take it no more. She glanced down at Ransil, who rode his mule alongside her own mount. The halfling looked lost in thought, but his small hand restlessly fingered Embrace, which was propped up on his lap by the saddle's horn.

"I'm still surprised you never mentioned that your mother had a keyshard in the Acreage." Anika didn't hide the annoyance from her voice, hoping to maybe stir the man so he would give up whatever else he might be hiding from her.

Oh, he's hiding plenty, that one, Stane assured her. As Ransil's shameful eyes found hers, Stane gave a chilling chuckle, forcing Anika to avert her own gaze, lest her anger get the best of her again. Part of her knew that however Stane's influence had infected her, it was determined to pit her against her allies.

Yet despite that, she could not let it go.

"Your brother tried to kill me, Ani."

The words quieted Stane's poisoned whispers, but the silence that filled its void was almost more terrifying to Anika. She jerked her gaze back to him to ensure that she heard him right. "When?"

He hung his head, unable to meet her eyes. "It was when you returned from Karrane, while you fought the incarnate. I was following Robin into the undercroft—Knife was taking him toward the gate." His voice cracked as he spoke of his apprentice, and when he looked back up to her, Anika could see he was crying. "I couldn't let him go back there, Anika. There's almost no coming back from that life."

"Gage tried to stop you?"

Ransil nodded slowly. "He stabbed me in the back—literally. I would have died if it weren't for Knife." He clenched his teeth as if he didn't want the name to escape his mouth. "I spent the last fifteen years of my life trying to stay out of that bitch's debt, only to be forced into it by—" He looked back up to Anika, catching himself before he cursed her brother. "I'm sorry, Anika. I didn't want to keep that from you…"

Whatever Ransil said next was lost to her.

The slow, ponderous clop of her horse's hooves mixed with the simmering rage the halfling's admission awoke within her to create a hypnotic effect that gripped all of Anika's senses. She faded from the world.

Stane spoke to her, but his words couldn't penetrate the primordial hatred that blossomed from the image of her brother putting a dagger in Ransil's back.

Suddenly, it felt like the storm had finally broken—as if the first incarnate's putrid sky was only a manifestation of the diseased atmosphere that had been hanging over Anika's entire life since being taken in by Bennik Lawson. All the pain and misery that had befallen her since her birthday was almost a culmination of being Gage Lawson's sister.

The Child of Shadow had truly cursed her. He had taken her mother, gotten their father abducted, ruined Ransil's home, and set her on the path that brought her here, riding to a war she didn't even truly understand.

Whether it was prophecy or Stane's wicked influence, Anika felt herself at the mercy of the Child of Light's true calling.

To kill the Child of Shadow.

"He deserves it."

The words came to Anika like a death cry, yanking her back violently to the present. She turned to see Deina on the other side of her, a puzzled look on her face.

"The warpriest," she said, nodding forward. "He wants to see you."

Anika turned again to see Ransil worrying after her, his concern somehow angering her even more than keeping this secret from her.

Without a word, she urged her mount ahead of the flanking mules and hurried toward the front of the column. The paladins were mostly on foot, with only a few rows mounted, trotting slowly. The chaplains rode ahead to serve as the scouting force. Anika found both Avrim and the High Warpriest at the head of the company, riding on either side of the carriage carrying the church's supplies. She welcomed their summons as a way to get out of her own consuming thoughts.

There was a darkness brewing inside of her that she didn't know how to quell.

"You felt something, didn't you?"

She looked at the High Warpriest, who only regarded her from the corners of his dazzling blue eyes. The man was too pretty for his own good. And his insinuation rankled her, as if he had been reading her thoughts.

"I feel my ass getting raw from this saddle," she decided to reply.

Avrim snorted a laugh before he could raise his hand and cover his mouth.

"Charming," Darrance said. "Don't be coy, you felt the Shadow just now, did you not?"

She didn't know exactly how to tell the man that she felt the Shadow all the time, assuming Stane's voice was an aspect of it. "I guess you'll have to be more specific."

The way he stiffened told Anika that Darrance didn't care for her attitude. He finally turned to face her. "I had always read that the Child of Light could always feel the Child of Shadow's presence. If both Avrim and myself could feel the sudden taint of the Shadow, shouldn't you feel it too?"

She looked at Avrim, who now had a much more stern look on his face.

"It was like the storm," he explained. "As if there were a sudden flash of lightning, but not from up there." He motioned north, toward Rathen. "It felt like it was far behind us." He cast a quick glance toward Darrance before adding, "Do you think we made a mistake leaving the city?"

"Of course not," Darrance snapped. "We've rooted out corruption there and now it comes from without. Bold action is needed. And if the Child of Light doesn't feel the same foreboding as us, it must not be too severe."

The rolling thunder of hooves up ahead begged to differ.

Instinctively, Anika drew Stormender, finally feeling some level of comfort against the oppressive dread that had fallen over their march. Even as the chaplains came into view, panic in their eyes, Anika still felt calmer than she had since falling in line with Ransil and Deina's mules.

"What is it, Jenore?!" Darrance kicked his massive white horse forward.

"The priory!" she called back, the four chaplains behind her reining in their mounts as their leader continued toward the warpriest. Anika and Avrim urged their own mounts forward so they could hear.

"There's movement," she continued through heavy breaths. "The place is a ruined heap—was totally abandoned last time I was here, but now there's horses outside the gates and smoke from a fire somewhere beyond the walls."

Darrance turned toward Avrim. "You continue the march with the main force." Pointing to Anika, he added, "Keep her here! Mallister! Your Brightriders are with me!"

"What's wrong?" Deina asked, riding up next to Anika with Ransil close behind her. "Trouble ahead?"

Anika noticed the look Avrim gave his friend—it was cold and fearful. "Someone's at the priory."

Deina growled and then spat. "They better not need our help. Swore I'd never go back there."

Part of Anika wanted to ask what happened there, but she could only guess they wouldn't be able to give her a full picture of it—not now. Besides, there were more pressing matters, such as all the talk of the Shadow the priests mentioned.

She felt the need to take action.

"I'll go check," she said, but Avrim's hand grabbed her reins before she could fully turn her mount around toward the priory.

"Darrance asked us to continue our march."

Anika snatched the reins back and turned her horse. "He may be your father, but he's not mine." But before she could properly get away, she felt hands on her shoulder and waist. Turning in the saddle, she saw both Deina and Ransil trying to restrain her.

"What are you doing?!" she asked, glaring at Ransil as the halfling clutched a hand securely through her belt.

"Can't have you goin' off alone, girl," Deina warned, wrapping her thick fingers around the leather strap over Anika's shoulder that kept her cloak in place.

Just as she was about to tell them how ridiculous they were acting—it wasn't like she was just going to ride off into battle without them!—a strange paranoia infected her mind. The same sensation that Stane's voice always accompanied sent a wave of dizziness over her, making her almost spill from the saddle. But her friends held her steady. They spoke to her, but their voices couldn't pierce the unnatural stupor she was falling into. The world fell away again, and she heard Stane's voice accompany a vision of Gage.

He's going to kill the next scion, the voice said as Anika watched her brother flying through the air like she had. It was as if she could feel the wind whipping through her own hair, feel the weightless ecstasy that had brought her all the way from Karrane to Sathford in mere moments—a journey that might usually take entire weeks.

Whatever Stane said next was lost to the sound of the open sky whooshing past her as she carried her companions up into the clouds above.

Gage landed weightlessly, his thin black boots touching the grass silently on the banks of a river. The trees above were losing their leaves, and a cool autumn breeze wrapped around him as the gathering powers exhaled and returned him to the ground's embrace.

There was a waterfall farther down the bank; a peaceful crashing of water accompanied the sounds of insects and rustling critters back in the woods that surrounded him now. He spun around twice, trying to orient himself, but he had no clue where he was or how far from Karrane he had flown.

All he knew was that he had to get back to Robin.

With no direction, Gage took quick strides down the banks of the river, looking for any road or other indication of where he might be.

Soon, the charred remains of a boat greeted him, the lazy waters of the river cascading around its crooked form. The nose of the vessel had run into the soft earth and gotten stuck. It may have once been a wondrous elven vessel, Gage guessed, but now it was an ashen ruin, burnt down to its skeletal frame.

It was an ashen grave.

Gage smelled the body before he recognized what it was. A sickly pleasant smell that reminded him how hungry he was. But his stomach turned an entirely different direction when he realized it was a person lying within the boat. He wanted to turn away from the remains, but the red gleam that pierced through the smoldering tomb would not allow it.

Not knowing why or how he knew what it was, Gage reached in and took hold of Ruiner.

An old man's voice told him what he needed to do with it. And instead of asking if it was just Stane putting on a different voice to fool him, Gage took to the air once more so he could get to Wick's altar before his sister.

CHAPTER TWENTY-THREE

A Study in Fire

Layla felt more at home than she could remember.

Waking up in the meager quarters she had taken in the Vestige reminded her of being below deck on *Severynth* when Valix had been alive, warming her bed as the ship swayed along on its doomed voyage. And despite the woman's absence, Layla could still feel the comfort she had provided during their short time together.

Not even the black book on her nightstand could ruin the cozy feeling permeating through her small little alcove of the Vestige. So she lingered in bed, under the heavy blanket Kartha had provided.

"I won't feel the chill," the green woman had said when giving her the covers. "I may look like a Daughter of Oakus, but this close to Wick's altar I feel like I'm about to burst into flames."

"Altar?" Layla had asked, unsure to which altar she referred.

Kartha had given her a curious look, as if the word she had just spoken was foreign to her. The moment stretched out uncomfortably until she finally just said, "It's late. We should all get some sleep."

The recent memory jerked Layla out of bed.

She couldn't remember exactly why she hadn't pressed the woman further. There was what seemed like a hole in her memory following that encounter. Layla could recall briefly sorting through what remained of the High Mage's study—remarkably, much of the books and scrolls in that room evaded the fires, likely due to wards being placed on the shelves. Maze went to meet with Reeve Jansen, and Layla spent the rest of the night alone in her room with a stack of books and a cup of wine.

Presently, she picked up the empty drink as if simply touching it might fill the hole in her memory. But no, it just made her thirsty.

Layla tried to put the curiosity out of her mind so she could focus on their current situation. The whole reason she decided to stay at the tower was so Kartha could begin translating *The Book of Stane*, and that was what she needed to direct her thoughts toward. She picked up the heavy tome and decided to go find the woman.

However, Layla's breath caught when she opened the door to leave her room. Maze was there with a fist raised, ready to tap on the charred wood of the door. They raised a finger to their lips before whispering, "I think the witch will be out most of the day. Care to join me for a trip to town? Not much food here, and I'd like to finish my discussion with the reeve concerning our residency here."

The mention of food made Layla's stomach rumble. She hadn't had a proper meal since their quick breakfast back in Waneport. But she didn't love the idea of taking *The Book of Stane* into a place like Stelmont.

Maze must have seen her looking down at the book. "I'm probably more paranoid than you, girl, but I think it'll be safe in your room. There's a key in the door there, just lock it up. I think we could both use some fresh air after sleeping in this chimney."

Maze was right. Even though the new residents had opened what windows remained in the Vestige to air out the stink, there was an odor of what Layla could only describe as burnt hair lingering inside the place. She set the heavy book back on her nightstand and locked the door as instructed, slipping the key into her robe pocket. She kept her hand over the comforting weight of the heavy piece of iron as she followed Maze down to the main floor.

"Morning," a dwarf grunted as they stepped through the front gates. He was one of the New Hold soldiers whose name Layla hadn't caught; there was a certain amount of guilt that plagued her from that realization, so she paused to regard him.

"Good morning," she said, as pleasantly as she could. "My name is Layla Abrigale, Court Mage for Queen Sopheena. We may have met before, but I don't seem to recall your name."

The dwarf gave her a puzzled look for a moment, flicking his gaze over to her companion before settling back on Layla. Then his face split into an honest, wholesome smile, his beard giving way to a row of crooked yellow teeth. "Bricky is me name, from Clan Bronkite in New Hold. Me kin helped hold the tower against the Burning Bitch and her hordes."

"We're grateful for that," Maze offered, making to continue their trek into Stelmont, but Layla lingered.

"I know you're busy with the repairs, Bricky, but if you would be so kind as to keep watch and make sure nobody else besides your kin disturbs our companion upstairs. She needs her rest."

"Certainly," Bricky said with a proud nod. "We'll keep the hammerin' to a minimum until everyone's properly awake. You can trust a Bronkite to keep their word," he added. "We ain't no oathbreakers like the Cleavers."

Layla thanked him again before she joined Maze toward Stelmont, who leaned closely to remark, "I didn't know you were so concerned with Kartha's beauty sleep."

Layla smiled. "I think that woman is the least of us who needs any beauty sleep. Besides, that was the easiest way to put the dwarves on alert without telling them about the book in my room."

Maze chuckled, leaning their head back to admire the cool autumn sky. "Clever."

Neither of them saw Anika or Gage flying through the clouds, each carrying their own burdens toward intertwined destinies.

Kartha knew she was dreaming, but it was one of those dreams that played like a memory, and with the fractured state of her mind, she did everything in her power to avoid waking up in the hopes that she might actually remember something.

This particular vision was of Ghulta, the underground city that was said to be the place where Stane was finally outwitted by the lich Gravern. But Kartha was skeptical that this was her own memory, because her own recollections of Stane during her time in Arkath were of him regaling her with tales of his time in Ghulta—a place she had never been.

But that doesn't make sense either, she thought, walking through the streets of the necromantic city that could potentially just be her own fanciful notion of what the place had actually looked like. Rather than try to work the timelines out in her slumbering mind, Kartha focused on navigating the vision that someone or something wanted her to see.

"You don't truly believe him, do you?"

Kartha froze mid-step as she was about to turn around a corner that would have put her on the path of the speaker. Instead, she spun slightly to join a group of hooded figures that walked in the opposite direction, away from a skeletal horse that turned the corner—behind the undead beast was an onyx chariot, carrying two colorful figures who stood out drastically against the grays and blacks that dominated the dark, gothic street.

"Why wouldn't I believe him?" a man answered. Kartha allowed herself a peek over her shoulder. The man was a beautiful young Eastlunder who had fiery red hair flowing to his shoulders in lazy curls. He wore bright yellow and orange armor, lightweight and flared at the edges like snapping flames. "Has Stane ever lied to us?" Kartha had to lengthen her strides to keep pace with the ambling carriage that navigated the busy streets of Ghulta.

"Not that we know of," the woman passenger replied. Her voice was musical and pleasant, but it had a sarcastic cut to it. From the edges of her vision, Kartha could see the woman's skin was blue—not like a corpse, but like a sea elf...which no living person had likely ever seen. Regardless, it's how Kartha imagined one looking. The woman's hair was darker blue, almost black, and she wore elegant aquamarine robes with plates of white armor at her shoulders, chest, and wrists.

It's Corsa, Kartha thought instantly. *Corsa and her lover, Wick.* Why was she dreaming about the old gods roaming the streets of Ghulta? It seemed like some fairytale imagination of what the gods might look like made flesh.

But Stane was the only celestial one made flesh, wasn't he? Kartha couldn't make sense of this vision, but she was determined to see it through as much as she could before she was ripped out of it by waking.

"These altars," Corsa continued, just on the edge of Kartha's hearing now that the carriage had cleared a group of (possibly undead) pedestrians. "You don't suppose—"

"Move it!" Wick shouted suddenly. "Hasn't your master taught you all how to use the walking paths?! Get off the road!" Kartha walked even faster around the unresponsive legions that clogged the wide streets of the city. She didn't even allow herself time to admire the dark and wondrous architecture that arose on either side of the bustling thoroughfare—her focus was purely on the gods and their discussion of her one true love.

"Stane says the altars are just for show," Wick said in a slightly calmer voice, though he still sounded furious. "It's all about faith, my dear. I mean, you can't deny that when we last visited Severynth, the way those Shadow priests were ready to swear off their old beliefs after witnessing you divert the tidal wave—I mean, you shouldn't even have been able to do that, right?!"

Kartha was close enough to the carriage now that she could hear Corsa let out a defeated sigh. "I just don't like his talk about sacrifices—how we are the ones that need to make sacrifices for these altars while he continues whatever affair he's having here with Gravern and Mural—"

Wick spun in his seat to interrupt her. "Easy, love. I know these people aren't all truly alive, but let's not invoke the Death Maiden's name so openly—not until we're out of the city."

"It's just curious, is all, Wick. Don't get me wrong, I still think we're on the right path. Like Myretha always says, there has to be some purpose we were all drawn together. But sometimes I just wonder what Stane's role in all of this actually is."

Kartha's heart began racing, thundering in her flesh-and-blood chest back in the burned tower. She was suddenly afraid that this dream would end before she truly understood what any of it meant. A sense of disembodiment overwhelmed her, and she found her legs no longer working. She began sinking into the solid stone street below her, slowly drawn down into its thick void.

"His role?" Wick was incredulous, and Kartha could hear his voice as if she were riding in the carriage herself, even though she watched it from where she sank into the nightmare below. "Sweet Corsa, don't tell me you want to wine and dine the Pillars. Just having to make an appearance here in front of Gravern is bad enough; imagine having to make merry with him, smell his maggoty breath. No, Stane was made for that tiresome labyrinth of ceremony and platitudes, and we were made to be out there. Having adventures! Showing the world that we are more than just the six most powerful sorcerers the world has ever known."

The voice finally began fading as Kartha felt her eyes begin to open. "We are gods."

"Are we not attacking?"

Veronitha put a warm hand on Melaine's shoulder, and the half-orc didn't smack it away as she once might have. In fact, the touch gave Melaine a sense of belonging, which reminded her of when the cult healed her burns on the Pyric Path. She looked down at her own hands, admiring the flawless skin before looking sidelong at her new leader.

The Combustress was still as scarred as she always was. It made Melaine want to ask why the woman hadn't healed her own skin like she had for her followers, but instead she just waited for the woman to explain her plans.

"We have everything we need from the Vestige," she finally said. "The altar waits for us farther east and we are running out of time."

Melaine turned back toward the tower to watch the dwarves toil away. Something about the sight of the short, stocky figures made her feel like she was forgetting something—a longing, just out of reach. She remembered her friend Brace, who had sacrificed himself so she could receive Wick's blessing. And she was from Wickham, she remembered that—but there was little else she knew about herself.

Not liking that feeling, she averted her eyes from the dwarves and waited for the Combustress to begin her sermon.

The cultists at the base of the hill seemed to be just as impatient, murmuring amongst themselves in hushed voices. A gnoll howled in the distance, reminding Melaine how glad she was that Veronitha didn't include those monsters in her main force.

"We make haste for New Hold," the Combustress said finally. "The altar will awaken soon."

Melaine wanted desperately to ask what that meant, but she had no other instinct than to trust the woman. That instinct felt...foreign somehow, but with everything that had happened, and the absence of her own memories, Melaine had little else to rely on.

The Combustress led her followers, and Melaine fell in line.

"We received a dove from the Brighthold."

Layla looked from Reeve Jansen to the Lightfather, who looked almost younger than her. She felt her pulse quicken at the mention of the Brighthold, unsure of what that meant. "From the Archbeacon?"

"That's right," the young priest said, folding his hands into the wide sleeves of his blue robes. He had a smug look on his face, as if he was savoring the suspense he held over the two outsiders.

They sat in the reeve's lavish parlor, which seemed far too extravagant for the otherwise rickety town of Stelmont. However,

Layla got the sense that Reeve Jansen had designs much higher than his meager station here in the Steddlewood. Jansen himself sat by the cold hearth in a lush satin chair, while his guests occupied the less exquisite seats that ringed the low refreshment table.

Maze took a cup of tea from Reeve Jansen's dwarven steward, who was making his way to each guest. "And what did our most luminous Luriah Vaughn have to say?"

Layla's companion sipped their tea loudly, souring the condescending expression on the Lightfather's face. But he nodded politely in response. "She has called all able-bodied errant priests to Sathford."

"Are you able-bodied, Father Shits?"

"It's Shence," the man said, his expression souring even more. "A common mistake to which I take no offense, my lady. My name is Veril Shence."

Maze uncrossed their legs. "Fair enough, Shence. Though, as ravishing as I may be, I am no lady. I don't mind the traditional lord or lady, but they are quite wasted on me. Just call me Maze."

"Very well," Shence replied, visibly uncomfortable by the notion. "But to answer your question: I am no errant priest. As a Lightfather, my place is here at the chapel. I have sent Keetha in my stead."

"Yes, and my own daughter has accompanied your companions to Oakworth," Reeve Jansen added. "I instructed her to confer with the new baroness to see if she is needed in Sathford as well."

"Is something happening in Sathford?" Layla asked, the nervousness from the Lightfather's news lessening now that the dove didn't concern her or the book she carried.

"War," Jansen replied, his expression tightening. "It seems Copera has taken Rathen, liberating it from the orcs. However, the Luminaura's foothold in the north was rooted in the free city, so it seems unsurprising that the Archbeacon wouldn't take kindly to outsiders claiming the city for their own."

"Not likely," Maze offered, loudly sipping their tea.

Layla leaned forward in her seat, hoping to establish a non-antagonistic presence to complement Maze's obnoxious demeanor thus far. "Has the queen herself called for war?"

Jansen regarded her curiously down the length of his pointed nose. "I was hoping you might be able to tell me—being her personal mage and all."

"In regards to her station, she has been otherwise indisposed," Maze replied quickly. "I am quite the handful, and she has been tasked to accompany me from Jath to Waneport, which is why we are traveling by land now. The Lord Mayor of Waneport wished to give us a tour of the Wane Coast."

Jansen nodded, taking a sip of his own tea before returning his gaze to Layla. "We have not received any official decrees from the queen. Which is quite odd, considering now many doves have come in from the Brighthold."

"It would not be the first time the Luminaura has acted as the throne's enforcers," the Lightfather added, declining to drink his own tea. His expression was sour as he glanced over at Jansen, as if they disagreed on this point. But when he looked back at Layla, his hollow smile returned. "Our gracious queen is most devoted to the Light, as you know."

"More than you know," Maze remarked, earning a sidelong glance from Layla. There was a rap at the door then, and Jansen's dwarven steward opened it to reveal Jaffron Casryk. Even Layla had to admit the man was handsome in his sea-green silks. He walked into the room as if he owned the entire manor, popping a piece of fruit into his mouth.

"Pardon my tardiness," he said, chewing loudly as he strode toward the seating area, motioning toward the reeve with both hands, palms up. "You have quite a prosperous little town here, Travith." He shifted slightly toward the Lightfather as he neared them. "And you must be Father Shits."

Maze snorted into their teacup.

"That's Father Shence," the man said without a hint of annoyance in his voice. "Veril Shence, Lord Mayor. Common mistake."

"Certainly," Jaffron said dismissively. "Look, I know we're all a bit disheveled by the recent events, not to mention the shakeup at the Arcania. However, as Lord Mayor of Waneport and governor of the Wane Coast, I am declaring these two—well, not quite women; one is, certainly, and the other is meant to keep you guessing. However, these two individuals will be taking up permanent residence in the Vestige. I will be staying as well, to oversee the repairs. The New Hold dwarves will be kept on as caretakers until the place is properly restored."

"And the Archmage?" Jansen interrupted.

"I have written to her myself, informing the High Sanctum of this new arrangement. So from now on, this is High Mage Layla Abrigale and Master Maze…" Jaffron made a motion for his companion to finish the title.

Maze just raised their tea in a toast and nodded with a smile.

"Master Maze it is," Jaffron scoffed.

The atmosphere in the room changed completely then, and Layla once more felt like she owed something to the son of a bitch that smirked at her. She didn't think she could ever forgive him for killing Valix, but maybe she could eventually recognize how valuable the man was to their cause.

Whatever their cause actually was…

Kartha burst into Layla's room, the unnatural strength in her limbs allowing her to knock the locked door from its hinges. Someone shouted downstairs in response to the racket she caused, but Kartha was too frantic to care.

She grabbed the black book off the nearby table and opened it on the bed, kneeling down so she could flip through its pages. The writing was still jibberish to her, as it always had been. But with each turn of the page, a piece of a memory would rekindle in her racing mind. At the moment, though, she didn't allow any of them to actually take shape. She didn't have time.

She reached the middle of the book, where blood stained the pages—blood of the scion. Words took shape on the crimson portions of the ancient-yet-durable paper, but they were of a language Kartha couldn't read—or, at least, couldn't remember how to read. Regardless, the message those alien words conveyed was clear.

"It was me," she whispered, her eyes rapidly jumping from one confusing word to the next. "I wanted to bring him back. We weren't trying to unthrone the gods, I was trying to make one."

She swallowed, remembering the hatred she had felt so long ago. Back when she was the old witch known as Kartha who had only one thing left in the world to live for.

Revenge.

She had known there were never any old gods, they were just pawns—her lover's followers who believed his lies just like she had. A fallen god's desperate gambit.

The so-called "old gods" were just witches and warlocks like her, who Stane had used to instruct the world how to worship gods—a practice the mortal consciousness no longer had use for. Stane forged their altars using aspects of his own broken body, a result of his own failures in godhood.

The truth was slowly coming back with every red word she failed to translate—because there was no hidden prophecy in the book—no godly wisdom or divine atlas.

The book was a prop, like everything else a deceiver like Stane would need to make the world believe in his bullshit.

None of it made sense to Ivy, the lost and confused green woman that knelt before a stranger's bed. Everything made sense to Kartha, the vile witch who had walked in Stane's footsteps just so she could hopefully make him suffer like he had made her suffer.

When she heard the heavy footsteps of the dwarves coming to check on the sounds, Kartha closed the book and returned it to the nightstand. Freeing herself from those pages allowed her to gather her thoughts enough to make a proper excuse, so the dwarves might not tell Layla she had been prying into her book.

She would need the woman's help to bring Stane low, and nobody would help her if they knew the truth.

And the truth was, Kartha brought the world to its knees just so she might bruise Stane's ego. There was no redemption for her, but at least she could help them defeat Stane before her own demise.

She was dead anyway.

CHAPTER TWENTY-FOUR

Home Alone

Quinn was restless despite the relative quiet that had befallen Raventhal Spire. With Anika, Ransil, and the rest of them marching to war alongside the Luminaura, there wasn't the same urgent energy that he had become accustomed to while roaming the halls.

He didn't like it.

Knowing he'd be unable to focus on any studies in their absence, he went to the one place that he thought he could be alone.

Since becoming High Mage, Quinn had to be around people much more often. While he was comfortable in the presence of Ransil and his allies, he found that being sociable with anyone else exhausted his mind worse than any spell could. While magic had always come naturally to him, people did not. And with Ransil gone, all Quinn was left with at the spire were people that exhausted him.

The rookery was his escape.

Unfortunately, he realized, as he heard the ravens above stirring from their midday meal, it was someone else's escape as well.

"Quiet down," a voice insisted. Quinn kept his steps silent as he ascended the last few stairs, wondering who else would be visiting the birds in the middle of the day—*Who else even knows their feeding schedule?* he thought to himself. "There's plenty to go around."

He turned the corner to see Raventhal's lone Oather feeding a strip of dried meat to Whitney, Quinn's favorite raven. The other birds were busy chewing on their own afternoon snacks, which were scattered across the perch in the middle of the room. The sky outside the wide windows of the rookery was pristine, and it framed the hard woman in a much different light for Quinn.

When Ransil had first urged him to allow Kasia Strallow to take the post at Raventhal—one that had gone unattended since the second Aberheim—Quinn was skeptical of allowing someone with her reputation to be his one and only Oather. However, regarding her now without her paralyzing armor, he saw a vulnerable side to the woman that made him suddenly understand why Ransil would chance to speak on her behalf.

"She's done some things," the halfling had told him, back when he originally posited her as someone that could help protect the sanctity of Raventhal Spire. "We've all done things we're not proud of. But I think she's someone you'd rather have on your side—especially considering what may come to pass soon."

Quinn hadn't asked what Ransil meant by that—there hadn't been much time for debate—but he would trust the man with his life (like he already had on several occasions).

Staring at the woman now, Quinn thought he understood what Ransil had meant—not in any specific terms, just that he was glad to have this woman pledged to his own cause as opposed to a foe's. After Whitney pulled the meat away from Kasia's fingers, Quinn stepped forward, loud enough to ensure that the woman heard him.

"High Mage," she said, stiffening her posture. "What brings you to the rookery?"

"I was going to ask you the same," Quinn replied, stepping forward to run a hand over Whitney's smooth onyx coat. "Usually no one is up here during midday, when they're back from their morning hunts. Besides, shouldn't you be part of the Luminaura's force?"

"Not unless you command me to," Kasia said, adopting a stern, official tone. "I report to the Arcania, not the Brighthold."

Quinn felt the jab, not liking the condescension in her voice. But could he blame her? He still felt far too out of his element in his new position, especially without Audreese or Ransil around to properly advise him. But he steeled himself internally, knowing that he would have to grow up eventually.

He was not one to admit defeat easily. Besides, he deeply cared about this place, as well as its former administrator, so he felt he owed it to Konrath Hoon's memory to be an equally effective leader.

With a firm expression, Quinn pet Whitney one last time as the bird feasted. He kept his gaze detached, staring out across the rooftops of Sathford and beyond. "The mayor overreaches," he finally said, thinking of the perfect cover for his shortcoming. "I assumed she might have stripped me of my Oather as she has my... Well, my other allies."

"The city is definitely in new hands," Kasia said, following Quinn's gaze toward the wide windows. "When I last came through here, the Tolle Collectors basically ran the streets, and Karlton kept to feasting and hosting nubile boys in his countryside estate."

Quinn wasn't quite sure what that last part meant, but he nodded and turned on his heels, deciding to escape this unintended social encounter while he could.

"How old are you?"

"I'll be eleven this winter," he replied, not surprised by the question—nobody believed someone of his accomplishments could be so young, and eventually he would have to explain himself. "My parents came from Vaina."

This drew her gaze; her eyes were wide, much like every other person's that learned of his ethnicity. "The dragon lands? Don't tell me you were born there…"

Quinn kept his gaze over the city as he shook his head. "The Shatterwood."

The usual silence fell. He had only truly divulged his heritage to a handful of people, including Fallon Shaw, Audreese Groaves, and Konrath Hoon, and the latter died pledging to keep the truth of Quinn Olivick's past a secret. However, Quinn himself was much less careful with the knowledge.

Finally, Kasia laughed, quietly and humorlessly. "I guess that explains how someone so young can work magic well enough to be High Mage."

"What's that supposed to mean?"

She regarded him curiously. "Surely you know about the places you're from? Vaina is ruled by dragons, and the only people that dwell there are said to be of draconic blood. Which means your parents were likely descended from the draconiths. And then the Shatterwood… You have learned of the Nether War, haven't you?"

None of this was new information to Quinn. "I've only been alive a short time, but in those ten years I've met maybe twenty other people from Vaina. One of them scooped sheep dung on a farm. Another makes a decent bowl of soup in the Five Casks. None of them can do the things I can do." He walked over to the window, boosting himself up on his elbows to get a better view of the city below. "I study hard here. If my heritage does give an edge, well, I don't see many others of my kind taking advantage of it similarly."

A moment of silence passed between them before Quinn added,

"Our makings don't make us. We have to do the work."

Kasia leaned against the wall dividing the windows, crossing her arms while she still stared at the boy. "You're certainly insightful, that's for sure."

"Insightful enough to know I'd rather have you as an ally than a foe," he admitted, surprising himself with his boldness. From the edge of his vision, he could tell that cut through her otherwise pleasant demeanor. It made him feel guilty—she hadn't necessarily been unkind to him. But for some reason, the talk of his own past reminded him of the things Ransil had told him about Kasia and her own past.

"We all make mistakes," he had said. "While not all of us deserve atonement, I don't know if it's for you or me to make that decision. Regardless, I've seen what you can do, Quinn. I do not fear for your safety on account of Kasia Strallow. My only advice is: keep a tight leash on her."

As if reading his mind, Kasia asked, "Why did you approve my appointment? Before even meeting me properly."

"Ransil Osbury," Quinn answered immediately. "He said you're the best at what you do, and with the new Archmage in control of all the remaining Oathers currently in Suthek, having the Lady Commander as an ally could prove useful."

She didn't react in any visible way to that response. But when she finally spoke, her tone had lost a bit of its edge. "I can attest to my usefulness." It sounded strange, like an admission of guilt.

Another prolonged silence fell between them, and Quinn found it oddly comforting. He didn't feel that urgent tension that usually accompanied most of his social interactions, especially with adults. Maybe that was why he liked Ransil so much; he was of a similar height, making him seem much less of an adult.

That thought made Quinn feel petty, but he couldn't deny the truth of it.

Finally, Kasia spoke again. "I understand the new Archmage has questionable allegiances. I want you to know, my loyalty lies with this tower alone—the Arcania cannot be tarnished. I may not have been the most ardent supporter of Fainly Lopke, but at least I could trust the man to keep the academies neutral. I do not know this Vera Mourgael at all, and if the rumors of her being a Shadowfiend are at all founded, I will do whatever I can to expose her." She returned her gaze out over the city. "I let my apathy toward the Shadow allow witchery to take root in Oakworth, and I will not make that mistake here."

The conviction in the woman's voice made Quinn shift his feet uncomfortably, as if she might suddenly try to toss him out the window if she decided she didn't like how he pledged his Oath of Sorcery. His hand went to the Arcanian mark around his neck out of instinct.

Kasia exhaled sharply. "Are the gates truly gone below?"

Quinn nodded. "Audreese said the one that the Guild used during the assault was the last one functioning in the undercroft. I heard rumors that House Grale has access to one in a ruined tower on their lands, but Ransil and I found no truth to that when fighting the gnolls." He finally turned to her. "Why do you ask?"

"Part of an Oather's duty is to protect their academy. Are the gates not the easiest way for unsavory visitors to infiltrate any of the Arcania's towers?"

"Do you fear another invasion? Aside from the Coperans, that is."

The cathedral bells rang then to mark the passing of midday. Kasia regarded the bones of the structure as she said, "I fear this new Archmage, if I'm being perfectly honest. Part of the reason I sought this station was to prepare for a rift in the Arcania. There are rumors that the Vestige has fallen outside of Stelmont, and I believe Oswald's tower in Harkand is infested with Shrouded agents. Say what you will about Fainly Lopke, but he was unwavering in his commitment to keeping the Arcania out of politics and religion."

"You think the rumors are true then? That Vera Mourgael is a Disciple of Stane?"

Kasia gave him a surprised look, clearly not expecting the boy to have been in tune with her own sources. "Whether she's a Disciple, a Shrouded, or one of those Circle of Oakus fanatics, I suspect she will not be impartial enough to prevent the Arcania from being corrupted from within."

Admittedly, Quinn hadn't given the subject much thought. He had quite enough on his plate with the daily operations of Raventhal, not to mention his and Ransil's recent excursions. If he was being honest, he was much more interested in the story behind the magic dagger that they had recovered from the cave than anything regarding the Arcania. Besides, he had never been a particularly ardent supporter of the previous Archmage either, so it was quite easy to put the new one out of his thoughts.

But Kasia's words and demeanor made him wonder if he had been shirking his duties as Konrath's successor by not keeping the happenings in Andelor top of mind. "So what do you plan to do from here about it?"

Kasia looked back over Sathford, the shadow of a smile touching her lips. "I intend to legitimize your position as the Archmage's Chosen—passed on to you by High Mage Konrath Hoon. That way, if Vera Mourgael proves to be a threat…" She regarded Quinn coldly, as if sentencing him to death. "I vow to make you the next Archmage."

Whitney cawed from behind Quinn, startling him from the Oather's paralyzing gaze.

Neither of them were looking into the sky when Ransil Osbury was pulled through the clouds overhead, one hand clutching the belt of the Child of Light while the other gripped a dagger trailing a tongue of fire.

Vera Mourgael felt the aerial disturbance from Andelor, but wasn't quite sure what to make of it. Her mind was otherwise occupied, pondering her next move in light of the city's recent events.

Two days ago, the king was formally charged with infidelity, sending riptides through the three high houses on Andelor's outskirts. House Durrask was obviously the first to oppose the charges, but Queen Sopheena had little choice but to take her husband into custody until such time that a proper trial could be carried out. Not since King Cedrius had a ruling body been charged with such an act of treason, so a great council would need to be convened to decide Markus Durrask's ultimate fate.

All of this had caused chaos among the throne, the Luminaura, and Vera's own High Sanctum—that worthless group of squabbling witches. Vera couldn't be more pleased about the uproar; however, her attention was needed to ensure the unrest continued in the city to prepare for Gravern's next move.

As she turned away from the clear autumn sky to return her attention to the map of southern Noveth, another strange sensation distracted her—one that she was much more familiar with.

It was Shadow magic.

There were others in her order that were far more experienced in the craft than Vera, but she knew its taste well. And someone was using it to contact her.

Instead of returning to the huge table in the center of her study, she retreated to her adjoined sleeping quarters. Fainly Lopke was a plain man that did little to add comfort to his dwelling, so Vera—likely out of pure spite—decorated her chambers with heavy velvet drapes and beaded curtains in the style of a Xe'danni witch den; it did little to assuage the rumors of Vera being a Shadowfiend, which was just an added perk to the comfort the decor provided her.

Even though she was hardly bothered by any Arcania dredges while in her chambers, she still secured the drapes behind her before unlatching one of Fainly's hidden passages near his old bed. Vera could only assume the elderly gnome used the concealed alcove as some sort of self-flagellation chamber, judging from all the illustrations she had found stored within, but she used it for her own more important rituals.

Such as replying to the Shadow-sent whispers in her head—the ones she wouldn't be able to decipher without the proper spells.

She shut the false wall behind her and prepared the small table in the hidden room with the necessary materials: shallow bowl, ebony-handled ritual knife, shadeleaf, and a dried rabbit's ear. The whispering in her mind intensified as she drew the blade across her palm, letting her blood drip into the bowl, which contained the other reagents. It took effort to concentrate on the Xe'danni incantation, but Vera managed to finish the ritual before the Shadow-borne message caused a splitting headache.

"The book is here," the voice said.

Vera's eyes rolled back into her head as the Shadow magic filled her. It was a familiar, nauseating feeling that she always dreaded. She was not some Light-blind Luminaurian, but she still had a certain amount of disdain for the Shadow, despite how many of her peers assumed she was a devotee of it. Yet she accepted how necessary it was to embrace the flexibility of those forbidden powers if she hoped to rise in Gravern's good grace.

And since the world would be his soon, that remained her sole focus.

"Price?"

"Do you have so many voices in your head that you can't remember mine?"

Vera scoffed, annoyed. "You'd be surprised. What book? *The book?!*"

"You looking for another?"

"Just give me the report," she snapped angrily, though her face didn't move; her voice was a thought carried all the way to Waneport by way of dark magic. "Did Valix's plan actually work?" Vera had her doubts when Price originally told her about the scheme to kidnap Sauthorn. She was skeptical of only a few powers in this world, but prophets and seers were counted among them, so she assumed Valix would only get insane mumblings from the old elf.

The thought of preordained events did not sit well with a person of action like Vera Mourgael.

"Valix is dead."

At first, Vera thought maybe Price's words were misinterpreted. She snapped her eyes open to observe the ritual components, ensuring nothing had gone wrong.

Unfortunately, everything was still in order. She closed her eyes again as she felt the tears come. "Are you sure?"

"I have no reason to doubt my sources," Price continued, sounding unbothered by the news. "The Lord Mayor himself is escorting one of the queen's mages—she's the one carrying the book."

"Escorting her where?"

"I've followed the party to Stelmont. They've taken up in that old academy of yours on the hill. But I'm at Crane's now since I couldn't risk trying to reach you while so near the witches in that tower—at least one of them might be in tune with the Shadow. Besides, the cult was on the march right behind me."

"The Combustress?" Vera had heard plenty about the fires in the south during the recent councils, before the king's treason was brought to light by the Guild. "Does she seek the book as well?" *Please no,* she thought. *I do not want to have to kill Veronitha. Not after what we did to her mother...*

"Not likely," Price replied, his voice weakening in her mind. "I overheard some of their followers back in the port; something is happening in New Hold. Sounds like the new clanmother running the place is a fire priestess now, stirring up a war with the miners. Should I look into it?"

"No," Vera replied, but she was certainly curious about what might be going on there. Unfortunately, she needed a trusted presence in

Suthek immediately. She was supposed to be there herself until Fainly disappeared. "Let me handle the book. If it's surely the queen's Court Mage, she will likely be bringing it to Andelor. If not, I'll send another Disciple. I need you back in Waneport—on the first ship to Suthek."

Price groaned in her mind. "Not there again. There's just dusty mines and dusty cunts there, V."

"The Oathers need to be brought in line with this new administration," she replied. "There will be plenty of dripping cunts waiting for you back in the city should you keep them in line for me. I may even give you mine."

Price laughed at that. "I may hold you to that, V. But there's something else."

"Make it fast, there's plenty else here vying for my attention."

"Knife's lieutenant was with the Lord Mayor's company—the dark elf. She gave me her Guildmark, saying she was done. But she also gave me some documents from the Shrouded."

Vera's heart quickened. "You mean correspondences?"

"Correspondences, pledges, confessions, you name it. I think these pages contain the names of every person in Vale pledged to the Shrouded, including the late Baron Caffery. I haven't had the time to sort through it all, but apparently Grip and her little Ruse snapped it up from the baron's manor before that incarnate attack."

Vera couldn't help but smile. With Grip out of the picture, she could put Price at the head of the Guild before Knife returned. And with those documents, she could blackmail any member of the royal council that was pledged to the Shrouded, ensuring King Markus would be either strung up or sent to the Sutheki mines—

Suthek, she thought, realizing she couldn't send him there now.

"Change of plans, Price. Bring those documents here immediately. I need you here instead. You're to take control of the Guild so we can properly prepare this city for Gravern's invasion."

Price groaned. "I hate Andelore, V. I have no desire to be Guildmaster. Even if Knife never came back, I don't want to be locked down in that sewer."

"Just get here as soon as you can, Price," she snapped back. "You'll have all that was promised, I assure you. Together we will rule this city and the Shrouded will be completely at our mercy."

Price didn't reply, but Vera could sense his apprehension. So she added, "Andelor will be Gravern's first foothold in Noveth. You'll want to be here with me when that happens, Price—it'll be the only way I can protect you."

"Fine," he finally said, "just keep it moist for me."

She smiled wickedly.

Desmond and Ruke wandered the empty hall, afraid to speak to each other. Since getting drawn into the altar, neither of them could even open their mouths without asking one of the following questions:

"Where are we?"

"What is this place?"

"Can you even hear me?!"

They could hear each other, but the bizarre atmosphere made everything feel fuzzy and delayed, so their voices swirled into a confusing noise.

Time passed at a confusing pace, and Desmond couldn't tell if it had been one minute since being in the mine outside of New Hold or one year. He was reminded of his experience being dead—the time between Layla Abrigale flaying the flesh from his body and Anika Lawson defeating the first incarnate. He felt removed from the world, despite his natural desire to be conceived of it. That combination made him retreat into his own mind, making the whole experience far too much like a dream.

Whatever their surroundings actually were, he and Ruke passed through what appeared to be a long hallway. Instead of walls, there were pillars of flames on either side, marking their progress in flickering beams of insubstantial heat.

It took a while, but Desmond was finally able to discern Ruke's voice.

"I remember this."

He managed to find his own voice soon after. "Are we inside Wick's altar?"

Through the smokey haze, he could make out her small face, turning to regard him. Her eye still twitched, pulsing with a faint green aura. "I think we are in Cindara. I was trapped in Elysun for hundreds of years, which is the domain of Oakus. It felt a little like this, so I can only imagine we have entered Wick's domain."

"Do we want to be here?" The question felt silly to Desmond—of course he didn't want to be here—but he was dependent on Ruke to guide him on this quest to discover the nature of the scions. He watched as her face regarded their surroundings, not coming to any formal conclusion.

"I think we *need* to be here, Desmond. I think our only hope lies in following whatever path calls to us."

As they continued walking through the fiery hall, Desmond couldn't imagine this place being their hope. But he continued on regardless.

After walking in determined silence, a figure took shape in the distance. It had a comforting presence to Desmond, which he attributed to his simple desire to break up the monotony of the fiery hall. But there was something else…

A gentle whistling caught his ear, softening the hard sound of the snapping flames on either side of him. It was a welcoming, jaunty melody, countering the gloominess that dominated his thoughts in this place.

"Pick up the pace," a voice called down, echoing strangely off the flickering walls.

Instinctively, Desmond quickened his step. However, a different voice—a slurred, drunken one—made him and Ruke both pause to regard each other with questioning looks.

"Don't rush me, Tinder. Keep yourself occupied by pouring me another drink."

"Oh, I'm occupied all right, Pops. You've kept me occupied for the past three hundred years and then some. It's time you shoved off, you old coward."

"It can't be," Ruke whispered, before swiftly making her way toward the dark passage ahead that seemed to swallow the firelight.

"Wait," Desmond said, moving to keep up. But something terrified him about whatever lay ahead; there was something eternal at the end of this passage, and it made his knees buckle as he tried to keep pace with the halfling. It felt like he was climbing a set of invisible stairs into the sky, leaving behind the firm, solid ground of reality. "What is beyond there, Ruke?"

"An old friend," she called back. The voices spoke swifter now, but their words became harder for Desmond to discern while his own heartbeat thundered in his ears.

It didn't take them long to get to that curtain of darkness at the end of the passage, and without a word, Ruke slipped into the awaiting black mists. Desmond stopped, dreading to see what waited beyond that oblivion. He may have waited there longer, but the heat from the flaming walls behind him intensified without Ruke there by his side, as if the passage had decided the sixth scion did not belong there without the first.

Desmond took a deep breath and followed the priestess.

The heat lessened slightly as he passed through the veil, and when he opened his eyes, he was greeted with a surprisingly cozy view.

It was an inn, not unlike The Wresting Tide in Caraby. But this one was brightly lit around the bar and main seating area, with heavy shadows in the recessed alcoves where misshapen silhouettes nursed their drinks without regard to the newcomers.

"Well, as I live and breathe," a voice called from the bar. "That is, if I did either of those things. Ruke Ebbers!"

Desmond's throat tightened when he regarded the speaker; he couldn't even manage a gasp of surprise. The figure behind the bar wore singed garments of vibrant yellow, red, and orange. The scarf he wore around his neck swayed as if it were caught in an updraft, the ends of it burning like candle wicks. However, what caused Desmond's throat to constrict was what hovered directly above that scarf: a disembodied blackened skull wreathed in flames.

"You're Tinder," Ruke exclaimed. Her voice was low despite her apparent excitement. It sounded as if it were a revelation to her.

"And you're quite early, my dear." Tinder poured the contents of a bottle into a decorative glass before flicking his wrist deftly and sliding the beverage down the bar toward an awaiting patron—one that Desmond couldn't even discern the shape of from their place in the shadows. "I didn't expect you until the rest of the scions were— Well, there I go again, spoiling things! But, since you're here, how about you two have a drink with your scared little friend over there."

Tinder motioned to one of the alcoves where a hunched figure sat alone in a circular bench that wrapped around a smoking table.

"Perhaps you two might be able to rouse him from that stupor," Tinder said in a lower voice. "He's really been icing the joy out of this place."

Desmond waited for Ruke to make the first move, not sure what he should do in this situation. But the halfling seemed frozen in place as she stared at the person in question. After a long moment, Ruke turned back toward the bar, stepping toward its hot aura.

"We've met before?"

Tinder's head seemed to rise farther from his shoulders as the black pits of his eyes grew wider. "Oh, come now, Ruke Ebbers, am I truly that forgettable?! I don't doubt the climate is more tolerable in Elysun, but don't tell me there was a nicer watering hole than Tinder's Flinthouse in that overgrown thicket. I'm truly hurt!"

Desmond approached the bar cautiously, not eager to draw the bartender's gaze. Heat poured off the surface of the bar as if it were an open oven.

"Apologies. When did you last see me?" Ruke asked.

Tinder clicked his tongue—*Does he even have one?* Desmond thought—and inclined his head as he reached under the bar to produce another bottle. "*When* is the wrong question here, toots. But if I had to guess, it was maybe the same time that old codger took up residence, some three hundred years ago. I suppose it may have been the night you and the Purveyors gave a toast to ridding the Abyss of that Stane fella."

The Unthroning, Desmond thought. He wanted to press for more, but he knew Ruke's memory was the key to understanding all of this, so he needed to let her set the pace; he waited for her response.

"Do you remember what we discussed then?" Ruke asked.

"Oh, I'm sure he does," Tinder said with a laugh, motioning toward the seated figure again. "It's all he goes on about. But here." He poured the contents from his bottle into two glasses, each one producing small clouds of smoke from the burning red liquid. "Sip this slowly, both of you. Wick's own concoction; we call it the Trubrew. Should help you better acclimate to the Flinthouse—usually only give it to those going to Cindara, but I reckon neither of you are passing the Burning Gates tonight…not until the other scions are in place, right?"

Ruke shot Desmond an excited glance, as if they had just learned some secret insight. Yet Desmond had no clue what any of this meant. His only knowledge of Tinder or Cindara were limited to the myths surrounding the lesser gods and beings that inhabit the Nethering—tales he never put much stock into.

He had trouble believing all this wasn't some elaborate dream—that he and Ruke hadn't knocked themselves unconscious by fiddling with Wick's altar and this was just some magically induced vision.

Regardless, he took the drink—surprised that it didn't burn his hand—and followed Ruke toward the seated figure.

"It is you, isn't it?" The figure's voice was reedy, struggling to form its words. "Ruke."

"Sir Pembrook," the halfling replied, climbing onto the cushioned seat next to him; Desmond slid into the seat on the other side so they were flanking the hunched figure.

"Just call me Branton now," he said, taking a sip of his drink—Desmond noticed the glass remained full, despite the old man's lips claiming some of its contents. "I have no right to a knight's honorifics anymore."

"Why are you still here, Branton? Did you get stuck here after the Unthroning?"

Branton looked up from his drink to regard Desmond with his small, beady red eyes. He licked his parched lips before looking over at Ruke. "I was too cowardly to pass through the Burning Gate like you asked. I don't know why; it would be the glory of my life to give myself to Wick's flames in his very own domain. But after we all swore to become the Scions of Stane in the name of each of the old gods, I sat down to drink away my nerves and just...never got up."

He took another drink before looking back at Desmond. "Is this who you chose to be my replacement? He looks a bit lanky—can he even wield a sword? Are you a knight, boy?"

Desmond shook his head. "I'm a Court Mage, or at least I was."

"Bah," Branton replied, waving his hand dismissively. "I never trusted a wizard in my day, they nearly burned Menevere to the ground when King Valton started that foolish alchemist guild—"

"Tell me about the scions," Ruke interrupted. "Were we supposed to free Stane from the Abyss?"

"Free him?!" Branton looked shocked. "Do not word it like that, as if we aimed to be his saviors. No, we were to draw him out from Mural's protective bosom so we could slay him properly. Don't you remember what happened during the Unthroning?"

Ruke shook her head, looking down as if ashamed. "I don't remember any specifics; my mind is hazy, and all the memories I do have are disjointed...like shattered glass."

"Drink!" Tinder called from the bar, clearly hearing their conversation. "I told you, it'll clear your heads, both of you! Two Trubrews for two looking for clues! Ha!"

Desmond stared into his glass, which looked like it was filled with liquid magma. But the drink only gave off a slight hint of heat.

"He's not wrong," Branton said, taking another drink of his own poison. "It will set your head right. It's just... I can't promise you'll like what you see."

Ruke gave Desmond a hesitant look before she drank. He brought his own up to his lips, watching her eyes grow wide with horrified realizations as her throat welcomed the Cindaran refreshment.

For Desmond, the lights went out and he fell back into the oblivion that had swallowed him when Layla Abrigale had first taken his flesh.

CHAPTER TWENTY-FIVE

Time to Burn

There was a clear, fleeting moment in which Dureen Cleaver questioned what in the Abyss she was doing. It came just as her double-bladed axe passed through the spine of her youngest clanson, Larsen. A clanmother was supposed to protect their sworn soldiers, and a clanson was supposed to be someone she would die for.

Instead, Dureen was executing each of hers after they had dared to oppose her orders. It didn't matter if her command went against everything a New Hold dwarf held dear: a clan followed their leader or they were lost.

In that brief moment of clarity, Dureen knew who she was before the Combustress came along and promised her a path to reclaiming long-lost Myrethold. She remembered the oaths she swore to the founders of New Hold, just like any other clanmother had to do when they were entrusted with their own mining operation.

But maybe most importantly, she knew the path she was on was blasphemous.

Fortunately (for her own sanity), the moment passed when her clanson's head tumbled from his armored shoulders, rolling to the ground to rest at a grotesque angle next to the four other bearded heads of his clanbrothers. Dureen straightened, ignoring the pinching pain in her lower back and the strange burden that tightened within her chest. Since her mind was engulfed in the fires of Wick once more, she didn't understand what clenched at her heart—it couldn't simply be grief for the dead men at her feet.

"What have you done?!"

Clanmother Cleaver looked up from the four headless traitors that bled on the tavern's floor to see a wide-eyed woman with the shadow of a beard along her jowls. Karla Cleaver stared slack-jawed at the massacre, her shoulders slumped in sorrow.

"They were traitors," Dureen said plainly, no longer feeling the grief that had infected her during that brief moment of clarity. "They would have had us kneel to Clan Bronkite."

A man screamed outside the window, followed by the sound of clashing weapons. Battle still raged throughout the city and would continue to do so until New Hold pledged itself to the Combustress, just as her clansons had refused to do moments ago.

Dureen's captain of her household guard continued gawking at the corpses of those clansons, ignoring the commotion outside. "Clanmother, this… This is…"

"This is war," Dureen finished. "If you're not ready to spill blood, Karla, you may as well join these traitors now. This city needs to be cleansed of the weak and disloyal before—"

"Disloyal to who?!" Karla snapped. "Larsen fought for Clan Cleaver during the Rebuilding! And Kary was my cousin! He would never betray the clan!"

"He did!" Dureen shouted, angrily pointing a finger at Kary's beheaded remains. A body slammed against the outer wall as if in response. Both women ignored it, just as they ignored the sounds of the dying outside. "He betrayed me! All of them did! I commanded them all to perform the rites that they knew were required! We all knew the plan! The Combustress comes!"

"Fuck the Combustress!" Karla screamed, raising her bloodied axe in both hands. "You are lost, Dureen! I thought this Wick business was some sort of act—gaining favor by appealing to the legends of Korinthy and Lena—but I can tell now that you're truly under that witch's spell!"

Dureen laughed. "An act?! How do you think we feed our great forges, stupid girl?" She raised her own axe, dripping with the blood of her executed kin. She held it up to point to the image above the bar, of the revered Wickan women that set Dureen on her own path. "The fires do not lie, Karla! Korinthy's daughter is the only one who can light the way to Wick's return! It's the only way we can take Myrethold back from the Shadow!"

Karla's eyes were wide with disbelief, struggling to make sense of the woman's words. "This is absolute madness, Dureen. You've disgraced your own clan, and for what? Some Xe'danni fire-dancin' whore?!"

Dureen lunged suddenly, bringing her axe around in an overhand chop that Karla managed to sidestep. Spinning, the captain brought her own weapon up to deflect the clanmother's next blow. But Dureen just rounded on her again, pointing again to the image of Korinthy Blaithe and Lena Osbury. "Blasphemer! New Hold would be a pile of ashes if it weren't for the Blaithes! We owe them everything we have and everything we stand to gain through Wick's vengeance!"

"Lies!" Karla snarled back. "You've been swindled, ya fat cunt! I let ya preach that fiery bullshit to me for over a year because I thought maybe, just maybe, it'd keep the Bronkites too distracted to vie for our holdings! But now you're just another fanatic that would rather set yourself on fire than keep a fucking oath!"

"Arrrrgh!" Dureen swung wildly at the woman, their axes crashing together. Karla deflected two more angry swings before losing her balance and falling against the bar. The clanmother took advantage of the misstep and smashed the captain's jaw with the butt of her weapon and then brought the axehead around in another overhead arc, burying its blade into the bar.

Two separate thuds followed: one from Karla slumping to her right side and the other from her severed left arm flopping limply in the other direction.

The door to the tavern was kicked in then. Dureen turned to see her husband, Garth. The grizzled man's beady black eyes regarded the scene from under his massive gray eyebrows. When his gaze settled on Dureen, he just nodded and said, "She's here."

Karla moaned drunkenly as she tried to get herself into a seated position against the bar. "Go bow down before your master, Dureen. You oathbreaker!"

"Another traitor?" Garth asked, drawing his thick Sutheki cleaver: a blackened blade that was part axe, part sword. The weapon was already coated in dwarven blood. "Shall I take her head here or give her to the Combustress?"

"Bring her," Dureen said through heaving breaths. "This one could use a few more sermons—maybe she's not quite lost."

"Give me that barbarian blade." Karla spat blood before using her remaining arm to gesture crudely toward Garth.

"Come and get it," Garth threatened.

The wounded captain sneered at him with bloody teeth. "I'd rather chop my own head off than listen to your burnt bitch try to convince me that torching a few farms will somehow give us back our homeland."

Garth made to lunge toward her before his wife interfered.

"Oh, come off it," Dureen snapped. "She's got an arm off, dear! Now, be a proper gentleman and escort her to the square. Let Veronitha decide her fate." Dureen kicked one of the severed heads; she couldn't tell which one of her clansons it had belonged to. "She's not as far gone as these fools. Perhaps witnessing the transformation will convince her which side she belongs on."

Karla spat again. "What transformation? Are you going to turn into a proper clanmother? One that keeps her oaths?!"

"I'm not the one transforming," Dureen said, moving to help Karla to her feet. The captain tried to slap the clanmother away, but lacked the strength. "Knock that off, fool. You lost the fight, live with the consequences. There now, put your arm around me, stubborn cunt." As they moved toward the door, Dureen whispered in Karla's ear, "You'll believe again when you see the incarnate, sweet sister. What Korinthy and Lena couldn't do, the Combustress will finally achieve."

Karla overcame the shock of losing her arm, feeling its pain almost all at once. She let herself cry, screaming with each step that Dureen forced her to take.

"The Children will come together," Dureen added, laughing at the other woman's agony. "And you will finally see why I chose to be on Wick's side—why the fire will remain when Light and Shadow die."

To say Tremly Boggs felt uncomfortable in his current situation was a vast understatement. Under Kathina Sulm's harrowing gaze, he did the only thing he could think to do: He followed.

He had followed Naya down the hill to join the Coperans on the Rathaway, then he had followed that strange company through the shattered priory gates, and he now followed as the Shadowfiends led him toward whatever dark designs they had for him.

As if just to mock his fear and anxiety, Ithakan had gone completely silent on Tremly. The last he had heard from the Shadowlord was taunts and threats that Nayamere Lahmoud would try to take the graystone from him.

"She wants my power to herself," Ithakan had said, while the Shadow priestess prepared his breakfast. Tremly had watched carefully to see if the woman was trying to poison him or otherwise attempt to subdue him through the food. So she could do what? Rob him? Tremly found the thought ridiculous, given how many chances the woman already had.

Ithakan's threats were once again unfounded: Naya had fed him a perfectly nonfatal meal of eggs, berries, and a crude Xe'danni hardbread, which was prepared the night before and warmed up on the fire until its crust cracked.

It was after that meal that Tremly convinced himself that he could truly trust Naya, as she was the only person he had encountered recently who hadn't tried to use him, shame him, or otherwise trick him.

Regardless of all that, Tremly now watched the Xe'danni woman carefully as he followed her from a distance, wondering why she hadn't told him about contacting the princess through whatever Shadow rituals she performed behind his back. While Kathina Sulm hadn't necessarily harmed him, she had certainly exploited his current condition, which Naya knew all about.

A sudden brashness overcame Tremly then, and he turned toward the princess, who also followed Naya through the ruins of the priory.

"How did you know about Ithakan?"

Kathina smirked at the question, not bothering to glance down at the halfling. "You think you're the only one he speaks to? Just because he's got his hand up your ass, working you like a gleeman's puppet, doesn't mean others that hear the Shadow don't speak with him."

"You worship the Shadow?"

She laughed at that. "Worship is for those that need something. I need nothing from the Shadow, aside from the occasional spell that might allow me to speak with certain Shrouded agents without having to ride several days first." She finally turned to him as she kicked aside a moldering orc corpse. "The Shadow can't do shit without someone like me to wield its power. Just like that crooked bastard wearing your skin can't walk around and carry out an assassination request for the new ruler of Rathen—he needs you, Tremly." Her eyes narrowed with sudden realization. "You grew your teeth back, huh?"

Tremly ran a tongue over the gaps in his teeth, only to find those gaps completely filled. *How did I not realize that?* he wondered. *They're all back! That's not possible.* He reached up with his gloved hand just to be certain. Ithakan had given him back his teeth somehow.

"I wouldn't be surprised if your eye popped back in as well,"

Kathina mocked in a harsh tone. "Like I said, the worshipping is done by the side that yearns the most. Shadowlords can't walk around under the Light without us, so expect gifts and flattery disguised as the opposite, because we hold the power here, my little assassin." She spat into Tremly's path, causing him to nearly tumble trying to avoid it. "But it seems only one of us knows how to properly wield it."

Tremly considered the woman's harsh words as he absently raised his eyepatch. He wasn't even surprised to find that his vision had completely returned, widening his view of the devastated terrain around him.

Sadly, such a miracle could not be properly appreciated in his current circumstances. Tremly felt tainted, as if his body itself was permanently given to the Shadow now. Even with his returned senses, he felt like Ithakan's presence within him was strengthened, as if the Shadowlord had gone silent to bide his time, gifting his host with wondrous works in hopes that his loyalty would be all but certain when the time came for another travesty that Tremly Boggs would have to carry out in the name of Ithakan.

"Such restoration is not supposed to be possible."

Tremly stopped to see Naya had turned around at the edge of the priory's cemetery. She was staring in shocked wonder at the halfling, her remaining hand motioning outward for him to join her.

Almost in a trance, Tremly did. He lost sight of Kathina as he approached the priestess. She gently touched the side of his face, running the soft tip of her thumb along the corner of his new eye.

"The Light works such miracles, Tremly. This is not the Shadow's way…"

He didn't know what to say to that, so he just asked, "What's that mean?"

"It means we are in the presence of something great," she replied, smiling. She was stunningly beautiful in the shaded mists of the graveyard, regarding him as a lover might, with passionate eyes that hid secret desires waiting to be unleashed. "Shadow becomes strongest in the presence of the malice of Light."

Like a sudden bolt of lightning, those words jolted something in Tremly's mind.

A series of visions assaulted him like recalled memories, but they were not his. Through the eyes of a child, he watched as his hand reached down and plucked the graystone from a pile of rubble. The scene gave him a sudden sense of warmth and belonging, and he wanted to protect that stone with his life. The next vision was through the same eyes, but the world had become twisted and corrupted. A woman's scream caused Tremly to double over into Naya's arms.

The visions continued. The boy he inhabited tore at a beautiful woman's clothes; a mother, screaming and weeping as her son ravaged her like some wild monster. Tremly could tell she wouldn't dare raise a hand to him, so the boy who Tremly possessed just laughed and tore his mother's garments away to reveal the breasts that had once given him life; he clawed at them with dulled nails, begging the Shadow to turn them into talons that could rip, rend, and ruin.

Tremly screamed, feeling Naya's hand caressing his face gently, trying to soothe his mind against the horrors that Ithakan unleashed on him. He knew the mother whose voice pierced his mind was the duchess of Rathen, Petrik's wife, who used to visit Tremly's old tavern, The Fourth Eagle, on occasion. It seemed like a lifetime ago, and his memories of the sweet woman were poisoned now by the visions of her young son trying desperately to kill her.

It was all too much.

Tremly let himself sink further into the Shadow.

Melaine kept her aim steady, refusing to fire the nocked arrow unless one of the dwarves truly posed a danger to the Combustress. But the fight had gone out of most of the New Hold citizens.

Bodies were strewn across the street as her fellow cultists made their way through the city. She tried not to look at any of the dead dwarves, fearing the inexplicable dread that came whenever she regarded a dwarf woman.

There were two members of the cult that she avoided for that very reason, and she didn't want to deal with that debilitating emotion at such a pivotal moment for her fellow Wickans.

"Combustress!"

Melaine shifted her aim from a kneeling dwarf man with arms raised in surrender to an armored woman dragging another similar figure who was missing an arm and was moaning incoherently.

"Quite the welcoming committee, Dureen," the Combustress said calmly, despite the other woman's urgent demeanor. "When I said to prepare the city, I didn't mean to commission a massacre."

"This was a long time coming," Dureen replied, casting Melaine a withering glare. "I see you've made some new friends."

The Combustress ignored that. "Has the altar been secured?"

Dureen deposited her load on the paved street, the woman letting out a pathetic wail as she slumped onto the bloody stump of her missing arm.

"The clanless Fowlers have barricaded themselves in there," she admitted, wiping blood from her cheek. "No matter. We can burn them out. The fools took their entire force, giving us the perfect opportunity to finally take the city."

The Combustress, who had been casually observing the wreckage of New Hold, rounded on the clanmother. "Do they know?" Her eyes were small slits of fire.

"They don't know which hole to shit out of," Dureen replied, hefting her axe over her shoulder. "They just think there's gold down there." She laughed, heartily and wickedly. "Locked themselves in the oven, I'd say."

The Combustress turned to Melaine. "Then I suppose it's time to light the fires."

Reaching into her pouch to produce a Wickan keyshard—one that she no longer remembered once belonged to Brace Cobbit—Melaine knelt and placed it on the ground. The Combustress spoke a single word that Melaine couldn't understand and the keyshard immolated, creating a small, sustained fire.

Drawing the first of the oil-soaked arrows from the small quiver at her waist, Melaine lowered its tip into the fire and prepared to turn the city into a burning monument to her new faith.

Tremly opened his eyes, stunned at first, until he remembered the restoration of his lost eye, and then panicked when he realized he didn't recognize his surroundings.

Did he take me again? Tremly wondered, sitting up in the grass. *Who have I been forced to kill this time?*

"Easy there," a familiar voice said. The princess was somewhere in the surrounding trees, her voice seeming to come from several directions.

"Where are we?" he asked the disembodied voice.

Naya emerged from the thicket then. "Still near the priory," she said, her voice much softer than Kathina's. "We are at the nexus— where the witch was forced from the stone."

"What witch?" Tremly's hand went to his pocket where he kept the graystone. But it was gone. "Where is it?!"

"Calm down," Kathina shouted in the same annoyed tone. "We're almost done. Dravor, mark that tree too! She needs a full circle, remember? Then go check on Horace!"

"What's happening?" Tremly asked, but when he started getting to his feet, Naya knelt beside him and put her hand on his shoulder to keep him seated.

"Do you feel that?"

He looked at her hand, wondering what she meant.

"No," she laughed. "Beneath you. Can you feel that presence?"

Tremly stared at the unremarkable grass that surrounded him in the clearing. Aside from feeling a little light-headed, he didn't know what the woman was talking about.

"This is where it happened," she continued. "Shadowlords were not meant to walk amongst us—they cannot take form under the Light. So they possess us, preying on our fears and secret desires. Promising us boons such as new eyes and teeth."

He looked at her, suddenly feeling accused—as if he had asked Ithakan for these things.

But she still smiled kindly, almost lovingly. "Only through acts of malice can Shadowlords break the rules imposed upon them. You're lying where Ithakan's host was murdered by a zealot of the Light, allowing the Shadowlord to retreat back into the stone, which it should not have been allowed to do. And it has led us back here."

"Why?" Tremly didn't know what the woman was saying; he just wanted to know what they were doing there. Why was he on the ground, and why had Naya summoned the princess here? "What do you want from me?"

Kathina Sulm emerged from the woods then, sword drawn, her face splattered with blood. "Should we expect more of them?"

"Likely," Naya said, still holding Tremly's gaze. "The gnolls are sure to be drawn to any threat to their champion."

"Who's their champion?" Tremly asked, afraid to know the answer.

"It *was* to be the Combustress," Naya said, as if the halfling would know what that name meant. "Or so she thought. But she did not understand what drew the creatures westward. It wasn't their devotion to her, nor was it their reverence of her power over Wick's blessings. They just chased power."

Tremly looked around again, not understanding. "What power?"

"The incarnate," Naya said in response. "Corvanna had to steal enough of Eyen's keyshards to gain his favor, which is why I assumed I would need Ruke's stone to create the Oakun incarnate. Yet, you delivered the answer to us, Tremly."

He looked from Naya to the princess, both of them staring at him as if he had some answer for them. "I don't understand…"

Kathina strode toward him then, quick for a woman of her size. "Dragging this out, Priestess…" She raised a heavy boot and planted it painfully on Tremly's shoulder, driving him back to the ground.

"Wait!" Naya cried, reaching out as the princess raised her sword with the blade down, hovering over Tremly's chest.

Before his vision even cleared from being so violently stomped to the ground, Tremly felt cold steel piercing his chest, driving his heart into the hidden grave of Percy Ambrose, who so recently embodied the malice of Light.

Melaine gasped as she watched Veronitha Blaithe levitate into the air, ribbons of fire pulled from the burning buildings of New Hold swirling around her. Her fanatic followers chanted prayers to Wick as they watched their savior become the next incarnate.

Everything that had happened to Melaine since leaving Wickham felt like someone else's life. She felt reborn in the depths of Kindler's Hearth, and this was the first wonder of her new life. Breathlessly, she watched as her new messiah ascended.

Somehow, Melaine knew something was wrong before the Combustress screamed. There was something in the air that changed; the exhilaration she had felt being in the presence of something so god-like turned into crushing dread just as Veronitha's fires dissipated.

"No!" Dureen rushed toward the falling form of her savior, discarding her axe and shoving her husband out of the way. Melaine was in position before the dwarf, dropping her own weapon so she could catch the Combustress.

"What happened?!" Dureen demanded.

"No, this can't be," Veronitha gasped from Melaine's arms, eyes skyward but seeing something far beyond. "Wick promised me—I was chosen! Mother sacrificed herself…"

Melaine couldn't follow the woman's rambling, but she eased her to the ground, hoping to calm her down so they could understand what went wrong.

"Was it the Fowler scum?!" Dureen demanded, turning to shout at the survivors of New Hold, who had huddled behind the Cleaver soldiers, watching the chaos that followed the failed ritual. "Get to the altar! Make sure they haven't done something!"

"No," the Combustress said, her voice low. "It wasn't them. It was a Shadowlord."

Tremly's dying was an unpleasant experience for him.

The pain from Kathina's sword cutting his small heart in two was brief and almost comforting compared to the inexplicable sensation of feeling himself melt into the earth. It was as if the princess had driven him so hard into the ground that he was swallowed up entirely and infernal hands pulled him deeper and deeper into the lower beyond.

And while the entire process of meeting his end was sickening and excruciating, it was almost preferable to what followed.

"It's thrilling, no?"

Tremly opened his eyes. He wasn't sinking into the earth below the priory or drowning in his own blood on Naya's lap. Instead, he was in a dimly lit chamber that had no walls, only inviting shadows. He heard a sound that was part whistle and part stringed instrument, plucking some forbidden melody that echoed softly from every direction.

"To know you're not supposed to be here," the voice said again, drawing Tremly's gaze to a dark figure emerging from the void. He was a youthful, pale man with a lazy curl of dark hair hanging over his brow. The rest of his boyish locks were pushed back behind his ears— human ears, though his features looked more elvish.

"Stane," Tremly whispered, not knowing why. He obviously knew the name, but he had no logical reason to attribute it to this man who strode toward him in shimmering clothing that was of a fashion completely alien to Tremly.

"There are rules up there," Stane continued, motioning to the darkness above. "They fought a war over it to make sure you, my lovely little friend, would never be able to be here. Doesn't that make your cock twitch just a little?"

Tremly had no response, except to slowly back away from the man.

"Oh, come now! You're not quite what I expected either," Stane continued. "With so many people desperate to stand where you stand now... Well, let's just say," he disappeared suddenly and then reappeared next to Tremly, putting a gentle hand on the halfling's head, "I had higher hopes."

Tremly jerked away, fruitlessly; it felt as if his limbs were sluggish and insubstantial in this place. "Where am I? Is this the afterlife?"

Stane laughed, spinning around like a young girl in a meadow. He threw his arms out and hung his head back in a show of ecstasy. "Oh, this is not the end, Tremly Boggs. This is just the beginning!"

A voice echoed from the nothingness. "Stane, dear?"

He stopped spinning, turning to Tremly with wide eyes. "Damn! She's usually asleep." He leaped over to grab Tremly by the shoulders, putting his youthful-yet-sinister face right in front of Tremly's. "Wake up."

Tremly tried to push the man away, but his grip was iron. "I'm dead! She ran me through!"

Stane grabbed his jaw and forced their eyes to meet. "They sacrificed you to appease the Light, to free that fondler of little boys from his rock. Now's our chance—to fight against cruel prophecy, even if it was by my own design. But that doesn't matter! Wake up!"

Tremly pushed again with all his might, but it was no use, the man was too strong. "I can't!"

"You can!" Stane screamed. "This is my only chance! Mural will be here in mere moments, Tremly, and she will demand things of us that I can't even describe. Now wake up!"

"How?!" Tremly cried. "They killed me!"

"Then, so you shall be reborn!" Stane screamed, releasing Tremly's face so he could pull his arm back and then thrust it violently in the halfling's chest, exploding his ribcage in a spray of blood.

Tremly tried to scream, but the man's fist wrapped around his heart—which was no longer severed—and squeezed.

The earth rushed past him as Tremly surged back up to the surface, driven by Stane's essence. He gasped violently, arching his back as he breathed air into his deflated lungs. He gasped several times as a woman's voice pierced his ears. It took a moment to regain his senses, but when he did, Tremly witnessed the birth of Wick's incarnate.

CHAPTER TWENTY-SIX

Conflagration

Geneva heard the fighting before Lexeth, since her husband was far too concerned with the visions he received from Reston. They had left the protective borders of Lohkrest on foot, forsaking the mounts that their friends at Lunath had offered in favor of taking the shorter path through the dense woods toward Blakehurst, where they hoped to find Bennik Lawson.

Scouting ahead over the open hills, Geneva now heard the desperate cries of townsfolk mixed with the clashing of steel and the squeals of what could only be livestock being burned alive.

"Lexeth, hurry!" she shouted, already racing down the hill toward the rising fires. Blakehurst was burning. She spun Brecka and Mara from the loops on her belt, eager to finally face the gnolls they had been tracking. "They're here!" She heard Lexeth curse from the other side of the hill, but she didn't turn to see him struggle to nock an arrow in his new bow; she was single-minded in her race to save the village before it was reduced to cinders like Rathen.

The first group of gnolls she reached were too distracted to notice her swift approach. One of the monsters used a shepherd's crook to pin down a struggling young man. Two other gnolls were hunched over nearby bothering with something. Geneva didn't care what it was, she leaped toward the one with the captive and swung Mara in a horizontal arc to remove the creature's head; its arms went limp and released its prisoner. The other two were so focused on their task that they didn't notice the intrusion until an arrow sprouted from one of their ears. The surviving gnoll spun to its feet just in time to catch Lexeth's next missile in its throat.

As the last of the monsters fell to its death, Geneva helped the young shepherd to his feet.

"Thank you," the boy said, prying his crook from the dead monster's grasp. "They chased off my flock—tried to burn them all!"

More screams came from Blakehurst, just beyond the next row of trees.

"I need to go!" he cried, making to flee. But Geneva caught his arm. "No!" he screamed in response. "Let me go! My sister's back there! They were chasing her back to town!"

"Let us help!" Geneva insisted, showing him the crossed hatchets she held in her other hand. "We're equipped to stop them; you're not!"

"Hopefully," Lexeth said from behind her.

She spun to see him looking up at her with fear in his eyes. He was kneeling down next to the dead monsters with two glimmering keyshards of Wick in his palm.

Who supplied them with keyshards?! Geneva asked herself, refusing to believe that such stupid beasts would know how to implement the things themselves. They either had to be taught or somehow compelled.

But there wasn't time to dwell on it. Both elves led the boy into the towering flames of Blakehurst.

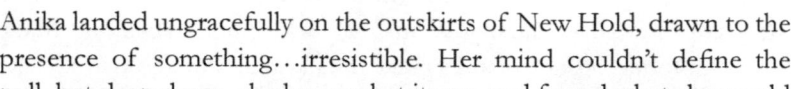

Anika landed ungracefully on the outskirts of New Hold, drawn to the presence of something…irresistible. Her mind couldn't define the pull, but deep down, she knew what it was, and feared what she would do should she encounter her brother.

Having retreated into her own mind during the flight, Anika had completely forgotten about her cargo, which now spilled to the ground in a combined heap.

"Myretha's dugs!" Deina cursed as she got to her feet, dusting herself off. "Never needed to know what a critter caught by an eagle felt like, but can't say I care for it!"

Ransil said something in response, but the voices were lost to Anika as the world began to swirl around her. She remembered what the flight to Karrane had done to her, and she was determined to persevere this time, refusing to lose consciousness. If she couldn't withstand her own powers, how could she ever use them properly?

A small hand on her arm allowed her to focus and endure the wave of nausea that desperately wanted to topple her.

"Are you all right, Ani?"

She blinked away the passing uneasiness to see Ransil—disheveled but unharmed—looking up at her with concern in his eyes. For a moment, she had almost forgotten where they had come from—what they had been doing before she forcibly dragged her two friends into the sky toward her brother.

But it all came back to her when she saw beyond the halfling, down the hill where Gage silently descended from the sky. Unlike her own landing, his was delicate and silent.

It infuriated Anika.

"Is that—" Deina's question was lost to Anika as she leapt into the air, drawing Stormender and spinning it in one fluid motion so its blade was aimed right for her brother's heart.

The sudden, raw emotion reminded her that this was why she had come: to kill her brother before he could do any more harm.

Seeing him now, she was convinced that Gage murdered their mother, more than likely killed Elza, and tried to slay Ransil beneath Raventhal. He was also the reason Matty died at the hands of Stane's scion—all because Anika thought she could save Gage from the Shadow.

But as she flew toward him, ready to finally end this all before her brother could bring any more misery into the world, she knew this was the only way to keep him from becoming the Shadow's pawn.

Even in her most hateful moment, she knew she was doing this for him.

There wasn't time for reflection, or to consider if something—or someone—was manipulating her to carry out this fatal judgement; the decision had been made.

It wasn't until Anika began her descent toward Gage that she saw the staff in his hand—an exquisite dark shaft that he spun in front of him when he caught sight of the threat. A thin ribbon of fire trailed a gleaming red keyshard affixed to the end of the staff, enveloping Gage in a spiral of embers.

Anika summoned the wind in response, whipping the fiery bands away so she could properly aim her knife toward Gage's heart. But his staff caught her blade just before it could meet its target.

"Anika, wait!"

Her brother's voice was shrill and desperate, but she didn't care; she may have snuffed out the fires surrounding him, but there was one that still raged inside of her. She landed beside him, gracefully rolling to her feet so she could meet his retaliation. But none came.

Gage just stood there, holding the staff defensively between them.

"Listen to me, Anika," he said, his voice calmer now, but still sounding wicked in Anika's mind.

"You killed her, didn't you?!" She didn't wait to hear his excuses; she had tried to plant the seeds of doubt that maybe someone else could have killed their mother, but deep down, she knew it had to be him. That was why when she threw Stormender at him, she aimed wide, hoping to use her bond with the weapon to bring it back to bury in Gage's back.

But Gage was too fast. He snapped the staff sideways and knocked the blade off its course; it went spinning wildly, out of Anika's control.

"You have to listen, Anika!"

"Why?" she snapped, ignoring the shouts from Ransil and Deina behind her. "So you can tell me more lies?! So you can deny killing our mother? Or Elza? Or trying to kill Ransil?!"

Even as the rage that burned inside her turned her vision red, she could see the familiar expression on her brother's face. It was the same expression he wore when he would lie to Anika about stealing her food or forgetting his chores. It flamed the fire within her that seemed to burn even hotter so near the fires of New Hold.

"I did kill Elza," Gage said, not even trying to show remorse; his expression turned hard, as if he was annoyed at Anika for reminding him of that atrocity. He glared up at her as he added, "But I did not kill Mother! She tried to kill me and—"

"Liar!" Anika let the fire surge through her, awakening the power of Eyen that called Stormender back to her outreached hand. That burning sensation inside of her also tapped into the dormant presence of Oakus, shaking the ground as Anika absently conjured twisting roots to grasp her brother's legs. "The Shadow has claimed you! And only the Light can stop you!"

Once she caught her knife, Anika made to launch herself at Gage again, ready to finish this. But something kept her rooted in place.

Literally.

Looking down, Anika noticed the snake-like growths wrapping around her boots. She turned to see Deina at the bottom of the hill, holding Harvester with both fists, the keyshard between its blade pulsing an emerald rhythm.

"Anika," Gage said, drawing her attention. "Father's alive."

The fire went out within her, which caused her grip to loosen slightly on Stormender. Almost immediately, it slipped out of her hands and flew toward Gage, who caught it by the handle deftly.

He smiled wickedly at her, the Shadow infesting his eyes. "But you'll never see him again."

Grip motioned for the others to hold. She could see from her vantage at the top of the hill that they weren't alone on the Valeway. They had made great time cutting through the woods and could be at Oakworth before dusk, but she didn't want them riding into trouble just to save time.

She was relieved to hear the company slow down behind her just as several cries rang out from the other side of the hill. Weapons clashed and something shrieked, dying loudly and grotesquely. Battle. A row of trees below screened her view, so she couldn't see clearly who fought, but before she could decide on a course of action, she heard one of the horses from her company break back into a trot. Turning, she saw that it was the Oather's young squire riding hard toward her, with the reeve's girl following.

"Dammit!" she cursed, wheeling her own mount around to meet them. "There's fighting ahead! Stay back!"

"I know," the boy replied. "We can hear! I'm going to help!"

"Help who?! We don't even know who it is!"

Jak didn't slow, steering his mount around Grip's. Claudia still followed, both of them drawing their notched swords as if they were Vale Knights out of legend.

"Fucking kids," Grip cursed, hearing the rest of their company approaching.

"What's the trouble?" Bennik shouted over pounding hooves as he and Grip followed the two glory-seekers.

"Some fighting that your brave companions couldn't see fit to avoid!"

"You didn't stop them?!"

Grip turned to scowl at the man only to see him smirking, toying with her. She smiled as well, not thinking the man capable of lightening up in the thick of it. It was a welcome reprieve. She rode with him eagerly, catching up to the younger riders who now turned around the bend in the road, out of their sight.

More shouts came from beyond the approaching trees, and Grip could hear Fainly cursing from behind them, likely struggling to keep up on his mule. She only hoped the gnome wasn't careless enough to leave the halfling girls alone in the wagon, but the two merchants who had joined their caravan would likely keep watch regardless.

A burning brand spun through the air as Grip and Bennik reached the hill, landing on the Valeway in an explosion of cinders.

"Whoa!" Bennik cried, reining in his panicked horse.

Grip was already slipping from her own saddle, drawing a dagger as she sprinted toward the cover of the trees. She could see Jak and Claudia, both dismounted and joining the fray. There were a handful of knights in gleaming emerald armor fending off three times as many gnolls that seemed desperate to get into a chapel. There were three other buildings near the place of worship—*An old Wick temple,* Grip noted, seeing the stone-carved flames framing the heavy doors.

"Vickers," Bennik said from behind her. He had the shortsword Reeve Jensen loaned him in one hand with his knife in the other. "We need to help him!"

Grip spun on him. "I'll help them, you get back there and watch Ransil's kin. Those girls need to get back to their mother in one piece, and I don't think those two swindlers we picked up are the best bodyguards." She nodded back down the road. "Sounds like the old wizard left them in the wagon alone."

Bennik cursed under his breath, but didn't argue. "Don't let anything happen to that kid, Grip. His father already lost one son."

She gave a shake of her head. "Would be a lot easier if he didn't ride off ahead like an idiot, but I'll protect him. Now go!"

Just as Bennik turned back toward his mount, Fainly rode up and dismounted. "Gnolls?"

"No time," Grip said, rushing toward the trees, not caring if the gnome followed. Through the leaves, she could see her allies joining the fight: Jak raked the back of a monster with a two-handed slash of his sword while Claudia drove hers into one of their backs.

"Timely aid!" one of the knights shouted, laughing heartily as he brought his huge greatsword around in a horizontal swipe. However, his joy was short-lived as his target avoided the lunge and brought its own weapon—a huge burning club—down on the knight's ornamented helmet. The green and white plumage on the helm—as well as the man's cloak—immediately caught fire, breaking the defensive line as he scrambled to put it out. Two monsters leaped at the advantage, ignoring the knights and pounding their giant torches on the temple's doors in an explosion of cinders.

What the hell do they want in there? Grip wondered, slipping behind the gnolls' siege lines and dispatching one of the reeking menaces without drawing notice. The next one was reaching for the gush of blood from its throat before Grip's first victim even hit the ground.

The rest of the battle was more of a massacre than anything else, with the gnolls being thrown back once their back line was thinned out enough. Grip wasn't spotted until one of the House Vickers knights removed his helmet.

"Brigand!" he cried, pointing at her.

It took a lot of restraint for Grip not to toss one of her concealed knives into his exposed throat, but Jak stepped between them, blood covering his face.

"She's a friend," he said through heaving breaths. "We're heading to Oakworth from Stelmont, where these things attacked us as well."

The helmless knight cast Grip another nervous glance before nodding his head reluctantly. "Apologies, milady. Don't see many Caimish elves in these parts is all. I meant no offense."

She ignored him, nodding toward the chapel they had been protecting. "What did they want in there? Keyshards?"

"Not likely," a muffled voice replied from within the chapel, followed by the sound of heavy wood dragging against stone. Two of the green knights moved toward the charred doors to assist whoever was inside.

"Lord Byron!"

Grip turned to see Bennik guiding their wagon down the narrow road leading from the Valeway. There was no sign of the halfling girls—Grip assumed they were hiding under the leathers so they wouldn't have to see the slaughter. The two merchants—a half-elf woman and a human girl likely no older than Bennik's daughter—watched from a safe distance.

"Is that you, Bennik?!"

The gruff old knight who had removed his helm now smiled brightly, moving toward Bennik as the chapel doors groaned open. Grip turned her attention back to the priest who emerged.

"We have no keyshards here anymore," the priest told Grip. He was a young dwarf with no beard, which seemed peculiar to her. Though she supposed most preachers were clean shaven, dwarf or no. He wore the blue robes of a Luminaurian, though Grip could tell the chapel beyond still bore all the red markings of a Wickan place of worship.

"What do you mean *anymore*?" she asked.

One of the green knights removed his helmet, revealing a face similar to the knight who now embraced Bennik Lawson in a bear hug.

"The cult took them last month," he said between deep breaths. He was still winded, despite how much he tried to hide it. "I'm Sir Laramy of House Vickers, milady. Sworn protector of the Caffery barony under which this chapel belongs, milady."

"Enough with the miladies," Grip said, sheathing her dagger. "Tell me about the cult—did they come with these cretins? If so, why would they return?"

"They didn't really come at all," the priest said, motioning toward the chapel's open doors. "My own brothers and sisters betrayed me. Taking all of the temple's shards—mostly depleted, they were; just used for worship. They killed my errant priest, Father Kreene."

Grip didn't pay attention to what else the dwarf said, focusing instead on the dead gnolls, wondering what drove them to such futile ends as sieging a meager roadside temple defended by armored knights. She looked back at the knight.

"Sir Laramy, was it? House Vickers is on the other side of Buckley Woods, is it not? What brought you over here?"

He motioned toward the dead monsters. "The've been burning every farmstead and hovel around the forest. We've been tracking them this past week and it led us here…just in time."

"And the Light thanks you for that," the priest said. "Good Lord Byron here and his boys are proper guardians of the realm, they are."

Grip turned to see the older knight join them with Bennik, the latter looking from the dead monsters to Grip before asking, "Any sign of the cult?"

"The Wickans?" Byron growled. "Fuck those maniacs—let them set themselves on fire all they want. It's these rotten fleabags who have been causing so much trouble in these parts."

"They're in league with each other," Bennik said, kneeling down to inspect the bodies.

Byron harrumphed. "How do you figure that, Lawson? We found a whole gaggle of those ash-robed fanatics slaughtered by these pests from Guyen."

Bennik peered up at Grip again, both of them turning toward Lord Byron.

"That's right," the man continued, pointing eastward. "We cut down three of these mongrels on the outskirts of Buckley, following their trail to a run-down turret that my sons keep chasing bandits out of—there were about a dozen of the Combustress's leavings in there, all torn apart and chewed on by these wretches."

"When was this?" Grip asked.

He straightened slightly, as if giving an official report. "Just this morning."

"They've turned on them," Grip whispered, wondering what that might mean. While it didn't seem too far-fetched that a bunch of savage monsters suddenly turned on their allies, the fact that it happened so soon after she felt the shifting of the Shadow...

"We should track where they came from," Bennik said, getting back to his feet. "Jak!"

"Here!" the boy called, stepping around the other knights that had encircled the scene.

"I need you to take the girls to Oakworth with Fainly," Bennik instructed, motioning to Grip. "We need to find out where these gnolls came from."

"I know where they came from."

They all turned to Fainly. The Archmage was staring wide-eyed at the bodies, but his gaze was somewhere else, some kind of realization settling on him.

Gage managed to drop the knife, clutching his hair on either side of his head in fistfuls, forcing the Shadow back into the recesses of his mind. It was an itch in the middle of his back that he couldn't scratch, but he desperately wanted to dig his nails into that blackness and indulge it.

He heard distant voices, knowing that the three people he once knew as companions could easily kill him in this moment of weakness. But he focused on keeping the whispered promises from Stane at bay, just long enough to tell Anika how she could stop the next incarnate.

Finally, he managed to look up at his sister, who watched him through slitted, angry eyes. Despite knowing the truth, he could understand why she felt such hate for him. She had lost everything, and when he gave her the smallest sliver of hope—that their father still lived—he poisoned that as well. In that moment, a torrent of emotions swelled within Gage and he tried to keep himself from crying—knowing he didn't have time for a breakdown—but seeing his sister now reminded him of everything that had happened since he stole that fucking necklace.

He fell to his knees. "I'm sorry, Anika," he said through restrained sobs. "Mother was right to try to kill me. As much as I try, I can't keep the Shadow from working through me…"

"Gage!" Ransil said, rushing toward him. "Are you hurt?"

The fact that the halfling who he stabbed in the back cared about his wellbeing made it even more impossible for Gage to fight back the tears. He felt the man's small hand on his shoulder and it was too much; he broke away, stepping back from the trio.

"Stay away from me! In case it happens again!"

"In case what happens again?" Ransil asked, keeping both his hands raised in surrender. "Tell us what happened, Gage."

He shook his head. "It doesn't matter anymore." Looking at Anika, who stopped struggling against the roots tangled around her legs, he said, "Someone named Reston Mauer wanted you to have this." He held up the fiery staff. "He's the one who told me father was alive."

Ransil looked stunned, lowering his hands. "You spoke to Reston?"

Desmond shook his head, not sure how to explain. "He sent me a message. I think… I think he's dead. But when I touched the altar in Karrane, I could—"

"The altar?!" Anika asked, struggling against the roots again. "Deina!"

The dwarf lowered her axe, causing the keyshard's glow to diminish and the roots to shrink away. Anika untangled herself, and the three of them encircled Gage.

"It called to me," he explained to his sister. "Which is why you went there and got married, right?"

"Married?!" Deina exclaimed. "When were ye—"

"Not now!" Anika snapped; she was still more angry than Gage had ever seen, but at least now she wasn't trying to kill him—yet. "What were you doing in Karrane, Gage?"

He wasn't ready to tell her about Knife and Robin's plans to go to

Xe'dann, so instead he pushed the staff toward her again. "Here, take it. You'll need it."

Anika looked at it suspiciously, glancing at Stormender with its blade stuck in the grass nearby. "For what?"

He didn't know how to explain it all to her, he just knew that she had to be the one to claim Wick's altar before he did, and he needed to get himself out of Noveth before the Shadow overpowered him again. He could only hope all the other altars were in Noveth for Anika to claim. "I don't know exactly, Reston just said you should have it. I think Father might know what to do with it. Maybe when you hold it, you'll hear Reston's voice like I do."

Slowly, Anika wrapped her hand around the staff. Gage saw something flicker in her eyes when she touched it, but she didn't say what she saw.

Someone shrieked in the distance, from the towering flames of New Hold.

"We need to help them," Deina said. "Me homeland is burning!"

"Claim the altar if you want to help them," Gage said, knowing they wouldn't completely understand, but he had to give them reason to hurry. "The Combustress will need the altar, and if I claim it for Shadow, she may be able to achieve her goal."

Anika looked up from the staff. "Which is?"

But Gage turned to Ransil, staring at the enchanted knife tucked into his belt. "It's the same as your mother's, before she died. She wants to set the world on fire."

Lord Byron led them through the ravine, knowing the terrain much better than any of them. But Fainly was close behind, certain he knew where they were going.

"I see no sign of their passing," Bennik told Grip, frustration evident in his voice. "What makes you so sure they came this way, Fainly?"

"You'll see," the gnome replied. Grip could see the man was trying to concentrate on something unseen; his sixth sense that his companions lacked guided him.

"We should be with the girls," Bennik said, not for the first time.

"Sir Laramy and Sir Tyril will keep them well guarded the rest of the way to Oakworth," Byron reassured from the front. "My sons are as valiant as they are capable. Rest assured, your companions will be feasting with the good Baroness Caffery in no time."

"They carry the Light's blessing," the dwarf priest, Simon, added, immediately muttering profanities afterward as he stumbled over a knotted root.

Byron's mention of food made Grip's stomach rumble, returning her thoughts once again to Ransil Osbury. Initially, she had been intent on going on to Oakworth with the others, ensuring that the Osbury brats got back to their mother safely. But something felt wrong about all this, and she knew as much as she wanted to return to Ransil, she wouldn't feel right looking him in the eye having ignored something that could possibly bring harm or dismay to the Lawsons. Looking over at Bennik, she thought of her own father, doing anything he could for his children.

She had to show Ransil she could be as good as him; she could set her own ambitions aside.

At least for the moment, she thought.

"There," Fainly said. "See those rocks."

Grip saw a stream running down the far side of the ravine, trickling over a jagged outcropping of stone. She could barely make out a dark alcove where a massive oak tree leaned precariously toward them.

"Seems a fine place for those cowardly cretins to hide," Sir Byron observed.

"I don't suspect they were the ones that were hiding," Fainly said, taking the lead now. The rest of the company followed, fording the shallow stream and climbing the wet rocks to reach the entrance to a surprisingly deep cave.

"Hold on," Grip told the gnome, gently pulling him by the shoulder so she could enter first. "I don't need you leading us into an ambush."

"If my suspicions are correct," Fainly said, shrugging out of her grasp, "then we're too late for the ambush."

Grip gave Bennik a confused look; the man shared her expression. Lord Byron just silently followed the gnome into the dark with Father Simon close behind.

Though she only had one good eye, it was the keenest in the party, and Grip could see a narrow passage sloping downward and wrapping behind the stream's small waterfall. There was faint torchlight illuminating the way ahead.

"Yet we're not too late for their fires to die out?" she whispered to Bennik.

As if in response, Fainly flourished his hand, giving life to a small orb of blue magic.

"The disturbance you felt last night, Grip," he said, not worrying that his voice echoed loudly down the passage. "It was a shift, which I felt too. Not for the first time."

"Meaning?" Bennik asked.

"I felt it when your daughter came of age, Lawson. Obviously, I didn't realize it then. I thought it was just the incarnate. But really, those…things are just the aftereffects. Your children are the ones that will decide the direction of the world, and I suspect we'll have our confirmation of that direction just around the bend there."

Grip scowled at the back of the gnome's bald head, wanting to smack it. She knew he was making this whole thing overly obtuse, toying with Bennik as if he had some sort of control over the vessels of Light and Shadow.

"I don't know what any of that means, Lopke," Bennik replied, stepping around the gnome so he could hurry toward the awaiting firelight. "But if this has anything to do with Anika or Gage…" The rest of what he said was lost to his pounding feet as he ran the rest of the way. Grip followed close behind.

The tight tunnel opened up to a wide chamber where knotted roots replaced the stone walls. A high fire in the middle of the space burned up into a blackened hole above, making Grip wonder how they hadn't seen the smoke on their approach. But what truly drew her attention were the bodies littered around the fire.

"I don't suspect this is the only one," Fainly said from behind them. "See that box by the fire?"

Grip and Bennik both moved toward it, stepping over the bodies of robed cultists, twisted, broken, and bloodied.

"Father Simon," Lord Byron called, "are your traitors here?"

The dwarf gasped as he entered the chamber, taking shuddered breaths like someone who had never seen death might do. *Poor wretch*, Grip thought, wondering what it might be like to be so innocent to the cruelties of the world.

"What about this box?" Bennik asked. "What's this have to do with my children?"

"This is a breaking ritual," he explained. "That box likely contained a Wickan relic—right, Father? You mentioned you were robbed?"

"Yes," the dwarf replied weakly. Grip turned to see Father Simon standing above a young halfling, stripped of her burned robes. It looked like her small breasts had been chewed off by the gnolls. "Sybil was one of my initiates from the Acreage. She always seemed so kind…"

Fainly cruelly ignored the man's grief. "Sybil likely brought a relic to the cult, and this ritual was meant to break it, returning its magic to the altar."

"The altar that you said was in Oakworth?" Bennik snapped. Grip could tell the man was too far out of his element; men always got angry when they felt stupid.

"I'm speaking of Wick's altar," Fainly corrected. "I only know the general area of Oakus' altar. But I assume the Combustress knows where Wick's altar lies; otherwise I don't see why she would arrange such a ritual."

"You said there would be other sites like this? Breaking rituals?" Grip asked, knowing Ransil would likely be involved in this already; her mind was racing with how she could maybe pinpoint where he might be.

"Encircling the altar, yes," Fainly said, scratching his head. "Wherever that is."

"Is that where I'll find my children?" Bennik asked.

Grip saw Fainly look up to Bennik, a pained look on the gnome's face. "I suspect your son will be there at least. He's already claimed an altar for the Shadow, and I can't imagine he wouldn't be doing the same for the others next…"

CHAPTER TWENTY-SEVEN
Shadow's Claim

Tremly backed away from the erupting earth, barely avoiding a chunk of molten lava, which landed on the patch of grass where he had died just moments ago. He couldn't breathe due to the thick smoke and clouds of dried earth, but that didn't stop his heart from pounding. Through the chaos, he saw two other figures. Naya raised her arms in exultation as the ground shook again, causing Princess Kathina to stagger toward a tree for purchase.

His body hadn't recovered from his resurrection, so Tremly lacked the strength to get to his feet; otherwise, he would have been fleeing what he knew would emerge from below. Instead, he pulled himself away from the tower of flame that now exploded up from the fiery wound that Naya's ritual had opened.

"Ithakan!" she screamed, her shrill voice oddly seductive. "Your time has finally come! Your shackles are broken and your paradise of carnal pleasures awaits! Come bring ruin! Sway this miserable realm to Shadow!"

In response, a massive hand burst out of the molten stew that splashed from the ruptured earth. The sight of those blackened fingers covered in cracked, smoking flesh made Tremly's own appendages lock up—he was frozen in fear, unable to do anything but watch as he, Naya, and Kathina birthed Ithakan into their world.

Stane laughed wickedly in his mind, filling the halfling with an uncomfortable elation that he tried desperately to suppress.

Get out of here, Stane said through his laughter. *You are all that matters in the world now, Tremly Boggs. Do not let that demon mistake you for a little boy . . .*

"We have to go!" Deina urged, moving toward the burning city. From this distance, they could see dwarven citizens fleeing from the thick smoke pouring from the front gates.

"She'll be coming here," Gage said, his voice sounding louder than it should have to Anika. "With your companion. The half-orc."

Deina spun around, eyes wide. "What'd ye say, boy?"

Anika picked up Stormender and sheathed it as she moved toward her brother. She still didn't know if she could fully trust him, but something about his claim awakened a…knowing within her. Somehow, she knew he was right.

Gage looked toward New Hold, his eyes seeing something beyond the flames. "Melaine. She's with the Combustress. I saw her when I flew over the city."

"You mean you saw a half-orc that looked like her," Ransil insisted. "Gage, you weren't beneath Oakhold when the incarnate—"

"I was," Gage said, turning to Ransil. Anika saw clear sadness in her brother's eyes, assuring her that he was still the boy she knew. *And I almost killed him*, she thought, wondering how she had let that anger consume her. But she tried not to dwell on it.

Ransil held his gaze for a moment before adding, "Then you saw what happened. Melaine and Brace both— There's no way they got out of there before it collapsed. The fire…"

Gage turned to Anika, motioning to the staff she held. "Listen to it. You think that fire itself lies?"

Looking from Ransil back to the staff, Anika slowly put her other hand on its smooth, burned surface.

When she focused on the heat beneath her hands, fire enveloped her as if she had begun burning alive. But there was no pain; rather, it was comforting, as if she had just recalled some lost, pleasant memory. In the flames she saw Melaine and a burned man in a cold dark cell, much like the one she occupied while in Karrane. The vision disappeared in a flash of fire, and then she saw them both, wrists bound, creeping naked down separate hallways.

Another gush of fire—she saw the man slit his own throat, bathing Melaine in a shower of warm blood, imposing upon her a new faith that would put her exactly where Gage claimed she was by the

Combustress's side.

Anika dropped the staff, turning to Deina with tears in her eyes. She opened her mouth to speak, but had no words for the woman—which ended up being of no consequence, since the dwarf turned and sprinted toward the burning city before anyone could say a word.

Ransil moved to chase after her, but Gage's words kept the halfling from leaving. "She'll have to come back."

"Why?" Ransil asked, rounding on him with a confused scowl. "Are you some kind of prophet now?!"

"He's right," Anika said, visions coming to her as she watched the city's flames rise higher. She saw the cultists gathering near the gates, following their leader toward...

Toward what? she wondered, looking at her brother. "Where did you find this staff? In Karrane?"

Gage shook his head. "Touching the altar there, seeing what you saw... It was too much, too fast. It weakened me, letting the Shadow take hold—over me and the altar. It convinced me that I had to kill you, Anika—it needs me to kill you so the cycle can continue. The destiny that exists between us is a monster, and it wants to survive, to continue. But I don't want it to continue, and I don't think you want that either. I can't imagine anyone in the world truly wanting this to continue."

She lowered her gaze, knowing that the same exact thing had happened to her. The Light had used her frustrations to its advantage, guiding her to this confrontation.

Gage bent to pick up the staff, presenting it to his sister. "I don't know where I was when I found this, but I think it was close to home. I could somehow feel Father's presence...like he was close."

Anika took the staff again, feeling the familiarity that Gage described, but she didn't feel close to her home; she felt close to *its* home.

"We don't have time—" Ransil began.

"No," Gage interrupted, "we need to go to the altar. Before the Combustress can get to it." He turned toward a path around the hill.

"To Pyram?" Anika asked.

Gage motioned for her to follow, leading her and Ransil toward the barricaded mines while New Hold continued to burn behind them.

Tremly was still pinned to the ground in terror when the paladins arrived. Several of the holy knights were mounted on horses, tearing through the thicket just so their mounts could rear back in fright as they entered the clearing, tossing their riders violently to the broken ground.

Kathina shouted commands to her soldiers, rushing to meet the intruders. But Naya shied away, focusing on the Shadowlord that pulled itself free of the burning sludge.

"Light's mercy!" someone shouted. Tremly managed to pull his frightened gaze from Ithakan to see one of the holy knights remove his helmet, revealing bright blond hair and piercing blue eyes that widened at the sight of a Shadowlord in the flesh.

"Avrim!" the man shouted over his shoulder, raising his sword to meet an attack from one of Kathina's men. "To the front! Paladins, channel the Light—banish that abomination!"

Ithakan let out a thunderous laugh in response, shaking the ground as he tore through it. "It's too late," he bellowed in a thunderous voice, scooping up a giant handful of lava to hurl at three paladins with their shields raised. The molten missile exploded on them sickeningly, setting the flesh within their armor on fire. The paladins shrieked and flailed into fiery heaps, dying before they could finish their prayers.

The horrid sight finally allowed Tremly's limbs to break free of their paralysis. He scrambled to his feet just as the battle began in earnest. He would have fled the clearing immediately, but the ground shook again and knocked him back toward a tree. Regaining his balance, he saw the blond paladin run his sword through his foe, shoving the dead Coperan mercenary aside to free his blade.

For a moment, their eyes met: Tremly's wide terrified gaze locking with the furious warpriest's. In that moment, the halfling saw the man's eyes burn with a hatred more primal than the Shadowlord's, and Tremly knew that the blasphemous scene had awakened a divine wrath in the man.

Whether it was Stane's presence within him or the lingering taint of Ithakan, Tremly knew that these priests would be his doom. They would summon the Light on the Shadowlord, and the clash of powers would obliterate them all.

He was finally able to break from the man's gaze and scramble back to his feet just as Princess Kathina's sword came around to meet the warpriest's.

Anika's stomach turned as she watched Gage wield Shadow magic so deftly. They were in the small chamber that served as the mine's entrance. Outside, they could hear the commotion coming from the city.

"We should be helping Deina," Ransil said under his breath, barely audible under the sound of Gage's dark summoned appendages, clearing away the rubble blocking their path.

"We *are* helping her," Gage said. His voice had a sinister edge to it while he harnessed those foul magicks. He kept his eyes from them, as if ashamed for them to see the darkness gathering within them. "Once she touches the altar, Anika can put out the fires in New Hold and undo the cult of the Combustress, releasing her followers from her hold."

Ransil turned to Anika. "Can't you just—I don't know, summon a storm? Make it rain?"

Anika looked down at her hands, wondering if she could work such a wide-reaching spell without Audreese or Quinn there to guide her. Every time she had unleashed magic, it would knock her out for days. But Gage replied for her.

"Not while the Shadow claims the altar. You feel it, Anika, don't you? Something's different, right?"

He was right, she knew; it did feel different. Even when she flew from the Rathaway, it felt…wrong. The flight to and from Karrane was terrifying in a different way, because she had felt so out of control. But her flight here felt like calculated rage.

The taint of Shadow.

"Then you put those fires out!" Ransil said, moving toward the mine's open doors as if he could see Deina; but the dwarf had already disappeared around the hills leading up to the front gates.

"No," Anika said this time, knowing that if Gage tried to harness that much magic from Eyen's altar, he would have to give himself entirely over to the Shadow.

And then she would have to kill him.

"We have to get to Wick's altar," she said, drawing Stormender. "Hold onto something, Ransil." She gripped the knife in both hands, the blade pointing downward; she looked ready to ritualistically stab someone. Just as she began to close her eyes, she saw the keyshard in her weapon begin to glow brightly. She remembered everything Audreese had taught her in the spire, clearing her mind of doubt and only focusing on the outcome of the spell.

She visualized a concentrated gust of wind pushing stones out of the way, working with tainted magic to clear their path. She could hear Ransil grunting behind her as the wind blew her own hair back, but she kept her eyes clenched shut so she wouldn't lose her concentration.

"To arms!" a gruff, muffled voice called. "They be sorcerers! Get Margie up here now!"

Anika finally opened her eyes, seeing figures behind the cloud of dust that now filled the tunnel. She let her spell go. "Wait!" she cried, realizing these were likely trapped miners. "We're here to help the city!"

Gage broke his own spell, the black tendrils turning to ash that blew away with the last of Anika's gusts. He stepped through the cloud of debris as if he didn't hear any of the dwarf voices beyond.

Anika had no choice but to follow, grabbing the staff from where it leaned against the wall. She passed through the thick cloud of dust, waving it away so she could see the gleam of the setting sun behind her, reflecting off the axes and shields that awaited them within the mines.

"Halt! Who are ye?!"

Anika was relieved to see that Gage had indeed stopped, raising his hands so the dwarves could see that he was not a threat.

"This is the Child of Light," Gage said flatly, motioning to his sister. "She has come to save your city from the Combustress, but she needs your help."

The claim was met with a wave of grumbles from the dwarves—Anika counted about twenty dirt-covered faces that she could see, most of them hidden under iron helms or behind raised shields.

"I heard the Child of Light was marching fer Rathen," a voice called from the back of the group.

"There's no time to address all the rumors you've heard," Ransil said, stepping up beside Anika. "My name is Ransil Osbury. I suspect many of you knew my mother, Lena. For any loyalty you have toward her, grant it to her kin. Your city needs your aid! It's burning as we speak!"

"They're right, I see the flames!" one of the dwarves called, pushing through the others. "Clan Bronkite will not hide in no hole while our kin burn! Come, oathkeepers! To me!"

Anika, Gage, and Ransil stepped aside as the dwarves all flooded out of the tunnel, clearing the path that led down toward Wick's smoldering vein.

Deina would have normally felt guilty cutting her way through a bunch of unarmored fanatics, but the rage that was awakened in her made her numb to such emotions. The thought of Melaine being alive should have filled her with absolute relief and joy, but instead it was anger that took hold; anger that she would have let the woman she loved suffer in the fires under Oakworth when she might have been able to save her.

Anger that she allowed her companions to convince her that Melaine perished, despite never truly letting herself believe it.

Mostly, though, she was angry that the world tried to keep them apart after finally finding each other, and she took that anger out on anyone and anything that stood in her way.

She cut through three screaming zealots before she came face-to-face with the truth; Melaine stood on the edge of a wall, an arrow nocked in her bow, aimed right at Deina's head.

Memories rushed back into Melaine's fragmented mind when she saw the dwarf woman, wielding an axe bloodied with the remains of her fellow cultists. Those memories kept her from firing, because deep down, she knew that she loved the woman.

"Deina…"

The dwarf's arms went limp, nearly dropping the axe as cultists circled her from behind. New Hold residents scrambled behind the encounter, looking only to escape from the fiery chaos. Melaine lowered her own weapon as full realization settled within her.

"Please tell me," Melaine said, leaping off the wall to stand before Deina, "that you're here to join us."

"Join?" Deina asked. The look of exquisite relief faded from her face, replaced with a pained look of confusion. "I'm here for you, Melaine. I thought ya were dead!"

Several members of her order closed in behind Deina, but Melaine motioned for them to stand back. "I *was* dead, awaiting execution in a cell. But Veronitha saved me, Deina. She can save you as well." She held out a hand, eager for her one true love to take hold of it. "Join us, Deina. Our moment is within reach."

Deina's eyes flared. "What are you talking about, Melaine?! Why are you even here?! Are you helping these lunatics burn my people's only home?!"

Her words cut Melaine, but she knew it would take some convincing to bring the dwarf to her cause—her kind were so stubborn, Veronitha was prone to saying.

"Just put down the axe," Melaine said, motioning to Harvester. "We need to get to the altar before the gnolls arrive. Someone has turned them on us…"

"Is that a fucking Brasson?!"

Melaine turned to see Dureen Cleaver approaching. The Combustress leaned on the short, powerful woman's shoulder. The cult leader's eyes were half-lidded, but she regarded Melaine and Deina with interest.

"She can walk the Path," Melaine insisted, turning fully toward her leader. "Let her come with us to the altar and she will show you how devoted to Wick she can be."

"Fuck that," Deina snarled, raising her enchanted axe. "We're not going anywhere with these demented firestarters, Melaine! Yer coming with me!"

"Cut her down!" Dureen called to her soldiers. "The Brassons are worse than those Bronkite scum!" Two Cleaver soldiers stepped forward with raised axes but stopped when the Combustress raised a hand.

"Bring her," the injured woman said, nodding toward Melaine. "She will be your charge—if she gets in the way, you'll both burn."

Dureen glared as she turned from Deina, guiding the Combustress toward the gates. Once they were gone, Deina stepped toward Melaine.

"All right, drop whatever act this is," she said, looking up into Melaine's eyes, searching. "What are ye doin' with these people?!" She motioned to the billowing smoke coming from the burning buildings. "How could you help them burn me home like this?!"

"It's all going to burn," Melaine said, repeating the tenets of the cult. "It has to, because only from ashes can the world truly be reborn as it should be."

"Oh, fuck that!" Deina shouted, tears welling up in her eyes as they narrowed on Melaine. "All the old gods have stupid sayings about how *they* are the ones that could save the world—no one else! It's how all their priests are able to pry coins from the purses of fools. This isn't you!"

Melaine smiled sadly down at Deina, knowing that she wouldn't be able to explain how important this was to her—not here, not now. She felt a compulsion from Veronitha; the same compulsion that moved several other cultists to take position behind Deina Brasson. They moved in unison, wrapping strong arms and hands around Melaine's lover, taking that wondrous axe from her hands.

To Melaine's surprise, Deina didn't struggle as they took her prisoner.

She just cried.

Avrim felt a poison infecting the Light. He had no frame of reference, but something told him it was the Shadow. Where he would normally feel white-hot certainty, he now felt a crippling doubt that caused him to pause mid-step while rushing toward the trees. The other paladins continued toward Darrance's battle cry, but Avrim faltered.

First, it was the sudden disappearance of Anika, Ransil, and Deina that caused him to doubt his path, but now it was something deeper that sapped his will to fight whatever trouble lay ahead.

When the earth shook once more and nearly knocked him off his feet, Avrim finally moved to follow the others into the priory's cemetery. He remembered the last time he was here, when he had exorcised the demon Ithakan from the duke of Rathen's son. He had thought the Shadow had touched him during that encounter, but now, as he moved through the thick and terrible atmosphere that strangled these woods, he realized this is really what the Shadow felt like.

Like doom and dismay.

He didn't dare summon the Light in this oppressive place; somehow he knew that would open him up more to the darkness that sought new hosts.

312 ~ B<small>RADY</small> J. S<small>ADLER</small>

Gripping his mace, he knew he was going into battle alone this time, regardless of how many Luminaurians surrounded him.

"Light, defend!" one of the paladins screamed from beyond the row of trees. Avrim's heart stopped when he saw the huge fiery hand reach up above the leaves—it was a giant's hand, with blackened flesh that cracked to reveal molten blood beneath.

"A Shadowlord!" another paladin cried. "Send it back to the Abyss!"

Despite his inability to breathe, Avrim pushed himself harder, racing to break through the trees. It felt as if he were rushing to his demise, but his conviction had returned in that moment—he was a warrior of the Light and would not allow for such blasphemy to take hold in the world.

Finally, he reached the clearing. But he couldn't believe his eyes.

The towering form of a Shadowlord crawled out of a pool of molten earth, its burning limbs smashing paladins and throwing globs of lava. One of the burning projectiles smashed into a paladin that was crawling toward Avrim for help; she let out a gut-wrenching shriek as the substance consumed her in a fiery blaze. He couldn't turn away from her dying, seeing the life go out of her terrified, pained eyes.

"Light above," Darrance's voice echoed, as if booming from the sky, "give me your strength! Make me your weapon!"

"No," Avrim whispered, looking up to the High Warpriest who stood before the towering Shadowlord, both hands clasping his sword to his chest. "Don't…"

But it was too late.

A pillar of Light cast down onto the clearing, focused on Darrance. Avrim had to turn away from the white-hot brilliance, but it didn't matter—he knew exactly what was happening.

The dread from passing over the cemetery lingered within him, and what he knew to be the Shadow was being repelled from the clearing, and from his heart.

They had stumbled upon a Shadow ritual meant to raise Wick's incarnate, but a shift occurred—by whom and from where, Avrim had no idea—and now something worse arose.

The malice of Light, Avrim thought, remembering the quote from the Luminary.

Ithakan screeched in pain as the High Warpriest of the Luminaura usurped his claim as Wick's incarnate.

It was different for Anika this time as she laid her hands upon the altar. In Karrane, she had been forcefully pinned upon the altar of Eyen, her blood fed into its veins by Stormender. She supposed that may have been why Stane could invade her mind.

But touching the warm red stone of Wick's altar actually cooled the fiery rage that nearly drove her to kill her brother. She calmly watched the flickering within the yellow veins that ran through the enormous ruby jutting out of the earth. The altar lit the wide chamber in vivid red hues, turning Gage's pale face bright crimson.

"Did it work?" Ransil asked. "I didn't feel anything, but something's happening, right, Ani?"

She wanted to answer him, but a vision took shape in the altar's depths and she was afraid if she did anything to break her concentration, she would lose it. Just then, the earth shook, ever so subtly.

"Can she hear me?" Ransil asked Gage.

"Wait. And I'm sorry for stabbing you, Ransil. You don't have to believe me, but it truly wasn't me."

"I know, kid," Ransil replied. "Believe it or not, I've survived worse."

Anika focused on the figures in the altar; a tall human man with scars and long white hair stood with a halfling woman whose green eye pulsated. They were trying to speak to her, but their voices were Gage and Ransil's; Anika wanted to tell them to be quiet, but her mouth still wouldn't obey her.

"Do me a favor, Ransil…"

"Assuming we get out of here?"

"If I reach for that altar, kill me."

"I can't—"

"Just do it," Gage insisted. "I've already claimed Eyen's altar for the Shadow—Anika needs to return there to take it back. Do not let me touch any others."

The figures were gesturing wildly to Anika to do something, but still she couldn't understand them. She felt panic rising and wanted to let go of the altar so she could speak again, but something kept her watching and waiting.

Wick wouldn't let her go.

Something needed the Light within her more than she did at the moment, so all she could do was watch the figures beg for her to listen while the Light shifted the balance of power.

Avrim's vision cleared after the first blow, so he didn't see what Ithakan's true face looked like. It was probably for the best, since it was said seeing a Shadowlord's face could drive a man insane. All he saw was the Shadowlord's massive arms go limp as his head flew through the air in a ball of fire.

Darrance Moore ascended on flaming wings, his blond hair replaced by a trail of cinders. The flesh beneath his plates of armor was now like the surface of the sun—an infernal angel of Wick wielding a sword of flames.

As the Shadowlord's body melted into a small volcano, Darrance began to descend back to the clearing. The surviving paladins raised their swords to their new champion.

"This cannot be," a voice said in a familiar Xe'danni accent. Avrim spared a glance from the incarnate to see the Shadow priestess who had corrupted Baron Caffery, looking awestruck at her second failed creation turning into a smoking mound.

Seeing the woman again filled Avrim with divine hatred, and he gripped his mace with both hands, knowing what that cursed woman forced him to do.

He charged forward, screaming, because he knew no other way to release the suffocating fury within. Gathering the abundant Light into his fists, channeling it into his weapon, he leaped off the hardened remains of a fellow paladin encased in bits of Ithakan.

The Xe'danni priestess screamed as the hulking Coperan woman tried to pull her to safety, but Avrim just focused on the target of his judgement: Darrance Moore's flaming head.

The incarnate of Wick fell to his knees, dead before truly born— denied the fate of being a living blasphemy.

Avrim had just a moment of reprieve before the High Warpriest's body sucked in all the Light surrounding them and exploded, banishing everything from the clearing in a heavenly blast.

CHAPTER TWENTY-EIGHT

Wreckage

Lexeth hadn't been to Blakehurst since accompanying his sister, Farrah, during one of her rangings. His memories of the place were cherished, since the quaint village had opened his eyes to what lay beyond the borders of Lohkrest.

Now, as he watched the place go up in flames, he felt a hollowness inside—the same feeling that he experienced when hearing the news of Farrah's death.

Maybe it's this place that's cursed, he thought.

For a moment, he stood frozen in place as gnolls and scavenging goblins chased after unarmed villagers while what few soldiers remained tried to drive the monsters back with whatever weapons they could find.

"Lex!"

He snapped out of his stupor to see his wife bury both of her axes into a huge gnoll, driving it to the ground in a lifeless heap. Blood sprayed across her lovely face, painting her like a feral huntress.

"Get the children!" She motioned with her gory weapon toward a small band of goblins banging on a barricaded door. A headless man's corpse was sprawled near that house while children shrieked in terror within the burning confines. He drew his bow and fired arrow after arrow at the horrid creatures, each missile finding its mark with a satisfying *thunk thunk thunk.*

While he wanted to rush over to help the children, one of the reeve's guards was already tending to them, and Lexeth was needed elsewhere. He followed Geneva toward the center of town, where most of the smoke billowed into the sky. Reeve Rupert Warner—a man Lexeth would be hard-pressed to ever forget—was barking orders as several of his guards escorted unarmed residents carrying buckets of water from the well.

"Reeve Warner," Lexeth began. "What's happening?"

The man turned on him, red-faced and bloodied. For everything that Lexeth could say about the reeve, in that moment, he was a man determined to defend his homeland; that was something Lexeth could respect.

"What are you doing here?!" he snapped. "How many more of you does it take to wreck our town?!"

"What are you talking about?!" Geneva replied, breathless. "We're here to help. From the look of things, it seems you need all the help you can get!"

"What are they doing here?!" Lexeth asked, firing an arrow at a goblin that tried to leap on a distracted guard. "What's drawing them?"

"They were scavenging Ransil's old place," one of the reeve's guards explained, cranking back her crossbow while looking up at the elves. "When we tried to chase them off, some old hag started with some of that swamp-speak and these monsters just started pouring out of the woods!"

Swamp-speak? Lexeth wondered, nocking another arrow to put down a gnoll coming toward them. "Is she still here?!"

The guard nodded, standing up to aim her weapon toward the fighting. "Probably still at the Mule. It was like she was looking for something there..."

Lexeth turned to Geneva, but she was already running into the thick of battle toward the halfling's old tavern. He followed, remembering how Farrah had bought him his first ale at Ransil's establishment. He shouldered his bow and drew his knife, feeling as if the occasion called for something a little more personal.

On the way to Oakworth, Fainly retreated into his own thoughts, not speaking to the others much. Bennik was even worse, brooding over the news that his children were at the mercy of grand schemes that none of them truly understood yet.

Grip had to make do with Lord Byron Vickers and his son, Sir Laramy. The latter had just returned from escorting the others to the Caffery's hold in Oakworth. The Vickerses weren't the worst of company, but for an agent of the Guild—or, former agent—it was unsettling making conversation with a man that would likely have sent you to his gallows under any other circumstances.

"I have heard Xoatia is an exotic place," Laramy said after joining them on the Valeway. He looked at Grip in an unsettling way, and she got the feeling that he was looking for his next conquest. "What brought you to Noveth?"

"If by exotic you mean war-torn and Shadow-taken," she replied, "then, yes, it's quite exotic. However, I didn't choose to come here. Through a series of preordained events set about by my mother and her five priests, I was exiled from home and forced to make a life in the Joined Realms."

Lord Byron made a grunting sound. "No better place to carve out a life, says I. Though, you have my sympathy in regards to the family trouble." He steered his mount closer to his son's so he could reach out and pat him appreciatively on the shoulder. "Family is something we should all be able to rely upon."

Grip couldn't help but laugh.

"You disagree?" Sir Laramy asked, trying to charm her with a dashing smile. And while his teeth were remarkably white and his eyes were pleasant enough, she had the desire to rake her fingernails across his pretty face.

"In my brief time here," she replied, looking over her shoulder at Bennik, who rode a good distance behind her, "I've seen families serve as little more than burdens to those who would seek that very reliance."

Lord Byron harrumphed. "Quite the dour outlook, I'd say. Perhaps you should keep better company, milady."

She thought of Ransil and his own family troubles and did everything she could not to slit the man's throat for such a callous remark. Instead, she took a deep breath and asked, "Have you heard the story of Korinthy Blaithe?"

"The savior of New Hold?" Sir Laramy asked. "Every dwarf I've ever met couldn't stop talking about her." He gave her a sideways look as their horses kept pace with each other. "Is she...a relation of yours?"

Grip shook her head. "Thankfully, no. She was Xe'danni, and I don't want to think what kind of monster I'd have become had I been born a Blaithe."

"Monster, you say?" Lord Byron seemed offended by the suggestion.

"I knew the woman's daughter," Grip explained, vividly

remembering the last time she had encountered Veronitha Blaithe. "The image Korinthy created for herself was an illusion; one so powerful that it fooled her own blood. It wasn't until the woman was murdered that the truth came out."

She looked at Byron and his son with her one good eye—the one Veronitha Blaithe did not take from her—and said, "So, yes. I've seen just how reliable a family can be, especially when it comes to dooming each other."

Ransil felt the earth tremble under his feet as he turned to see shadows stretching down the hall toward the chamber leading above. Just as he was about to warn the Lawsons, Anika screamed. Red beams of energy shot out of the altar as if it had just been shattered, but Ransil didn't have the chance to see. The ground beneath gave out and he had to scramble toward the altar to avoid falling into the furnace below.

The chamber suddenly felt like an oven, and Ransil spared a look down to see a molten river flowing through a vast underground tunnel. Before he could even rationalize that, he heard a familiar voice cut through Anika's pained cries.

"Why did you bring that here?"

He turned to Veronitha, drawing Embrance from his belt in one fluid motion. His mother's keyshard sparked to life, glowing as bright as the altar.

"Ransil," Anika said weakly, pulling herself up from the ground. "Don't…"

"Leave this to me, Ani," he said, narrowing his eyes on the Combustress and her robed companions packing the tunnel behind her. "I should have done this fifteen years ago."

"You fool!" Veronitha shouted. She pushed away from the armored dwarf that helped her through the passage, her golden eyes smoldering on Ransil. "Do you realize what you've done?! That was to be unmade where our mothers first swore their lives to Wick—you're undoing their work by bringing it here before the altar!"

"Ransil," Anika tried again, but the halfling raised the weapon threateningly toward the Combustress, ignoring her.

"Don't you dare speak about my mother's memory! You soiled her legacy when you lied to me about the shard! You tricked me and my father into letting you corrupt it!"

"Let me gut this runt," the dwarf said, hefting her heavy axe with both hands.

Veronitha stayed her with a raised hand, stepping toward Ransil, her eyes fixed on Embrance. "Give it to me, Ransil. Before you, too, fall under its sway! We are joined to that thing and it needs to be broken! You know it does! You must feel it too!"

"Ransil!"

He turned toward Anika, hearing the desperation in her voice. She held out a hand, looking too exhausted to even get to her feet. There was no sign of Gage beyond the altar; he had abandoned them as before. At least this time he didn't leave a knife in Ransil's back.

Despite the desperate urge he felt to take vengeance on Veronitha, Ransil could not ignore Anika's pleading eyes. He spun Embrance and presented the handle to her, glaring at Veronitha, expecting her to react; but the Combustress just stared at Anika with wide, terrified eyes.

She knows what she is, Ransil thought, wondering how that was possible. But as Anika took the blade from his hand, he found his answer when he caught sight of two familiar faces among the cultists.

"Melaine?"

Ransil's question was lost as the ground beneath them gave way. The last thing he saw before tumbling into the fiery depths below was Anika jamming Embrance into the altar just before a ball of fire engulfed her...

The scions watched helplessly as the world outside rushed past them beyond the crimson veil. Desmond still didn't know if he had woken up from the stupor he had fallen into while drinking with Sir Branton, or if he was still dozing in a state of bizarre drunkenness. Everything felt like some strange dream.

"I remember now," Ruke said, a reassuring sound in the insubstantialness of their surroundings. "Korinthy Blaithe was chosen to be the scion, but not by me. Wick deceived us. He was always the most burned by Stane's betrayal. Vengeance is his nature."

Desmond turned from the scene beyond the altar's confines to face the priestess. "I can't follow anything you say, Ruke. I still don't even know if you want to help or hinder Stane."

She laughed, despite her eyes widening in red terror as she watched the events surrounding the altar of Wick. "That's exactly his nature. Only by having his allies think they're foes and vice versa can he keep his secrets while pitting them all against each other."

Desmond knelt down and grabbed her firmly by the shoulders, tired of these riddles. "What secrets?!"

Her eyes found his, her gaze steady and calm. "As I told you over drinks. There are no gods, Desmond. There never were."

He pulled back from her, confused and unsettled. Something about that wild claim felt familiar, but it was a concept that made him now feel suddenly hollow.

"Stane was meant to be a god," she continued. "The one and only god. But he was unworthy and could not gather the faith needed to ascend. So his only hope was to deceive those who had the power to make him a god."

"Who?" Desmond whispered. He didn't look at the world beyond their void, but the flashing lights told him magic was being unleashed; likely a battle for control of the altar.

"Us," Ruke said with a smile. "All of us. Humans, halflings, elves, dwarves, gnomes... All of us. Only we can give him what he wants. Faith is a currency, and Stane is the greatest swindler. He made the old gods out of the six most powerful sorcerers in Aetha by forcing the world to see them as such"

Desmond let go of her. He stood up, feeling as if he might empty his stomach. Having never considered himself a person of faith, the whole concept of magic being tied to the old gods was such a core element of how he understood the world, he suddenly felt adrift.

Being trapped in a hallway of fire did not help the matter.

"They must have discovered his scheme," Ruke continued. "Because Stane had to build these prisons to lock them away, not knowing he was creating the very chain that would allow Gravern to imprison him."

Desmond felt dizzy, unable to even form words in response. The heat was intensifying in the passage, as if Wick wanted to burn these intruders out of his domain.

"Sir Branton down there was waiting for the scion I chose," Ruke continued. "But she never accepted the Shadow like you and I did, Desmond. She left the door open for her daughter." She raised a stunted finger, pointing toward the scarlet barrier blocking them from Aetha. Desmond saw the Combustress rise up from a shroud of smoke and debris, the glow of the molten river turning her scarred flesh gold. Time slowed as he watched the Child of Light get to her feet, a deadly key in each hand: the burning staff and the windblown knife.

"What happens if she kills one of us?" Desmond asked, remembering his confrontation with Anika—how she sacrificed love for the belief that she could save her brother with Desmond's existence.

"Then the balance is broken," Ruke whispered. "What was once Wick's will become Stane's. He will consume each of the old gods until he is whole, complete in his power and ascension." She looked from Wick's scion to Desmond. "We are the last locks on his prison, I'm afraid—the only thing standing between him and the godhood he so desires..."

Desmond turned back to the confrontation, realizing now why she had urged him to try to get Anika's attention. But at that moment, time seemed to warp, as if everything they were witnessing was just a vision. It all played out backward, with the altar rushing back up through the cave-in; back to when Anika took the enchanted dagger from the halfling, raised it, and drove it into the altar.

The scions screamed as they were engulfed in fire.

Lexeth grabbed Geneva and pulled her away just in time as a goblin's crooked knife slashed at her back. He drove his own blade into the creature's throat before kicking it back into the bushes. The gnolls were closing in, throwing burning brands at them as the elves reached the blackened husk that used to be The Early Mule.

"Get back out there!" a screeching voice instructed from within. There were sounds of rummaging around and scampering feet. Lexeth didn't wait, kicking the scorched door open to get a jump on this swamp witch.

The elves were greeted by a strange sight.

A hunched halfling woman in a tattered green cloak pushed aside crates, broken tables, and other remains within Ransil Osbury's ruined tavern. She had moss and tangles of lichen wrapped around her muddy robes, her ratty gray hair fraying out of her hood in all directions. Four humongous scaly creatures moved about, each on four webbed feet, ramming their frog-like heads into various objects as if they were helping the woman.

"You there!" Geneva called out, stepping into the tavern. "What is the meaning of this?!"

The witch didn't seem bothered by their presence, nor did her reptilian companions. "Like I told the fat man," she replied in a Guyenish accent, "I'll help put out the fires once someone tells me where Lena's son hid that damn dagger."

Lexeth gave his wife a curious look before turning back to the halfling. "What dagger?"

She finally looked at the elves; her huge bulbous nose had several unsightly warts on it. "His mum's dagger, of course! Embrance! These dumb dogs have been sniffing it out for me."

"You're leading this filth?!" Geneva asked, spinning her hatchets as she approached the woman. "I name you foe on that account, witch!"

The halfling produced a short, crooked staff from her cloak, which had a cracked bell hanging from the top of it; the bell's clacker was an aquamarine keyshard.

A Corsan hag, Lexeth thought, reaching out to pull Geneva back. But he was too late.

The gnome spoke a word and her keyshard gleamed as it rang the bell. The frog-like dogs scampered away as if they sensed trouble. Before Geneva could take another step, a globe of water encased her head like a glass sphere. Lexeth gasped in horror as his wife turned to him, dropping her weapons so she could splash the water from her face, but her hands went through it uselessly. He moved over to help, but similarly, his own hands just went through the water without breaking its shape. He grabbed her face to try to pull it free, but the water moved with her as if attached.

Lexeth let go to draw his bow, nocking an arrow fluidly before taking aim at the hag's head. "Undo the spell, witch! Don't make me kill you!"

The halfling cackled, giving him a wicked smile. "You kill me, she dies too. Such a pretty elf-maiden to waste, if you ask me, sir."

He lowered his bow, fighting back tears as he watched Geneva fall to her knees, unable to breathe.

"Tell me what you want! Please!" he begged.

"You're gonna help me find that dagger, yes?"

"Fine!" Lexeth said, ready to agree to anything. "Release her!"

The witch clanged the bell on her staff again and the water around Geneva's head splashed into a puddle, allowing her to gasp for air.

"Now, snap to it," the halfling said, as if once again unbothered by the intrusion. "It's a fine dagger, about yay big with a huge hunkin' red keyshard in it. Lena promised it to me—the keyshard, that is; don't much care about the blade. You can have that for all I care. But the keyshard is mine! Since my foolish brother took my family's from me."

The sounds of battle outside in Blakehurst seemed to be dying out, as if the gnolls and goblins had lost the will to fight.

"We better hurry," the witch said, going back to tossing and kicking aside anything she could find. "It sounds like my diversion has just about run its course out there."

Lexeth helped his wife to her feet. "To what ends do you seek?" he asked the witch, keeping his eyes on Geneva to ensure she recovered from the spell. "Even if you find this dagger, do you suppose the reeve and his guards will just let you leave after such destruction?"

The halfling went about her business without responding, merely grunting to her familiars as they returned to their previous efforts of head-butting anything their master tossed aside.

"You're a Corsan priestess," Geneva said, her voice raw from coughing as she got to her feet. "And yet you're in league with gnolls and the Combustress?"

The halfling spun toward them, fury in her eyes. "I ain't in league with no Blaithes! They double-crossed me! That filthy bitch Korinthy went back on her word, and that daughter of hers... Well, let's just say I ain't looking for this dagger so I can butter my toast better." She cackled at that, returning to her search. "After the deal me and Korinthy made with Corsa, Embrance is the only thing that can actually kill her little spawn..."

Embrance turned to fire in Anika's hand, but she held on as the altar dragged her into the fires below. She heard a chorus of screams, piercing the thunderous sound of the mines caving in on them.

Anika heard whispers enter her mind again, but she refused to let Stane taunt her—not now. Focusing on the lessons she had with

Audreese at the spire, she cleared her mind enough to conjure a vortex around the altar to slow its descent. Just as she was about to shout for Ransil, she felt his small hand grab her boot. She curled her legs in to help him brace for the landing, which came just as the halfling hugged her waist.

They landed roughly, but not violently—the same could not be said of the cultists who fell to their deaths around them. Some were crushed under huge chunks of rock, while others tumbled into the molten currents, screaming as they burned alive.

"Combustress!"

Anika knew that voice, but couldn't place Melaine through the debris that clouded the cavern. She got to her feet, leaving Embrace jammed into the altar so she could draw Stormender. The staff Gage had given her was still in her right hand—*Ashrender,* she thought, not knowing where the name came from—its keyshard glowing like a small sun so near the altar.

"You killed her!" Melaine cried, stepping through the shroud of swirling rockfall dust. She had her sabers drawn, several bleeding cuts on her face and arms. "She was our only hope against the malice of Light!"

Ransil coughed behind Anika. "Are you truly the same Melaine from Wickam who helped us battle two incarnates?!" He had two of his knives drawn as he stepped protectively around the Child of Light. "Or did she actually die down there in Oakhold? And you're just some twisted monster wearing her face?"

Melaine readied her blades and crouched low to engage, but a soft voice steadied her.

"I am not allowed to die," Veronitha said, struggling under the weight of her dwarven protector. Melaine sheathed her swords to go help her messiah out from under the dead woman's weight. "Not until Wick's work is done."

Veronitha Blaithe was a mangled corpse that still drew breath. Her broken limbs didn't seem to bother her.

"It is done," Anika said, stepping aside so they could see Embrance returned to the altar. "You wanted to break your mother's dagger because of the Light it contained, didn't you? That was what prevented you from using Wick's power for your own sick pursuits."

Veronitha glared at Anika with those inhuman golden eyes. "You know nothing of my mother…"

"I know she deceived you," Ransil said. "And she must have deceived my mother—I refuse to believe otherwise!"

"Our mothers were joined in purpose!" she screamed, causing Melaine to flinch back from her. The Combustress's tattered robes left most of her burned body exposed, but she stepped toward Anika and Ransil as if she wore a full suit of armor. "*I* refuse to believe otherwise! She would have never killed my father unless..." Her furious gaze faltered, shifting slightly from Ransil to something that wasn't there. "She would not lie to me..."

Something about the way Veronitha said that made Anika recall Matty's death, when the scarred man begged her to kill him. She turned to find Gage, but he was nowhere to be seen in the cave; the only thing behind the altar was a molten river dragging most of Veronitha's followers into the dark.

"Who wouldn't lie to you?" Anika asked, turning back to the Combustress.

She met her gaze to reply. "Ruke Ebbers."

That name ignited a memory in Anika's mind, from just moments ago.

"She's the scion!" Ruke had screamed from the depths of the altar. "She's not the incarnate! She's the scion!"

Anika spun around to look into the altar again, but all she saw was the wound that Embrance had made; a vacant crack from which smoke poured out.

"No!" Melaine screamed.

Anika turned just in time to see Deina—face bloodied and bruised—grabbing what remained of Veronitha's hood.

"Give her back to me!" she yelled, tears cutting through the smeared ashes on her face. Embrance flickered just for a moment before Deina thrust it into the Combustress.

CHAPTER TWENTY-NINE

Change of Plans

Maze tapped their fingers on the table, staring into the chipped glass that contained the worst wine they had ever tasted. Silence hung between the three individuals who were now likely the only ones in the world who knew the truth about the Unthroning.

That is, Maze thought, looking up at Kartha's lovely, green, borrowed face, *if this creature is even capable of honesty.* But as their eyes shifted to Layla, flipping through *The Book of Stane* as if she could suddenly understand its contents, Maze was reminded not to cast stones at glass towers.

"It's quite a tale," they finally said, braving another sip of the reeve's wretched vintage. "If I understand it all correctly, you schemed to carry out Stane's will just so you could thwart it in his presence?" They snorted a laugh after another sip. "Quite the revenge."

"It's hard to believe," Layla said, still turning pages. She finally looked up at Maze and then to Kartha. "No gods? What about all these priests? I've seen faith do incredible things, just like magic. How do you explain that?"

Kartha gestured to the elf. "Like you said: magic. Just a different kind. All these powers in the world come from all the same aspects of creation. It's just the manner in which they are channeled. Wizards are able to harness it through focused spells learned through study, while priests tap into it through their belief in something greater than themselves."

Layla scoffed, letting her hands fall defeatedly on the open book. She turned to Maze. "Then what is faith at all then? If there are no gods?!"

Kartha seemed offended by the question, leaning away from Layla as she raised a skeptical eyebrow. "Faith is the greatest power in the world, child."

"Afraid she's right," Maze added, raising their glass toward the woman. "For better or worse."

"Faith is what made Stane's plan viable," Kartha continued. "The world believing in gods is truly all it takes to create a god. That was at the crux of his efforts, and why the old gods truly came into being."

Layla looked doubtful, but Maze could see there wasn't much fight left in her; *Poor thing.* How someone so young could have already gone through so much, Maze couldn't imagine. Despite their own struggles, Maze still felt like Layla Abrigale had dealt with more than any one person had any right to.

"So where does this leave us?" Maze asked, diverting the conversation to the present. "We can pontificate all we want, but shouldn't we figure out a plan given all these memories coming back to you, Kartha?"

"It's still in motion," she said flatly, pushing her own glass of wine away. "We bring the scions together as Anika Lawson slays each of the incarnates. It can't be her brother, since the Shadow's motives are much harder to discern. Then, when Stane is released from Mural's Gates, we can stop him from killing them."

Layla looked up at that, eyes wide. "Killing them? You mean the scions?"

"Yes, precisely," Kartha replied.

Maze closed their eyes, knowing things were about to get difficult. They were just glad Jaffron wasn't there to make matters worse.

"No!" Layla said, pushing herself away from the table to stand up. "Desmond dies! If he truly lives like Jaffron says, I will kill him again myself!"

"You don't understand—" Kartha began.

"No! You don't understand!" she shouted, tears filling her eyes. "He raped me! Over and over! Isn't that worse than what Stane did to you?! He cursed your child, but he didn't force himself on you! He didn't—" Layla began to sob, turning to hide her face from the others.

Maze moved to comfort her, but Layla rushed from the room, slamming the door behind her. They turned to Kartha instead. "She's done enough, hasn't she? Can't we just leave her out of the rest of it? I can help you take care of Stane—I'm guessing by now you know what I'm capable of…"

Kartha wouldn't meet their gaze, her eyes conveying more emotion than Maze had seen from her since their meeting. Whether it was guilt or just frustration, Maze couldn't tell, but Layla's distress clearly affected her.

"It has to be her," Kartha said. "She bound herself to the scion when she spilled his blood on the pages. I know she didn't understand what she was doing at the time, but these old spells don't care much about intent, do they? The deed is done."

"So what happens if one of these scions dies then?" Maze asked, not seeing how she could ever convince Layla Abrigale not to flay one of them on sight. "Where would that leave us with Stane?"

Kartha turned to look out the window, admiring the eastward view over the sprawling Steddlewood. "Each of the scions represents an aspect of Stane—the same aspect he used to create the old gods. As long as those aspects are kept from him, he is just a mortal man—powerful, but mortal enough to be killed. Unless each scion is present when we usher him back from the Abyss, I can't say for certain he can be killed."

Maze saw her ancient eyes become distant as she added, "I think I had a chance during the Unthroning, when the Nethering Gates were weakened—I felt a connection to Stane... He seemed terrified. But then Myretha gave birth to the Children."

A gust of wind blew in from the window, turning the pages of *The Book of Stane*. Maze and Kartha both watched with bated breath to see what would be revealed.

But, as before, neither of them would be able to read whatever page it settled on.

Not without Layla.

Melaine felt dizzy. Something pulled her eyes back into her skull, something that was desperate for her to lose consciousness. But she was able to withstand it once she felt Deina's powerful hands on her.

She jerked her eyes open to see the bloodied face of the woman she loved. For a moment, though, it became Brace's horrified face, just as blood fountained from his slashed throat, and then everything from the past several days flashed through her mind. From her pledging herself eternally to Wick's service to Deina killing the Combustress and freeing Melaine from whatever dark magic had turned her into a brainwashed zealot.

It was all too much for her to endure, and she swayed, knees buckling. She fell into Deina's arms.

"Mel!"

The sturdy dwarf managed to ease Melaine to the ground—a woman who was nearly thrice her height.

"Are ye all right, Mel?! Speak to me!"

Melaine was coherent enough to say, "I'm so sorry, Deina. The Path… They made me…"

"Hush now," Deina said. Melaine's vision was spinning, but she could tell the dwarf was crying, her voice thick with emotion—that pained her more than the exhaustion wracking her body. "She's dead now—that wretched bitch! Yer back now, with me."

Melaine let herself melt into the woman's embrace, feeling safe and protected for maybe the first time in her life. She finally allowed herself to properly mourn Brace's sacrifice; too exhausted to even cry, but silently thanking him for letting her have even just one more moment with Deina.

"I love you," Melaine whispered, not waiting for a response before finally drifting off as the Shadow fully released her.

"She'll be fine," Deina insisted stubbornly, clearly not wanting their help as she rocked on the ground with Melaine. Ransil could tell the dwarf knew exactly what she had done to the Lawsons by killing a scion, and he didn't want her to have to face that guilt while having her moment with Melaine.

He would not ruin that, so instead he joined Anika, who stood over the Combustress.

"You know what this means?" she asked. Her eyes were fixed on the bloody dagger in the woman's back, but she was looking at a doom that was much further away.

Or maybe much closer.

"I do," Ransil said, feeling a tingle on his back where Gage had inserted his own dagger not long ago. "But if I learned anything from meeting Veronitha Blaithe, it's that nothing is ever as it seems, kid."

"You believe that?" She turned to him, her eyes wet and hopeful. "You think we can save Gage after all this? Do you… Do you think he's even worth saving at this point?"

"Of course he is!" Ransil snapped, unreasonably angry at the girl's question. But he immediately regretted his tone when he saw her reaction, shying away from him, reminding him that she was still so young—thrown onto a cruel path that he wouldn't wish on anyone. "I'm sorry, Ani. It's just…" He looked back down at Veronitha, seeing what the Shadow did to people who had the best intentions. "I refuse to accept that killing your brother is the only solution. Besides, that won't kill the Shadow."

Anika turned to look at the smoking altar. "Well, if you have any ideas…"

"I don't yet," he admitted, kneeling down to remove Embrance from Veronitha's back. The dagger felt different in his hand, but he couldn't decide if it was more or less powerful.

It was just different.

"I have to go," he said, still staring into the depths of his mother's keyshard resting in the crossguard of the weapon, seeing questions that needed answers.

"Yeah," Anika said. "We should get back to Sathford to consult with Audreese and Quinn."

"No," Ransil said, dreading what he had to say next. "I need to go home."

"To Blakehurst?"

He stood up, using his cloak to wipe Veronitha's blood off Embrance so he could tuck it into his belt. "The Acreage. Back to Bramble Nook—to see my father."

"I can take you there," Anika said, a hint of desperation in her voice. It made Ransil's decision that much harder.

"No," he said. "You are right to consult with Raventhal, they need to know what's happened. And you'll need their wisdom."

"Ransil, please."

He turned to look up at her, fearing that her face might weaken his resolve. But even seeing her stand there in front of Wick's burning physical presence, he knew he owed it to her to do his part. Only by learning the truth about his mother would he be able to truly help her cause.

"I promise to return once I have the answers I need," he said, offering a weak smile. "I owe it to you," he said, motioning to the Combustress. "I owe it to her. And I owe it to my father. I think he tried to warn me about all this, but I thought I knew it all back then." He laughed without mirth. "Kids think they know everything. I need to do this alone, Anika." He stepped toward her so she could see his face lit by the warm glow of the burning river. "I need you to trust me."

She nodded, trying to stay strong even as tears ran down her ash-coated face. "I trust you, Ransil. More than anyone else."

They both turned at the sound of Deina gasping. Melaine was waking.

"Mel! Are ye all right?" Deina pushed the half-orc's hair out of her bloodied face.

Ransil hurried over to help the women to their feet.

"I'm fine," she said. "Thanks to you." She kissed Deina deeply before allowing Ransil to help her up. "Thank you all," she said. "I don't know how to begin apologizing..."

"Then don't," Deina snapped. "We know it wasn't you, Mel." She got up to find her axe amongst the cultist corpses. "It was the Combustress—working some kind of spell on ye."

"She truly thought she was a savior," Melaine said, sounding to Ransil as if she were deeply affected by the woman's death. He empathized, obviously, but he felt compelled to tell her not to mourn Veronitha's death; at least now she was free from the burden her mother left her with.

If only he could free himself from the one his own mother left him.

"I know what it's like to hear the whispering that likely plagued her mind," Anika said. "Stane has been taunting me since Karrane; I wouldn't be surprised if it was him that twisted her mind, convincing her that she was saving the world by burning it to the ground."

"They truly did believe that," Melaine added, still staring down at the Combustress. "They all believed it. So did I..."

"Enough!" Deina shouted, drawing all their attention. Streaks of ash ran from the dwarf's eyes, which were tight black slits of fury. "We won't mourn someone that gave in to the Shadow like this! She was wicked! Weak! Power-hungry! Look what she did to Mel! Good riddance, says I!" She kicked the corpse of Dureen Cleaver. "Let 'em all burn with their precious Kindled One!"

Ransil could tell the outburst was only a charade as the dwarf fell to her knees. Melaine went over to embrace Deina. He had seen grief like this—it was just a way for Deina to reassure herself that murdering one of her own kin was the only answer.

He wouldn't let Anika go through that.

Killing Gage was not their answer.

He just needed to prove that.

Ransil stood with Anika as they all properly mourned who they once were and contemplated what they would each have to soon become.

The search for the dagger came to an abrupt end when a chorus of howls shook what remained of The Early Mule's walls.

Geneva saw Lexeth ready his enchanted bow, and she drew her hatchets as well, turning to meet whatever spells the hag would use on them this time.

But they were alone.

"Where—?" Before she could finish the question, a goblin smashed through a wall wielding two bloodied maces of vastly different sizes. Lexeth fired immediately, but the arrow just sprouted from the muscled goblin's chest, seeming not to faze him. Geneva spun her weapons and engaged, slashing across with her right hand. Brecka slid between the creature's ribs with a wet thud, but still the monster stood, bringing one of his own weapons around to smash into the leather armor covering her shoulder. Geneva screamed in pain, feeling bones breaking as she rolled away from the blow.

"No!" Lexeth shouted.

The searing pain blurred her vision, but Geneva could hear her husband make noisy work of killing the monster, likely carving him up with his knives. She felt his hands on her shortly after, helping her to her feet.

"We need to go," Lexeth said, leading them back outside.

"No," she said through clenched teeth, determined to fight through the pain. But she could barely even hold her weapons, cradled in her good arm. "We can't leave—have to save them."

She felt the life go out of her husband then, causing her to blink away the dizziness to see what caused him to freeze up. As her vision cleared, she gasped.

Blakehurst had been nearly completely razed, with fires burning everywhere. *How?* she wondered, knowing that they would have heard the raid escalating to this point—unless the hag cast a spell...

"She tricked us," Lexeth whispered. "There's nothing left for us to save..."

Crying, Geneva moved toward the nearest gnoll that raised a gore-covered maul in both hands, ready to crush the skull of a screaming woman. But Lexeth pulled her back. The last thing she saw as he dragged her toward the trees was the reeve dragging himself across the village square, both of his legs in useless bloody ruin, leaving a gruesome trail in his wake.

She wept as Lexeth guided her toward safety; she cried not just for the devastation they might have avoided, but also from the excruciating pain coming from her shoulder.

"We need to find Bennik," Lexeth told her. "His children aren't safe."

Geneva clenched her teeth, each step sending a stab of pain through her left side. "Those things were there because of that hag," she managed to reply. "Whoever has that dagger isn't safe…"

As if in response, the gnolls howled in elation as they brought Blakehurst to ruins, ready to follow the trail toward Embrance.

Avrim nearly collapsed as he pulled the last paladin away from the blasphemous remains of Ithakan. He didn't truly believe the Shadowlord was vanquished, but he wouldn't let any bright knights rest so near that terrible husk. So he endeavored to account for each fallen warrior of the Light, dragging armored bodies until the sun began to set.

There was nothing left of the High Warpriest, not even his sapphire cloak. The power Darrance summoned had completely consumed him.

In the moment of impact, when his mace connected with Wick's incarnate, visions assaulted Avrim. Whether they were sent to him by the Light or the Shadow—or possibly both—he believed them to be the truth of what happened on this corrupted patch of earth.

He saw how his trusted accomplice Father Josaiah secretly executed poor Percy Ambrose, simply for falling victim to a Shadowlord's influence. That horrendous act, done in the name of the Light, had allowed this travesty to unfold. Avrim couldn't bear the thought of returning to his role as beacon in Sathford now, to serve an order he no longer even recognized.

Looking out across the ruins of the Rathaway priory, he vowed not to leave the place until he restored it to how it should be: a sanctuary.

A place of healing.

The world needed a pure source of Light, untainted by whatever the Archbeacon's schemes were and unburdened by the politics that pulled Avrim away from what he should be doing.

Looking down at his bloodied hands, he didn't know exactly what that was yet. But he was eager to find out.

Leaving his bloodied mace on the ground, he began taking off his armor as he went to find a shovel.

He had a lot of graves to dig before he started rebuilding his faith.

CHAPTER THIRTY
The Other Half

Gage walked, refusing to embrace Eyen despite knowing it would take him weeks to get to Pyram on foot.

That is, if he intended to return to Robin at all.

Knowing what he knew now—after holding that staff and learning what he truly was—he was afraid of what would happen. He felt the Shadow coiling within him, yearning for him to feel any significant emotion so it could infect it, poisoning all of Gage's thoughts to bend him to whatever whims it fancied.

Using magic or being near people he cared about would only give the Shadow a foothold; it couldn't control him if he chose solitude.

But what kind of life is that? he wondered.

Or is that Stane wondering that? He grabbed handfuls of hair on either side of his head, ready to pull it all out.

Instead, he took a deep breath; he was intent on beating this.

He decided back at Sathford that he was done being an instrument; the events back at New Hold only reaffirmed it.

Let Anika see this prophecy through without him. He knew she could; she was so much stronger than him.

Then, once it was all settled, he could return to Robin.

He watched the sun begin to descend behind the trees along the coast, wondering where he should go to find the solitude he needed. Thoughts of Robin just twisted into visions of Knife, dying by Gage's vengeful hands. He hardly escaped his most recent encounter with Anika without killing her with her own knife.

And even though his father was alive (according to the voice of a dead man), Gage knew seeking the man out would only doom him.

Nobody could help him.

Nobody could understand him.

You're wrong, Stane said. *I am the only one who will understand you, Gage. And I know exactly what you need. I'm the only one that the Shadow can't control—who better to show you how to break free of its hold?*

Gage stopped there in the middle of the Valeway, staring at the road ahead leading to Westerra. He could continue on, wandering aimlessly in hopes an answer came to him. Or, for once, he could truly listen to Stane and decide what path he should take.

What harm could come from listening?

A brisk autumn wind blew in, whipping his dark cloak in front of his face. When he reached up to lower it, he wasn't even surprised to see a figure standing on the road before him.

"Hello, Gage," he said, standing half his height and resting his little hands on his hips as if he had been waiting there for a while. "Honestly never thought you'd actually summon me."

"You're Stane?" he asked, incredulous. The middle-aged halfling looked like a commoner, even though he dressed like a Guild agent. He smiled at Gage, revealing unnaturally bright white teeth.

"Well," he chuckled. "That's a bit complicated. Let's just say I'm a friend. Here to show you the way."

"The way to what?"

He laughed harder at that, shaking his head as he turned to continue down the Valeway. "You Children just always want to spoil the surprises, don't you?"

The Shadow didn't seem to want Gage to follow the little man, so he did.

Anika watched from the gates of New Hold as Ransil rode for the Acreage. He packed lightly, just enough food for the day, his weather-beaten green cloak, and his blades (including Embrance).

"I'll return with answers," he had promised her, trying not to meet her eyes.

She didn't press him, not wanting the little man to see how badly she wanted him to stay. Anika knew he was trying to do the right thing—to help her understand—but it didn't make the parting any easier.

"He'll be fine," Deina said, grunting as she tossed another bundle of burned wood into the cart. "You should be gettin' some rest, kid. That is, if you're still fixin' to go back to Sathford on the morrow."

"Aren't you?" she asked, turning to help clean up the city.

"Sure," she said, "once we're done here. Might be a while though—

lots of fixin' up to do."

"It's the least we can do," Melaine said, dropping her own haul into the cart.

"Ah! Now quit that!" Deina snapped. "I told ye to go see the priestess. I saw how you landed when that mine caved in. I won't have ye pushing yourself—I'll take care of this."

"I'm fine," Melaine said with a smile, returning her gaze to Anika. "We'll be sure to come join you at Raventhal once we help Hank restore order here. And once we retrieve Brace's remains and his keyshard from that cultist lair on the coast."

"Let me help with that," Anika said, knowing she couldn't risk flying while the Shadow still claimed Eyen's altar, but she couldn't just leave them to clean up after all of this.

"It's our task," Deina insisted. "You got yer own, don't ye?" She gave a crooked smile, despite her gruff insistence.

Anika grinned in turn, just now realizing that she hadn't heard a single whisper from Stane since the encounter with Gage. She looked south, toward Karrane, wondering if that's where he went.

She would find out eventually, because she refused to allow the Shadow to retain its claim on Eyen's altar. But for now, she had to get back to her training; she knew she wasn't yet ready for what lay ahead.

She looked once more toward the Valeway to catch a last glimpse of Ransil on his mule, but he was already gone.

Walking back toward the smoking remains of the city, Anika felt grateful. With one hand on Stormender and the other holding Ashrender, she felt more complete than she ever had. Despite walking alone, she knew she wasn't on her own.

Glancing over her shoulder to see Melaine and Deina embrace once more, she felt like she had so much more to fight for now.

Something about that made the unknown less frightening.

It made her want to be something she never considered herself capable of until now.

A hero.

EPILOGUE

Troubled Waters

Madison Wright pulled her hood forward as the rain continued to mercilessly fall. The road into Hookport was nearly flooded, with her horse having to trot along the very edge of the packed earth to avoid getting stuck in the sodden mud.

Normally, she wouldn't have risked such a trek in such perilous conditions, when the winds had been acting so oddly, but trouble seemed to never be far from her town. Since Morty's untimely death—ripped apart by some unknown monster stalking the outskirts of Roskaway—it had fallen to her to serve as outrider.

Mistbrook was only about a day's ride from the larger town of Hookport, and the latter's position along the lake made it a much more appealing stop for traders. And yet, Madison felt like something was diverting all the devilry of Guyen's northern borders to her front porch.

At least she had the road all to herself—no one else seemed stupid enough to ride in a storm like this. Lightning flashed across the night sky, with a thunderous boom quickly following; she could tell she was in the heart of it. It felt the appropriate weather for the news she carried.

"Oy!" a voice called from the gates ahead. Only a few torches remained burning in the deluge, likely warded by magic. But those small sources of light were enough to guide Madison through the sheets of rain separating her from a warm meal, a hearty ale, and a dreadful display of begging on her part. "Who goes there?!"

"The Reeve of Mistbrook!" she shouted in reply. "Come to speak to the constable!"

"Ha!" the voice called back. "Join the throng!" The gates began creaking open. "Come on then! Let's get that mount in a dry stall and maybe a bit of soup in ya!"

She wouldn't say no to that.

342 ~ B<small>RADY</small> J. S<small>ADLER</small>

Accepting the generosity of Hookport's guards didn't drop Madison's guard; she knew exactly what she was walking into. If anyone thought they were truly the ruler of all of Guyen, it was Constable Niklus Reinhart. Many thought the halfling was prickly due to his stature not rising to the heights of his own self-importance, but Madison truly thought that the man believed all the old rumors that the Reinharts were cheated out of the sunken throne.

No one had truly ruled Guyen, aside from the three constables that were appointed by the Menevere throne to govern the wetlands when the naga queen was finally vanquished. The marsh kings of old were just a legend, sucked into the wet earth with the aptly named throne that sank with the Maiden's Hall during the Nether War.

None of that mattered to the Reinharts, who traced their ancestry back to the first marsh queen, Wynonna Reinhart.

Regardless, Madison knew she needed Niklus to see her plight. Unless he provided the protection they needed against these constant raids, Mistbrook would never survive the winter.

Maybe that's fine, she thought as she hurried from the stables toward the nearest inn, The Drowned Woes. *Maybe then I can chase after that Eastlunder who was the only one to leave me satisfied after a night of passion.* Oddly, she hadn't thought of Bennik Lawson in the past couple days, which seemed even more peculiar given the recent troubles. If that man and his allies were truly able to put a stop to the undead threats coming from Arkath, certainly they would be more than suited to assist with the kobolds and troglodytes invading from the swamps.

However, that green woman was very unsettling...

Before Madison could reach the Woes, a massive half-orc man with a wide-brimmed hat blocked her path, startling her.

"The constable wants to see you."

"How convenient," she replied. "I was hoping to see him. Can I dry myself off at the Woes first? I'm wetter than a bride on her wedding night here."

The man just motioned for her to follow, leaving her little choice. The streets were mostly vacant, with just a few covered wagons rolling slowly through the muddy thoroughfare and some hooded laborers carrying their soaking loads to the various warehouses that lined the streets.

Lightning streaked across the sky again, reflecting off the still surface of Hook Lake. It looked to Madison like a huge sheet of glass separating her from some swallowing abyss. She looked away from it, not liking the feelings it evoked.

Perhaps if it was any other night, she would have noticed that the rain didn't disturb the lake's surface...

The half-orc led her to the constable's meeting hall, which sat atop a great stone keep overlooking Hook Lake. A strange hooded figure with their hands tucked into the wide sleeves of their robes looked down from the turret just above the constable's office, filling Madison with even more dread. Another vein of white cut across the sky behind the person, adding to their menacing presence.

"Who's that?" Madison asked the half-orc as they reached the stairs leading up to Niklus' keep.

"An envoy from Vaina," the man grunted. "Don't ask the constable about it—they're not getting along well."

When Madison looked back up at the mysterious figure, they were gone.

Wonderful, she thought. As if her task here wasn't already facing unreasonable odds, might as well add a Vainese dragon mage to the mix.

Finally, Madison found refuge from the storm. The constable's hall was warm and welcoming, with lush tapestries hanging from the high wooden walls depicting heroes in aquamarine armor battling the serpentine naga that had once dominated these lands.

As Madison shook the rain off her heavy cloak, she looked around the great hall to see she wasn't alone with the half-orc guide. A dwarf with a monocle jammed into his eye was having a drink by the fire, a huge furry fist planted on his hip as he raised his mug in salute to Madison.

"Picked a fine night for travel," he said with a strange accent she couldn't place. "Good sir Prall, would you mind getting the lady a proper meal and a proper drink, eh?"

"I ain't your servant," Prall replied back, removing his hat to reveal a length of black hair plastered to the bald scalp on the side of his head. "Feed her yourself. Just tell the constable it was me that found her, not Ryson, that miserable prick—he's probably whoring under the docks. I'll be checking on my dogs."

"You do that, you miserable brute," the dwarf replied as Prall disappeared through a heavy door to the side of the hall. "I do apologize for his manners. Things have been a little tense around here since I delivered the bad news."

"What news is that?" Madison asked, not really wanting to hear the answer—she carried enough ill portents already.

He gave her a shocked look, adjusting his monocle. "Where are you coming from, my dear? If you don't mind me asking?"

"Mistbrook," she replied, confused. "About a day's ride northwest. Why?"

Before he could answer, the doors at the other end of the hall were thrown open. Two armored guards flanked the small constable as he walked down the length of luxurious carpet. As Madison expected, he was dressed like some great Eastlund duke with a clean aquamarine tunic emblazoned with a leaping fish in golden thread on his chest. He wore a silly hat that was cocked to one side of his youthful head, the huge yellow feather bouncing with each of his steps.

His expression was restrained fear, which unsettled Madison.

"Good, you've come," he said, though Madison couldn't tell if he was looking at her or the dwarf.

"Was I expected?" she asked.

Niklus looked at the dwarf and then back to her. "Are you not here to answer my summons?"

She shook her head. "No, I'm here to ask for aid. Mistbrook is under constant assault by all manner of creatures from the swamps. We don't have the means to keep throwing back their raids."

Niklus waved his hand. "Oh, we can help with that. I'll send patrols immediately and garrison the town accordingly. You will be safe under my protection."

Madison was dumbstruck, looking from the constable to his peculiar dwarf companion. She had expected a series of pleas and negotiations; what she hadn't expected was to ever find such an agreeable Niklus Reinhart.

She was momentarily worried that she was speaking to an impostor, but the success of her mission was enough for her not to care.

"If that's settled," the constable said, snapping his fingers at his guards, "on to more important matters." One of his armored attendants was carrying an ornate chest, and the other guard moved to begin opening its lock as the halfling stepped aside, allowing his guests a proper view.

"If you didn't receive my summons," he said, "then you likely hadn't heard that my sister had finally been found. Thanks to my fellow

Constable Throne here and his rugged band of mercenaries, the hunt has finally ended."

"The Murkreavers, they call themselves," Constable Throne said proudly. "Best band of ne'er-do-wells you can buy this far from Jath."

Niklus nodded in agreement. "Coin well spent, sir! Anyway, she had taken over a half-sunken tower in the wetlands practicing whatever Shadow magic she dug up from those naga ruins."

"Sister?" was all Madison could think to say.

Niklus raised an eyebrow. "Nancine Reinhardt. Don't you know your local lineages, Reeve Wright?!"

Stop acting like a king, she thought, but she just inclined her head for him to continue.

The lock on the chest clicked open and the guard moved aside as he opened it.

"Well, amongst the other treasures my wretched sister was hiding in that sloppy dungeon of hers, the Murkreavers were successful in finally uncovering my family's lost crown!" the constable proudly announced.

Madison couldn't help but gasp when the aquamarine keyshard set in the crown gleamed at the same time that lightning struck outside. It was an exquisite headpiece, wrought out of twisting iron latticework in the style of seaweed, all reaching toward the massive Corsan keyshard affixed at its apex.

"It's quite a sight, is it not?" Niklus continued proudly. "We are still making proper arrangements, but I summoned you here to invite you into my first council, as the sprawling lands around Mistbrook will be crucial for my cause."

"Your cause?" Madison asked, still staring at the crown.

"As it always has been," he replied, as if it were a silly question. "To reinstate my rightful position as king of Guyen."

Thunder seemed to shake the keep then, giving Madison the distinct feeling that she just experienced the first decisive strike of a terrible war.

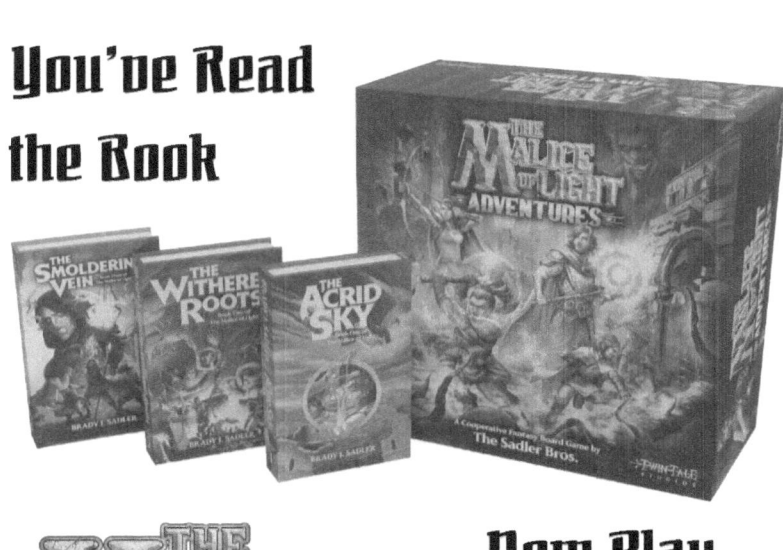

Please Review

THE SMOLDERING VEIN

About the Author

Brady J. Sadler is a drummer, game designer, and author. Along with his twin brother, Adam, he is the co-founder of the fantasy metal band Lorenguard and the publishing company Twin Tale Studios.

In addition to his novels, he has designed dozens of tabletop games and expansions and written for various TTRPG lines.

Brady lives in Indiana with his wife, two kids, and, unfortunately, a couple cats.

www.bradyjsadler.com
www.twintalestudios.com

www.ingramcontent.com/pod-product-compliance
Lightning Source LLC
Chambersburg PA
CBHW021957130726
47903CB00014B/1557